Dear Readers:

Please, come and join us at the beautiful, Victorian-style Seascape Inn, a magical bed-and-breakfast nestled on the Maine coast. A short walk from the graceful and alluring inn lies Sea Haven Village, where Fred and Lucy will welcome you to the Blue Moon Cafe, a picturesque eatery where you can dine in summer by the gentle ocean breeze and, in winter, be intrigued by the shroud of mystical fog and crisp, cool sea mist.

After your meal, stop across the street at The Store, a fairly modern grocery and gas station owned by Mayor Horace and Lydia Johnson. There you can pick up most any incidental you might have forgotten in your haste to pack. Should you arrive by car, rest assured it'll be in good hands with Jimmy Goodson at Jimmy's Quick Service Garage.

Other residents ready to welcome you to the peaceful village include Pastor Brown, a handsome, young minister; Miss Millicent Thomas, the elderly owner of Miss Millie's Antique Shoppe; Bill Butler, resident poet and manager of the Fisherman's Co-op; Sheriff Leroy Cobb, who stops in at the cafe every afternoon for a slab of Lucy's homemade blueberry pie; Hatch, who maintains the lighthouse; and, of course, the ever-nurturing Miss Hattie, caretaker of Seascape Inn. Oh, and do try to ignore the rantings of Miss Hattie's neighbor, Beaulah Favish, insisting that strange things are going on at Seascape Inn, mmm? She's reportedly a touch eccentric—even when it comes to relaying the Seascape Legend.

Please, come join us by reading the fourth *Seascape* series novel, *For the Love of Pete* by Rosalyn Alsobrook, and let the magic of Seascape Inn work for you as it is rumored to have worked for those special few who've dared to . . .

Live the Legend

From the *Seascape* Creators,
Victoria Barrett and Rosalyn Alsobrook

For the Love of Pete

A SEASCAPE ROMANCE

ROSALYN ALSOBROOK

St. Martin's Paperbacks

FOR THE LOVE OF PETE

Copyright © 1997 by Rosalyn Alsobrook.

Excerpt from *Beside a Dreamswept Sea* copyright © 1997 by Vicki Hinze.

Cover photograph by Steve Terrill, courtesy The Stockbroker.

ISBN: 0-312-96136-7

Printed in the United States of America

St. Martin's Paperbacks edition/March 1997

10 9 8 7 6 5 4 3 2 1

Miss Hattie's Red Velvet Cake

Cake

   ½ cup shortening
1¾ cups sugar
  1 teaspoon vanilla
  3 eggs, separated
2½ cups sifted cake flour
  ½ cup unsweetened cocoa powder
1½ teaspoons baking soda
  ¾ teaspoon salt
1⅓ cups cold water
  ¼ ounce red food coloring

Preheat the oven to 350 degrees F.

Cream the shortening with 1 cup of the sugar till light. Add the vanilla and egg yolks, one at a time, beating well after each addition. Separately, sift together the dry ingredients; add them to the creamed mixture alternately with cold water, beating after each new addition. Beat the egg whites till soft peaks form. Fold the whites into the batter. Blend in the red food coloring. Bake in 2 greased and lightly floured 8×1½-inch round pans at 350 degrees for 35 to 40 minutes. Set the cake aside to cool.

Frosting

   1 cup granulated sugar
⅓ cup water
¼ teaspoon cream of tartar
   Dash of salt
   2 unbeaten egg whites
   1 teaspoon vanilla

Combine the sugar, water, cream of tartar, and salt in a saucepan and bring to a boil, stirring until the sugar dissolves. Very slowly, add this sugar syrup to the unbeaten egg whites in a mixing bowl. Beat constantly with the mixer until stiff peaks form, about 7 minutes, then beat in the teaspoon vanilla. Once blended, frost the cooled cake.

❧ *Chapter 1* ❧

"So why should *you* look so unhappy?" Pete grumbled, scowling from across the rented car as he muttered the first words spoken to his mother, Jillian Westworth, during the past twenty miles. "*You* aren't the one who had to go and give up two whole weeks of baseball just when the best part of the ball season really got going good just so you could fly way up here and be nice to a bunch of grown-ups you don't even know."

"Coming here also pulled you out of your last two weeks of school," Jillian pointed out, forcing what she could of a cheerful smile. She had to keep a brave front. It would serve no purpose for Pete to know just how heart-wrenching it was for her to return to the Seascape Inn, even after all these years. "If it weren't for this trip, you would never have been allowed to finish out your work or take your tests early."

"Yeah, that part was pretty neat, I guess." He shifted away from the passenger door where he had slumped since having left the airport an hour earlier. He craned to get a better look at the tiny pinpricks of ocean flickering through the tall pines and ancient oaks shading the narrow tar-patched road.

Despite Pete's determination to be miserable, the rugged countryside and the quaint, colorful houses nestled in the trees had caught his interest, coming as no surprise to Jillian. Pete loved the outdoors and had always yearned to live in a small town or somewhere out in the country, but the suburbs was as close as they'd ever gotten.

Even his pouty disposition couldn't keep him from appreciating the beautiful countryside.

"Besides, I thought you were supposed to like this place," he continued while stretching his neck to get a look at a fat raccoon that obviously had its days and nights confused. It paused in its waddling trek along a roadside path to glance at the passing car. Pete's attention locked on the peculiar animal as they passed at a moderate speed. Although they had raccoons in Texas, they weren't as fat, nor as dark and shaggy as this animal. "I thought this was one of the places where you and Grandpa and Grandma used to come on vacation when you were a kid like me."

"It is." Jillian glanced again at the painfully familiar woodlands as she turned off the main highway and headed east toward Sea Haven Village for the first time since that fateful summer nearly nine years earlier—returning *only* because Reynold insisted she meet him there. "Your grandma and I often spent months at a time up here during the hottest part of summer when Dallas becomes such a broiler oven." The afternoon sun splashed through the glass across her bare arm and leg just below the cap sleeve of her turquoise and pink plaid shirt and the one-inch cuff of her pink shorts. "Your grandpa would join us during his regular two-week vacation plus whatever weekends he didn't have hospital call."

"Why'd you ever stop coming up here?"

Jillian paused, then decided on a partial truth. "After Grandma died, Grandpa lost interest in this place." No reason to divulge that she had stopped coming even before then, or hint that Pete was in any way connected to her last summer there.

Losing sight of the raccoon, Pete straightened and again stared at the curving road ahead. His forehead notched as he readjusted first the seatbelt then his backward red baseball cap, worn haphazardly over a thick, wavy shock of dark brown hair that had not yet been cut short for the summer. "Yeah, I miss Grandma sometimes."

Pleased he remembered her so well, for it had been over three years since the accident and Pete had been only four at the time, Jillian's smile turned sadly genuine. "We all do."

Pete fell silent for the next several miles, giving Jillian freedom for thought again. Nearing the small community of Sea Haven Village, her memories tumbled forth with such vivid clarity it felt almost like the past nine years had never happened.

First came memories of the happier visits, when she was a child and had often hiked into town to buy an ice cream soda at the Blue Moon or visit Miss Millie's Antique Shoppe for the fresh-baked cookies the dear woman often furnished those who stopped in to shop or chat.

But on the tender heels of those heart-warming images came the unwanted memories of that last, devastating summer: the summer she discovered Brad Pierce did not really love her.

It was those bittersweet memories of the two summers spent loving Brad that made her so reluctant to return now—which she did solely at Reynold's request. Her fiancé had been so very sweet to her during the several months she had known him—and to Pete—she could not very well deny him such a small favor. Especially when Reynold had asked so little of her until now. Besides, it was not like she had to face actually seeing Brad again. Just those places that reminded her of him.

Even so, she dreaded the next two weeks. How long could she pretend not to be adversely affected by all the places she and Brad had been? How long until Pete and Reynold guessed there was such a shocking secret connected to the place?

Tears stinging, Jillian turned away from Pete. She did not want him to see how very emotional she had become in the last few minutes. He had enough to deal with, having to miss such a large part of his very first baseball season to come to this place. He did not need to bear the weight of knowing his mother was every bit as miserable—nor did he need to know the regretful reason why.

"Is that what's making you so sad?"

Fearing he'd somehow peeked into her thoughts, Jillian's heart jumped to her throat. The boy had amazing insight sometimes. "Is *what* what's making me sad?"

"Missing Grandma. Is that what's making you so sad?"

Rather than deny her emotional state when obviously he had already picked up on the approaching tears, she latched on to that reasoning. "I guess. Although I don't mean to be so sad today. It's bad enough that you're in such a sad mood. We certainly don't need me sad, too."

Pete twitched his freckle-spattered nose while he thought about that. Obviously, he hadn't considered how his sulky mood might affect anyone else. "Tell you what, Mom. I'll try real hard not to be sad while we're here if you will."

"That's a deal." Jillian glanced over at him and winked, her heart rushing to give her pint-sized hero an invisible hug. He could be such a sweetie. "No more of either one of us being sad or grumpy. We are here to have a good time."

Pete grinned dimple-deep, then nodded. "Deal."

Relieved that at least she would not have to worry about Pete's foul mood anymore, Jillian's focus shifted again to her all-too-familiar surroundings.

So much about the place had not changed in the past nine years, yet certain specifics were not quite the same. The small, white-steepled church still sat off the village road to the left, its front doors open to catch the cool ocean breeze, looking much as it had the afternoon she was nineteen and had gone there to pray for the strength to do the right thing and put Brad Pierce out of her life forever. But the windows looked different somehow. Driving closer, she saw why. The old beveled windows had been replaced with brilliant arrays of stained glass.

So the young Preacher Brown did finally get his windows. She smiled. How proud he must be. Did he also have the padded pews he'd always wanted? Checking the church sign to verify that Preacher Brown was indeed still pastor, she made a mental note to try to attend at least one of the services while she was in town or at least go by and visit long enough to find out about the pews first hand, and to see if Preacher Brown was still as incredibly charming as she'd thought him to be back when she was a teenager.

After passing the tree-dappled church, Jillian's gaze moved on to the old redbrick post office and city hall, also on the main road. No obvious changes there. Was that sameness because the post office part was still run by old Vic Sampson, the man who had forever had a crush on Miss Hattie, the dear woman who'd become the lifelong caretaker of the Seascape Inn? Vic had had his eye on Miss Hattie for as long as Jillian remembered. Had those two finally allowed their close friendship to flower into something more?

Not likely.

Miss Hattie would forever mourn her lost soldier, Tony Freeport—sad for old Vic, but beautifully true. Miss Hattie had never gotten over her fiancé's untimely death.

Knowing what it was like to lose one's only true love, Jillian shifted her gaze to Pete, who looked more like his father with each passing year. At least *she* had Pete, the only true joy left in her otherwise lonely life. Miss Hattie would be forever childless, though she had semi-adopted different children in the village through the years. She remembered how Miss Hattie had doted on Jimmy Goodson. Poor Jimmy had one of those mothers who was never around and Miss Hattie had tried to make up for that by always being there for him. Miss Hattie had such a loving heart. She would have made a wonderful mother. But all hope of her having children and living a normal, happy life had died the day her soldier was killed.

Jillian sighed. How very like Hattie she was, never marrying because, sadly, she had never found anyone to touch her heart in quite the same way Brad had. Even now that she was twenty-eight and had finally relented and gotten engaged, it wasn't so much because she had suddenly found true love.

Oh, she cared for Reynold, but she had agreed to a marriage more because her son needed a father than because she needed a husband. Especially now that Pete was growing older. He needed the sort of influence and confidence only a man could provide in his life. A man who was not his doting grandfather, spoiling him rotten as a way to compensate for having so little time to spend with him. No, Pete needed a strong, responsible man to spend quality time with him while loving him for the wonderful little guy he was. He needed Reynold.

Forcing such unwelcome thoughts aside, the threat of tears returning, Jillian glanced out across the street, catching sight of an auto repair garage she didn't remember being there: *Jimmy's Quick Service Garage.* Curious, she peered into the two large, open bays to get a closer look while they passed in front. Could the Jimmy on the sign be little Jimmy Goodson all grown up? Jimmy had always been curious about the way mechanical things worked. Or had someone new moved there?

Spotting a man in dark clothes leaning over the engine of an old beige Dodge, she tried but couldn't make out the mechanic's face. Who she did recognize though was the stooped, elderly woman standing beside him, wagging a gnarled finger as if scolding the car itself.

"*Beaulah Favish, as I live and breathe.*" Jillian took her foot off the gas to slow down for a better look at the astonishing sight.

"Huh?" Pete glanced first at his mother then at the garage.

"That woman over there." She pointed with a quick flick of her hand. "I can't believe she's still alive. She looked to be a month older than dirt way back when I was a kid."

Pete leaned toward the window to have a closer look, pressing the tip of his freckled nose against the glass. "She looks pretty old, all right. Who's she to you?"

"Nobody, really. Just the town snoop. I wonder if she's still trying to run everyone's business the way she used to." Jillian chuckled at the thought, feeling a great relief to be laughing instead of weeping like she had feared. "Poor Sheriff Cobb used to catch the worst of her rantings. Probably still does."

"By the way she's flapping that finger of hers, I'd say she hasn't changed much," Pete replied, then pointed farther down to a tall, dark-skinned black man and a small lighter-skinned black boy. Both were standing outside the local grocery. Both carried large paper sacks. The boy also carried a half-eaten strawberry ice cream cone. "Who's that over there?"

Jillian's gaze shifted to yet another familiar face. "The man's name is Bill Butler. I don't know about the boy. Maybe one of their sons. Can't be Aaron, though. Aaron would be about twelve by now. And George would be just turning ten. That boy appears to be closer to your age. I guess Bill and Leslie didn't stop at two children after all. Maybe Bill wasn't teasing when he said he wanted his own basketball team."

"I wonder if the boy plays baseball," Pete asked, shifting in the passenger seat to get a better look as they passed in front of The Store, still the most modern looking of the handful of buildings that made up the small village. "How far are we from the place where we're going to stay?"

"Not far. The Seascape Inn is up on that rise over there. See? You can see part of the roof and several windows from here." She pointed toward the large, old Victorian house that long ago had been turned into a quiet haven for city-weary vacationers like her and her family.

Although they had yet to pass Landry's Landing still bulging with its odd assortment of local curios and fishing needs, or the Blue Moon Cafe with a huge iron ship anchor propped out front, or the freshly painted Fisherman's Co-op built along the edge of the ocean cliffs, Pete's attention remained focused on the tempered, three-story gray clapboard house where they would spend the next two weeks.

Jillian, too, stared ahead to the familiar high-pitched roof, the enchanting widow's walk outside Miss Hattie's bedroom, and the large round tower coupled to the Great White Room on the north side. She tried not to glance again toward the co-op where she feared she might see images of Brad, tall, lean, and sun-bronzed from hours at sea, swaggering off one of the larger boats.

"I wonder if there are any other guests here," Pete said, rolling down the window to stick his head out for a better look at the different outbuildings. He caught his baseball cap just as the car draft plucked it off his wavy hair.

"At this time of year, I doubt there will be anyone else. It's still early yet for the local tourist season to be underway, or what there is of it. I imagine it'll just be us three and the Nelsons during our two weeks here."

Pete sank back again but tried not to look disappointed, clearly determined not to be the first to go back on their bargain to not be sad. "Well, at least it's not far to town. Maybe I can make friends with that boy we saw back there."

"That's true. And I'm sure there are other children here. But do keep in mind, they're all still in school. During the most of the day, you'll pretty much be stuck with me."

"Well, you're not so bad. I just wish Mr. Johnstone and his new friends weren't coming here on Friday. I'd rather it just be you and me."

"And for the first two days it will be," she reminded him. "But after that we'll have to share our time with Reynold, who is really looking forward to this chance to get to know you better. And we'll have to share some of our time with the couple he's invited here because they are very important people to him. Mr. Nelson's company could end up being a multimillion-dollar advertising account for Reynold, and his wife supposedly has lots of influence over him. Besides, it won't be so bad. In fact, I think with all we have planned to do, you'll enjoy yourself a lot. Before you know it, it'll be time to go home and you'll hate the thought of leaving here. Everyone does."

"We'll see," was all Pete had to say on the matter as he turned his attention to a small black cat lying on the front step. As soon as the car stopped, he popped the door open and hurried to see if he could pet the animal without it running off.

As expected, Hattie Stillman greeted them at the front door, delighted to see both.

"I see you remembered the way, Jilly," she called to them.

No one had called Jillian Jilly in ages. Jillian fought a fresh onslaught of tears as she hurried across the yard and up onto the chair-scattered veranda where she'd spent many a lazy afternoon as a child.

In the nine years Jillian had been gone, Hattie hadn't changed a bit. She was still huggably ample and round, still had a lacy white handkerchief peeking out of one apron pocket while the imprint of her reading glasses rumpled another, and she still wore her feathery white hair in a simple, grandmotherly bun at the back. Although her black shoes were different—these a bit more fashionable than the old matron shoes she had worn ten years ago—her dress was still as comfortably cut and her smile as welcomingly warm.

"How could I possibly forget my way here?" Jillian asked, her heart rushing out to encompass the dear woman she had known practically all her life. She hurried forward for her usual hug. "I've been here far too many times to ever forget something like that."

"But it's been nearly nine years." She spoke with her usual spritely clip common only to Maine. "I thought maybe you'd forgotten all about us old Mainiacs by now. But then I guess you've been too busy with this one to have had much time for vacations and the like." She gestured to Pete, who stood cautiously off to one side, a black cat with goofy-looking eyes draped over his arm. "I gather he's not much for hugging strangers." She made no move toward him. "Is this by chance Pete, the boy who'll be needing a rollaway?"

"Yes, this is Pete. And you're right, he's not much for hugging strangers," Jillian agreed, then winked at Pete to relax him a bit before following Hattie inside. Pete took a moment to stroke the cat's gleaming black fur, then set it down and trailed the adults into the foyer.

"I see nothing has changed," Jillian offered, scribbling her name into the registration book while waiting for Hattie to pull a room key out of the old ceramic boxes that lined the registration desk. As she set the pen back in its holder, she glanced at the grandfather clock that had fascinated her so as a child. Funny, it didn't look nearly as large as she remembered it. But it was every bit as stately.

"Oh, I'm sure you'll find some things have changed, but mostly this place remains the same. I see no need to tamper with perfection." Hattie quirked a quick smile as she plucked the key she wanted and held it out. She turned her attention to Pete, who stood near the front door, quietly studying his new surroundings. "But I see things have definitely changed for you. How old is your son?"

"Eight." Pete piped in, answering for himself, then looked a bit embarrassed when he quickly amended. "Well, I will be in just over a week. For now, though, I'm still seven. But I'm so short, most folks think I'm only six. I hate that, but I'm pretty much used to it."

Jillian shifted uncomfortably. Would Hattie do a quick bit of math in her head? Counting back the nine months plus would easily reveal that Pete was conceived the latter part of July or the early part of August during her last summer there.

"Is this key to the Great White Room?" Jillian asked, quickly diverting Hattie's attention, hoping Reynold had remembered to make the request when he phoned in the reservations. She had always loved it those summers they managed to have the big front room on the second floor with the charming, windowed sitting area attached.

"Yes, you two are in the Great White. Your friend will have the Shell Room. And the New Yorkers will have the big suite out in the carriage house, which has now been updated to include a microwave and a telephone. Your friend wanted to be sure the New Yorkers had the best while they were here. I have those other three all scheduled to arrive sometime Friday afternoon. Is that correct?" She narrowed her eyes as if unusually interested in the answer.

Jillian nodded. "Yes, Reynold is coming here straight from a business meeting in New York City with David Nelson, the president of a large corporation Reynold has been trying for months now to win over for the firm. And you're right, he wants nothing but the best for them."

Which was why Jillian had come early. To set up a full schedule of events, then help Reynold entertain David Nelson and his wife, Shelly, who was also to meet them there late Friday afternoon.

Willing to help in any way she could, Jillian had already memorized not only their names, but their favorite foods, their favorite topics of conversation, and the awkward fact the wife hated the ocean almost as much as her husband loved it.

That alone should make it quite an interesting two weeks. Jillian was just glad she and Pete had been asked to arrive early, more so she could have a needed adjustment period to get over the disturbing effect that being there again caused than to have a day or two to set up the fishing trips, island tours, picnics, and such. By the time Reynold arrived Friday afternoon, she should be back to her old self and ready to take on her hostess duties with a smile.

Well remembering *the couple that got away*, Hattie waited until she heard the door close upstairs before reaching for the telephone. She had considered the meddlesome plan for days now, ever since hearing that Jillian Westworth was about to return with friends. But now that Hattie had seen the boy for herself, she knew it was the thing to do.

Having memorized the telephone number, she happily dialed Brad Pierce then waited for someone to pick up.

"Dr. Pierce, here," Brad answered, sounding extremely tired for so early in the afternoon.

Hattie wondered why an assistant or nurse hadn't answered the telephone, as busy as Brad must be taking care of the general medical needs of two rural counties in northern Maine. "Dr. Pierce? It's Hattie Stillman. I hope I'm not bothering you, but I have some wonderful news."

Because Brad returned to Sea Haven Village every year to visit with the friends he'd made years earlier, he had little problem recognizing the voice. Suddenly, he didn't sound so tired. "And what good news is that?"

Since Brad did not like to talk about Jillian, or how the two had parted Sea Haven Village not speaking so many years ago, Hattie did not mention her current guest. She didn't dare. Nothing clammed him up quicker than to mention Jillian by name. Instead, she went right to the plan. "There's been a little prize drawing involving the names of all the guests who stayed here last year and guess who won?"

"Me?"

"That's right. You. You've just won a week at the Seascape in addition to all the other surprises that go with it." She pressed a hand over her mouth to keep from giggling at that last comment, thinking herself quite witty. *Surprises indeed!*

"I have?"

"A-yuh, but there is one catch to this. I know you usually like to come in late summer, but for this, the week has to be taken right away, before the busy season starts. Are you at all interested in collecting such a nice prize?" She held her breath and awaited the answer.

After an unbearably long pause, Brad responded, "To tell you the truth, you couldn't have called at a better time. As it turns out, I'm just coming off a very emotionally draining week and could really use a little R & R. And Dr. Mack still owes me from having covered for him a couple of weeks back in March." Another bit of silence was followed by a deep laugh. "And my nurse has already deserted me for the rest of the month, having just had that baby of hers. Yes, this is definitely doable. Unless I call you back, expect me sometime tomorrow."

Hattie felt light as air as, seconds later, she plopped the receiver back into its cradle. Tomorrow was perfect. He'd be there a full day before this Reynold Johnstone fellow arrived, whoever *he* was.

Glancing ceilingward with an impish grin, she wondered what her Tony thought about all this. He had always considered Jillian and Brad one of his few failures. She knew that was why Tony had never tried to pair Brad with one of the other guests at the Inn during the nine years following. They all felt Brad had belonged with Jilly.

Tony must be delighted to have this second shot at the pair—and even more delighted to see that they shared a son. Dressed the way the boy was, in a baggy white Astros T-shirt nearly as long as his shorts, and wearing a Rangers ball cap turned backward, the small seven-year-old looked amazingly like his thirty-one-year-old father, though there was plenty of his mother in him, too. Such a handsome child.

What would Brad's reaction be when he arrived that next day and discovered not only was his lost love there, but so was his son?

A son Brad obviously didn't know existed.

❧ *Chapter 2* ❧

Adjusting to the familiar surroundings more quickly than she had expected, Jillian pushed aside her sad memories of Brad and the summer-gone-awry long enough to enjoy this time with her son. She and Pete, who had also long since overcome his sulky attitude about the place, returned to the Great White Room to change out of their wet swimsuits into dry clothes, eager to hike into the village for a couple of midafternoon snacks.

"I'm fre-e-e-zing," Jillian chattered as she tried to stab the key into the lock with a trembling hand. "I can't believe you dared me into doing something like that."

"I can't believe you let me," Pete laughed as he pulled his beach towel tighter around his shivering shoulders. "How should I know the water would be that cold? Back home, Troy and I have been swimming since before ball season started."

"But that's in Texas. This is Maine. There's a world of difference."

"So I just found out." He laughed again when his mother shoved the door wide and raced to the blue-covered bed to grab her clothes and shampoo, then raced immediately back out into the hall, her damp beach towel knotted around her hips, flapping at her heels.

"Laugh all you want, but at least I thought to claim first

dibs on the bathroom. You just sit here and freeze your little freckles off. I'll be back in a minute.''

Opting for a quick, hot shower rather than the long, soaking bath she would have preferred, Jillian was in and out of the bathroom in less than ten minutes. Accustomed to sharing the only bathroom on that floor with whatever guests had the other two rooms, she quickly wiped the shower stall with her damp towel, then returned to the bedroom to put on fresh makeup and blow-dry her hair.

''Your turn,'' she told Pete as she draped her wet swimsuit over a hanger and placed it near one of the open windows in the turret. ''I left the shampoo in there for you. *Use it*. Then bring it, your swimsuit, and your towel back with you.''

''I know, I know. We have to leave the bathroom clean,'' Pete said, already headed for the door, a wad of clean clothes under his arm.

''And take the key with you. Don't forget, for some reason that door has been locking on us even though it doesn't have an automatic lock, and I'll be drying my hair and might not hear your knock over the noise.''

Shrugging, he detoured to the small table where she had tossed the key beside his favorite baseball cap and grabbed both before leaving.

Alone again, Jillian headed for the antique vanity. Sitting, she quickly combed the tangles out of her wet hair, applied fresh makeup, a layer of moisturizing insect repellent, then located the plug for her blow dryer. Shuffling through her accessories bag, she pulled out the round brush and the hair-pick she needed, then went to work styling her thick, shoulder-length brown hair into soft, dark waves away from her face. Already she could taste the old-fashioned strawberry ice cream sodas they planned to order in town.

How wonderful that she had finally been able to push aside most of her earlier heartache and frustration. This vacation might turn out to be a good thing after all.

* * *

Due to a late start, Brad arrived at the familiar little bed-and-breakfast tired but happy, wearing a comfortable pair of faded jeans, a Pirate baseball shirt, and a Pirate cap turned backward so the bill did not block part of his vision. He didn't question Hattie when she met him at the front door with a key to the Great White Room already in her hand. It was the room he always had whenever there. Nor did he question her oddly intent expression as he slid the key into his front jeans pocket and quickly scribbled his name onto a fresh page of the register.

"I parked the Blazer around back in the usual spot," he told her as he reached down to grab up the only bag he had brought. Although he planned to take advantage of the full week offered, he saw no reason to pack more than the one large satchel. With Sea Haven's relaxed atmosphere, there was no reason to take up space by packing anything dressy, and he kept a light jacket, a coat, and medical supplies in the Blazer, so he had not needed to pack any of that. All he had needed to throw together was his favorite sneakers and an assortment of comfortable jeans, shorts, and shirts. "If you want me to move it for any reason, just let me know."

"It'll be fine. Enjoy your stay," Hattie assured him as he hastened toward the stairs, eager to make himself at home. "And enjoy all the wonderful surprises that go with it."

Feeling rejuvenated just being near the ocean again, Brad jogged up the stairs, taking them two at a time. He paused near the alcove windows to stare out at the water a moment, then pushed aside the unbidden feeling of sadness that always washed over him whenever he first arrived there. Rather than become bogged in bitter memories that twisted at his heart and thrashed his pride, he took a deep breath and turned away. It did no good to live in the past.

A quick glance at his watch revealed there was enough time for a brisk, invigorating swim before supper. Just the thing to discourage any further melancholy thoughts. He would take a quick swim in the icy water to get his blood stirring again then head over to the co-op and see who was there. By then a few of the boats should be in.

Unbuttoning his shirt with his free hand as he headed toward the bedroom door, he already pictured having the entire beach to himself. Being the off-season for tourists and a workday for the locals, there would be no one else there to bother him. With the way part of the beach set in a tiny inlet, he could swim nude if he wanted, although the thought of entering that frigid water without at least a swimsuit for protection wasn't all that inviting. Invigorating was one thing. Purposely freezing off vital parts of one's body was quite another.

Outside the familiar door, Brad paused long enough to fish the room key out of his pocket with his free hand and noticed a low, steady humming noise inside the room. Attributing the sound to a small vacuum, and not really caring that the room was still being cleaned, he slid the key into place, turned it, retrieved it, then stepped inside.

Seated on the small chair upholstered in the same restful shade of blue that accented the rest of the spacious room she had often shared with her parents, Jillian still faced the mirror, finishing her hair, when she caught a glimpse of movement behind her. Shifting her gaze to the reflection of the now-open door, she expected to see Pete, fully dressed, baseball cap in place, ready to hike into town. He so hoped to run into a few of the local boys so he could get to know them. She just hoped they would not be too busy with chores and homework to spend at least a little time with her son. It might help him get over missing Troy so much.

Discovering the area near the door empty, she turned her attention further into the room, to the area where the dresser stood against the far wall. Her heart slammed high into her throat, cutting short her next breath, when instead of her impatient short-for-seven-years-old-son, she saw Brad Pierce. All six-foot-two of him.

Unable to form a rational thought at such an unexpected

sight, she cut off the hand dryer and set it down as she stared round-eyed and unblinking at the unmoving reflection. There being no real logic to what she saw, for Brad lived in a completely different part of the state; her pulses throbbed with a strangling combination of hope, anger, disbelief, and fear.

Worried he was just another apparition, having seen his strong, handsome image in so many places since her arrival, she didn't move. She feared if she turned around for a better look, he wouldn't really be there. Yet, at the same time, she feared he *would*.

Struggling to calm a maelstrom of battling emotions, and still unable to speak the words to express her jumbled musings, she continued staring dumbfoundedly at the reflection of the man she had never fully banished from her heart. How wonderful and sexy he looked, standing on the opposite side of the room, a billed cap turned backward anchoring a soft hank of curling, dark brown hair in need of a trim—*exactly like Pete's*.

Comfort appeared to be more important than tidiness because, also like Pete, he wore his black baseball shirttail out and unbuttoned, exposing a still flat stomach and a lightly haired, muscular chest—although not nearly as sun bronzed as in years past, it was every bit as manly.

Jillian's fingers itched with the memory of how warm and comforting that strong chest had felt nine years earlier—a chest she had thought would always be there for her cheek to find solace.

Not wanting to be reminded of their two summers together, or of his eventual betrayal after so many words of love, she pushed the unwanted memories aside. Memories that only hurt her more.

"*Jillian?* What on this green earth are *you* doing here?" Brad asked, first to break the taut silence. He took a step in her direction, but only a step.

"Drying my hair," she answered the obvious, still staring into his incredibly blue eyes through the mirror. She set the hairbrush down, her hand now too weak to hold even that.

His having spoken meant the apparition was real. Brad Pierce stood just the other side of the tall, double bed, staring at her with as much uncertainty as she stared at him.

Her heart hammering madly beneath her white silk blouse, she finally managed a breath as she slowly turned to face him. "How'd you get in here?" She indicated the spacious white room with a quick wave of her hand as she caught sight of the large, unfamiliar black travel bag that sagged on the braided rug at his feet. "How'd you get inside my bedroom without me letting you in? That door has been locking on us automatically ever since we got here."

"Your bedroom?" Brad peered down at the key still in his hand then held it up as if that should explain. "Hattie told me this was to be my bedroom for the week. It's the room I always have when I come here. She's the one who gave me the key." His forehead notched with a combination of confusion and suspicion when he lifted his blue gaze to Jillian again. "Did you win a week's vacation, too?"

"No. We paid to be here."

For some reason, it hurt to know he still came there. The place obviously did not affect him as painfully as it did her. "We?"

His gaze snagged the rollaway folded against the far wall. *Pete's* rollaway. Her heart cringed.

"Who's we?"

Not wanting to answer, Jillian ran her hands nervously over the smooth surface of her summer-pink gabardine slacks, then hurried to ask a question of her own. "Am I to gather by what you said that you've won a week stay here?" Her stomach knotted at the thought. If true, Brad would be there half the two weeks she and Pete planned to be there.

What dreadful timing. How could she ever hope to keep Pete and Brad apart in such cozy surroundings for an entire week? Talk about asking the impossible. It would probably be better for everyone concerned if, instead, she faked some sort of an emergency and took her son home now. Before he and Brad had an opportunity to see each other.

But that would mean deserting Reynold in his hour of need. She could not in good conscience leave Reynold there to entertain the Nelsons alone. Especially not after having also promised him this chance to get to know Pete better. Pete hadn't quite accepted Reynold yet, and this trip was supposed to rectify that somehow.

"Yes, I did win a week here. Or so I was told." Brad glanced at the clutter on the bed and the personal items scattered across the desk near the window. "But apparently some sort of mistake has been made with the room assignments. Since you have obviously been here long enough to be well settled, I'll go downstairs and swap keys for a different room."

"Thank you. I'd appreciate that." *And hurry. Before Pete comes back from the bathroom and you see each other.* Her pulses pounded with such fearful concern, she felt the throbbing in the hollow of her throat. She reached up to touch the delicate heart-shaped pendant that rested just below her collarbone to hide the pulse point from Brad's penetrating gaze.

Brad studied her an endless few seconds longer, then bent for his bag and turned to leave. He tensed after having gone only two steps toward the doorway.

Jillian glanced at the still-open door and silently gasped, her worst fear realized.

There stood Pete, staring at Brad with a pair of dark-lashed eyes the exact same shape, and glimmering the exact same shade of blue as his father's.

Eight years of protecting Pete from the truth stood on suddenly shaky ground.

While Jillian's heart struggled for its next beat, Brad's puzzled gaze cut to Jillian's left hand, obviously looking for a wedding ring. Not finding one, he cut back to Pete's curious expression.

In turnabout, Jillian glanced at his finger to see if he wore a ring. He didn't. But that was no surprise, considering his view of marriage.

"Well, suddenly it all makes more sense," Brad said, his

body rigid when Pete moved a few more steps into the doorway.

Pete glanced at his mother across the room as if trying to decide if this man meant to harm them. She tried to appear calm, for his sake.

"What makes more sense?" Jillian asked, before realizing that whatever Brad had to say could be ugly enough to cause severe emotional trauma for Pete. When she did realize how the wrong answer could devastate Pete, her stomach clinched. *Please don't let him say the word bastard.* Let him call her all the names he wanted, but don't let him refer to Pete as his bastard. Pete knew the word only too well.

Brad looked at her again, studying her, then at Pete, just a few feet away. "Everything."

Ill prepared to have both Pete and Brad in the same room intently staring at each other, and fearing Brad would eventually react to the uncanny resemblance between him and his son and say something angry or hurtful, Jillian did not know what to do. Part of her wanted to go ahead and get everything on out into the open, letting the chips fall where they may. Nine years had been a long time to harbor such a secret. But a larger, more protective part of her feared one of those falling chips might pierce right through Pete's tender heart.

The many insecurities connected to Brad kicked in. Brad had not wanted a family. He had made it clear he especially didn't want children. And here he now stood faced with a son.

But obviously he hadn't caught on to that fact yet. If only she could keep it that way.

With no idea how Brad might respond once he realized the truth, she dared not chance a negative reaction. She had never asked Brad for help in supporting or raising the child, and had no intention of doing so now, but still he might see Pete as a threat. She would not chance that reaction.

Not with Pete right there to witness it.

What she needed was more time to think through this unexpected turn of events. Another nine years would do nicely.

"Weren't you on your way downstairs to solve the room problem?" she asked as a way to nudge him on out of their sight.

When Jillian showed no intention of introducing the two, Brad took it upon himself to determine more about the boy's identity. He knelt, facing Pete more than her, his taut leg muscles stretching the soft fabric of his jeans. "Hi, there, young man. What's your name?"

"Pete," he answered, looking first at Brad, then at the clothing bag beside him with a puzzled expression. "Who are you and why are you in our room?"

That was Pete. Never too shy to ask questions when it came to a situation he didn't understand.

"My name is Brad Pierce. Dr. Brad Pierce. I live here in Maine, although a good distance north of here. I'm an old friend of your mother's."

Pete's eyes widened upon hearing Brad's name and occupation. "You know my mom from when she used to come up here on vacation a lot?" He looked at his mother questioningly but didn't voice any suspicions—for which she felt deeply grateful. Jillian wasn't certain he had made the connection, having not asked about his father in over a year, but worried he would eventually. How would Pete take to finding out that the biggest reason his father did not know about him was because he did not want children? Ever. Children were a hindrance to men like Brad.

No, it was better Pete believed that the only reason she had not married his father was because there had not been enough love between them. He was still too young to understand the rest.

Again, she tried to hurry Brad out of the room by reminding him about the key, but Brad wasn't to be hurried. Was that because he had finally guessed Pete's true identity?

"I see by your shirt and cap that you are a Rangers fan," Brad commented, then gestured to his own shirt, still open and exposing a strip of taut male skin. He smiled a dimpled smile, much like Pete's. It was a smile that had touched Jillian's heart in a way no other could. "I'm a Pirate fan myself."

"I like both the Astros and the Rangers," Pete explained, then unwadded his beach towel and the shirt he had worn to the beach to show him the Astros emblems since at the moment all he had on were Ranger clothes. "But the Pirates are okay."

"A Texas man all the way, eh? Have you ever been to any of their games?"

"Sure, my grandpa takes me when he can."

"What about your father?" Brad stood again and glanced out into the hall as if expecting to see someone else enter the room. "Doesn't he take you to any games?"

Jillian held her breath, praying that Pete had yet to make the connection. How would she handle it if her son responded to Brad's questions by asking him if maybe he was his father? Would she quickly lie, knowing eventually Brad would figure out the truth? Or would she face the awful showdown now?

It was not a decision she was ready to make.

"I don't have a father," Pete answered simply. "At least not yet."

"Yet?"

Pete nodded then quirked a dimple that was in no way associated with a smile. This time, the dimple reminded her more of herself. "There's a man Mom met a few months ago who says he wants be my father and has even asked Mom to marry him, but for now we go it alone. Always have."

Brad studied the boy with a guarded expression while Jillian prayed he wouldn't guess the truth, and if he did guess it, that he would keep silent for now. Her heart cringed with each word that fell from his mouth.

"So, you are the only man of the house right now?"

Pete eyebrows arched as he tossed back his skinny shoulders and puffed his chest at that last question. "That's me."

Brad studied him a moment more, filled his lungs with a deep breath, then held out his hand for an official greeting.

"Glad to meet you, Pete. I hope we see more of each other during the next several days."

He tossed Jillian a quick, probing look, then grabbed up his bag again and left.

Jillian released the breath she had held about three seconds too long in a soft, audible rush.

Safe.

For now.

Furious couldn't begin to describe Brad's feelings as he marched back down the stairs in search of Miss Hattie. Guessing the boy upstairs to be about five to six years old, he would have to be an idiot not to realize the implication. The pain from it cut so deep, he felt it from the inside out.

Jillian had a son. A son who was undoubtedly conceived within that first year after they parted.

For someone who had once pledged her undying love, she had certainly managed to replace it and him quickly enough.

During all those years he had pined away, miserably wishing their situations could have allowed a more permanent relationship between them, she had already found someone else. No wonder she hadn't bothered trying to contact him again after their last summer together. Jillian had deceived him from the start. Since she had never really loved him, she had probably not given their summers together a second thought before entering into an intimate relationship with whoever eventually fathered her son.

Had he really thought she might have been miserable, too? Boy, that was sure a joke.

Having just faced the very human evidence of how little he had meant to her back then—how he had been so completely duped by her sweet mutterings of love and devotion—it felt like someone had just driven a stake right through his heart. The pain was so intense he wasn't sure he could bear it.

She could at least have waited a couple of years before falling that deeply for someone else. After all, he had gone the full nine years and had not found anyone to compare yet.

But, too, if she had cared enough about this other man to have had such an intimate relationship with him, why hadn't she married him? Pete had mentioned he and his mom went it alone and always had. Could it be the man who replaced him had used her in much the same way she had used Brad? Had her second lover wanted a little more than someone to help pass the time?

"Dr. Pierce, you look unhappy," Hattie said, glancing up from where she had just written something on a small piece of scratch paper. "Is there a problem with the Cove Room?"

Brad had paused on the bottom step, his hand holding the banister in nothing short of a death grip, but moved forward again at the sound of Hattie's voice. "I'm sorry, but you didn't give me the key to the Cove Room. You gave me a key to the Great White."

"I did?" Hattie's lily-white hand fluttered to her lace-edged collar. "But how could I have made a mistake like that? I already have guests staying in the Great White."

"So I found out," he replied, leveling a gaze at her. Although he had never really considered Miss Hattie the conniving sort, she did have the reputation of being somewhat of a matchmaker. Just how innocent was she in all this? And how innocent was Jillian? Was it possible Jillian paid to have Hattie call and pretend he had won a week's stay?

But, no, that concept didn't quite fit with the way Jillian had all but tossed him out of her room a few minutes ago. Still, it seemed a bit too coincidental that after all these years they would both return there at the same time like that—and that they had both ended up being handed a key to the same room.

But then, in truth, the Seascape Inn was known to have stranger things than that happen.

"Here's that key you gave me," he handed it back, watching while she scrambled through her ceramic boxes with a crooked finger, looking for a different one.

"You are certainly right. That was indeed a key to the

Great White. I guess I'm so used to giving you that room, I handed that key to you by mistake. I wasn't really thinking. I'm so sorry. So very truly sorry. Especially when you consider who is up there right now. *Oh, my.*''

Hattie's string of apologies fell on deaf ears. Falling under their own direction, Brad's thoughts became lodged in the past while waiting for the correct key.

Vividly remembering the day he first saw Jillian standing along the cliffs, watching the boats dock all those years ago, he did little more than thank Hattie when she finally handed him another key, then he headed back up the stairs. Clearly, he had been just as awestruck by Jillian's beauty back then as he was now, because in the nine years since he had last seen her, she'd hardly changed.

Nor had her effect on him.

Which angered him more.

Even as he slid his key into the lock of the new room, his pulses raced like some young schoolboy's. Just from having seen her again. Oh, how he resented her for that.

Glancing across at her closed door, one thing rang clear. He would have to be very careful during the coming week or chance losing his heart to the beautiful Jillian Westworth all over again. If that happened, he risked suffering an even worse heartache than the first time.

Old wounds, once reopened, were the hardest to heal.

''Mom, we gotta eat,'' Pete complained when his mother suggested they skip supper downstairs and instead bring the checkerboard upstairs and play a friendly game of checkers in their room. He pressed his nose against the window screen so he could see the black cat crossing the yard below, the same goofy-eyed cat that had followed them back from town earlier.

''Pete, how can you possibly think of food when it has only been a few hours since we had those ice cream sodas?'' she asked, patting her stomach with the flat of her palm. ''Aren't you still full from that?''

Pete pushed away, the cat having finally moved out of sight. "Not really. Besides, you told Miss Hattie at lunch that we'd both be there for supper tonight. Don't you remember? She asked if we'd rather have fish or ham and you asked her if she had any salmon? Remember? You said something about how she used to fix it when you were a girl. Isn't it wrong to promise one thing then turn around and do another?"

"But—" she started to argue then shrugged, surrendering. "Okay, you're right. I did say we'd have dinner here. We will indeed go downstairs for supper at the appropriate time."

"I thought she said supper was at seven. It's nearly that time now." He pointed toward the digital clock, the only kind he knew how to read, then waited for his mother to suck in and release that long, slow, deep breath she always sucked in and released whenever she was more irritated than usual about something. "Doesn't that mean we should go eat now?"

"Just a minute." Making Pete wait, she stepped over to the mirror and brushed hair that didn't need no brushing, smoothed a couple of wrinkles out of the pink pants she wore that didn't need no smoothing, then powdered the tip of a nose that didn't need no powdering. Finally, she turned away from the mirror and plucked Pete's hat off his head just before they headed out the door. "You don't wear your hat at the dinner table, remember?"

"You sound like Mr. Johnstone," Pete muttered, snatching the red cap from her, folding it in half, and tucking the bill into his waistband so he would have it for later. A guy had to stay prepared.

"It's proper advice for anyone who wants to show good manners. Reynold is just concerned with how others perceive you."

With the stairs just wide enough for two, they walked down together, but paused halfway just long enough for his mother to straighten a crooked painting of the smiling woman who used to own the house, the one his mother had told him such funny ghost stories about the night before—all having to do with this lady and her meddlesome grown-up son, Tony.

"I wonder if Dr. Pierce will be at supper tonight," Pete commented, checking his mother's face to catch her reaction as they started downstairs again. Ever since the doctor had poked his head into their room earlier, his mother had been acting a lot like Tweetie Bird in a room filled with Sylvesters. Which was why Pete suspected this Brad guy now staying in the room across the hall just might be more than some old friend. It just could be that he was the same Brad guy who was also his father.

Pete remembered his mother telling him once how his father, Brad, had been a real serious medical student all those years ago. So serious in fact that going to college to become the doctor he had always wanted to be was part of the reason he never married his mother and became his real father. Being a doctor was more important to him than having a wife.

"I don't know if he will be there or not," she answered after a pause, giving no real insight into how she felt about that. But then, she was awful good at not looking angry even when she was. Scary thing, that.

"I sure hope he's there," Pete offered just as he leaped from the squeaky third step to the floor below, just to prove he could jump that far and still land on his feet. "I like him."

"Why? Because he's a baseball fan?"

"Yeah, and 'cause he's a friend of yours." He headed automatically for the dining room. "No offense, Mom. But you don't have all that many friends."

She arched her eyebrow in such a way that it made Pete laugh.

"Well, you don't. Except for Mr. Johnstone, Grandpa, and those people you work with over at Great-Grandpa Bailey's charity foundation, you don't have many friends at all. Not like Troy's mother." Troy's mother had lots of friends, so many she sometimes didn't have time to do the laundry or cook a meal, which was okay with Troy since he didn't mind dirty clothes and his mother was one lousy cook anyway. That was one reason Pete like eating over there so much. They had pizza a lot.

"I have enough friends to suffice," she replied with a sharp wag of her head. "Besides, you left my very best friend off that list entirely."

Pete paused in the doorway, puzzled. "Who's that?"

"You, silly."

Grinning, he continued on into the room. "Oh, yeah, I forgot." He paused just inside the room to breathe deeply the smells coming from the kitchen.

"Forgot what?"

Pete hadn't noticed Dr. Pierce standing over by the big double doors made mostly of tiny windows with his back to the room. Sure enough, neither had his mom. They both jumped at the sound of his deep, man's voice. His mom maybe even more than him.

"That I'm my mother's best friend," Pete answered, hurrying to see just what it was Dr. Pierce stared at through the windows in the door. He laughed when he spotted a short, fat, black and gold dog stretched on its side with Candy the Cock-eyed cat perched across his belly, eyes closed, as if she had every right to be there. He guessed Dr. Pierce liked to look at animals, too.

"Odd sight, don't you think?" Brad asked, tilting his head to the right as if that might help him make better sense of the pair. Until then, Brad had stood board stiff, but with Pete laughing beside him, his shoulders relaxed some.

Pete laughed again. "What we need now is for some bird to fly down and settle on top of the cat's head."

"Yeah, that would be something, wouldn't it?" Brad chuckled, too, then reached down to rumple the top of Pete's head.

Pete flinched when he first saw the hand coming, used to Mr. Johnstone's constant attempts to tidy his unruly curls, then blinked in surprise when instead Dr. Pierce had tousled it more. Grinning, he peered up at his new friend. The guy liked to look at animals and didn't worry none with slicked-back hair or dressing up for supper. Although he had thought to take off his baseball cap, Dr. Pierce still wore the same pair of jeans and the same black and white baseball shirt he'd had on earlier that day. *Mr. Johnstone would not approve.* "You know, you're all right, Dr. Pierce."

"Thanks, but call me Brad. We're friends now, aren't we?" Returning Pete's grin, he turned away from the door. "And you're pretty all right yourself." He glanced briefly at Pete's mom before heading for one of the ten cushioned, straight backed chairs surrounding the dining table.

Friends? With an adult? Pete knew right then he liked this Dr. Brad Pierce. Whether the man turned out to be his father or not, he liked him. Liked him a lot.

But obviously, his mother didn't feel the same way. She had already sat down in the same chair she'd sat in during their last three meals there—the same one she said she had sat in as a girl—and now stared so many angry daggers through her water glass, Pete was surprised it didn't pop a half-dozen leaks.

Having gotten used to sitting in the chair right beside her, he pulled it back and sank onto the pink and dark blue flowery cushion. Then, knowing his mother would do it for him if he didn't, he took his napkin, shook it once, and plopped it in his lap before sitting a moment, kicking his legs.

"Where's Miss Hattie?" Pete really didn't much care where she was, but the room seemed just a little too quiet without someone talking about something.

"She's gone to remind Cora it's time to serve the meal," Brad answered, settling in a chair across the table. "She'll be back in just a few minutes."

He, too, thought to put his napkin in his lap, which Pete thought would score points with his mom. But it didn't. She continued to look just about ready to explode.

Again, the room fell so quiet they could hear the slow ticking of the big clock out in the hall.

Pete twisted his mouth, looking around for something else to talk about, clear that unless he kept the conversation going, there'd be none at all. But what could they talk about? What did his mom and this man used to talk about?

Pete chuckled to himself when he looked again at Brad and noticed, he, too, was searching the room as if looking for something to discuss. It was then that Pete noticed Brad had the same color eyes as his and, without a ball cap, Brad's dark hair parted in the exact same spot as his, not quite in the middle, but not really to the side either. The color of his hair was just a little different, but not too much different.

How he longed to know if this man might really be his father. But at the same time, he feared asking. He did not want to take the chance of being told different. He wanted it way too bad to chance being told it was not true.

Glancing again at his mother, he saw she still refused to look at Dr. Pierce. It was like she was pretending the man wasn't even in the same room with them. He chuckled again, quiet like, so no one would notice while he thought about what would happen if he suddenly screwed up his courage enough to just up and ask his mother out loud if this man was by some chance his father.

She would sure have to give the man some notice then.

It was an idea certainly worth some pondering.

❧ *Chapter 3* ❧

What normally was Jillian's favorite meal of the day turned out to be nearly a solid hour of silent torture. No matter what she did, or how hard she tried to act unaffected by Brad's presence or by the friendly rapport developing between him and her son, she couldn't quite seem to pull it off. Every time she glanced up from her plate, her gaze went involuntarily to the strong lines of his lean face, which, incredibly, had become even more endearing with age.

How annoying that those perfect-shaped curves in his cheeks had deepened and that his impossibly blue eyes with the long, curling dark lashes were even sexier than she remembered. He also looked more wizened somehow. No longer was he the carefree young man from the two summers she had known him. He was a doctor now. He had achieved the goal he had fought so hard to have, and now faced all the many crises a medical doctor faced by dint of his profession.

Seemed fair, she thought, perversely hoping he was at least half as miserable as she had been these past several years. If it had not been for Pete, she would have been unbearably lonely and unfulfilled.

But *was* he miserable? What *was* his life like now that he finally had what he had wanted more than anything else—even more than he had wanted her? Was he as happy as he had expected to be? Or had he discovered being a doctor not quite what he had thought it would be? Like some of her father's friends.

Judging by his jovial nature while bantering with Pete or teasing Miss Hattie, she supposed he was indeed very satisfied with how his life had turned out. And that irritated her to no end. How could he be so happy without her when she had been so miserable without him? It didn't seem at all fair. But then it was her own fault she had fallen in love with him those many years ago. She'd known from the first day they met, his becoming a medical doctor had meant the world to him, and justifiably so. She had just hoped she would come to mean as much.

But she hadn't.

How foolish she had been to think he cared enough about her to want to marry her.

How foolish she was even now, wishing he would have a miraculous change of heart and suddenly decide he did love her and couldn't live without her after all. Why couldn't she just be a realist and accept what was never meant to be? But then, too, why couldn't she keep from looking at him every time she lifted her gaze from her plate? What was it about him that jammed every logic-related frequency in her brain? And always had.

Fortunately, Brad had become so involved in his conversations with Pete and Miss Hattie, he rarely glanced in her direction long enough to notice her unexplainable interest.

Clearly, he wasn't in any way as affected by her presence as she was by his. And that wounded her pride as much as it battered her heart. He could at least pretend he noticed she was there. Instead, a majority of his attention went to Pete, which seemed a little odd to her.

For a man who had never wanted any children in his life, he certainly got along well with this one. He and Pete had struck up an amazingly quick friendship. Which wouldn't be so worrisome if not for the constant fear that Brad would eventually see something in the child that triggered the truth.

A resemblance that would make him aware he had a son, one he had never been told existed.

Jillian dreaded what would happen should Brad figure out the truth about Pete's parentage. Pete would be the first one he'd hurt. She'd come in a close second.

Brad never wanted a child, but he also wouldn't like finding out that a child of his did exist yet had been kept from him all these years. Brad wasn't the type to tolerate having had such a secret kept from him—no matter how noble the reason.

But then again, he had seen Pete twice now without making a connection. Maybe they would make it the entire week without him discovering his special connection to her son. Possible, if she could just keep the two apart for the rest of the week. But fat chance of that, with Pete having taken such an instant liking to Brad. Maybe her best bet would be to try to catch Brad alone and explain the truth to him in a mature, calm, adult, rational way.

And hope he didn't kill her.

She shuddered, figuring Brad would react to that in one of two ways—of which she was prepared for neither. He would either reject her again, rejecting their son as well, or he would suddenly reenter her life, but for all the wrong reasons. If he found out about Pete, would he then demand his rights as a parent? And turn their serene world upside down in the process?

She couldn't chance that. She couldn't risk having to share Pete with a man who lived thousands of miles away. The same man who had turned her away so callously after having used her in the worst possible way a person could be used. The same man who had made it perfectly clear that he never wanted children. Or a wife.

In truth, Brad would have no moral right to intrude upon their lives to such a degree. But he would certainly have a *legal* one.

Jillian blew out an anguished breath as she set her fork

aside, her apple pie not half eaten. She had had enough emotional torture for one night. *Time to retire.*

"That was certainly a delicious meal," she said to no one in particular as she neatly folded then set aside her lace-edged napkin.

"But you hardly touched your dessert," Hattie complained. Her soft green gaze fell on Jillian's plate. "And after not eating but half your salmon. Aren't you feeling well?"

"Oh, no, I'm fine." She couldn't have Miss Hattie worrying about her health, not when there was absolutely nothing the sweet woman could do to cure what ailed her. For once, even the gentle magic of the Seascape Inn could not soothe her troubles away. "The truth is Pete and I decided to be a little naughty this afternoon and went into the village for giant ice cream sodas, and I guess mine affected my appetite."

"Strawberry, no doubt," Brad remarked, then quickly tensed, making her wonder if he had meant to comment at all. He refused to look at her.

"Yeah, you're right." Pete piped in, clearly impressed by Brad's insight. "They were both strawberry and they had real strawberries floating in them. Big fat ones you had to fish out with a spoon. You should go try one sometime."

"I've had them in the past." Brad admitted, his handsome face rigid as he, too, folded his napkin and set it aside. He laced his hands and rested them on the table in front of him while looking at Pete. "And you're right, they are good."

Jillian shifted uncomfortably, knowing they had shared many a strawberry soda during their two summers together. She tried not to remember the laughter and murmurs of love that had accompanied those times.

Worried Brad was about to mention those shared sodas to her already inquisitive son, she sought to change the subject. But Pete was too quick with his next question.

"Well, then, next time me and Mom go into the village to have more of those strawberry sodas, you want to go along with us?"

Brad's pale blue gaze cut to hers, then quickly darted away.

He ran a hand through his thick dark hair, pushing it away from the strong lines of his face with a practiced swipe. "I don't think your mother really cares to share any of her time here with anyone but you. This is your vacation together."

"Oh, she doesn't mind. The more the merrier, isn't that right, Mom?"

Jillian forced a tenuous smile as she struggled to draw that next breath into an extremely constricted pair of lungs. Suddenly, the room felt hot. Stifling. She had to find some way to nip this latest idea in the bud. "The truth is, Pete, we do only have one more day to share together before the others arrive."

"Others?" Brad frowned. Clearly, he had not expected there to be more people coming.

Why? Did he think she couldn't possibly have any friends of her own? Just because she had foolishly allowed him to be the only person in her life during those two summers so long ago, didn't mean he had remained the only person during all these years. Didn't he remember Eve and Trana who had come to visit her for a week during the early part of that last summer? She *did* have a life of her own. Even back then. And she *did* finally get over him.

Brad, having studied her with those penetrating blue eyes a moment, quickly returned his attention to Pete, his expression unreadable. "You have more people coming?"

"Yeah, Mr. Johnstone and two people I don't know are coming up here tomorrow. Mr. Johnstone is Mom's fiancé." Pete made it clear by the sharp twang in his voice that he wasn't exactly pleased by the prospect.

"Fiancé?" He looked again at Jillian's bare ring finger, then lifted an eyebrow as if to question the validity of that last statement.

"I'm having it resized," Jillian stated pointedly, letting him know she had not missed the insinuation. Just because she wasn't worthy of him didn't mean she wasn't worthy of all men. Her worst insecurities reborn, she reached up to play nervously with the gold pendant at her throat, the one her mother had given her the day Pete was born. "We've only been engaged for four days."

"Interesting." Brad's facial muscles turned to granite as he shoved his chair back, but didn't stand even though he had clearly intended to. It was as if something held him back.

His scowl deepened.

"Yeah, remember? I told you upstairs about the man who wants Mom to marry him. He's also the one who wants to be my father. Or so he says." Pete offered the explanation for no apparent reason. He had certainly not been asked. "I just wish the guy knew how to do stuff, like play baseball."

"He doesn't know how to play baseball?" Brad's angry expression faded as he turned his focus back to the boy.

"What a shame," Hattie put in. A pensive expression pulled at the soft wrinkles in her face. Her glittering gaze missed nothing of this exchange as she reached up to pat a stray wisp of stark white hair back into place. "Everyone should know how to play baseball."

Pete's mouth flattened as if he considered the situation downright ludicrous. "This man doesn't even want to go to a ballgame and learn about it. My grandpa tried to get him to go to a big game there in Dallas a few weeks ago, had free tickets given to him by one of his patients and everything, and Mr. Johnstone wasn't interested."

"He didn't have time," Jillian inserted in ready defense of Reynold, resenting that these two thought it their business to discuss someone Brad didn't even know. At least *Reynold* didn't shun the idea of having a family. *He* wanted a son in his life. "I've explained; Reynold is a very busy man with a very important job."

A muscle that curved through Brad's cheek twitched, but he said nothing in response.

"Busy? I'll say he is." Pete screwed up his face to show further disapproval, then dropped the discussion of Reynold all together. "Do you like to play baseball much, Dr.—I mean, Brad?" He quirked a grin, clearly liking the idea of having been asked to call a grown-up by his first name.

Jillian waited for the answer to Pete's question, glad for now Reynold was no longer the center of conversation. She didn't want to have to think about her fiancé at the moment, or what he might do after he arrived to discover her there with an old boyfriend. Would he turn out to be the jealous type? Or would he believe them meeting there was indeed unplanned, and at the same time understand just how foolish and naïve she had been back then—how she had truly thought Brad loved her. How she had foolishly thought that she and Brad were destined to be together forever.

Quietly, she studied the man she had thought one day she'd marry. Brad stared, unseeing, at the buffet on the far side of the room, as lost to his thoughts as she had been to hers, then blinked after Pete's question finally registered. "Know baseball? You bet I do. I'll admit I haven't played in awhile, but in my younger days I was one darned good little shortstop."

"You? A shortstop?" Pete looked truly bewildered by such a comment. "As tall as you are, I would think you'd have played outfield. Or with arms like those, maybe the pitcher."

Absently, Jillian glanced down at those arms and felt a deep, familiar fluttering in the vicinity of her stomach. Brad may not be working the fishing boats anymore, but he had certainly managed to keep in shape somehow. Could those strong arms possibly feel the same draped possessively around her shoulders as they had nine years earlier?

Her eyes widened, alarmed by the frightening direction of that last thought. Good grief, but she needed to get out of there! Before she became any more aware of Brad as a man. Or worse, as a lover. Why couldn't she just remember him as a callous heartbreaker and be done with it?

Struggling to do just that, Jillian cleared her throat, expecting to break the conversation long enough to make her excuses. But no one noticed.

"Oh, but I wasn't always this tall," Brad pointed out to Pete. "Right up until my last year in high school, I was one of the shortest boys in my whole class."

"I know how *that* feels. If it wasn't for Eric Goodman, I'd sure be the shortest boy in my room.'' Pete scowled, then hiked an eyebrow. ''When'd you get so tall?''

''I'm not exactly what's considered tall, but during my senior year I did suddenly shoot up about four inches and then grew another two inches after that. It drove my mother nuts trying to keep me in clothes that year.''

Pete considered that a moment and grinned. ''Maybe there's hope for me yet.''

Jillian studied her son quietly. With Brad having already been six-foot-two when she met him, she had forgotten all about his being short as a boy. There really was a good chance Pete wouldn't always be so short compared to the other boys. Knowing how much his lack of height bothered her son, she was glad for this new hope.

But afraid this discussion of similar problems in height might trigger other discussions of similarities between them, she quickly intervened. ''So, Pete, are you ready for our checker game rematch?''

''Sure. If you think you can stand losing again,'' Pete said, already pushing back his chair. He plucked his cap out of his waistband and slapped it back on his head as soon as he slid to his feet.

Glad finally to be able to leave behind Brad's disturbing presence, and all the painful memories associated with it, Jillian again complimented Hattie on the meal, and stood, only to find herself needing to sit again with Pete's next question.

''You wanna come, too, Brad? You could watch the first game, then play the winner. That's the way me and Troy and Jeffry do it when there's more than two of us.''

Jillian clinched a fist. What was it with Pete and all these blasted invitations? Why couldn't he just leave Brad out of their plans? ''Pete, I'm sure Brad has other things to do.''

When Brad didn't comment right away, Hattie took the opportunity to speak for him. ''Oh, but there's not much else to do around here this time of year. It still gets pretty chilly at night. I think a checker tournament would be fun. I'd love to play, too.'' She clapped her soft, weathered hands then rubbed them together in anticipation. "The first one to win three games is the declared champion and gets to say what dessert we'll have tomorrow night. If I win, it'll be apple crumb pie again." Eyes glittering, she glanced from Jillian to Brad to Pete. "What are your favorites?"

"I like chocolate cake." Pete put in quickly, not giving Jillian time to protest. "What about you, Brad? What dessert do you like."

"I like chocolate cake, too. But I think I like Miss Hattie's red velvet cake even better." He turned to look at Jillian as if to ask her if she remembered it, too. "With piles of white icing."

Hattie smiled. "So, it'll be chocolate cake if Pete wins or red velvet if Dr. Pierce wins. What about you Jilly? What'll it be if you win?"

Jillian had never felt so trapped. By declining, she would disappoint both Pete and Hattie, two people she really had no reason to disappoint. But if she agreed, she would be stuck in Brad's stifling presence the rest of the evening. Neither possibility appealed.

"Chocolate fudge," she finally relented, deciding she might as well make the stakes worth winning if she was going to have to participate. "With nuts."

"Yeah, she likes lots of nuts in her fudge," Pete agreed, his blue eyes sparkling at the prospect of a four-man checker tournament.

"Pecans, as I recall," Brad muttered as he pushed himself out of his chair to join them, but before anyone questioned how he knew, he had picked up his plate and glass and headed off toward the kitchen.

Reminded that Cora normally left as soon as supper was served during those months she worked, leaving Hattie to have to clear the table, Jillian, too, picked up her plate. She felt guilty for having forgotten until now.

Pete screwed his face, puzzled to see everyone suddenly grabbing up dirty dishes, but didn't ask any questions as he headed back to get his plate and glass, too. As soon as they had the table cleared and dishes soaking, the four headed for the front parlor to start the checker tournament.

Two painfully long hours later, Pete emerged victorious and Jillian wasted little time retiring them to their bedroom. Having spent most of the evening with Brad, being reminded of his quick wit and how very similar Pete's quirky facial expressions were to his father's, had caused her more heartache and misery than she cared to bear right now. She had come there hoping to enjoy herself. Not be so blatantly reminded of a love that would never be.

"That sure was fun," Pete said, obviously appraising the evening's activities from a different perspective. "Can you believe the stupid move Brad made there at the last?" He paused in his attempt to unfold the rollaway. "He almost had me cornered again, then moved right in the way of that perfect triple jump. I sure had him after that."

"A good thing you were able to get the best of him, since you were both down to such few pieces and it was for the world-global championship," she pointed out, although she suspected Brad had thrown the game on purpose. Brad enjoyed competition, but winning had never been all that important to him; it was the game itself he loved. To a certain degree, that explained the reason their relationship had ended so abruptly. He had enjoyed the game—the challenge of winning her heart—but in the end, the victory itself had meant very little to him. He had tossed her away like yesterday's bath water.

Determined not to think about Brad again that night, Jillian promptly grabbed up her nightclothes and headed for the bathroom to change. By the time she returned wearing her favorite beige nightgown and matching cover-up, Pete was in his Astros pajamas, sitting cross-legged on the rollaway, going through the baseball cards he had brought with him. With Pete, everything centered around baseball or Nintendo.

Glad to have his attention elsewhere, so tired all she wanted to do was put the horrible events of this day behind her and go to sleep, Jillian paused to breathe in the cedar-scented night air before closing two of the three windows she had left open. Leaving one half open so she could continue to breathe the tangy air during the night, she kissed Pete good-night and turned out all the lights but the one closest to him.

"If you feel cold during the night, get up and close that last window," she told him. "And as soon as you finish with those cards, be sure to turn out the light."

With Pete's head in those cards, Jillian expected no further conversation as she slid beneath the lemon-scented covers.

She had barely closed her eyes and settled into the most comfortable position when Pete evidently found something to quiz her about.

"Mom?"

Thinking it would be too obvious to try to pretend she was already asleep, Jillian responded, but without bothering to shift positions or open her eyes. "What?"

"Why are you so angry at Dr. Pier—ah, I mean, Brad?"

The question came out of nowhere and—knowing where the answer could lead—slammed like a fist into Jillian's stomach. It took a moment to catch enough of a breath to respond. "Why do you think I'm angry at Brad?"

Her blood trailed icy paths below the surface of her skin. This was not a conversation she wanted to have. Not yet. Not until she'd had more time to think about how to better explain everything.

"I don't know. It's just the way you treat him, I guess. And the way you don't smile whenever you are around him, like being around him makes you mad for some reason. And he acts the same way. I don't understand. He said you two used to be friends a long time ago. Why aren't you friends anymore?"

"Isn't it a little late to be asking all these questions?" she prodded, hoping to avert his attention. "We have a long day tomorrow."

"It's only ten o'clock."

"And well after your usual bedtime. We can talk about this later." *After* she'd spent half the night figuring out a safe but logical answer. She refused to just come out and tell him the truth, that his father never wanted him anymore than he had wanted her. That she had completely misread him.

"Is it something he did to you?"

"*Peter Alan*," she tried again to dissuade him, this time by using his full given name, something she did whenever she dangled at the end of her rope. "It's late. And I'm tired."

"I just want to know why you don't like being around him. He's really a nice guy."

"*Pe-ter*." She curled her hands into tight fists beneath the crisp white sheets that smelled like fresh lemon. "Put the cards away and go to sleep."

"I can't. I'm thirsty. I haven't had anything to drink since supper."

With a heart thudding hard and fast from a very real desire not to talk anymore, especially about Brad, Jillian fought to keep her voice calm and her words clear. "Then pour yourself a drink. There should be fresh water in that porcelain pitcher on the dresser. The one over there by the yellow flowers."

"But what if I'd rath—?"

"Water will have to do. There are glasses beside the pitcher."

Wide awake again and staring at the high, spackled ceiling—Pete's latest string of questions having effectively jump-started her pulses—Jillian listened with as much patience as she could muster while Pete dragged the desk chair across the floor, then checked the water pitcher.

"It's empty." He clattered it back into its bowl and climbed down from the chair. "Can I go downstairs to the kitchen and get a drink out of the refrigerator? Miss Hattie said it was all right to do that."

"Yes. Go on," she told him, puzzled. What had happened to the water that had been in there earlier? It couldn't have evaporated in so short a time.

But, then, she had to admit she was glad the water was gone. By the time he returned from downstairs, she could reasonably pretend to be asleep. That should avoid further questions for the night. "Just don't forget your key. That door is still locking itself automatically for reasons unknown to man."

"Maybe it's those ghosts you told me about last night," Pete offered, sliding the key into his pajama shirt pocket. "Maybe they are the ones tripping the lock. As some sort of prank."

"Pete, the ghosts are just make-believe. The stories aren't real, just tales the locals like to tell. The only person who thinks those ghost stories are in the least bit true is Batty Beaulah, that older woman I pointed out in town yesterday." *Ghosts indeed.* She'd given up believing in the ghosts of Seascape Inn a long time ago. "Go get your drink then come right back *and go to sleep.*"

"Whatever you say," Pete responded cheerfully, then quickly slipped out of the room.

Brad sat in the dark sipping a small glass of thick, cold chocolate milk, having found nothing else in the refrigerator other than tomorrow morning's orange juice.

There was little point going to bed yet, as hyper as he felt. He would never be able to fall asleep, not knowing that Jillian Westworth and her son slept right across the hall. A son he had never known existed until now. A son born of a relationship that had to have occurred within that first year after they had parted.

Barely noticing the muffled thud on the other side of the room as the icemaker dumped ice in preparation for another day, Brad took another long sip of milk, wishing he had something stronger to fill his glass. Something that might help numb the maelstrom of emotions plaguing him. He had been too ill prepared for the powerful feelings Jillian still aroused in him. Even after nine years.

Why hadn't he gotten over those emotions yet? Why did it have to hurt all over again just seeing her?

Resting his wrists on the kitchen table, he cupped his hands around the nearly empty glass, then tilted his head back and moaned softly. How could he still be in love with her? After all the pain he had gone through because of her, all those years of suffering but convincing himself he had done the right thing, how could he still possibly be in love with her? Was he doomed to feel this way forever? Would he still long for her even after she had married this Reynold Johnstone and made the man Pete's father?

Brad glanced again at the dark shape of his glass and frowned. It could be Reynold Johnstone really *was* Pete's father and deserved the right to be in their lives forever. But, no. Hadn't Pete mentioned they'd known the man for only a few months?

Then who was Pete's father? Was he some important business tycoon who had not only fit Jillian's lifestyle better than he ever could, but who had found Jillian to be every bit as irresistible as he had? A man who had enjoyed her lovemaking in the same depth he had? How long had it taken the new guy to break past her barriers? Obviously not the full year it had taken him.

Brad drew a deep breath, hoping to relieve the misery twisting painfully inside his heart.

He had never really had a chance, being a small-town boy with small-town values, and small-town significance—not at all the type to make a sophisticated, urbane young woman like Jillian Westworth happy for the rest of her life. He never should have allowed himself to get to know her. He should have realized he could never compete against her lavish existence.

They were too different. He would have always been a misfit in her life, someone who eventually would have brought her down. After all, he had grown up the only son of a poor, hard-working rural mail carrier with no means to furnish Jillian with the sort of extravagant and important lifestyle she was accustomed to living.

He had known from the onset he could never provide for her in the manner she deserved and rightfully expected, at least not for the following eight to ten years—and even now that he lived comfortably by his own standards, it in no way compared to the way she lived. He never would have fit into her social level. He'd seen that when two of her college friends had visited the inn for a week. Her world was too different. Even before Jillian's father had become one of Dallas' most prominent surgeons, the Westworths and Baileys were worth millions. And her friends' families were worth about as much.

That was why he did what he did that last week of their final summer together. There was no way he could have asked her to live the life of a pauper while he struggled through medical school, and he wouldn't have felt right taking money from her parents so she could live in a manner more befitting her needs. Had he done that, he would have always wondered if he could have made it on his own. That would only have caused resentment between them later on.

Clearly, it had been in Jillian's best interest as well as his own to end it when he did. Had he lured her into an even deeper commitment, into a more lasting relationship, she, too, would have regretted it later.

Still, letting her go had been the hardest, most painful thing he had ever done in his life. It didn't seem fair that he had to face that pain all over again. Especially now that he knew it had been more for his *own* good than he had realized.

Even now, knowing her love had not been true enough to last her even a year, it still hurt seeing her again. Hurt like hell.

He clamped his eyes shut, though all he gained by doing so was a deeper darkness. The images waited for him behind his closed lids. The morning she had hinted for a stronger, more lasting relationship, it had broken his heart, but somehow he had found the words needed to set her free. He had lied and told her he wasn't ready for marriage, that marriage and a family would only get in his way right then—but he had done so for her sake. Or so he'd thought.

Turned out, it was a good thing for himself he did, considering how easily and completely she had removed herself from his life after that. Although he had asked her to keep in touch, inwardly hoping there would be a chance for them yet, and although she knew which college he had attended as well as his parents' home address, he had never heard from her again. How better to prove just how right he had been to break it off when he did? They were never meant to be. In hardly any time at all, she had cast aside the memories of their intimate moments together and replaced him with someone else. Someone who had given her Pete—her little southern charmer.

He pressed his glass-cooled hands over his face as the image of the bright-eyed, inquisitive boy came to mind. Pete looked and sounded so much like his mother that it was impossible not to be touched by him. Impossible not to open his heart to the handsome child.

Still, Brad had to keep his priorities straight.

But what were his priorities?

Rubbing his stubbled chin, for he had not shaved since five o'clock that morning, he could not decide whether to leave gracefully or stay. If he left, it would be the same as admitting Jillian had run him off—or rather the painful memory of how it had once been will have run him off. It would certainly be the coward's way out. But if he stayed, he risked a worse heartache than before, for this time he would have to bear seeing her with another man.

The man destined to be her husband.

Before, he could pretend for his own sake that she missed him and thought about him as often as he thought about her, but seeing her with that other man would mean living with the reality that she had never missed him at all.

He could always do everything possible to avoid her, *avoid them*, but the inn was small, as was the village. He would run into Jillian and her fiancé again and again. There would be no way to stay and not see the two together. Still, he refused to run—refused to let her, or even Miss Hattie, know just how strongly and adversely affected he was by all this.

Sitting forward, he planted his elbows on the solid oak

table and again buried his face in his hands. How he wished he had never met Jillian. How different his life could have been.

Bitterly, his thoughts drifted yet again to that afternoon he first saw her, standing on the cliffs with the wind in her soft, dark hair, watching the boats dock late on one afternoon in the early summer. He had never really had a chance that day. She had claimed his heart immediately—claimed it, branded it as her own, and, in the ten years since, had not yet let it go.

"Why does it have to hurt so?" he asked aloud, not expecting an answer. Although he had felt a odd presence in the room upon entering, that was nothing new for Seascape and he had thought himself still alone in the darkness.

"What hurts?"

Brad dropped his hands and glanced toward a small shadow in the doorway. *Pete.*

❧ *Chapter 4* ❧

Pete felt for a light switch, but when he didn't find one, entered the kitchen anyway, headed straight for the breakfast nook in the far corner. Just enough moonlight spilled through the windows to tell exactly where Brad sat. "Do you need a Band-Aid? If you do, I've got some upstairs in one of my bags. They got Rangers printed all over them, but they're good Band-Aids."

"Pete, why are you down here so late? I thought you and your mother had gone to bed an hour ago."

Pete couldn't see Brad's face because he sat with his back silhouetted against the moonlit windows, but could tell by the way Brad stretched his neck, he'd peered off into the hallway behind him, probably expecting to see his mother trailing in after him. "Yeah, we'd both gone to bed, but I got thirsty and decided to come get something to drink before going on to sleep."

"Are you here alone?"

"Yeah." He shrugged. "Don't worry. Mom's still in bed. She won't be following me down."

Brad cleared his throat then lifted something toward his mouth.

Wishing he could see better, Pete glanced around for a light switch. Thinking maybe there would be one over by the walk-through pantry, which he remembered also led out into the storage garage and the basement, he walked over and felt of the wall. "So what are you doing down here all alone and sitting in the dark?"

"I was thirsty, too. I came down for a glass of milk."

"Why didn't you turn on the light?" Pete's fingers finally struck a wall switch. Flipping it, the overhead lights flooded the kitchen, one over the table where Brad sat squinting, one over the stove in the middle of the room, and one over the sink, where they had all left their dishes earlier.

But the dishes were gone now. Miss Hattie must have taken time to wash them before heading on upstairs for bed. All that was left was a wet rag hanging over the faucet.

"I didn't really need to turn on a light. There was more than enough moonlight for me to find my way over here."

Pete glanced at Brad's almost empty glass on the table and wet his lips in anticipation. "Chocolate milk?" Sure was better than plain water any old day.

"On the second shelf."

Remembering where the glasses were, he hurried to help himself to a sizable portion and left just enough in the carton for one more person to have a serving. He took a quick sip before starting across the floor toward Brad, his toes curled against the unexpected cold. Maine had a real problem with understanding it was nearly time for summer.

"So what did you hurt?" he asked as he set his glass down on the table. He glanced at Brad's face, neck, and hands but saw no blood or bruises. Not even a red mark.

"Nothing."

Pete noticed how saying that answer had made Brad look away, just like Troy did when he wasn't telling the whole truth. "But I heard you say something about hurting when I walked in."

"Don't let that bother you." Brad quickly reached for the chair closest to the glass and pulled it out so Pete could sit. "I was just talking to myself about nothing in particular. I'm one of those people who mutters a lot. Ask any nurse I've ever worked with. I'm really okay."

"Are you sure? I got those Band-Aids if you need them. Mom is always telling me it's smart to be prepared, so I brought the whole box." He frowned at how nervous Brad acted whenever he said something about his mother. Like she was someone he didn't want to talk about. "Why are you and Mom so angry with each other? I asked her earlier, but she wouldn't tell me."

"What makes you think we're angry with each other?" Again, Brad looked away—this time at his hands, folded on the table in front of him.

"By the way you act around each other. You both will talk to me, and you'll both talk to Miss Hattie, but you almost never say something to each other. That's the way me and Troy are when we're mad at each other about something. Otherwise we got no trouble at all finding things to talk about."

"And who's Troy?"

Pete paused to take a long drink of his chocolate milk, then wiped his mouth with the hem of his Astros pajama sleeve before remembering he was not supposed to do that anymore. Mr. Johnstone hated it when he did that. He cut his gaze to Brad, expecting to be nagged for what he had done, but Brad didn't say a word. "Troy is my new best friend back in Texas."

"Your *new* best friend? Why's that?"

"Troy's father works for some big company that makes him move around a lot. Troy has only lived near me since Christmas. He's on my baseball team and he lives closer to me than most the other boys in our neighborhood."

"You play on a baseball team?"

"Yeah. On the Red Sox. His dad's my coach." Pete took another drink of his milk, but this time he thought to use one of the paper napkins in the center of the table instead of his pajama sleeve. "Troy's got a great dad. He lets me come over and pitch ball with them whenever I want. He's the one who taught me how to bat without closing my eyes. I got a real problem with closing my eyes whenever there's something I don't want to see, so he taught me how not to do that.''

Brad leaned forward, smiling for some reason. "That's pretty important. Being able to bat without closing your eyes.''

"I'll say. Before, I had a jim-dandy of a time trying to hit that stupid ball. I'm still not good at it, but at least now I hit some of the pitches. I just hope I don't forget everything I'm supposed to remember before I finally get to go back. We're supposed to be here two whole weeks. With my luck, I'll be back to sitting on the bench again.''

"If we had a bat and ball, I could pitch you a few to keep you in practice,'' Brad offered. "That is, if your mother doesn't mind.''

"Really?'' Pete sat forward, then glanced off at his reflection in one of the nearby windows. Somebody had left the white lace curtains open and the sudden movement across the blackened glass had caught his attention. "I got a bat and ball. And I also got my new fielder's glove. But I don't have one for you.''

"I can catch bare-handed.''

"Great. Maybe I won't have to go back there having forgotten how to do everything after all. Troy's dad is going to be so glad. So's Troy. He just knew I was going to come back ruined again. Two weeks is a awful long time to go with no practice at all, and because of school taking up most of the day around here, I don't think I can get up a gang of boys to play with me much while I'm here. If at all.''

Brad studied him a moment, then asked, "Why aren't you in school? This is only the second week in May.''

"Because Mr. Johnstone wants to bring some man here for us all to be real nice to—some man real important to his work.''

"The trip here wasn't your mother's idea?''

He moved his hands from the table to his lap, just out of Pete's sight, so Pete stared up at his eyes instead. Again, it struck him how much like his own they looked, exact same color, shape, and all. This man had to be Pete's father. *Please, let it be that.*

"Nope. I don't really think she wanted to come much. This place seems to make her sad now that Grandma's not around anymore. No, coming here was all Mr. Johnstone's idea. You see, Grandpa has always said how this place has a special magic that makes people feel good, said it was just the medicine for whatever ails a person, which is why he sends patients here sometimes to recover from stuff they need to recover from. Mr. Johnstone wants this place to work that special magic on the man coming here with him so that man will have his company do business with him."

"I see. It's a business trip."

"Yeah, that's what Mom called it, too. But she said we'd have fun anyway, especially after the man's wife got here because she's supposed to just love little boys like me." He wiggled his eyebrows in the most adoring manner he knew, making Brad chuckle. "I'm supposed to help make them want to do all their advertising business with Mr. Johnstone—which might not be too easy considering the woman's supposed to hate the ocean almost as much as her husband loves it." He paused for another drink of milk, then added, "But don't worry. We'll still have time to practice baseball. I won't have to spend every minute with them. Mom's already promised me that. She knows I didn't really want to come."

Brad pressed his lips together a moment, then opened his mouth as if about to ask another question when the echo of telephones ringing stopped him.

He and Pete looked at each other, then out into the dark hall, as the second ring sounded, then there was a minute of silence followed by a softer ring upstairs toward the front of the house.

"Must be Mr. Johnstone calling Mom," Pete offered, then quickly drained down the last two of gulps of his milk. "He probably wants to be sure we're getting things all set up the way he wants them. I guess I'd better get on back upstairs. Mom told me to come right back after I got a drink and now she's going to realize just how long I've been gone.''

Remembering the new rule to put dirty dishes in the sink, Pete hurried over and set his glass just to the right of the drain. "You want me to turn out the light on my way out so you can be in the dark again?''

"No, I think I'd better go on up to bed, too. Wait a second and I'll walk up with you.''

It wasn't until several minutes later, when Pete was back in his room listening to his mother explain on the telephone why she had not done everything she was supposed to do after they got there, that Pete realized Brad had never answered any of the questions he'd asked him about his mother. What was it that kept those two from talking about each other?

Jillian felt more than a little guilty when she hung up the telephone. She and Pete had been there a day and a half and she still hadn't done everything Reynold had asked her do. And why? Because since having bumped into Brad again after all these years, she had not thought about much of anything or anyone else. What was worse, except for the incident at dinner in which Pete and Brad had verbally chastised Reynold for having the audacity not to know anything about baseball, she hadn't given her own fiancé a second thought.

Why hadn't she at least remembered to set up Saturday's boating excursion and Sunday's picnic? Thankfully, she had thought to give Miss Hattie a list of the Nelson's favorite foods, so the meals could be more along the line of what he wanted. But that was about all she'd done.

"Was that Mr. Johnstone?" Pete asked at the same time he turned out his light, casting the room in shadows again. Seconds later, the rollaway creaked as he crawled into bed.

"Yes, it was.''

"He still coming tomorrow?''

"Yes. And he's looking forward to spending some time with you.'' She trounced her pillow into a more comfortable shape and laid back down. "He said to tell you he plans to take you to the local tackle shop on Monday and buy you all the right fishing gear for Tuesday.''

"We're going fishing Tuesday?"

If I don't forget to set it up. "Yes. I'm supposed to charter a boat to take us offshore. Won't that be fun?" Lying on her side, she stared idly toward the turret where moon-drenched windows glowed silvery blue on one side. She wondered why she herself wasn't all that happy with the prospect of a day or two on the water. As a girl, she'd loved fishing with her father.

"If you say so, Mom."

Jillian didn't like the sigh in his voice and shifted so she could better see the rollaway. A tiny streak of moonlight from the window nearest the desk caught one corner. "I wish you'd try a little harder to like Reynold. After all, he's going to be part of the family soon."

"Not till November," Pete was quick to point out. A little *too* quick. Why couldn't Pete see all the good that would come of the marriage? This was the answer to a lot of his problems.

"Why do you say that as if you don't want it to happen? You've said again and again how much you've always wanted a father."

"I know, and I do. But I want one like Troy has. Not one like Jeffry's. Mr. Johnstone is just exactly like Jeffry's dad and nothing like Troy's."

Aware Reynold and Jeffry Craig's father did have a lot in common—both young, energetic vice-presidents working their way to the top of their respective corporations—she asked, "And what's wrong with Jeffry's dad?"

She sat up, hoping to have a better look at Pete's face, but it was too dark to detect more than where his body made a small bump in the middle.

"Nothing, I guess. It's just that neither Jeffry's dad nor Mr. Johnstone know anything at all about baseball or even soccer, and they don't like to play Nintendo either."

"There are other things in life besides playing sports and Nintendo."

"Yeah, but he doesn't like doing things like catching lightening bugs or bumblebees either. Shoot, even *you* will go catching lightening bugs with me when I want."

"But he does like to fish occasionally. And we both know how much you like fishing. Next week, he'll be able to show you how to catch those really big ocean fish. That's something any boy would love to do."

"I suppose."

"And he'll be able to teach you other things—things you otherwise wouldn't have the chance to learn; things I'd never be able to teach you. It'll be nice having a man around the house. A man you will be able to talk to whenever you want about things only guys can talk about."

"It could be worse, I guess."

Jillian settled back onto her pillow again, thinking progress had been made, however small. "You'll see. Reynold will be good for us both."

At least Reynold cared about them enough to put them on equal footing with his career—unlike *someone else* she had known. She cringed at the memory of that day in early September nine years ago when Brad suddenly let it be known he did not want the burden of a wife hanging around his neck while he struggled through medical school. His education was too important to him. Becoming a doctor was too important to him, which of course meant she was not so important. That had had a lot to do with her insecurities, and even more to do with the reason she had yet to tell Brad about Pete, for he had also said he didn't want any children getting in his way.

She couldn't bear the anger she'd feel, or the pain, should her sweet, precious Pete turn out to be no more important to Brad than she had been, and she sure didn't want Pete facing such cruel rejection. Something like that could be emotionally traumatizing to a boy so young.

Her stomach wound into a tight, rigid knot at the mere thought. Pete would never understand not being wanted by his own father. He'd had a hard enough time understanding that his father hadn't loved his mother enough to want to marry her.

That was why she prayed nothing happened to reveal her son's biological identity over those next six days. The time wasn't right for Pete to have to face something so hurtful.

Pete woke early the next morning, eager to see what he could do about making his mom and Brad get along better. If they would just spend some time with each other, they might get over being so angry at each other and be friends again. Since it had always worked for him and Troy, it would probably work for adults, too. But first he had to find some way to make them spend time with each other.

Beating his mother out of bed, he hurried to the bathroom to brush his teeth and comb his hair, then returned to the bedroom to put on insect repellent and dress for the day. Because the morning was a lot cooler than the one before, he set aside the shorts he had planned to wear and instead put on a pair of jeans, cuffed to fit his short legs, and his red and white Red Sox team shirt. On the back was his name and the number 18.

By the time his mother had woken enough to find what she planned to wear for the day, he was ready to go downstairs.

"I'll be out on the front porch," he told her, hoping to find either Brad or the cat there. Either one would help pass the time until breakfast.

To his disappointment, neither was there. Nor was either to be found in the flower gardens, off toward the ocean, or out by the pond. After checking behind the carriage house, the hothouse, and the place where people parked their cars, he gave up and returned to the house.

Entering through the mudroom, he found Miss Hattie in the kitchen baking blueberry muffins. She had just pulled one tin out and set it aside to cool.

"Those sure smell good," he told her as he took his cap off and sat at the table to watch in the exact same spot where

Brad had sat the night before. From there, he could see the main part of the kitchen as well as the large empty fireplace and a rocking chair with red-checked cushions where Miss Hattie sometimes sat to read her magazines. Right now, the old-timey radio that stood over near the rocking chair and fireplace played old-timey music, but so low he could hardly hear it. "I wish Mom knew how to make blueberry muffins as good as you."

"Would you like one now?" she asked, peering at him while she poked at the steaming tips with her finger. Why that didn't burn the heck out of her hand, Pete had no idea.

"No. I guess I'll wait until the others come down," Pete informed, reaching for a bowl of fresh daffodils that sat in the middle of the table beside a smaller basket of porcelain ones. He was curious to see if the fresh flowers smelled as pretty as they looked. Something he had noticed about this place was that there were always yellow flowers in every room. "I'll need to be there with them when it's time to eat."

"Oh? And why is that?"

"Because if I'm not there, those two won't talk to each other much." Having discovered hardly any smell at all to the fat, lacy blooms, he put the flowers back where they were but continued to sit forward. "I don't know why it is, but they act just like me and Troy do sometimes when we've had a big fight about something."

"And that bothers you?"

"Sure it does. I like Brad. And I want him and Mom to be friends again. Like they used to be." He twisted his mouth while he thought more about that. "Did you know them much way back when they used to be good friends here?"

Miss Hattie smiled that smile that reminded Pete of his Grandma. It made him want to run over and hug her close, but he resisted the urge. She might not understand why.

"Yes, I certainly did." She stood and smoothed one of the pockets on her white apron. "I've known your mother since she was your age or younger. She used to be a regular guest here. And I've known Brad since he was in his mid-teens, when he started spending his summers working on the boats. As I recall, he worked for Wilson Ruby, who eventually sold his two boats to Mike Mitchell before he went away to live with his brother. Brad was a good friend of Wilson's nephew, Heath, and both boys spent their summers around here.''

''Then do you know what it is my mom and Brad are so mad about?''

''No, I'm afraid I don't. But I'm like you. I do wish they'd forget whatever it was that happened back then and be friends again.'' Her smile deepened. ''Maybe it would help matters if today we found something for them to do together.''

Amazing, she'd think that. ''That would be great. But what?''

''Surely, if we put our heads together we'll think of something.''

Pete leaned back in his chair, glad to have someone else wanting to help. With both of them trying to help, he bet they could get something done.

But as it turned out, even Miss Hattie's suggestions to Brad and his mom didn't work out. Neither wanted to be around the other no matter what anyone suggested to them. Shortly after breakfast was over, Brad headed off to someplace called the co-op to see if any of his old friends were around while his mother sat down at the telephone to finish making the arrangements dorky Mr. Johnstone wanted her to make.

Disappointed, and wanting time to sort through all the different feelings he had stirring around inside him, Pete sneaked upstairs into the attic, thinking it the perfect place to be alone. He was surprised to find the space just below the high-pitched roof to be set up like a bedroom with dusty white cloths draped over most of the furniture and what few boxes were stored there.

Looking for a place to sit, Pete headed for the twin bed and sent up a layer of dust when he plopped down on one end. While scooting back so he could prop his shoulders against the planked wall, he thought he caught a glimpse of a man moving in the shadows over in the windowless corner of the L-shaped room.

Thinking he should apologize for coming in without knocking, Pete squinted to get a better look through the dust motes swirling in the slanted rays of sunshine streaming through the arched window above and saw no one was really there.

"Figures. No one is *ever* there for me," he muttered, feeling particularly sorry for himself and continuing to mope while wondering how he was ever going to figure out if Brad Pierce was his father. The way the two adults kept ignoring any questions about each other, just coming right out and asking them would never work.

"What about Reynold Johnstone?"

The voice startled him, causing him to jump so hard he popped his head on the wall behind him and knocked his Rangers' cap clean off his head.

"Who's there?" Again, he squinted through the fat, dusty sunrays spilling into the room. This time he made out the shape of a man in what looked like might be army clothes seated on a large sea trunk.

Thinking it was a little scary he hadn't spotted him before, Pete swallowed hard as he slid his cap back down over his unruly hair. "Who are you? What are you doing here?"

"The name is Anthony Freeport. Tony to my friends. And I live here—*sort of.*"

"What do you mean 'sort of'?" Pete leaned forward to get a better look at this Tony guy, but the dust caught too much light to let him see clearly.

The man hesitated just a second, then answered. "I'm a spirit."

Pete frowned. The only spirit he knew about was team spirit. "I don't understand."

He could make out enough about the man to tell he had reached up and taken off his hat and now held it in his hands. Thinking it the thing to do, Pete followed suit by pulling off his baseball cap again. Manners were real important to some folks. "What do you mean you're a spirit?"

"I'm a ghost."

Pete was still choking on all the dust he'd suddenly sucked down his throat when Tony explained further, "But, not to fear. I'm not the type to want to harm little boys. I'm what you'd call a *friendly* ghost."

"No, you're not." Pete fanned his face with the cap, his cheeks suddenly as hot as if he had just run a whole set of bases. "Ghosts don't exist. My mother says so. Who are you really?"

"I told you. My name is Tony Freeport, and despite what your mother says, I really am a ghost. I'll admit I don't normally materialize for mortals—usually a voice is enough— but in this case I felt I should make myself seen."

Pete's jaw dropped like a metal bat on homeplate after a bunt when Tony moved to stand over a cloth-draped dresser but without actually getting up. It was like he just drifted up and over with no effort at all.

"How'd you do that?"

"Do what?"

"Are you really a ghost?"

"Yes. You remember the two ghosts your mother told you stories about your first night here?"

"Yeah."

"Well, I'm one of them. Remember? She even told you my name. Tony. My grandfather is the one who built this place."

"Cool." Pete scooted to the edge of the bed, eager to find out more about this. In all his days, he'd never met a ghost before. "So, where's the other ghost Mom told me about? The one who used to be your grandmother?"

"Grandmother Cecelia divides her time between this and another world, giving most of it to the other world these days; but she's normally around when I need her. So are others in the family, though I'm the one with the strongest reason to remain."

"Way cool. How'd it happen? I mean, how'd you ever get to be a ghost?"

"It's a long story having to do with love and loyalty, but what it amounts to is that I was shot to death *long* before I was ready to leave this earth."

"In a robbery?"

"No, in a war that happened over fifty years ago."

"Super cool. Did you die a hero?"

"Some say I did. But that has nothing to do with you or your problem; and you are why I've surfaced. I want to help if I can."

"How?"

"First, I need you to tell me who Reynold Johnstone is to you and why he's the one who called to make your reservations."

"Wow, do ghosts know everything?"

"No." Tony chuckled. "But we know more than you'd think. Who's this Reynold Johnstone?"

Pete scowled as he sank back on the bed again. Mr. Johnstone was the last person he wanted to talk about. "He's the man my mother said she's going to marry come November."

"I gather you don't really like him."

"What's to like? The man is a total dork. He's always saying he likes me and wants to get to know me better, but then never wants to do anything with me. He hates all the things I like and is always telling me what to do. He doesn't want me to wear my clothes the way I want to, and is always either turning my cap around forward or taking it off my head entirely so he can slick my hair back out of my face with his fingers. He also refuses to call me Pete like everyone else. To him, I'm always young Peter." He rolled his eyes to show his disgust. "It's always 'young Peter' this, or 'young Peter' that. It's enough to make me want to throw up."

"But if he'll make your mother happy—"

"That's just it. She's not all that happy when he's around. Not anything like Troy's mother is when she's with Troy's dad. Or even the way Jeffry's mom is with Jeffry's dad. Oh, Mom and Mr. Johnstone get along and all, but they don't laugh and tease each other, or play games together, or even kiss."

"Maybe they do their kissing when you aren't around."

"Oh, yuck! Don't say that." The thought of those two kissing on the mouth the way some silly adults did made him squint his eyes shut tight. Nothing made him more sick than to see two adults kissing on the mouth. It's what ruined almost every movie he ever saw.

"Don't you want your mother to get married and be happy?"

"Sure. But not to someone like Mr. Johnstone."

"Oh?"

Pete wagged his foot while he tried to decide just how much to tell his new friend—the ghost. "I'd rather she married someone like Dr. Pierce."

"Brad?"

Pete's face lit just hearing the name. "Yeah, Brad. He's nice. I didn't even meet him until yesterday and already he's willing to play baseball with me. He told me to have my bat and ball ready later this afternoon and he'd pitch me a few."

"That should be fun."

"It would be even more fun if I knew for sure—" He hesitated telling the rest. What if Tony didn't understand? What if he laughed at him for even thinking such a thing?

"If you knew for sure what?"

He wagged his foot harder. "Can I trust you to keep a secret?"

Tony chuckled. "Funny, I was just going to ask you the same thing. You see, I don't like most people knowing I'm here so I'm hoping you'll promise not to tell anyone you met me. Please, don't even tell your mother we talked. It would just cause problems." He stroked his face, which was still hard to see because of all the sun-glittered dust floating between them. "Tell you what. I'll promise to keep your secret if you'll promise to keep mine. How's that?"

When Pete didn't answer right away, Tony prodded. "I'm your friend. You can trust me. Just ask Vic the mailman. Or ask Hatch over at the lighthouse the first time you meet him what he thought of me. He'll tell you what a trustworthy friend I was. Or ask Hattie about me. It might make her a little sad, but she'll tell you the same thing.''

"Hattie knows you?''

"She was my girl.''

"*Miss Hattie?* A girl?''

Tony chuckled again. "So what's the secret?''

Although it was hard to imagine Miss Hattie having been anyone's *girl*, Pete needed to trust someone. He needed to talk about what all he felt inside. "It's just that I think Brad might be my father. I can't get Mom to talk about it, but I think he's the same Brad guy Mom told me she fell in love with a long time ago, the one who stole her heart then broke it by telling her he liked her and all but didn't want no wife getting in his way. If he is that Brad, then I sure do wish there was some way to get him to change his mind about not loving her back enough to ask her to marry him so we could finally be a *real* family. And even if he's not my real father, I would sure like him to be.''

He twisted his ball cap in his hands. "But I can't even get them to talk nice to each other. If only there was some way to get them to spend some time together so they can get over being mad, but there's not. Even Miss Hattie tried to get them to take a walk together today, and they wouldn't do it. Wouldn't even think about it.''

"Maybe you two need some help. I'll see what I can do. Maybe if we form a conspiracy of sorts against them, we can find a way to make them do exactly what we want. I'll give it some thought.''

Pete took in a quick breath, hopeful again despite not really knowing what this conspiracy thing was. "But you'll have to hurry. This afternoon, Mr. Johnstone is supposed to show up here with his friends. After that, Mom will stay busy helping him entertain them. She won't give any time at all to Brad after everyone else gets here.''

"I'll sure do what I can. In the meantime, try not to let on that you may know the truth. I think secrecy is best at this point.''

❧ *Chapter 5* ❧

Friday afternoon and all day Saturday, all efforts to throw Jillian and Brad together for any worthwhile length of time failed, frustrating both Pete and his new ghost friend, Tony, to no end. It had been hard enough to get the two into the same room before Reynold Johnstone and the Nelsons arrived, but after the newcomers had settled into their different rooms, it became downright impossible.

Pete was about ready to give up.

"Tony? You up here?" he asked as he slipped into the attic bedroom shortly after supper that Saturday night. Because it was not only already dark but also cloudy outside, no light came through the windows, making him have to feel his way inside.

"I'm here."

Not knowing where a light switch would be, Pete had only the light coming up through the opening in the floor to guide him across the room. He walked as far as the bed and sank down, dejected. "This is not working out. Mom and Mr. Johnstone are headed for a nighttime walk with the Nelsons and Brad is headed over to one of the neighbor's houses to play cards."

"I know. I tried to keep them from leaving by whispering cautions to both Mr. Johnstone and Mr. Nelson, but that didn't work. Either the men don't hear well or they attribute my voice to some abnormality in the wind, like so many people do. After that failed, I tried hiding Mrs. Nelson's sweater and Brad's jacket, but somehow your friend, Johnstone, found where I'd put them.''

"He's *not* my friend." Pete wagged a finger sharply in Tony's direction. Although he couldn't actually see him in the darkness, he could tell the voice came from over near the trunk again. That seemed to be Tony's favorite spot.

"Sorry. Poor choice of words."

"What are we going to do?" Pete played with a button on his shirt. "Nothing you or me or Miss Hattie has done so far has worked."

"I know."

"It's like they are both dead-bent on staying away from each other no matter what anybody else does."

"I know."

"If we don't find some way to get them both together and off by themselves, they are never going to get over being mad at each other."

"I know that, too."

"And, if they don't get over being mad at each other, there's no chance they'll ever be friends again."

"I know."

Pete sighed, thinking for someone who knew so much, Tony was being of very little help. "So what are we going to do about it?"

"*That* I don't know."

Pete slouched down until his head stayed propped against the wall but his shoulders touched on the bed, tapping the rubber sole of his shoe on the wooden floor. "Well, we've got to do something. Can't you think of a single plan that will get my mother away from Mr. Johnstone long enough to spend some time alone with Brad?"

When that question was followed by the sound of only a gentle night breeze whisking across the high-pitched roof, Pete's heart jumped. The last thing he needed was for Tony to ditch out on him. "You still there?"

"I'm thinking."

"This just isn't fair," Pete continued, after Tony again fell silent. "Tomorrow's Mother's Day and it looks like Mom and I are going to have to spend the whole thing on some deserted island with Mr. Johnstone and the Nelsons, eating strange food I never heard of and talking about stupid stuff that makes no sense. We're supposed to be gone almost all day."

"That's right." Suddenly, Tony sounded encouraged. "Once they have been taken out to the island, there won't be any way back until the boat returns late in the afternoon. The island is completely deserted at this time of year. No other tourists will be there. That gives them no other means of returning."

"So?"

"So, I think I have a plan that just might work. But this time it'll be solely up to you to pull it off."

"Me?"

"Yes. How good are you at play-acting?"

Unable to sleep with such an important business deal still pending, Reynold paced the floor of the Shell Room, mulling over the day's events. During the afternoon boat ride to New Harbor and Long Cove, he had scored definite points with David Nelson. He was certain of it. The man was so easy to work, it was hard to imagine his father, Joshua Nelson, ever having helped put him in charge of such a large and nationally important company. Joshua had to be getting senile in his old age.

Reynold chuckled silently as he ran his finger along the beveled edge of an antique writing desk in passing. By the time the Nelsons leave Seascape Inn, he should have gained so much ground, David will be begging him to take over the company's advertising. He shouldn't even need the two weeks he had set aside for this.

The vice-presidency of Stuart, Crusie, and Taylor was as good as his.

Pausing in front of the mirror, he locked his hands behind him and chuckled again. Not only had he made such obvious headway with David, Jillian and Peter had also scored well with David's wife, Shelly, who had taken to Peter's puzzling charm precisely as predicted.

He laughed out loud at his own cleverness.

Shelly Nelson's fascination with children was the primary reason he had asked Jillian to bring young Peter along, although he doubted Jillian would have agreed to the two-week scheme had it meant spending Mother's Day apart from the boy—much less Peter's birthday next week. Jillian was loyal that way—which he considered a worthwhile trait, as long as she directed a good part of that loyalty toward him, and so far she had.

Leaning closer to the scrolled mirror while smoothing an errant wrinkle from his shirt, he smiled. Jillian was the ideal asset to his rising career. She was poised, intelligent, and beautiful, plus she came from a wealthy, well-respected family.

None of which described his ex-wife.

Poor Karen had been pretty enough, although not in an elegant sort of way—and she was a damn good lay—but she simply had not satisfied his executive needs, nor had she met his changing lifestyle. Karen had been far too happy with her common way of life, so happy she had wanted to bring children into it. And he didn't. That had been one of the main reasons he finally divorced her four years ago.

Children had never fit into his plans, which was why he'd had a vasectomy so early in his marriage. With all her talk of motherhood and biological clocks, he had worried Karen might try something foolish and become pregnant on purpose. That never could have worked into his plans. He knew from watching others that children took unnecessary time, money, and energy away from the more important aspects of life. They were distractive, messy, and demanding—and not worth the bother.

The only reason he put up with young Peter, at least for

now, was because he had discovered being nice to the boy was the quickest and surest way to Jillian Westworth's heart. She loved to hear him praise the boy, even though there was so little there to praise—and she loved hearing him discuss activities they could all do together, like a family.

But a family was not at all what he wanted. As soon as the boy was old enough, Reynold planned to hire a woman whose sole job would be to keep the boy occupied and out of their hair, unlike the housekeeper Jillian employed now, who only occasionally watched the boy and even then without a firm hand. That and make sure he spent a lot of time at summer camps. The farther away the better. Reynold refused to have the loud, unruly boy in his way for long. Once legally married to Jillian, he would see that the recalcitrant brat no longer remained a disruption—for either of them. Soon after the marriage, young Peter would be out of there.

Growing more pleased with himself by the moment, his business plans falling right into place, Reynold stepped out on the small deck attached to his bedroom and breathed deeply the cold, invigorating, pine-scented sea air. How right Jillian's father had been about this place.

It had a magic all its own.

Jillian awoke to a bedroom filled with brilliant splashes of morning sunshine and a large bouquet of fresh yellow jonquils still damp from an early morning rain, shimmering just inches from her nose.

"Here, Mom, for you. Happy Mother's Day." Pete's beaming face appeared just above the fistful of flowers, his blue eyes dancing with merriment. Jillian was surprised to find him already dressed in a pair of jeans and a white baseball style shirt exhibiting a popular cartoon character at bat. He had also slicked back his unruly curls with water in an added attempt to try to look neat.

Quite a difference from the sulky boy he had been the night before. *Thank goodness.*

"You remembered. How sweet." Warmed by her son's

thoughtfulness and happy that his annoyance for having been left behind to watch television with Miss Hattie the evening before had disappeared, she pulled him into a playful hug. She hadn't really looked forward to a third Mother's Day without her own mother around to dote on, especially while being in a place they'd shared so many happy hours. That made Pete's surprise all the more uplifting. "Thank you. The flowers are beautiful. What a wonderful Mother's Day present they are."

"But they aren't all you're getting. Miss Hattie and I have a special breakfast waiting for you downstairs." He pulled away, leaving her with the bent-stemmed flowers, already headed for the door he had left open. "Hurry up, get dressed, and come downstairs."

"Why?" Still holding the flowers, she tossed the covers aside then stretched the muscles in her back, tight from inactivity. "What are we having?"

"It's a surprise." He looked excited enough to burst. "Just hurry up and come downstairs. I'll be in the dining room waiting."

Having said that, he disappeared.

Curious about this surprise breakfast, Jillian quickly tossed her legs over and slid out of the enormous four-poster bed. After putting the flowers in water, using one of the drinking glasses for a vase, she put on the lightweight pleated slacks and long-sleeved, pearl-buttoned blouse she had picked to wear that day for the picnic. Though stylish, the material was a little sturdier than what made up most of her outfits, and the light beige color brought out the contrasts in her dark brown hair. It also made her poolside tan all the more noticeable, which was why Reynold liked her so much in light, muted colors.

After buckling her feet into a pair of comfortable bone-colored sandals, she headed to the bathroom to wash her face and brush her teeth. Because Brad had already been there—that fact obvious by the lingering scent of his tangy cologne—and because Reynold had not yet left his bedroom, evidenced by the Do Not Disturb sign still hanging from his doorknob, there was nothing to delay a quick return to her bedroom to put on her makeup.

Within a very few minutes, she had finished the makeup, shaped her hair into a simple style swept away from her face, and headed downstairs to see what wonderful surprise awaited her in the dining room.

"Good morning, Jilly," Miss Hattie called to her from the right side of the room where she and Pete stood side by side facing her, blocking the view of whatever was on the buffet behind them.

Hattie smiled that mischievous smile of hers as she tucked the lace hankie she had just used to dab at her temple into the front pocket of her sea-green church dress.

"Good morning," Jillian returned. She drew in a deep breath as she stepped farther into the room. *Fresh, hot pancakes.* Had to be.

She glanced beyond the two conspirators. The only other person in the dining room was Brad. Like before, he stood near the closed French doors that looked out onto the south wing of the veranda and across to the ocean. He had his hands locked behind him, his usual noncommittal expression in place.

Her heart did its customary leap when she noted how relaxed he looked in a snug pair of faded-denim shorts with a loose-fitted, white cotton shirt tucked in but left open at the collar. Watching her, he didn't speak a word when she headed toward her smiling son, but nodded in her direction when she glanced at him a second time.

She sucked in a quick breath, appalled she still couldn't keep her gaze off him.

But why would she want to? Why would any woman want to? She wrinkled her lips at that last thought, wondering for the first time since seeing him again how many other women had entered and been callously dismissed from his life since her. Was there, by now, a special one? One that he cared for enough to keep? Or had he stayed true to his bachelor ways?

She thought about that, picturing him with beautiful women draped on either arm, and felt a quick stab at her heart—and the unexpected desire to scream at him.

Darn the man for still causing her such emotional turmoil. And darn him for staying so desirable. It wasn't fair. How could anyone look so casual and unassuming in his everyday clothes and yet at the same time still look so incredibly sophisticated and sexy? The man virtually oozed sensuality— the kind that could make any woman ache.

"Go ahead and sit down, Mom," Pete said, gesturing to her usual chair, the second from Miss Hattie's end, with its back to the buffet as always. "I'm going to serve you your breakfast myself."

"Shouldn't we wait for Reynold and the Nelsons?" She glanced at the empty chairs the others should fill. Since arriving the afternoon before, Reynold had taken the seat beside her, opposite Pete, while the Nelsons had sat directly across the table, beside Brad. "It would be the polite thing to do."

Pete looked deeply wounded by that suggestion. "If we wait, the food will get cold. Besides, it's after eight o'clock and Miss Hattie told everyone last night how breakfast was going to be served at eight o'clock sharp because she's got to go to church earlier than usual today because it's her day to take the flowers. They were all told if they weren't here at eight, they'd be eating cereal, cold muffins, or fruit."

True, Miss Hattie had said just that. If Reynold and his friends missed this special breakfast, it was their own fault. Besides, how could she possibly do anything to disappoint her precious Pete, especially after all he had gone through to please her?

"Okay, I'll sit." She reached for her chair only to have her son leap forward and pull it back for her. "Thank you, sir."

"You sit, too, Brad," Pete called over his shoulder as he returned to the buffet where large shiny domes covered the food. "You, too, Miss Hattie. Today, I am serving everyone."

Brad and Hattie exchanged grins as they, too, took their seats, catercornered to each other.

"The juice and coffee has already been poured, but there's more on the table. Now, everyone gets however much fruit they want and a heaping stack of these pancakes," Pete announced as, first, he set a bowl with strawberries, cantaloupe, and blueberries halfway between his mother and Hattie, then returned to the buffet for the still steaming platter of pancakes.

With a napkin draped over his arm in what he clearly thought waiter fashion, he moved to the table and scooped the odd-shaped cakes directly onto the four waiting plates, including his own. Before returning the last of the pancakes to the buffet, he gestured to three small porcelain pitchers already on the table, near where Miss Hattie sat unfolding her napkin. "Everyone gets a choice of blueberry, or strawberry, or maple syrup. Mom, of course, will want strawberry."

"This looks delicious," Jillian said as she accepted the tiny pitcher of strawberry syrup from Hattie, who had insisted mothers always go first on Mother's Day. "And, I must say, the table service is exceptionally wonderful this morning. What a fine waiter we have."

"I even helped cook the pancakes," Pete put in as he set the metal dome back over the platter to keep the remaining pancakes warm, then headed for the table. "Didn't I, Miss Hattie?"

"And an expert cook he is," Miss Hattie agreed. "He didn't spill the batter once, did he, Brad?"

"Not once," Brad said and winked at Pete as he cut into his maple-drenched pancakes with the side of his fork. "Although he did miss the pan by just a little when flipping that first pancake."

Jillian glanced up from her plate, surprised. She hadn't expected Brad to have been involved in her Mother's Day breakfast. "You were there?"

"Sure," Pete answered for him. "He's the one who showed me how to flip and catch them without using a spatula. Just like the cooks in restaurants do."

Jillian looked down at her misshaped pancakes with that new insight, then cut a questioning gaze to Brad.

"It's something my father taught me to do when I was about Pete's age," Brad said, as if his knowing how to flip a pancake needed explaining. "I used to make pancakes for my own mother on Mother's Day. Just like my father did for his mother, only he called them skillet cakes."

Jillian's insides fluttered at the thought that a family tradition had just been passed down from one generation to another with no one aware of it but her. Suffering a twinge of guilt, she looked back at her pancakes, not quite as hungry as before.

"Go ahead," Pete said, taking the pitcher she had just set aside and pouring a thick coating of strawberry syrup over his plate as well. "Eat up."

Not about to disappoint Pete after all this trouble, Jillian stabbed a bite of pancake, dragged it again in the dark red syrup, then placed it in her mouth. Pete waited until she had chewed and swallowed appreciatively before bothering to cut into his own food with typical vigor.

Before long, the four of them had eaten their fill of pancakes and fruit, so much so that Jillian felt the strain of her waistband when she finally set her fork aside.

"I don't know about you three," Miss Hattie said, also setting her fork aside, "but I'm full to the gills."

"I am, too," Jillian admitted, glancing at her son. "Pete, we shouldn't have eaten so much. We still have that picnic ahead of us."

"Yeah, well, I don't really want to go. Those people are too boring. There's not much for me to do when we're with them. Besides, Mrs. Nelson is the only one who even notices I'm around."

Brad cut his gaze to Pete, then to Jillian, but said nothing.

Jillian frowned, certain he was silently judging her behind those big, lash-fringed baby blues. "Pete, don't say that. I've already told you what fun we're going to have today."

"Just like I was supposed to have fun yesterday when we

went on that boat ride over to Long Cove? Yeah, that was a real blast. I've never had so much fun listening to two men talk constantly about things I don't even understand. I'd rather stay here and have Brad pitch to me some more when he gets back from his hike than sit around with you guys and be ignored. At least Brad talks about things I know about.''

"Pete," she chided, shifting uncomfortably beneath Brad's studious gaze. Had Reynold and David really dominated the conversation that much? She stared through the multitude of windows in the French doors, trying to recall exactly what had been discussed and by whom. "That's not nice to say.''

Pete thrust out a stubborn jaw, then sulked.

"Nice or not, at least the boy's being honest about how he feels," Brad put in, his voice deep and his expression rigid with unexplained emotion.

Not having expected his interference, Jillian clenched her jaw. This was really none of his business. "Maybe he's being a little too honest. It's certainly not something he has to say in front of others.''

"Oh? Would you rather he be deceptive and pretend to enjoy something he doesn't?" He set his fork down, giving her his full attention. His blue eyes glinted with something she couldn't quite identify—and really didn't want to. Her heart gave a perplexing little leap. "Would you rather he lied to you about his feelings? Would you rather he pretended to be having a great time, if in fact he was not?''

"No. Of course not.''

"I'm glad to hear it. There's nothing I despise more than to be around a person who purposely lies to, or otherwise misleads another.''

Aware by his deliberate, icy glare that there was a personal message there for her, however vague, Jillian swallowed hard. Suddenly, he looked nothing like Pete.

Had he somehow guessed the truth about his son? *Please, no.*

"Not even if there's a good reason for someone having done so?''

"There's *never* a good reason for deceit."

How much had he figured out?

Heart twisting, Jillian chewed on the tender corner of her lower lip while she studied his grim expression when an unexpected voice from the hall doorway stole her attention. A female voice, followed by footsteps.

"Did we miss breakfast?"

Smiling, Shelly Nelson paused near the end of the table, waiting for her husband to move ahead and pull her chair back for her, which he promptly did.

Once seated, and the Nelsons served some of Pete's pancakes, the conversation at the table shifted to the beautiful weather and to the fact David Nelson had not remembered to call his mother yet to wish her well. Shortly after he had jotted himself a note to do just that, Reynold appeared, dressed in a pair of crisp white slacks and a green and white striped pullover shirt, eager to discuss their plans for the day.

He refused the offer of the last two still-warm pancakes and opted for a couple of slices of cantaloupe instead. "So what time are we supposed to be at the pier?"

Pete, clearly sulking again, asked to be excused at the same time Miss Hattie left to finish getting ready for church. Once given the nod, he disappeared outside through the French doors. Brad soon followed.

Distracted by the sight of her son and his father sitting out on the veranda talking about something obviously serious, Jillian missed most of the discussion at the table. She was too curious about what was being said outside to give full attention to her current surroundings. Too curious about the bond growing between her son and his father, her first-and-only true love.

It was odd how often during the two short days Brad had been there that he and Pete had found occasions to be alone together. They would either walk out along the granite cliffs or the beach below, watching boats or collecting ocean drift, or they could be found out on the sloping front lawn, practicing baseball.

Both situations had made her nervous, but seeing them outside now made her even more apprehensive. Did Brad suspect? Was that what had prompted that little speech about deceit? If not, why did he spend so much time with the boy? Brad didn't even like children. He had made that clear nine years ago. Had he changed his mind about that?

With a tight knot worrying her throat, she reached for her water glass and took a sip, her gaze never leaving the French doors. What *did* those two find to talk about? Did their conversations ever lean toward the physical similarities between them? Had either caught on to the biological link between the two? Or were they too trusting to think she could have kept something so vital a secret? Pete might be that trusting, having never been given a reason to question her, but Brad didn't appear to be the type to trust anyone.

Her stomach flipflopped at that thought, for in truth she did not deserve his trust. And judging by their earlier conversation, Brad did indeed suspect a physical link between him and her son.

But as long as the subject of Pete's age or his birthdate didn't surface, Brad would have no way to be sure. Was that what they were out there discussing right now? Was Brad pumping Pete for the information he needed to prove parentage?

No, Pete wouldn't be laughing so hard if the conversation were at all serious. Either she had read more into Brad's earlier comments than she should, or Brad was biding his time.

A chill skipped down her spine, causing a scattering of tiny bumps under her skin. If only there was some way to keep those two apart until Thursday afternoon or early Friday morning when Brad was scheduled to leave. Or at least ensure that they spent very little of that time alone. But what could she do short of be a personal chaperone for them? Pete liked Brad. And evidently Brad liked Pete. That meant they were going to spend time together. And with her commitments to Reynold, who had yet to realize that she and Brad had once been lovers, she couldn't very well hope to be around every time Brad and Pete were together.

She sighed inwardly. At least Brad and Pete would be spending that afternoon apart. Pete would be with her on the island while Brad stayed mainland, hiking the nature trails.

"So what do you think, Jillian? Should we do that then?"

Reynold's unexpected question jerked her attention back to the present. Not wanting to admit she had not followed their conversation for fear Reynold might ask why, she blinked then smiled. "Of course. Whatever you want."

She had no idea what she'd just agreed to, but did not want to chance having to tell Reynold about Brad just yet. She was not ready. Reynold already knew they had been friends during their younger days, and for now she would leave it at that. In time, she would tell him everything, but for now she had enough problems to deal with.

"Good, that settles it. After the picnic we'll have the boatman drive us on around to Indian Point to see the big lighthouse from the water. I hear it's a lot larger than the one here, and quite a dramatic sight in the late afternoon."

"Fine." Jillian met his gaze, feeling horribly guilty for where her thoughts had strayed, then looked across the table where David and Shelly sat sipping their second or third cup of coffee. She had no idea which.

She really should give these three her undivided attention, but a movement behind them, off to the right, caught her notice. She glanced over in time to see Pete and Brad returning inside, Brad with his electronic pager in hand.

Uncommon relief washed over her when Brad explained he was headed upstairs to make a couple of telephone calls, if his phone was working again, then would take off for the day.

It would be easier to set him out of her thoughts after he had gone.

Out of sight, out of mind.

Or so the saying went.

Maybe this once it would prove true.

Glancing at Pete, Jillian felt further relieved. His impassive expression revealed that nothing had been said outside to raise his suspicions. Unlike his father, the ice god, her son was not very skilled at hiding his emotions. If he had a serious question plaguing him, it would be evidenced in his pale blue eyes.

Good. At least her son hadn't picked up on any suspicions Brad may have. Pete could enjoy the day without worrying about Brad's true identity. She smiled at that, thinking he deserved to make it through at least one more day without chancing Brad's anger, and his rejection.

After Brad headed toward the hall, Pete slanted a gaze at Reynold, and obviously remembering Reynold's aversion to wearing a cap in the house, yanked his off his head and held it precariously in his hands. "Mom, since it's over an hour yet before we leave for the pier, can I go out by the pond and skip rocks for a while? Miss Hattie said it's all right to do that."

As long as Brad was not going, too. "Sure. Just try not to get too muddy." She glanced back at Brad to make sure he had not changed directions and was still headed toward the hall. Those two had spent enough time together for one day. Her nerves could take only so much. "But be sure to come running when we call."

Pete nodded, then glanced up and smiled at Miss Hattie, who had just entered after having gone upstairs to find her purse and gloves.

Brad paused several feet away, long enough to let the older woman pass.

"Miss Hattie?" Pete called for her attention. "Who's that lady out by the pond? The one out in the trees with binoculars and the funny-looking hat with pink flowers sticking out of it?"

"Beaulah Favish." Brad, Hattie, and Jillian all answered clearly and in unison, then laughed as they exchanged knowing glances. The others looked at them with baffled expressions.

"Couldn't be anyone else," Miss Hattie continued the explanation, wrinkles shaping a soft smile. "That's Beaulah's favorite Sunday hat, which means she is already dressed for church. But, since she was not appointed to take flowers today, she probably won't actually leave for twenty or thirty minutes yet. If she doesn't see something out there she thinks momentous enough to keep her glued to the edge of my property, she'll be gone in just a little while."

"Amazing that she never gives up her vigils," Brad said, with a shake of his head, his eyes sparkling at the memories associated with the crotchety old busybody. "You'd think after all these years, she would have relinquished the idea of there being ghosts here and quit trying to find proof."

Pete's eyes widened at hearing Brad mention ghosts, but he didn't question him about them. Instead, he cut a quick gaze ceilingward, as if double checking to be sure none were hovering about watching him, then moved closer to the French doors, toward the outside, at the same time Brad disappeared into the hall.

The melancholy that washed over Jillian the moment Brad left her sight was immediate. She hated being at odds with him and wished there was some way for them to be at least friends again. How wonderful it had felt to enjoy a mutual laugh with him again. How nice that for one brief moment they had again shared a cheerful memory—one that had caused neither of them any pain.

And how sad.

She glanced again at Pete, who now had his hand on the doorknob while looking back at Miss Hattie, who continued to answer his question.

"If one good thing can be said about Beaulah Favish, it's that she rarely misses Sunday services. Nor do I," she added, glancing quickly at her locket watch. "Speaking of which, I'd better be on my way. And, don't forget, should any of you return early and need me, I'll be at Millie's most of the afternoon." She started toward the mudroom, where two large floral arrangements awaited her. "Millie's son, Richard, is here for Mother's Day and she's having a special gathering at her house. I can hardly wait to see that boy again. He's such a dear.''

Without being told, Pete released the doorknob and hurried off to help Miss Hattie carry the flowers to her car, waiting until he was just inside the mudroom to slap his baseball cap back over his head.

Jillian smiled. What a helpful little gentleman her son had become in the past several months. She glanced at Reynold, certain he had a lot to do with Pete's sudden behavioral growth. The common courtesy and proper etiquette that were so very important to Reynold had clearly begun to rub off on her son.

All the more reason to marry the man.

❧ *Chapter 6* ❧

Jillian returned to the now empty dining room from the kitchen to call for Pete. As promised, a food-filled picnic basket and the quilts they needed for the picnic were waiting on the oak counter, to the left of the large double sink near the window. All she had had to do was remember to fill the Thermos with the icy lemonade Hattie had made earlier and left in the refrigerator; and they were ready for the daylong excursion.

In fifteen minutes, they would be on their way.

Barely seconds after she stepped out the double French doors, the late-morning sun slid from behind a fat cloud, washing away the soft shadows that had blanketed the yard. Catching a movement off to her right, she glimpsed Shelly Nelson returning from the carriage house where she and David occupied the only full suite. Shelly had paused on the path that ribboned through one of the brilliant flower gardens to gaze off toward the endless ocean. A sun-warmed breeze lifted her stylishly cut short blond hair away from her perfectly sculpted face.

Shelly was probably two years younger than Jillian, and had to be a good six years younger than her husband, but her natural poise, good humor, and sophistication helped her fit in with any age group. Jillian admired her for that.

"David's coming," she called after spotting Jillian on the

veranda. She gestured to the carriage house behind her before she started toward the house. "He's just changing his shoes. After hearing Miss Hattie say how rocky and steep the shore will be where we'll dock, he decided to put on sturdier shoes."

Jillian noticed Shelly had also changed footwear, choosing a pair of strong-laced shoes made from hard white leather over the slip-on white canvas shoes with blue-anchor appliqués she had worn earlier. The morning having started out cooler than the day before, she had also changed from shorts to a pair of light blue pleated jeans that fit her trim figure perfectly.

If she were not so nice, Jillian could find plenty of reason not to like such a beautiful young woman.

"Reynold, too," she called back, pointing in the general direction of the second-floor windows near the back of the house, then glanced again at the small, picturesque pond with its stone benches and latticed gazebo as she descended the steps.

Pete was not there.

Annoyed, she scanned the sloping lawn, looking for the sight of his bright red baseball cap while an uncomfortable feeling gnawed at her. Remembering how adamantly he had not wanted to go with them that day, she shifted her gaze toward the towering evergreens that formed a dense forest in the distance.

Surely he hadn't tried to follow Brad down the nature trails. If he did, the child could be anywhere. Those trails led in all directions. So many directions, a novice had to carry a pocket map to keep from getting lost.

But that was a senseless concern. Wanting to know the second it was safe to put her guard down, she had watched Brad disappear into a section of forest north of the inn only a few minutes ago—*alone*.

Wherever Pete was, he was not with Brad.

At least she didn't have *that* worry.

"Have you seen Pete?" she asked Shelly and walked out

into the yard. With a curved hand, she shaded her eyes from the late-morning glare. With the earlier clouds now mostly gone, warm sunlight bathed the countryside, causing the cooler temperatures to climb to a level more in line with what she preferred for this time of year.

"Not since breakfast." Shelly glanced toward the pond, too. "Isn't he where he's supposed to be?"

"Evidently not," Jillian muttered, then called out, hoping he would answer from somewhere nearby. "Pete, where are you?"

No response.

She closed her eyes briefly to listen. The only sounds were the cries of gulls and the gentle roar of ocean waves splashing against the rugged shore some distance away.

Pete wasn't coming out from wherever he'd gone.

Her stomach knotted farther. How would she ever explain this act of rebellion to Reynold? He had so looked forward to everyone enjoying a fun, trouble-free day. "Pete, wherever you are, it's time to go." She moved farther from the house.

Shelly followed, straining on tiptoes to see down by the pond. "There he is!"

Wrinkling her forehead, Jillian stared in the direction Shelly pointed. She didn't see him. "Where?"

"There." Shelly had already started to run. Panic filled her voice. "On the ground, near the gazebo."

On the ground? Heart frozen in mid-beat, Jillian sped off, passing Shelly in seconds. "Has he hurt himself?"

Fighting a mother's hysteria, she crossed the sloping lawn toward the pond along the southern part of Seascape land with amazing speed.

Despite her desperate calls for him to answer her, Pete didn't move—or utter a sound.

Jillian's body literally trembled by the time she reached the patch of tall grass that had all but obscured his small body. Her heart lurched to see him lying on the ground, doubled over with a tight grimace on his face. His ball cap lay on the ground beside him, littered with grass.

Kneeling, she searched his body for any obvious signs of injury but saw none. No cuts or abrasions of any kind. "Pete? What happened?"

"My middle. My middle hurts something awful," he whimpered, his pain too severe to open his eyes and look at her. "I can't even stand up."

Terrified, she ran her hand over his face and felt the cool sweat drenching his body. Geez, but she had to *do* something. "When did it start?"

"I was already hurting some when I first got down here, but the pain didn't get real bad until few minutes ago." He still did not open his eyes.

"He needs a doctor." Shelly stated the obvious, having finally caught up with them. She, too, knelt and wrung her hands with worry. "Maybe we should call an ambulance."

"I wonder if they have 911 here," Jillian responded, sliding her arms under the backs of her son's legs and behind his shoulders. She was so shaken, she had trouble lifting him, but eventually managed to stand with him in still her arms. "Run ahead and call for help."

Shelly was off like a streak.

Pete moaned with each jarring step Jillian took as she hurried to carry him over the uneven ground toward the house. They were still a good distance away when Shelly came running back out of the house, her husband right behind her.

"The phones aren't working. What'll we do now?"

Jillian didn't know. With Hattie gone, she had no way to find out where the closest hospital might be. If only her father were here. He would have his medical kit and would know exactly what to do to help Pete.

Struggling, she continued toward the house, stumbling when her foot met a particularly uneven piece of ground, relieved when David rushed forward and took Pete from her. Her arms had started to ache from strain and she had feared dropping him.

"Momma?" Pete called to her while David continued on toward the house only a few steps ahead of her.

Jillian's throat constricted at hearing his pitiful voice. It had been years since Pete had called her Momma, since the day he had staunchly proclaimed that only little kids called their mothers Momma. Big kids like him called their mothers Mom. Knowing Pete would never revert back to that reference while in his proper mind, her heart twisted hard beneath her lungs, hampering her next breath. "What, son?"

"Brad's a doctor. Why don't you go get him? He'd help me."

Jillian pressed her hands to her face with relief. Why hadn't she remembered that? Brad *was* indeed a doctor. A general practitioner. He could help Pete. But where was Brad? By now he could be either halfway to the lighthouse to visit with Hatch or well into the stretch of thick, forested hills that ribboned between Sea Haven and New Harbor.

He carried a beeper, but without access to a working telephone, and not knowing his beeper number anyway, that fact was worthless.

How could she possibly reach him?

Suddenly remembering the ship's bell attached to the far corner of the front porch, she ran to it and wagged the worn, leather cord with all her might. Her already aching arms wrenched tight spasms with the added strain.

Surely Brad would hear the bell's peal, and realize something was wrong, as should any neighbors not at church.

Somebody would come to their rescue.

Seconds later, just as David, Shelly, and Pete neared the front door, Reynold hurried outside to see what all the ruckus was. His expression went rigid when he spotted Pete in David's arms, folded in a tight ball.

Jillian rested her arm long enough to listen for Brad. Had he heard the bell and realized it meant trouble? Or was he too far away? *Please, God, don't let him be too far away. Please.*

"What's wrong with the boy?" Reynold asked, narrowing his gaze with obvious concern when Jillian glanced his direction.

"I don't know," David replied, brushing past, headed for the parlor. "All I know is when I came to the house looking for Shelly, I found her trying to use the phone to call 911."

"*911?* Is it that serious?"

Whatever the response was to that, Jillian didn't hear, for she stayed on the porch and kept ringing the bell in short cycles. She scanned the wooded area north of the house where she had last seen Brad, and where so many of the nature trails began. She cried aloud with relief when a minute later she spotted him trotting out of the forest. He was too far away for her to see his expression, but he was curious enough about the noise to head directly toward the house at a steady jog.

Wanting to relay what had happened as quickly as possible, she leaped from the porch and started toward him, skirting the half-dozen flower gardens that grew in small, lush islands along the north side of the lawn.

"Something's happened to Pete," she called out when she grew near enough to be heard. "He's ill." By then she could see his face. His expression shifted immediately from questioning to concerned. He broke into a faster run.

"Where is he?" He didn't slow his pace—not even as he passed her, his hiking sneakers digging deep into the grassy lawn for traction.

"David carried him into the parlor." Shifting directions, Jillian ran as hard and as fast as she could to keep up, but found it impossible. The distance between them grew until, by the time she had arrived inside the house, breathless and still panicked, he was already in the parlor examining her son.

His son.

Their son.

But did he know that? Was parentage what had caused him to run so incredibly hard? Or was that the result of his natural doctor's concern? She wished she could see his face to better judge, but he was turned away from her.

"Pete, does it hurt when I push here?"

When she entered the brightly lit sitting room, still gasping for her next breath, Pete lay on his back, knees bent, across one of the two facing settees that formed part of a small sitting area in the middle of the room. Someone had thought to pull off his sneakers and unbutton his jeans and shirt, but he still gripped his middle with both arms, his eyes pressed so tight with misery it made her mother's heart ache.

She paused just inside the doorway long enough to gather a semblance of composure while Brad, down on one knee, shifted his weight from side to side, carefully examining Pete.

David and Shelly stood directly behind the damask-covered settee, watching Brad focus his full attention on Pete. Reynold stood away from the rest, in the turret area, beside a winged chair. Rather than watch, he stared out the window, his hands clasped tightly behind him. Clearly, he didn't know how to handle such a frightening and intimidating situation. Probably hated the helpless feeling they all felt.

Rather than chance getting in the way of Brad's examination, Jillian joined Shelly and David on the opposite side. She rested a hand on the soft damask and watched while Brad carefully pressed skilled fingers against different areas of Pete's body. He tested the lower abdomen, both sides of Pete's middle, then felt along the sides of his throat before pulling his eyelids back to observe the pupils.

"You going to have to give me a shot?" Pete asked, clearly not happy with thought. "Because if you are, you got to tell me ahead of time. There are just certain things I don't like to watch."

"I promise," he said, stopping to tap Pete lightly on the nose. "If I have to give you a shot, you won't have to watch."

After a few minutes more, Brad stood and faced Jillian. His troubled expression sent yet another ripple of worry though her.

"I'm not sure what's causing his pain. There's no accompanying fever. No muscle aches. No swollen glands. And the pain he's having doesn't seem to be associated with any of the related organs. My guess is that it's a simple stomachache from having had too much strawberry syrup on his pancakes this morning, followed by a little too much activity out by the pond. I have medicine I can give him but all he probably needs are a few sips of ginger ale and some quiet time. But I can't be sure of that just yet."

Hoping Brad was right, that it really was nothing more serious than a stomachache brought on by too much sugar and sun, Jillian reached for the gold pendant at her throat and toyed with its smooth edge. "How long until you do know for sure whether that's the problem?"

He shrugged, cutting a glittering blue gaze to Pete, who now lay with one eye squinted partially open. "How long it takes depends on his metabolism. If it is just his stomach, he could feel better in only a couple of hours, or if it involves his intestines, it could take most of the day before he's completely over this." His gaze shot past her toward the turret where Reynold stood, as if some movement had caught his eye. "How long a recovery takes is really out of my hands."

The muscles in Brad's lean jaws tightened while he continued staring in Reynold's direction. "I can see what a damper this puts on your plans for the day. If you four want to carry on with your picnic, do so knowing I will stay right here and take care of Pete. Just leave me a handwritten letter with your insurance information, and stating I have permission to admit him to a local hospital just in case this turns out to be more than an overly active appetite. It'll save a lot of aggravation and paperwork."

Jillian shook her head, not to the request for a letter, but to let him know she wasn't going anywhere. She crossed her arms over her aching heart when she glanced at her son, still grimacing with pain. "We can't possibly leave here now, not knowing Pete is this sick."

Shelly moved closer to rest a supportive hand on her shoulder. "Jillian's right. We can reschedule the picnic for another day. We really should stay here."

"But that's so ridiculous," Reynold spoke, finally moving away from the windowed nook. Everyone turned at the sound of his voice. "The boy doesn't need us all here, and we already have the boat chartered, the food packed, and a perfect day outside. If Dr. Pierce really is willing to stay and watch over young Peter for us, I see no reason why we can't continue our day as planned.''

He raked a hand through his immaculately cut blond hair while he stared first at the back of the small sofa where Pete lay out of his sight, then at Jillian. ''Going through with the picnic would help you take your mind off his pain. And it's not as if our being here will help the boy's situation any. Truth is, us being here might cause more harm than good.'' His questioning gaze darted from Jillian to David and finally to Brad. ''Didn't you say he needed quiet?''

''I did,'' Brad replied, his tone flat. Shifting his weight to one well-toned leg, he continued to stare at Reynold with a noncommittal expression.

Jillian uncrossed her arms while trying to figure out what sort of emotions hid behind that carefully controlled expression. Were they a doctor's troubled emotions? Or a father's?

There were no true clues, not even when he elaborated. ''You four can leave here assured I'll take good care of him. Pete, here, is my friend, and I always take good care of my friends.''

''Then it's settled.'' Reynold clapped his hands together, then rubbed them briskly as he moved forward again, standing now where he could see Pete. ''We go ahead as planned and let the good doctor do his job. Maybe by the time we've returned, the boy will have—''

''Momma?'' Pete interrupted in a weak voice, restoring everyone's attention to him. ''Momma, are you going, too?''

With Brad having moved aside, Jillian was free to kneel in his place. She took Pete's tiny hand in both of hers and noticed how cool it felt. Damp. Clammy. ''Of course not. I'm not going anywhere until I know you are completely well again. I guess I'm a little like Brad. I can't very well leave my very best friend in such a time of need, now can I? ''But Reynold was right about Pete needing quiet. There really was no point in everyone forfeiting their plans for the day.'' I'll stay here and help take care of you, but everyone else will probably still go.''

"But, Jillian . . . ,'' Reynold inserted. But whatever argument had occurred to him, he curbed it. After a pause, he finished with, "I hate leaving you behind.''

Pete's hand balled into a tight fist inside Jillian's as he grimaced again, then moaned softly, drawing Reynold's bothered gaze to his contorted face. "But if the boy is really that sick, I understand. We'll miss having you along.'' He took a deep breath and returned his attention to Jillian as he motioned to the other two with a quick wave. "The rest of us had better get moving. We were supposed to be at the pier five minutes ago.''

David headed immediately for the door, but Shelly tapped her tented fingers together while watching Pete's latest grimace. "I think I'll stay here and keep Jillian company. You two go on without me.''

Pete's eyes flew open, clearly upset by her generous offer. His balled hand tightened harder inside Jillian's while he gathered the strength to speak. "No, Mrs. Nelson, please don't stay behind because of me. You go on and have some fun like you planned so you can come back here and tell me all about what I missed.''

Shelly studied Pete hesitantly. "But I hate running off to have fun while you are so sick and your mother is so concerned.''

"Oh, but it's bad enough I'm ruining Mom's day. It would make me feel even worse if I knew I was ruining your day, too. I want everyone else to go on with the picnic and have loads of fun. Bring me back some seashells if you find any. I promised Troy I'd come back with a suitcase full.''

Jillian's heart soared with pride. Such a warm, caring young man her son was turning out to be. There he lay in incredible pain, faced with spending the rest of this beautiful day in bed miserable, and his concern was for everyone else. It made her want to hug him close, but she didn't dare. Pete thought such overt displays of emotion were for babies.

"Yes, Shelly, do go on and enjoy the picnic," Jillian encouraged, smiling while she studied her little hero's truly concerned expression. "After all *someone* has to help with the food. You know how inept these two are when it comes to serving themselves."

Shelly cocked her mouth to one side a moment, clearly undecided, then finally nodded. "Okay, I'll go. But I'll want to find our young man in much better health when I return." She bent over the back of the baroque settee to stroke Pete's damp curls with caring fingertips. "I'll be very upset if I come back and find out he's not well. He's such a sweet boy." Her eyes glistened when she straightened. "How I long to have a son like him one day."

Instinctively, David returned to his wife's side and slid a comforting arm around her slender shoulders.

Remembering the Nelsons had tried unsuccessfully for three years to have children, Jillian hurried to change the subject—before Shelly slipped into a mood too melancholy to overcome. "Oh, but your time at motherhood isn't all that far away, and with your poor luck, you'll end up with a whole houseful of boys one day. All of them every bit as active as Pete. Meanwhile, the basket with the food and the Thermos needing lemonade are waiting inside the kitchen, as are the quilts. Reynold's right. You three are already late. You'd better get a move on."

"Well, we can at least give up the trip to Indian Point afterward," Shelly insisted, already on her way toward the wide hallway door flanked on both sides with stately floor to ceiling bookshelves, David's arm still curled lovingly around her shoulders.

"But why give up that?" Reynold asked, following only a few steps behind. "It's not like we can do anything here and the view of the point at sunset is supposed to be nothing short of spectacular. Jillian's father told me it might be a little out of the way, but it was not to be missed."

Jillian grinned. Reynold felt so obviously helpless in situations like this—although he had sure better get used to them.

Fatherhood was jam-packed with many such emotional trials.

"Tell you what," she called after them, hoping to spare Reynold any more of that helpless, incompetent feeling he now endured. Reynold was far too unaccustomed to not being in full control of a situation. "If Pete isn't any better by midafternoon, I'll send word to the Butlers, and Bill can tell you when he comes after you on the island later. You can then come on back here, if it'll make you feel better about Pete. But if he's better by then, there's no reason you three should give up your trip to the point. It truly is a beautiful sight from the water, what with the sky filled with colors, reflecting off the water as it splashes dramatically on the rocks below."

Reynold glanced back at her with a grateful smile. "And by then, I'll bet young Peter will be feeling so much better that this Bill fellow will tell us we might as well stop off at that big inn there on the point for cocktails." He winked, then looked a lot less troubled when he sauntered out of the room, toward Shelly and David, already in the hall.

"Some fiancé you have there," Brad muttered, as he, too, headed for the door.

Jillian felt no inclination to discuss Reynold's obvious insecurities so she let the comment pass. "Where are you going? I thought you planned to stay and watch over Pete?" Not that she couldn't do so herself. But that was what he had told the others.

He jerked to an indignant stop then spun around, glowering at her. "Earlier, Pete said something to me about having lost his favorite baseball cap out by the pond. I told him I'd go find it for him. It should take me all of ten minutes." Having said that, he bunched his shoulders and promptly left.

Jillian stared after him, baffled by such an unjustified outburst of emotion. Why was Brad so angry? Because his plans to spend the day hiking the trails was now ruined? Or was he angry because of her secret? Because she had never told him about Pete?

Her heart fluttered while she again worried Brad had somehow guessed the truth.

❧ *Chapter 7* ❧

By a little after noon, Brad had Pete settled into bed, sipping small amounts of chilled ginger ale at regular intervals. Although Pete's ailment never advanced enough so that he lost any food and his color had soon returned, he still grimaced and complained a lot. Even so, the pains had diminished enough to allow him to sleep, which he did off and on while Jillian and Brad both waited nearby in case he needed one of them.

Until certain Pete's symptoms weren't related to something more serious than having had too much strawberry syrup for breakfast, neither Brad nor Jillian wanted to be too far away should he awaken from his nap and call out. But neither wanted to stay in the room with him either, for fear their presence might keep him from a restful sleep. As a compromise, they blocked the bedroom door open with the desk chair and moved out into the alcove near the stairs.

Destined to spend the next few hours in each other's company, they waited together in the lofty, sunlit area of the second floor but chose to sit on opposite ends of the wide, comfortably cushioned window seat.

With a bank of guillotine-style windows making up part of the main wall, all open, a gentle breeze drifted in off the ocean and ruffled the curtains tied back on either side. The breeze felt warm and comforting, and carried with it the be-

guiling scent of cedar, honeysuckle, and brine. Had anyone
else been at Jillian's side, she would have closed her eyes
and reveled in the silky caress of moist sea air, and the steady,
tranquil sound of the distant waves lulling her. As it was, she
tried not to be affected by the sensual surroundings while
waiting for Pete's call should it come.

She also tried not to be affected by Brad, who sat sideways
with his back propped against the window jamb, his knees
folded and tucked nearly to his chest. He had peeled his feet
bare, placed his shoes and socks neatly to one side, and now
sat with his feet beside him on the cushioned bench, staring
idly at the rippling sea.

She refused to wonder what sort of thoughts had so effectively captured his attention, refused to worry that he might
be trying to figure out what he wanted to do now that he was
faced the possibility of having a son. Instead, she glanced
through an interesting old reference book about the history of
ocean vessels she had found on the neatly kept bookshelf
beside her and thought back to a similar day when her own
mother had sat right there while she lay in the Great White
Room recovering from a late case of chicken pox.

For the first hour, neither Brad nor Jillian spoke, each pretending to be unaware of the other, despite the fact that Jillian
couldn't remember ever having been more aware of anyone
in her life. Without actually turning in his direction, for fear
he would notice, she glimpsed first his slender feet baring
long toes buried deep into the soft cushion, then his hands,
resting lightly on his raised knees.

There was as much contradiction in those hands as in the
man himself. Such strong, skilled, yet gentle hands. Hands
attached to a man who had claimed to not want children in
his life, yet had formed a friendship with Pete so quickly.
Brad, the man she had fallen in love with so many years ago.
Brad, the guy who, when not working, loved to wear his jeans
faded and cap backward just like his son. Brad, the father of
her child. Brad, the doctor he always wanted to be.

That last thought took some getting use to, but after having watched Brad examine Pete downstairs, it had finally struck her that Brad was a real doctor now. Like her father. And a good one at a that. He had known exactly what to do to find the source of Pete's pain, and even what to give him to lessen that pain immediately. Imagine something as simple as ginger ale having eased Pete's cramping enough to let him rest. She'd never have thought of it.

Once she had finally figured out that all Pete suffered from was an old-fashioned stomachache, she would have dug through her suitcase for a bottle of that pink medicine, and would have given him a liberal dose, even though he hated the stuff and would have fought her tooth and nail before swallowing any. But Pete didn't hate the chilled ginger ale. They had had no problem getting him to drink that. No problem at all.

With Brad still staring vacantly out across the sun-sparkled ocean, Jillian lifted her gaze higher long enough to study his strong, achingly familiar profile. It was the handsome but solemn profile of a man who had raced to her son's aid as if fearing his very life itself had depended on it.

That memory comforted her.

Brad's decision to become a doctor had indeed turned out to have its advantages, although it had certainly brought along its disadvantages, too. It was that obsession to become a doctor, that steadfast determination to graduate from medical school with high marks and in record time that had driven a wedge between them. It was what had left her the single mother she was today.

At least he had been honest with her from the start. Becoming a medical doctor had always been the most important thing in the world to him. Having a wife and children would never fill a place of any importance to him.

She blinked to keep from crying as a result. If only she could have experienced one of those famed Seascape miracles she had heard about all her life. If only Brad had come to love her with the same depth and intensity she had loved him.
And still did.

That much was obvious.

In all these years, she had never stopped loving Brad Pierce. She had tried. Thought she had succeeded. But she realized now, she had never even come close.

How sad that in all this time, she had never let go of those many emotions so deeply associated with Brad. Never freed her soul of the hurt and harm he could do to her. *Did* do. And could yet do.

Even now, Brad had the power to hurt her more than anyone else could. She sensed that in the way her heart still fluttered and her stomach still churned whenever she as much as looked at him. If only hurting her had not been what he had wanted to do. If only he had longed to make her as happy as she had wanted to make him.

Aware by Brad's continued distant expression that his thoughts were anywhere but in that alcove with her, Jillian leaned just a little closer, then shut her eyes and breathed deeply his familiar cologne, wrapping herself in old memories. Old memories of what it had been like before she had found out she was pregnant—before she had ever mentioned the word marriage to him.

What fun, loving, carefree days those had been. Every moment spent together had been a moment to treasure, whether it had been spent walking along the cliffs exploring each other's lives, or sitting in the Blue Moon sharing their laughter over an icy root beer or a frothy strawberry soda.

She smiled despite the ache that filled her heart, barely conscious of her current surroundings until Brad finally chose to break the collective silence.

"I don't want to make you angry, and I know it's not really my place to say anything, but there's something bugging me and I won't feel right until I've gotten it off my chest."

Surprised he had spoken, Jillian's eyes flew open. *Now what?* She made a wild grab for the book that had unexplainably jumped out of her lap, but missed by inches, startled when it hit the wooden floor with a crack. Her heart pounding hard, she looked down at where the book landed but was too focused on the fear of what Brad planned to say to bend over and pick it up.

"That sounds ominous," she replied, amazed at how calm she sounded when inside her pulse pumped frantically.

Anything that had to be offset by the phrase, "I don't want to make you angry" could not bode well. Was he about to ask her about Pete? Had he finally clued in on the fact he and her son had a lot more in common than baseball? "What exactly is your problem?"

"That's just it. It's not really *my* problem," Brad started, then swung his feet around to the floor and scooted closer to pick up the book for her. He waited until she had taken it from him and returned it to her lap before explaining further. "It's more Pete's problem. And yours."

He paused a minute, then rubbed his face with his hands, sitting close enough now his elbow brushed her arm, sending an unexpected shockwave up through her shoulders. She tried to scoot farther away to prevent more of the same, but the side wall prevented it.

"Hell, maybe it is my problem, too. But only because I care about your son. I care about him a lot."

Care about *your* son? Not *our* son? Encouraged by the implication, she sucked a deep breath, held it long enough to steady her rapid heart rate, then quietly released it. Was it possible he still hadn't guessed who Pete's father was? But how could he not? The evidence was so strong. "I don't understand. What problem are you talking about?"

"Reynold," he answered simply, saying the name as if just speaking it aloud left a bitter taste in his mouth. He narrowed his gaze as he wrinkled his nose, bringing her attention to the three faded freckles there.

"Reynold?" She stared at his troubled expression, baffled. Was Brad jealous? No. Couldn't be. He would have to love her before he possibly could be jealous. "How is Reynold a problem?"

"He's not good father material." Brad leaned forward, resting his forearms on his parted knees, but continued to look at her with an amazingly sincere expression—considering his words. "The man is far too involved with himself. With his work. I'm sorry, but I've seen Reynold's type before. Too many times. He's so far into himself, he is incapable of ever putting anyone else's needs above his own—not even the needs of a child. He can never give Pete the amount of time, or level of attention a boy like that needs. Reynold's own needs are too likely to get in the way."

Jillian nearly choked. *Now there was a pot calling the kettle black!* "And I suppose in the nine years since I saw you last, you've become an authority of some sort on what makes a good father."

His expression turned granite-hard as he sat back again. "No, I'm not an authority. But it doesn't take a genius to see that Reynold doesn't care enough about your son to be a good parent to him." Brad waved his hands to emphasize his words. Again the side of his elbow brushed her arm but this time it was Brad who leaned back to prevent it from happening again. "Why, just a couple of hours ago the man you plan to marry was far more concerned over the possibility of failed picnic plans than he was about the fact Pete was in serious pain. Doesn't that tell you something?"

"Just that you've become a poor judge of people—because you're dead wrong," she responded, absently rubbing the spot where their arms had touched. Why she suddenly felt so compelled to defend Reynold when what she should do was refuse to listen to Brad at all was beyond her. "Reynold was very concerned about Pete. Didn't you see how troubled he looked?"

"Troubled, yes. But about what?"

"About Pete. What else was there to be troubled about?" Fighting to keep her anger in check, she explained further. "You obviously don't know Reynold. He's a man of quick and decisive action. He is used to being in complete control no matter how serious the situation. He was out of his element earlier. And because of that, he couldn't help but feel helpless and uncertain with Pete lying there so ill. He's not used to facing personal dilemmas like that and didn't know how to deal with the situation.''

''And you think a man like that will make a good father?''

Frustrated that Brad continued to doubt Reynold, she curled her fingers around the leather binding of the book still in her lap. ''You are wrong. About this whole thing.'' She glared at him, her eyes narrowed. ''Reynold loves Pete. And he loves me. That's all that matters to me.''

Brad's eyes turned dusky gray while he studied her a long moment more. When he spoke again, he sounded so quiet she almost did not hear him.

''And do you love him?''

Jillian's heart skipped two beats. She had not expected him to ask that personal a question. ''That is none of your business.''

''That may be, but it doesn't keep me from asking. Or from wondering. Do you love him? Or haven't you yet figured out what love really is?''

What's that supposed to mean? Looking down at the hand that should carry her engagement ring, she darted the tip of her tongue back and forth across her lower lip to buy a few more seconds of time. Just how should she answer that? Should she admit the truth and chance him asking why she would marry a man she didn't love, or let him believe whatever he wanted? ''I've already told you about that. Reynold and I are engaged to be married. In November. Don't you listen?''

Refusing to let it go at that, Brad lifted a gentle hand to her chin and cupped it with his fingers, forcing her to look at him. ''That's not what I asked, Jillian. I asked, Do you love him.''

Reluctantly, Jillian met his searching gaze and felt that old familiar spark when he dipped closer to see into her eyes more clearly. The intoxicating scent of his cologne invaded the intimate space between them, distracting her long enough to forget the primal urge to run away.

Why did the man have to look and smell so good?

"Just tell me the truth," he prodded and continued to search deep into her soul, his blue eyes dark and probing. All but the fingertip directly beneath her chin fell away. "Do you love him?"

Why do you care? Jillian's mind screamed, uncertain why he would ask such a thing. It wasn't as if her loving Reynold would take anything away from Brad. He had thrown her love away years ago.

Baffled, Jillian shifted her gaze to the base of Brad's well-sculpted throat, the masculine shape of his collarbone prominent between the opening of his plain white collar.

The familiar bong from the grandfather clock at the foot of the stairs saved her from having to answer. Her heart sang out in gratitude. "It's one o'clock. Time to check on Pete again."

Brad continued to study her a moment, then suddenly shoved away. Without another word to her, he jerked on his footwear, tied the shoes with quick, sharp movements, then seconds later was on his way into the bedroom to check on his patient.

Jillian followed quietly behind, not certain why he should act so annoyed—after *he* had been the one to end their affair all those years ago, not her.

Pete quickly snapped his eyes shut and pretended to be asleep when he caught the sound of two sets of soft footsteps headed toward his room. Having detected the angry tone of their voices just moments earlier, he knew it wasn't time yet for his recovery. His mother and Brad still had problems to work out and if he pretended to be well again now, they would probably just go their separate ways and not say another word to each other in the four days Brad had left.

Pete didn't want to take that chance.

Waiting on someone to wake him from his pretend nap, he concentrated on lying perfectly still and listened while one set of the footsteps came right up to the bed.

"He's still asleep." Brad whispered so as not to disturb him.

Aware Brad was now right over him, Pete tried not to grin over the fact he was play-acting—and obviously doing a darn good job of it.

"Does he look like he's still in any pain?" That whisper came from his mother, who sounded a little farther away. Maybe over beside the open door.

"No, not in any pain; but judging by the twitch under his eyelids, he's having a very intense dream."

Pete's pulses jumped at hearing that last comment. His eyelids were twitching? How come? He tried harder to lie perfectly still so Brad wouldn't guess the truth. He already knew what Brad thought of deceptive people and sure didn't want Brad to figure out he was never really sick. That would ruin everything.

Brad fell quiet a moment, then murmured in a questioning voice, "I wonder what he's dreaming about." He tilted his head. "What exactly do six-year-olds dream about?"

Jillian purposely did not correct the mistake concerning Pete's age.

"With Pete, it probably has to do with either baseball, swimming, or Nintendo. I can tell you a few things it doesn't deal with—there's eating broccoli, cleaning his room, or kissing. He hates all three."

Pete felt inclined to agree, but didn't dare. He lay quietly and wondered why his mother hadn't corrected Brad about how old he was. Maybe it was something she didn't want him to know. If that was so, it might be smart of him to be real careful and not go letting his age slip.

Pete next wondered when one of them would wake him so he could tell them his stomach still felt a little bad. Obviously, they were in no rush to find out.

He hoped Tony was somewhere close by, cheering him on like he was supposed to. His question was answered when he felt a cool, reassuring hand on his shoulder. Without opening his eyes, he knew it was Tony's hand and that somehow he had heard his thoughts.

Again there was several seconds when nothing was said until finally Brad commented, "It's amazing how very much Pete looks like you."

"Like me?" Clearly, that comment had taken his mother by surprise.

"Yes, he's a very good-looking boy. You must be very proud to have a son like him."

The sounds that followed indicated that one of them was already leaving. Without having bothered to wake him. Curious to see who it was, he squinted his eyes open just a little and spotted Brad moving toward the door. His mother now stood only a few feet from the bed, but since her attention was focused on Brad and not him, he opened his eyes just a little more to get a better look at her puzzled expression.

"Yes, he's a handsome one all right." She continued to stare at Brad without blinking, as if she couldn't quite believe she had heard him right. Or maybe she had too many thoughts going through her head at the same time and she didn't know which one to latch on to. "But I don't think he looks all that much like me."

Just before Brad stepped out into the hallway, he turned to face her, but continued on his way. "How can you say that? Except for the color of his eyes, the spattering of freckles on his nose, Pete looks just like you. Right down to the playful dimples when he smiles."

"Not to me. To me, Pete looks more like his father."

While his mother followed Brad out of his sight, Pete noticed her back suddenly stiffen, like maybe she hadn't planned on saying that. She followed the unexpected comment with a quick change of subject, "Since he's sleeping so peacefully right now, and it's now after one o'clock, I think I'll go downstairs and see if there's anything left to make a few sandwiches for lunch. If Hattie still has the makings, which do you prefer, ham or turkey?"

By then Brad was too far away for Pete to hear what he

said after offering to go down with her, and Pete was caught too off guard by his mother's comment to care.

She had said he looked more like his father.

Intrigued, he waited until he heard the loud squeak of the third stair from the bottom to be sure they were far enough away, then sat up in bed and stared at himself in the oval mirror just above the vanity table nearby.

Jillian's heartbeat still raced at an uncontrollable rate when she and Brad entered the kitchen only minutes after returning downstairs. Although she had not yet figured out how to broach the subject of her son's yet undisclosed parentage without causing more trouble than she cared to face, in the past few hours she began to hope the topic would arise of its own accord. After three days of worrying about the consequences of having kept such a vital secret, she wished Brad would finally suspect the truth and question her, but do so while they were safely out of Pete's earshot. Like now.

Although not yet prepared to volunteer the information—not wanting to shoulder the responsibility of having made such an altering decision—if Brad would just question her, it would force the issue at last. Once confronted, she would have to tell him. She would have a *reason* to tell him. And in truth, he had a right to know.

If only she hadn't lived all these years without telling him. That was what made it so tough to approach the subject now. Even though she had never come right out and lied to him about Pete, she had never volunteered the truth, either. That omission, by its sheer serious nature, was as wrong and as harmful as having lied, and she knew it.

But she had kept the secret for all the right reasons. Maybe Brad could be made to see that. Oh, sure, he would be angry when he first learned of her treachery. No doubt about that. And he would be angrier still, when the full magnitude of what she had kept from him all these years struck him—and rightfully so—but that sort of reaction couldn't be prevented now. She would just have to suffer that anger, then try to explain. She had kept her dark secret for their son's sake. She did not want Pete as badly hurt as she'd been.

But would Brad listen? Would he at least try to understand that her reasons were noble, even though her actions were not? Or would he hate her immediately for what she'd done?

There was no way to second-guess his reaction.

But at least questions would force that reaction and get everything on out into the open so they could deal with it. That disclosure either would bring Brad permanently back into their lives in some fashion—an intrusion she did not dread nearly as much as she had in the past. Or it would drive the final wedge between them—for Brad had since made it quite clear what he thought of deceitful people.

Mulling over the different possibilities, she opened the refrigerator, found a small platter with lunch meats, sliced tomatoes, and sliced cheese on the second shelf near the front. She pulled the waxed paper off and set both on the counter, still considering what it would be like to finally have her secret out in the open. No more deceit. No more avoiding Pete's questions about his father, a man he had a right to know.

If Brad would just ask the right questions, she would have no choice but to tell everyone the truth at long last. The gut-wrenching limbo she had lived in for so many years would finally end. With the truth finally revealed, she would know how or if Brad would eventually fit into Pete's life. All those years of agonizing would be over, though the heartaches themselves might have barely begun.

Perhaps it was that growing desire to put the long-kept secret to rest that had compelled her to point out to Brad that Pete looked a lot more like his father than her. Perhaps she had hoped Brad would respond by asking her who that father was.

But he hadn't. He had let it pass.

Was the man oblivious?

"I'm not really all that hungry yet," Brad said, breaking her troubled thoughts as he crossed to the cabinets near the sink to retrieve two glasses. "I'm still pretty full from that breakfast Pete made earlier."

"Me, too," she admitted as she reached into the refrigerator for the mustard. The only reason she had mentioned lunch at all was because she had surprised herself with the comment about Pete's resemblance to his father. She hadn't planned to say that. "Want to just split a sandwich?"

"Works for me. But you might go ahead and make Pete a whole one. As soon as he feels up to it, I'm going to want him to eat something a little more substantial than that half-gallon of strawberry syrup he had for breakfast."

Spotting a bread box across the room, Jillian brought out a loaf of wheat bread, then pulled out four slices, enough to build one sandwich for Pete and one for her and Brad to halve. She had just located a table knife and the salt shaker when she heard Brad chuckle.

"Can you believe it? Church has barely been out an hour and already Beaulah Favish is back at it."

"Is she?" Unable to resist, Jillian left the knife sticking in the freshly opened mustard and moved to stand beside him at the sink. A gentle breeze curled through the window and tugged at the ruffled white curtains as she leaned closer. "Where is she?"

Brad pointed to a thicket of woods just beyond the gazebo. "Right there."

Jillian squinted but didn't see anyone. "Where? I don't see her."

Brad moved to stand more behind her than beside her then leaned forward until his chest pressed warmly against her shoulder, and pointed again. "Right there."

Trying desperately not to react to the familiar sensations now rekindled inside her—just from the fact they now touched—Jillian followed the direction of his arm, but still saw nothing out of the ordinary. "Are you sure you saw her out there?"

"Just wait." When he spoke, his breath felt warm and vibrant at the back of her right cheek, making it hard for her to concentrate on anything other than how close they now stood. And how marvelous it felt. She fought the desire to close her eyes and pretend they were still lovers. She refused to be swept away by the many giddy sensations building inside her.

His finger hovered then moved to the right half an inch. "Right there."

Jillian saw it. The reflection of the sun off the glass in Beaulah's binoculars. With the position now pinpointed, she could make out the woman's tiny form moving about in the brush. "Oh, I see her now. I can't believe that little snoop is still out there patroling the perimeter."

Brad chuckled again as he lowered his hand to the edge of the sink just inches away from Jillian's tension-knotted midriff. "Do you remember the time that the little busybody caught us kissing out in the gazebo at night and marched us to the house to tell Miss Hattie, thinking Miss Hattie would be so appalled she would in turn tell your parents?"

Jillian nodded, laughing along with him even though at the time she had been petrified for they had very nearly progressed past the point of just kissing when Beaulah had suddenly appeared out of the foliage like a small piece of the forest that had suddenly come alive. "Of course, I remember. I also remember how, instead, Miss Hattie told Beaulah it was none of her business what went on in her gazebo, and if her guests wanted to strip off and run buck naked into the pond, it was no concern of hers."

Relieved to have something to break her exhilarated concentration, Jillian's gaze followed the movement of shifting limbs in the brush while she spoke to Brad still standing behind her. "Miss Hattie told her just as long as what happened didn't harm or offend the other guests in any way, she didn't care what went on out there." Still laughing, Jillian spun around to face him, eager to break their touch, but unprepared for the startling effect of finding his translucent blue eyes studying her from only inches away. Her heart rate doubled. "Do you remember how Beaulah gasped right out loud when

Miss Hattie actually dared to use the word naked?''

"Yes, and then she threatened to go tell Preacher Brown that Miss Hattie was promoting promiscuity among her guests, only to be reminded that Preacher Brown was out of town for two weeks." Brad's blue eyes glittered with more than mirth while he, too, thought back to those happier times. "If seeing us kiss like that was enough to send that old busy-body into such a flying tizzy, it's a very good thing she didn't have a telescope in addition to those binoculars. She would have had a heart attack to see what went on during our picnics out on that little island."

His gaze narrowed almost imperceptibly while Jillian fought for her next breath. Images of their lovemaking filled her thoughts.

Swallowing hard, Jillian's gaze shifted to his parted lips, lips that just seconds ago had been stretched into a dimple-deep smile but now registered no expression at all. Suddenly, she wished he would kiss her. If for no other reason than for old time's sake. He stood more than close enough. All he would have to do was bend forward a few scant inches. She would tilt her chin and meet his mouth halfway.

Her insides fluttered like a fallen bird at the thought of what it would be like to be encircled by Brad's strong arms again, feeling the overwhelming magic of his embrace, the dizzying wonder of his kiss. How sadly exciting that would be. Even though, now, she understood there was no unspoken commitment between them, and that their futures were not forever entwined like she had once thought, she longed to feel him close to her just once more.

But in the next instance, she felt guilty for even having considered such a thing. After all, she was an engaged woman now. After nine years of floundering, her life finally had direction. Kissing Brad would be wrong.

And foolish.

What if it led to something more? What if she gave into the overpowering desires building inside her only to have him touch her heart then cast her aside again? The pain and humiliation would be too great, her losses too many. She might not love Reynold, but she needed him. She needed his stabilizing effect in her life, as did Pete.

She loved her son and would do *anything* to see him happy.

That included walking away from Brad at a time he looked to be right on the verge of kissing her.

❧ *Chapter 8* ❧

While Pete continued his slow but steady recovery from what could not have been a more badly timed stomachache, Jillian spent much of the afternoon in the alcove, talking with Brad. After halving the turkey sandwich she had made for them, and making sure Pete ate at least part of the ham sandwich she had brought upstairs for him, they settled next to the open windows again. There, they continued to listen for Pete while taking short, careful jaunts down memory lane.

Catching up on some of the more major events in their lives during the past nine years, Brad was surprised to learn Jillian did not live in quite the grand lifestyle he would have expected all these years, given the wealth at her disposal. Jillian was just as surprised to discover that perhaps Brad had had a worthwhile reason to want to become a doctor. He honestly enjoyed taking care of his patients and worried about them much like a parent would.

Eventually, the animosity they had shown each other during their first few days there fell away, and for several hours they truly enjoyed each other's company.

Jillian laughed upon hearing about Brad's hectic days as a lowly intern, while Brad chuckled over a few of the humorous incidents Jillian had caused during her years as the director of Bailey Foundations, which now governed a wide assortment of charities, each set up by the generous endowment left by her maternal grandfather.

The caution flag did not pop up again until shortly after Brad returned from one of several trips to the bedroom to make sure Pete's recovery continued.

"He's sitting up now, going through those six packs of baseball cards I bought for him earlier when I drove into the village to get more ginger ale. He's all excited because he found a Nolan Ryan in one of the first packs he opened."

"A Nolan Ryan?" She turned away from the window where she had been watching a pair of masked terns play in the gentle breeze. "Pete idolizes Nolan Ryan. I guess now you'll be Pete's friend for life."

Brad chuckled, then crooked one leg while he sat facing her on the bench-style window seat. This time he did not bother to take off his shoes. "He's already checked it against his most current Beckett and found out it's worth over twenty-four dollars. Seems those cards I bought are already well over two years old. I guess the Johnsons don't bother updating their baseball card stock very often."

"I'll bet Pete's glad they don't."

Nodding, Brad shifted his weight toward the back of the window seat to make himself more comfortable as he glanced back toward the door which was still propped open. From where they sat, they couldn't really see Pete, but could view a corner of the large double bed where he had made himself at home. "I'm amazed every time I look at that boy. I know you said you think Pete looks more like his father, but I find it hard to believe he resembles anyone but you. It's amazing how much alike you two are, right down to the dimples and shy smile."

His own smile widened, shaping dimples she thought looked far more like Pete's than hers ever did. Long, deep, and adorable.

"Jillian, you've got yourself a great kid in there. He makes me wish I'd found time to marry and have a son just like him. That's exactly what's missing from my life."

Having just been handed the perfect opportunity to tell

Brad the truth, Jillian's heart struck with such fury against her ribs, the resulting jolt shook her right to her toes. Stunned, she did not know whether to make use of the opportunity as it was and blurt out what she now longed for him to know, or question him further—to clarify that he actually meant what he had just said. After all, the words just spoken did not in any way emulate those said nine years ago. Truth was, they were the exact *opposite* of what he'd told her all those years ago.

Who was he trying to kid? Nobody changed that much. What was the point in lying to her now?

"Brad, how can you possibly say something like that?" *Didn't he realize who he was talking to?*

"How can I possibly say something like what?" His forehead creased between two perfectly shaped eyebrows, as if he had the audacity to be baffled by her sharp tone. "All I said was that I wish I had a family."

His pretending not to understand her emotional outburst upset her even more. Did he really think she would forget the horrible things he'd told her that day? She came unglued.

"I know. I heard exactly what you said," she responded, her voice far louder than originally intended. "But I don't understand how you can possibly say something like that to me and sound so sincere."

"But I am sincere." He raised his voice to match hers. Clearly, he didn't like having his lies pointed out to him.

"The hell you are."

Brad's blue eyes stretched to their limits as if unable to believe what he had just heard, then narrowed again, shading his emotions with those long, silky eyelashes. "What's got into you?"

"What's got into me? Try the fact that you're sitting here lying to me with such careless indifference." Jillian virtually trembled with anger and renewed hurt as she jabbed her finger in the direction of the window. "In case you've forgotten, nine years ago, you stood right out there on those cliffs and told me that one of the reasons it was over between us was because you didn't have the room for children in your future that I did. Remember? You said your life was all mapped out to take a completely different direction than mine. That you couldn't possibly be hampered by the responsibility of a family. Remember? You said a family would do nothing but get in the way of your precious career. Or have you conveniently forg—?''

An unexpected creaking sound not too far away pulled her attention away from Brad's dark glower long enough to spot Pete standing just inside the hall, an assortment of baseball cards in one hand and his dog-eared monthly price guide in the other. His pale blue eyes stared wide and unblinking at Brad, then slowly shifted to look questioningly at her. ''What's going on out here?''

Jillian's outrage changed immediately into concern for her young son. How much did he overhear? ''Nothing is going on out here, Pete. We're just having a discussion about something.''

''But you're yelling at each other.''

''It's a *loud* discussion,'' Brad put in calmly, then stood. ''One we really shouldn't be having.''

''About you once saying you didn't want children?'' Pete asked.

Brad's forehead notched as he cut a concerned gaze to Jillian then back to Pete. ''How long have you been standing there?''

''Long enough to hear how you once told my mother you didn't ever want to be saddled with a family, especially children.'' Pete's voice trembled with the strain from having to say such awful words aloud. ''I don't understand. I thought you liked kids.''

Jillian's heart ached at the sight of her son's stricken expression. This was exactly the sort of hurt she had hoped to avoid for him. Shifting her weight forward to the edge of the seat, she prepared to rush over and comfort him, but Brad beat her to it.

''Oh, but I do like kids.'' He knelt so he would be eye-level with Pete, then rested a comforting hand on the boy's slender shoulder. "Try to understand, it was nearly nine years ago when I said that to your mother. I was still very young. I was also very wrong. I spoke the truth a minute ago when I told your mother how I'd dearly love to be a parent and have someone like you in my life. But my problem is, I never found the right person for me like your mother did. Still, that doesn't keep me from wishing I had a child of my own. We all wish for things we can't have."

Bracing herself, Jillian pressed her palms into the cushions beside her, not prepared to accept the sincerity in his expression. If what he had just told her was true, it would mean she had been wrong all these years. Wrong about him. Wrong about how he would react to unexpected fatherhood. Wrong about *everything*.

Judging from what Brad just said about children, the reason he had so unceremoniously dumped her was simply because she was not the right person for him, not because he had developed any real, lasting aversion to having children in his life. Evidently, he had only used that as an excuse to get rid of her, knowing how she longed to have a family of her own one day.

Could she really have misread Brad so completely? Was he really not opposed to having children of his own? If so, she had kept these two apart for no valid reason. Rejection and unrelenting anger had never been a possibility.

As dumbfounded as she was guilt-ridden over the very real disservice she may have done these two, Jillian watched, unmoving, while Brad rocked forward on his knees and pulled Pete into a loose hug. Strong arms circled skinny shoulders, reminding Jillian that the one thing father and son didn't have in common was build.

"That's why your friendship is so important to me," Brad continued with all candor. "For the past few days I've pretended that you are that son I've always longed to have."

Jillian clenched her teeth against the piercing pain that simple statement caused, but she tried not to appear dazed or heartsick by any of this. Not even when Pete turned his blue eyes toward her, then for some reason stared up at the vaulted ceiling above her head and nodded once before shifting his attention back to Brad.

She glanced up almost expecting to see someone there.

"So is *that* what you and Mom fought about those nine years ago? She wanted children and you didn't? Is that why you two suddenly decided to quit being good friends?"

When Brad shifted his gaze away a moment, there was such sadness there, Jillian resisted a very real urge to rush over and pull both of them into her arms. She was too curious to hear the answer.

"Yes, Pete, that was part of it, I think. But there were other reasons, too."

Jillian could tell by his pained expression, his thoughts relived that last time they were together, much like she had so many times in the past.

"And we're still friends? You and me?"

Brad's smiled returned as he met Pete's hopeful gaze. "Of course we are."

"And you're still going to pitch me a few later, after we're sure that sandwich I ate is going to stay down like it's supposed to?"

"I wouldn't miss it."

Pete looked happy again when he slid out of Brad's easy embrace and headed to where Jillian still sat, her stomach holding her down like lead. "Mom?"

Afraid of what he might say to her after she had caused such a childish scene, Jillian responded cautiously.

"What?"

"Can I call Troy tomorrow and tell him about these new cards I just got? He's not going to believe some of the players here." He held the handful of cards out, clearly more excited about their content than he was distressed by her behavior. "I also want him to know that for the first week at least, I'll be getting in a little batting and pitching practice while I'm up here so he can tell his dad. I want them to know how I'm not going to be coming back from Maine ruined after all.''

Glad she wasn't getting a well-deserved lecture for that outburst, especially knowing he'd been right there in the next room where he could hear every angry word, she smiled. "Why wait until tomorrow? Why don't we go call him right now?''

It would give her something to do other than face Brad after everything the three of them had just learned about each other. She needed more time to think about what had been said, more time to consider its value and its ramifications.

"But how can we call Troy when the phones aren't working?''

"You look well enough to ride into town with me and use one of the telephones there, and tomorrow you might have a hard time catching Troy home. He'll have school and baseball practice to go to. And I did promise Shelly I'd stop by the co-op and tell Bill whether or not you had started along the road to recovery so they could decide whether to go on to Indian Point or return here.'' She glanced at her watch. "He'll be heading off to the island in just a little while.''

"Great. Let me go get my shoes on.'' He took only two steps toward the door before spinning around to face Brad. "What about you? You said earlier that you wished the phones would start working again so you could check in with that other doctor who is taking care of your patients this week. Do you want to come with us? If we behave real nice and smile a lot, Mom might let us stop in the Blue Moon for a couple of those strawberry sodas like I had on Thursday.''

"Strawberry sodas?'' Brad asked, one eyebrow arched in disbelief. "With you just getting over a stomachache from having eaten far too much strawberry syrup? *Not* a good idea.''

"Oh, but I feel all fine now.'' He patted his stomach soundly to prove it. "You were right. A few hours of rest is all I needed.''

"Still, you should probably lay off heavy sweets for a day or two. No sense inviting trouble.''

Pete pursed his lips at an angle while he considered Brad's advice, then beamed again. "Okay, you and Mom can have the sodas. I'll have some of that white soup they make, the kind Mom says Grandma always ordered whenever she went there."

Not giving Brad a chance to agree or decline, he hurried off to put on his shoes and find his cap. "We can go just as soon as I'm ready."

Brad yearned for a few moments alone with Jillian, but could not very well ask Pete to go get lost for awhile, not after having discovered how important it was to the boy to be with him. Clearly, Pete longed for a father figure, and during the next few days, he would provide that. Gladly.

Still, he needed a little time alone with Jillian, time to finish the discussion they had started earlier in the alcove. He wanted a chance to explain why he had told her he did not want children when it was in no way true—not even then. Nor was it true that he had thought his education more important than his love for her. Quite the contrary. Nothing had ever matched the importance of what he felt for her. It was because he loved her as much as he did that he had lied.

But *he* had lied for a good reason, while *she* had lied to suit her own selfish needs. Jillian *had* indeed cared for him, he knew that, but she'd purposely exaggerated what she felt toward him as a way to assure he fell in love with her so he would provide her all the diversion a bored little rich girl could want during their two summers together.

Brad's heart ached with the memory of how easily he had been sucked in by her sweet words and adoring looks. How he had *wanted* to be sucked in. So, why was it he felt so guilty to have lied to her, too? Probably because until then he had never lied to anyone before in his life; nor had he lied to anyone since. Even with patients facing inevitable death, he avoided skirting the truth.

Like his father, he prided himself on his honesty. That's why it was time to correct the lie he had told Jillian. She deserved to know the real reason he had set her free, although in retrospect, he hadn't really protected her from anything, not when she hadn't truly loved him to begin with. Even had he screwed up his courage and asked, she would never have accepted a proposal of marriage from someone like him. She would have continued playing him along a few more days then; had he not been the one to provide a reason to break up, she surely would have supplied one of her own. The summer had been nearly over by then. She would have cut the ties binding them before that week's end.

Still, Brad wanted to clear his conscience of the lie. He was not sure how she would react after she discovered he had deceived her, too, but it was time they discussed the truth. Time they brought all that old bitterness out into the open, so they could get over the animosity and the guilt and reach an understanding. For little Pete's sake, they should at least try to be friends.

If they returned to the inn early enough, maybe he could find a way to be alone with her before the other adults returned—if only for a few minutes. He had to try.

But for now, it was the three of them. They had made their phone calls from the pay phone at the post office and were headed into the Blue Moon Cafe, laughing over the comical way Candy-the-Cock-eyed-Cat lay draped like a wash rag over the part of the huge ship anchor out front. Pete laughed especially hard, claiming the animal looked ridiculous.

Laughing together. Like a family.

Amused by that thought, for he would love to be a part of a family who enjoyed its own company like that, he waved to Lucy Baker as they entered.

"Well, bless my soul if it isn't Dr. Pierce," she said, coming around the counter with bright smile and a lively bounce. As usual, she had a pencil stuck behind her ear. "Wrong time of the year for you to be here, isn't it?" She grabbed up a wet rag off a nearby table and headed for Brad's favorite spot near the jukebox. "Bill told me you were here. Or would 'complained' be a better word?"

"Complained?" Pete asked, peering at him quizzically as he took his red cap off, folded it in half, and tucked the bill into his waistband exactly like Brad had just done to his own. "What did you do?"

"What'd he do?" Lucy repeated, commenting before Brad could. "Why, sweetie, Dr. Pierce here had the audacity to win last night while playing Bill, Jimmy, and Bill's Uncle Mike in a big game of rummy. And poor Bill was just so sure he had the winning hand."

"I'm surprised Bill admitted it." Brad laughed, knowing the man had his pride.

"Actually it was Leslie who said something first," she admitted with a playful toss of her head, causing the golden-red hair pinned high on her head to shimmer beneath the overhead lamps. "But when I asked him outright, he finally admitted that it was true. He admitted right out how you'd beat the socks off him."

"Who knew they were his only pair?" Brad laughed again, trying not to conjure up a visual picture of Bill Butler standing around in bare feet. As he recalled, Bill had a pair of the knobbiest brown feet he had ever seen. "Besides, if I'd known ahead both of his socks had holes in them, I'd have thrown the game."

Lucy giggled at such a pitiful attempt at humor, but then Lucy giggled at everything. Originally from the South, it was just in her nature to be cheerful all the time.

"So, I guess you three are here for supper, what with Miss Hattie having such a good time over at Miss Millie's this afternoon. I just got back from taking them some eggs they needed, and I do doubt that Miss Hattie will be back home until nearly dark, if then. Richard had them talked into making a couple of batches of homemade ice cream since he won't be able to get back up here until July Fourth."

"Supper?" Brad hadn't thought about it, but if Miss Hattie was not going to be back in time to eat with them, he saw no reason why they should wait to eat supper there. Especially when all she had left behind was cold sandwich makings and they had already had one sandwich meal. "What time is it?"

Lucy glanced at the neon clock on the wall behind the counter. "Nearly five-thirty. Almost time for those heading for Sunday night services to stop in." She hurried to wipe the table, although Brad couldn't see that it needed it. "You three better hurry and get your order in if you want to avoid any big delays. You won't be the only customers in here before long and it is just me and Fred here tonight. Nolene's gone off with friends to Augusta to visit some craft show and go to that movie Andy's been talking about all week. She left out early, early this morning."

Even though Nolene was now nearly seventeen, Brad couldn't imagine Fred letting her go with friends to a city that far away. No wonder Jimmy had said he wasn't looking forward to getting up today. He probably already knew Nolene would not be at church that day. Poor Jimmy. Why didn't he just admit to that girl that he was in love with her and ask her which one she liked more—him or Andy?

"Which explains why the tables need wiping," Lucy went on. "What with it being Mother's Day an all, we've been busy, busy, busy. I know it doesn't look it now, but right after church today this place was so swamped that some people had to wait fifteen minutes to have a place to sit. Even the upper deck was filled to overflowing. Then all afternoon long those who didn't eat lunch here have been stopping in to treat their mothers or wives to a piece of cake or a slice of pie." She gestured to the glass domes on the counter. "In fact, I ran plum out of pie a little over an hour ago and haven't had time to even roll out a fresh crust to bake more. And that huge meatloaf I made for lunch didn't last an hour."

Used to Lucy's talkative nature, which had always been a large part of her sassy charm, Brad didn't interrupt while she went on to tell about the pretty pink blouse Nolene had bought her for Mother's Day.

They waited until Lucy gestured they should sit, before taking to the red vinyl chairs.

"Since you've all been in here before, you know the drill."

She gestured to the menus tucked sideways between the chrome napkin holder and the large, knob-style salt and pepper shakers. "I'll go get your drinks and your silverware while you look through and decide what you want to order." She smiled at Pete, who already had his menu open and was busy pouring over the writing, even though he was obviously not old enough to read much more than a few key words. Brad had already guessed him to be about six.

"Let's see," Lucy continued, "as I recall from the other day, the young man here likes Dr Pepper, and you two will both ask for Diet Coke, only tonight it'll have to be Diet Pepsi because we're all out of Diet Coke and Lydia closed The Store early so Horace and Andy could take her out to the point for a special supper. Is Diet Pepsi okay? Or would you rather split a large root beer like you used to a long time ago? You remember?" She winked. "One big glass? Two *very short* straws?"

"Diet Pepsis will be fine," Jillian answered quickly, looking a little distressed by the time Lucy hurried back to the counter.

"That woman sure talks a lot," Pete said just loud enough for Brad and his mother to hear, as if that obvious fact needed pointing out. "And she sure seemed happy to see Mom in here today. Kept looking at her and grinning."

"I imagine she was a little surprised to see us come in together," Brad admitted. "It's been quite a few years since that's happened."

"I just hope she doesn't get the wrong idea about this and start placing bets on us," Jillian muttered, watching while Lucy clattered ice into three plastic glasses. Like Pete, Jillian held a menu open in front of her, but she had yet to look at it. "Maybe I should let it be known that us being here together was Pete's idea and save her from wasting her money."

Reminded of the town's pastime, Brad glanced over his shoulder to make sure Lucy wasn't at the bulletin board doing just that. "I don't think you have to worry about Lucy. She lost too much money on us the first two times. A lot of people did. Truth is, the only one who made money off of us at all was Lydia Johnson, and I hear she made quiet a haul at the end of that second summer.''

''Oh?'' Jillian cut her gaze to the open menu, as if suddenly more interested in its contents than the conversation. ''Why is that?''

''Seems she's the only one who had guessed from the very start we weren't destined to be together and placed her bets accordingly.'' His stomach twisted from the painful memories this discussion evoked. ''I think she took one look at me, then took one look at you, and knew we were too different. Because she was the only person betting against us getting together, she ended up raking in one big bundle.''

Frowning, Jillian glanced in the direction of The Store, owned by Lydia and her husband, Horace. She peered through the window only a second before returning her attention to her menu. ''At least *someone* profited.''

''What are you guys talking about?'' Pete asked, clearly puzzled by their discussion. He wrinkled his freckled nose, reminding Brad of Jillian's playful expression when she used to flirt with him. ''Who's Lydia and what did she bet on?''

He looked up at Brad as if expecting him to answer.

Brad hesitated, not sure what to tell him. Or even if it was his place to tell him. He and Jillian had enough problems to work through. He didn't need to add another by saying something to Pete he shouldn't. Not after deciding he wanted to be friends with Jillian again.

''Lydia Johnson is Sea Haven's repressed socialite,'' Jillian put in, relieving Brad of the necessity to answer. ''She and her husband own The Store across the street, just down from here—you know, the place where we had those Slurpees late in the afternoon during our first day here? Where I stopped in to find out if there's an ATM machine anywhere nearby.''

Pete nodded that he did indeed remember. ''The lady with the dark hair who looks like she doesn't get near enough to eat? The one with the long pink fingernails who kept looking through the window to the parking area, trying to see what kind of car you'd rented? What was it she bet on?''

Jillian thought a moment, then went ahead with her explanation, choosing not to lie to her son. Obviously Jillian's deceit was directed only to those outside her family.

"On us, Pete. On Brad and me. You see there's a long-time tradition around here in which the locals bet on whether or not certain guests at the Seascape Inn will come together, make a match, and find true love. It has a little to do with the legend I told you about, the one where certain people claim the Seascape Inn holds a special magic. Well, some say that magic is only for lovers.''

"Lovers?'' Pete wrinkled his nose tighter. "You mean the kind that kiss?''

Her mouth twitched as if fighting a grin. "Yes, Pete. The kind of lovers that kiss. When the locals decide a particular couple is destined to be together like that, they make bets, guessing how long it will take the two to become aware of their deep attraction and announce an engagement. The residents keep up with those bets by pinning notices with names, dates, and times to that bulletin board over there. If an engagement is announced, the person whose guess is closest to the exact time wins.''

While Pete turned his attention to the old, worn corkboard behind the counter, littered with various pieces of paper and business cards, she cut her gaze to Brad. "Seems most of the people around here decided Brad and I would be one of those couples, so a lot of them started placing bets as to the date and the time we'd finally announce our big day.''

A sudden catch in her throat kept her from continuing, so Brad took it from there. "But Lydia Johnson knew from the start we would never make a permanent match. She knew we'd leave here without ever setting a date. Fact is, she was so certain of our differences, she offered to match *everyone's* money who had favored us getting married. She wanted it so if she proved right, and we didn't announce an engagement before leaving at the end of that summer, she would collect on every wager pinned to that bulletin board.''

''The people here thought you two loved each other enough to want to marry?'' Pete studied his mother carefully. ''Why is that?''

Jillian's shoulders tensed, letting Brad know it was not a question she cared to answer yet. To help her out, he changed the subject. ''You better be deciding what you want to eat. Lucy will be back here in just a few seconds with her order pad.''

''I want to know more about you and Mom,'' he protested, but when he looked beyond Brad and saw that Lucy was indeed on her way back with the drinks and flatware, he let the first subject slide in favor of the second. ''I am pretty hungry.'' He looked questioningly at his mother. ''Can I have both a bowl of that white soup Grandma always used to eat here and a hamburger?''

Brad watched the changes in Jillian's beautiful face while she looked first as if she might try to talk him out of ordering so much food, but in the end agreed. ''Okay, if you really think you can eat that much.'' She smiled at her son.

How Brad longed to reach out and touch that sweet face. How he longed to trail his finger down the soft curve of her cheek while he gazed deep into those dark brown eyes like he used to.

But now didn't dare.

Even if he thought there was a way their diverse lifestyles could fit together now that they were both much older and his situation considerably different, Jillian belonged to another man—one who did not deserve her, but who was going marry her just the same.

He would be wise to remember that.

''Chowder and a hamburger sounds good to me, too,'' he said, but in truth he suddenly had no appetite at all. ''I think I'll order the same.''

Returning the menu to where he had found it, he couldn't decide if it was being again with the woman he had loved and lost so many years ago, or knowing she had become engaged to a man who clearly did not deserve her or her son that had so quickly diminished his appetite. But when the food arrived fifteen minutes later, just as other people finally drifted into the restaurant, dressed for church, Brad had to force himself to eat.

❧ *Chapter 9* ❧

$\mathbb{P}$ete broke from yet another daydream about Brad and continued up the stairs. Since they had returned from the village a half hour earlier, he had not been able to keep his thoughts on the here and now long enough to accomplish anything of much use.

"So, how'd it go?" Tony asked just seconds after Pete entered the attic.

Once again, Pete plopped down on the dust-scattered bed near the wall. "Pretty good, I think. Weren't you there?"

Pete glanced around the shadowed room, looking for Tony's shape. Although he had yet to get a good look at Tony's face, he was quite familiar with Tony's broad shoulders and immense height. He spotted him in the far corner, seated in his usual spot on top of the trunk.

"No. I was over at Millie's watching them make blueberry ice cream." He laughed, his voice so deep and likable, Pete smiled. "It reminded me of the time Hattie and I made ice cream for a church social just before I was shipped overseas. Of course, we spent more time making—" He paused, then cleared his throat. "Never mind about me. Did Brad and your mother get along while you three were in Sea Haven together?"

"They seemed to. At least they acted like they were over being angry with each other—although a few times they did seem kind of nervous around each other. While we ate supper, they picked at their food as if *they* were the ones who had suffered a stomachache instead of me.''

Pete leaned forward on the bed, pressing the toes of his sneakers to the wood floor for balance. "Did you know everyone thought Mom and Brad were once in love? People around here even made bets on them getting married!''

"They weren't just *thought* to be in love. They *were* in love. Deeply in love. And until today, I had no idea what might have caused them to break up like they did. I wasn't around at all that last day they were here. I was away from the inn seeing what I could do to keep a woman I knew from drinking so much that she neglected her son. When I returned here the following morning, your mother was already gone. She left three days before her parents did. And by that afternoon, Brad was gone, too.''

"Then you've figured out for sure what broke them up? Was it because Mom was a person who had always wanted kids, but he wasn't?'' He sneezed, the dust having finally gotten to him, then blinked twice. "Do you think he got so upset to find out I was already inside her stomach that he got angry about it and broke up with her because of it? Do you think Mom made up that part about my father not ever knowing about me?''

"No, I don't think he *was* told about you. I think the discussion where he informed your mother he didn't want any kids must have occurred before she had quite gathered the courage to tell him she was already with child. Maybe his telling her all that resulted from her testing the water, so to speak, with talk about children in general. Which would explain not only why they broke up, but why he has yet to figure out you're his son. He never knew she was already with child when she left here.''

Pete's heart leaped with so much hope he thought it would bust wide open. "You think so? You think he really is my father?'' Although it still did not really prove anything, it made him feel better to hear that Tony also thought such a thing could be true.

"Yes, Pete, I do. I know them. Your mother adored Brad. You could be no one else's child. But the problem now is how do we get Brad to figure out that same thing."

Pete thought the answer to that question pretty simple. "Why not have me just come right out and tell him about it?"

"No, that won't work to our advantage. This is something your father has to find out from your mother. If he doesn't find out about the secret from her, he's going to be extremely angry, and properly so. He will resent your mother a long, long time for never having told him what he has every right to know."

That made sense. He kind of resented that himself. "So, how do I get her to tell him about me? Ask her to?"

Pete could see just enough about Tony in the growing shadows to tell he stroked his chin thoughtfully. "No. It would be better for everyone if she decided to tell him on her own."

"So what do we do?" Pete sniffed loudly, the sneeze having made his nose run. Stupid thing about sneezes. "Got any ideas?"

Tony shrugged. "All we can do is make things right for her telling him."

Pete's stomach fluttered with yet another rush of hope. "Maybe she's downstairs telling him right now. When I left, they were alone in the front room, sitting in those chairs that look out over the ocean. That's why I forgot on purpose about Brad promising to pitch to me today. I figured it would be a good idea for them to be down there by themselves for awhile. Maybe with me gone she's telling Brad all about me right this very minute." By bedtime, this whole matter could be resolved. Would she then tell Mr. Johnstone to get lost? Naw, she would probably be a lot nicer about it than that. Too bad.

"No, I'm afraid not. While you were daydreaming your way up here, the others returned from their day trip and joined them in the parlor. Your mother is not the type to tell Brad anything so important or so personal unless she is completely alone with him, and the mood is just right."

That made sense. "So what we gotta do is find more ways to get them alone?"

"And in the right mood."

"Any ideas?" He flatted his eyebrows when he looked at Tony then. "Ideas that don't involve me running in place until I'm covered with sweat, and you poking me real hard in the side while Brad examines me so I'd whine at just the right times?"

"Not at the moment." Tony chuckled at the memory of what they had done. "But when something presents itself, I'll let you know." Having said that, he stood just inches off the floor and floated toward the wall nearest the door Pete had left open, about to leave.

Aware in a couple of more seconds Tony would be gone again, Pete's stomach shot up into his throat with such force it pitched him right off the bed and onto his feet. "Tony, wait."

Tony paused several feet above the stairs, his face high into the lofty shadows when he turned back around. "Pete, if you're planning to ask me what will happen after Brad finally knows about you, I have to be honest and tell you that I haven't a clue. I know you are worried sick that as soon as your mother finally does tell Brad the truth, he will become so angry about it, he won't want to have anything else to do with her—or you. I'm sorry, I can't tell you for certain that won't happen, though I hope it doesn't. Even so, he needs to know. One way or another, this matter has to be resolved before Brad leaves here this Thursday."

Pete thought it odd that Tony knew just how worried he was about the outcome, but shook his head, "That's not what I was going to ask."

"Then what did you want?"

Pete looked down at his right sneaker, untied as usual, then tucked it behind the other so Tony wouldn't notice. "Can I ask you about something that's got nothing to do with the problem with my mother and Brad?"

"Sure."

He fidgeted a moment longer, hoping his was not a dumb question. "Do you ever get to visit with other ghosts?"

"Yes, I've made contact with other spirits from time to time and am in constant contact with my grandmother, who is in and out of this house pretty regularly. Why do you ask?"

"I sort of want to send my Grandma a message." He finally looked up from his shoes. "I want her to know Grandpa, me, and Mom miss her plenty but that we're all doing real good so she doesn't need to worry about us."

Tony drifted down into the dim light from outside, allowing Pete to see his face for the first time. Although his image was faded—like peering at an old photograph—Pete studied his features attentively, surprised by how young Tony looked. Why, he didn't look like he could be even as old as his mother, though something about that face showed the wisdom of someone who had lived as long as his grandpa. Pretty darned handsome for a ghost, too. His cheeks were long and thin, but strong-boned; his neck solid and lean. In his eyes was a shimmer of tears. Did ghosts actually cry?

"I can assure you that your grandmother already knows all that, but I'll see what I can do about getting the message to her so you can be sure she's not worried."

Pete's heart swelled with happiness. "Thanks, Tony. If you do that, I'll sure owe you one."

Tony, still hovering near the door, smiled and nodded. It was the first time his lips had moved at all, even when he spoke, making Pete aware that somehow Tony had talked to him without once opening his mouth. *Cool!*

Tony chuckled, as if having heard his thoughts. "Just do a favor or two for Miss Hattie and we'll call it even."

"Great." Pete liked doing favors for Miss Hattie anyway. Mainly because she reminded him so much of his grandma. Even though the two dressed and walked completely different, there was just something about Miss Hattie's eyes and especially her smile that made him think of his grandma. "I'll go down and find something to do for her right now. Maybe

I can get it done before she ever gets back and surprise her."

Tony's smile widened but dropped when a creak sounded on a stair just below him. His eyes rounded when Brad appeared, passing right through him. Pete grimaced, worried that sort of thing could hurt, but Tony looked more startled than pained when he watched Brad come to a stop just beyond the stairs.

Pete also worried that Tony would be upset to have had his existence accidently revealed to yet another person. But, then, Brad was the type who could be trusted not to tell anyone else. All they would have to do is explain how important it was to Tony that nobody else know he was there.

"Hi, Pete. Miss Hattie told me you were probably up here," he said, glancing at their dark, gloomy surroundings. "Why are you up here hanging around the attic all alone?"

"Alone?"

Tony waved his hands to catch Pete's attention. "Brad can't see me."

And obviously Brad couldn't hear him either because Brad never turned around to figure out who had spoken.

"In need of some quiet, thinking time?" Brad must have figured that had to be the reason because he immediately went on to explain why he looked for him. "Miss Hattie just returned from the village and told me to tell you she brought one of Miss Millie's chocolate cakes back with her, and two kinds of homemade ice cream."

"The blueberry is the best," Tony put in, distracting Pete from answering right away.

Brad—clearly not having heard that either—mistook Pete's lack of response as a sign of worry. "I know, you're probably concerned about getting sick again, but judging from how much food you put away a few hours ago without causing as much as a stomach twinge, I think it should be safe enough for you to have a little dessert. She told me there is plenty for everyone, but she wanted you to have a try at the first slice of cake or the first scoop of ice cream. That's for having carried her flowers to the car this morning."

Cake *or* ice cream? Not having had anything sweet since breakfast, thanks mostly to Tony and his idea to play sick, Pete was all for having *both* the cake and ice cream. "Great."

Waiting until Brad had turned to go downstairs ahead of him, he glanced in Tony's direction and waved. Remembering that Tony had the weird ability to read his thoughts, he reminded him without ever opening his mouth, "Don't forget. You're supposed to be trying to come up with some way to get Mom to tell Brad about me."

Although they still ran the very real risk of Brad becoming so angry he might never speak to him or his mother ever again, Tony was right. If Brad really was his father, then he needed to know it for sure.

They both did.

Unable to concentrate, Jillian pretended to listen while Reynold paced the veranda, bragging about how much he had accomplished during the picnic and boat outing that afternoon. Her tormented thoughts were too ladened with guilt from everything she had learned that day to allow her to grasp more than the fact Reynold and David Nelson had found plenty of time to talk about business, time Reynold had obviously used to full advantage.

Although glad Reynold had made a lot more progress while he was gone, she just couldn't focus her thoughts long enough to participate in a real conversation. Not after finding out about the mistake she may have made.

Oddly enough, Reynold never noticed.

"You wouldn't believe how much David likes me," he continued. Walking over to the banister, he stretched his tired muscles while he looked toward the moon-bathed carriage house where David and Shelly had retired early for obvious reasons.

Since returning from the island, Reynold had showered, changed clothes, and restyled his blond hair to its usual perfection. Again, he looked quite impressive in his white pressed slacks, soft leather dress shoes, and his designer-brand pullover shirt.

"It's really amazing how easy it was for me to get on the inside tract with that man."

Jillian nodded, and continued only half-listening while he went on to recount several of the more important conversations they'd had that day. She was too busy recounting her own conversations that day to hear much of anything else.

It was not until she recalled some of what Brad had said to her while they sat in the alcove together that she realized Reynold had not asked about Pete's recovery; nor had he asked how she had spent her time. They had been apart for over eight hours in all. Wasn't he at all curious about her activities? Didn't it bother him even a little that she had been left there alone all day with a man as extremely handsome as Brad Pierce?

"I can hardly wait until Tuesday," Reynold continued, unaware he had come under such scrutiny in her thoughts. He narrowed his green eyes with conjecture. "Once we're all out on that water fishing, I plan to flatter David beyond belief. No one will have casted a line more beautifully than that man." He chuckled at the thought.

"Reynold, you haven't asked about Pete since your return. Why is that?"

"What's to ask?" He shrugged and glanced at her only briefly, his attention unwilling to leave the lighted windows of the carriage house for long. "It's obvious by the way the boy scampered up those stairs earlier that he has fully recovered. Plus, he said something to Shelly about having had a hamburger and soup at the local restaurant after it became apparent Miss Hattie wasn't returning in time to prepare a meal here. How long did it take for him to start feeling better? An hour? Two?"

"Actually, it was midafternoon before he felt well enough to get out of bed. By then, he had eaten part of a ham sandwich I'd made him and I think the solid food is what finally made him feel better. That, and the prospect of driving into the village with me to call Troy.''

''Troy?'' Reynold wrinkled his forehead at what was obviously an unfamiliar name when he turned to face her again. This time he managed to keep his attention on her.

''Troy is the boy on Pete's baseball team.'' It annoyed Jillian to have to remind him of someone so important to Pete. In their small subdivision, residents moved in and out with unsettling regularity, but Troy had been Pete's closest friend since well before Christmas. ''The one whose father is also Pete's baseball coach.''

''You mean the little black-haired boy who never wears a belt with his jeans and chews gum with his mouth open? Why would Peter want to call him?''

''Because they are good friends, and I think Pete is feeling a little homesick. You have to remember that because school is still going on, Pete is up here with no children to play with. He's bored.''

''Bored?'' Reynold studied her a moment as if unable to believe anyone could possibly be bored with such an important business deal coming together. ''Well for the next few days he certainly won't have much of a chance to be bored. Tomorrow morning about ten o'clock, we'll go into the village and rent Peter all the proper fishing equipment he'll need from that little sundries shop Hattie told me about and then we'll return here to practice working with it. Then Tuesday and Wednesday, we'll spend both days out on the water fishing from sunup to sundown. He'll have so much fun, he'll forget all about missing his little friend.''

Glad to see some concern for Pete after all, Jillian smiled. Obviously, she'd misread his reason for not having asked about them. ''I'll need a line, too.''

Feeling guilty to have allowed Brad's earlier comments to influence her perception of Reynold so unfairly, she stood and walked over to join him near the edge of the lighted veranda. The cool air coming across the mainland felt good against her skin. ''I haven't been ocean fishing in years. Not since my father last took me. I guess I was about seventeen then.''

''And are you a good fisherman?''

She wagged her head proudly and smiled. ''Pretty much.''

Her smile faded when he reached out to touch her cheek with a curved palm. Why didn't his touch affect her in quite the same way Brad's had earlier? She flashed anger at Brad. Until today, she hadn't noticed that Reynold's touch lacked spark. But then Reynold was not a touchy-feely sort of person.

''Well, try not to be too proficient on Tuesday, sweetheart,'' he said in a deep, coaxing voice. ''We do want David to catch the biggest fish.''

''Or Pete. Pete would get a real kick out of catching the biggest fish. It would be just the thing to have made this whole trip worthwhile.''

''I suppose.'' His hand fell away as he looked again at the carriage house. ''Whatever serves the best purpose.''

Pete's sneakers skidded to a squeaking halt when he hurried through the foyer searching for his mother. He had come downstairs to tell her he was ready to take a bath and go on to bed but was sidetracked when he caught a glimpse of a small photograph that until now had sat facing the other direction, so that only whoever stood behind the desk saw it.

''It's him,'' he said aloud, truly amazed. He walked closer to have a better look. Sure enough, it was Tony, dressed in his officer's uniform, smiling as if he had some special secret to tell. Although the photograph was old, it was a clear picture, the every detail in sharp focus. Even sharper than seeing him upstairs in the attic.

Mouth gaping, Pete tiptoed and pulled the photograph off the desk and stared at it.

''Be careful,'' Miss Hattie told him, causing him to jump nearly out of his skin. He had not seen her sitting behind the tall desk, but obviously she was. ''That picture is very special to me.''

Aware he had no right to be touching it, he quickly put it

back then wiped his hands on the back of his blue jeans as if to rid himself of any noticeable evidence.

"I'm sorry, ma'am. It's just that when I saw—" His heart jumped a foot. How did he explain why he had been so startled to see that photograph without letting on he knew the dead man pictured there. He had promised Tony not to tell anyone about their friendship. Not even Miss Hattie. It was one promise he intended to keep.

A few seconds later, Miss Hattie came around the end of desk where he could see her. None of the worry or anger he expected to see creased her crinkled face. Instead of scolding him for having touched something so important, she rested her hand beside the shiny frame and smiled. "A handsome man, wasn't he?"

"Yeah, real handsome. I like that uniform. As my grandpa would say, 'Real snappy.' "

She laughed and a dimple curved into her soft cheek. "Oh, he was a snappy one all right. That's Tony Freeport. He was my boyfriend back when I was much younger. We were engaged."

Don't I know. Weird, for a second there, Pete could almost picture Miss Hattie young and pretty and smiling that same sort of smile at Tony. He glanced again at the photograph and for a moment could have sworn it winked at him. He covered his mouth with both hands to keep from laughing.

"I imagine you felt drawn to the picture since your grandfather was a Captain in the army, too. He was stationed in Panama during the war, as I recall."

"Yeah, that's right. *That's* what made me want to take a look at it. Your boyfriend is wearing the same type clothes Grandpa is wearing in the photograph that sits over his desk at the hospital." If that explanation worked for her, it worked for him.

"The one that sits beside your grandmother's graduation picture?"

"Yeah, how'd you know that?" Was she also part ghost or something?

"Your grandmother told me about it one day after she saw this very photograph. She was so proud of your grandfather; she talked about him a lot during those weeks he couldn't be here with her."

Miss Hattie slipped her lace hankie out of her pocket and fluttered away a layer of dust Pete couldn't even see from the glass protecting Tony's bright smile. When she finished, she pointed the frame so it faced the area behind the desk again, like it had until tonight. That was the thing about Miss Hattie, she liked things to be orderly. "Your grandfather is quite a handsome man. And, oh, how he loved your grandmother. When they were up here on vacations, he shared every moment with her. Or with your mother. Usually both. Such a happy family. It was always a true joy to have them as guests."

"So you knew my grandma pretty good?" Pete wet his lips in anticipation.

"I should say so. We had many a long chat out on the front porch late in the afternoon. Oh, how she loved to watch the shadows creep across the lawn late in the day while talking about what all she planned to do once your grandfather arrived. She would sit and rock with me for hours while your mother played with whoever she could find to play with. One summer, your grandmother even took up crocheting with me. In fact, I think I still have the doily she crocheted for me. I put it away after her death, not wanting it spoiled."

Signaling him to follow, she headed toward the living room where there was a big cabinet with a shiny glass front that displayed all sorts of really neat items, mostly things the man who had built the house had carved out of big, useless chunks of wood. There were birds of all shapes and sizes, tiny ships like the ones they used to show in old movies, fish of all kinds with their tails curled high, but best of all was an old clock with a door near the bottom that Pete was sure hid some marvelous treasure.

"I like to keep my memories out of harm's way," Miss Hattie explained. She tucked her hankie back into her pocket as she bent to pull open a small drawer just below the wide glass doors. She slid a hand inside and carefully came out with what looked like a potholder that had been flattened paper thin by a steamroller or something. She held it out to him. "Your grandmother made that."

Awed that she would let him hold it, Pete's eyes stretched wide as he watched her place the thing in his hands. For a moment, it felt as if his very own grandmother was handing it to him. Checking, he quickly glanced back up at her face, and was a little disappointed to see Miss Hattie still there. The strange way things happened in that place, there was that slight chance he had been right. "It's pretty."

It was white, round, and bumpy with pink roses around the edge. Sorta like those fancy placemats on the tables in the front parlor.

"It was the second thing she made. The first was a jacket to go around your grandfather's coffee mug at work to help keep the beverage warm while he was off seeing his patients."

Pete pressed it to his face and breathed deeply. It still smelled like his grandmother. "This is so neat." He took several more deep breaths before reluctantly handing it back to Miss Hattie.

"No, you keep it."

Miss Hattie's eyes were all watery, like she had just sneezed. Or was about to cry. As bad as he wanted the thing, he couldn't hurt Miss Hattie like that. "No, she gave it to you. It's yours."

"I think I was just meant to keep it until you came along. It's yours now. My gift to you." She took that hankie of hers and dabbed lightly at the corner of one eye then at her temple. "I'll have no arguments about it young man."

Pete stared at the gift, his heart soaring. "Thank you, Miss Hattie. I'll take good care of it."

"A-yuh, I know you will."

Pete pressed it to his face and breathed deeply again. This

had to be the best gift he had ever gotten. "I'm going to go show it to Mom."

"You do that. She'll love seeing it again."

Eager to share his wonderful gift, Pete hurried out onto the veranda where he had seen his mother talking to Mr. Johnstone earlier, but nobody was there. Frowning, he headed out into the garden. Sometimes the grown-ups like to sit out there. But nobody was there, either.

Frustrated, he hurried back into the house, through the mudroom, and was excited to find not only his mother over by the refrigerator, but Brad was there, too, sitting at the table. Terrific.

"Look, Mom, look what Miss Hattie gave me," he said, breathless from a combination of excitement and having run so hard. He crossed to where she had just poured herself a glass of milk and held his prize high so she could see.

"Oh, Pete, it's the doily my mother made." She set the glass aside and knelt, touching the edge with the tips of her fingers. "Miss Hattie gave that to you?"

"Yeah, said something about she figures she's been keeping it for me all these years," he explained then held it up to her face. "Smell it. If you breathe real deep, it smells just like Grandma used to."

Doing as told, she closed her eyes and smiled affectionately. "You're right. It does smell just like her."

He turned to go show Brad, but at that moment Mr. Johnstone and Mr. Nelson came in from the main part of the house, laughing about something. They walked right into the path he planned to take, blocking his view of Brad completely. He frowned, waiting for them to move on across the room and out of his way.

"Reynold, look what Miss Hattie has given Pete," his mother said while Pete continued to wait for the two men to pass. She stood again and now walked over to where Reynold and David had stopped right in the middle of the room, still laughing about something.

Reynold glanced briefly at what Pete held in his hand and

nodded. "That's nice." He immediately returned his attention to Mr. Nelson.

"But you don't understand," she continued, glancing first at Pete, then at Brad with a troubled look on her face. "My mother made that."

"She did?" Reynold glanced at it again, but didn't move closer for a better look. "Fine job. Very domestic."

Again, he returned his attention to Mr. Nelson. "You said Shelly wanted something to drink. Milk, orange juice, or lemonade?"

Pete jutted his chin out, insulted that Mr. Johnstone had thought so little of his wonderful gift, but he didn't say anything about it. He was in no mood to make trouble.

Finally, the men moved far enough out of Pete's way, he hurried around to where Brad sat staring at the back of Reynold's head as if the horrible man had suddenly turned into a space invader. "Did you want to see it?" He climbed onto the chair beside him and held out the doily.

"Of course."

As expected, Brad leaned forward for a closer look. "May I hold it?"

"Sure." Pete sat back and watched proudly while Brad held the doily carefully with both hands, then lifted it to his face and breathed deeply like Jillian had done earlier.

He smiled then handed it back. "Yes, I do remember your grandmother wearing that perfume. It always reminded me of summer flowers. Does it you?"

Pete breathed it again and laughed. Not because what he said was funny, but just because it made him feel good. "Yeah, it does." He had forgotten that Brad knew his grandmother, too. For some reason, it was comforting to know he remembered how she smelled. "You know, Brad, I sure do wish you were going fishing with us Tuesday."

Mr. Johnstone spun around, somehow hearing that last comment, though Pete would have sworn he wasn't paying attention at all. "Peter, the man's name is Dr. Pierce to you, and I've already explained to you once that there won't be room on the boat Tuesday for one more."

Brad's hands flattened against the table, as if he was about to push himself up out of his chair, but didn't. "I'm the one who told the boy to call me by my first name because we've formed a special friendship, and I already understand about the size of the boat. I have plans to go inlet fishing with friends Tuesday anyway."

"Still, I don't think the boy should be whining about something I've already explained can't be. He has to learn that he can't always have things his way. That's not the way real life works."

"That's for sure," Pete blurted out, before he realized he had spoken out loud. "Because if I could have things my way, you'd be on another planet."

"Pete!" His mother's shocked voice verified he had indeed said that out loud.

Afraid she was about to ask him to apologize, and not wanting to, he turned and ran out of the room as fast as his little legs would let him. He would rather eat worm dirt than tell that man he was sorry.

He heard footsteps behind him.

Worried Reynold had come after him, he ran all the harder, darting outside into the dark.

❧ *Chapter 10* ❧

Even though Brad had soothed Pete's hurt feelings enough that Pete eventually returned to the kitchen and apologized to Reynold for what he had said, and Reynold had graciously accepted the apology and offered one of his own, Jillian had a hard time falling asleep that night.

Reynold had not meant to hurt Pete intentionally, but he had—and for reasons that in a way supported what Brad had said about him earlier. He had been so involved in making sure David found whatever he had come out of the carriage house to find, it simply had not occurred to him how important that doily might be to a sensitive child like Pete.

He had admitted it. And he'd apologized for it. But still Pete had been hurt. And still Brad had glowered at him.

But Brad had no way of knowing. The real reason behind Reynold's behavior was he had never known either of his own grandmothers, therefore he had no notion of the close, unbreakable bond that developed between a doting grandparent and a loving grandchild. If he had understood that, he would have known to stop talking to David long enough to praise the wonderful gift Pete had been given.

Like Brad had.

Instead, Reynold had been too concerned over the fact that David had emerged from the carriage house needing something. Devoted to meeting the man's every whim during their two weeks there, Reynold had taken it upon himself to see that David returned with the refreshments he had sought. It was not until after Pete had gotten so upset over his lack of attention that Reynold recognized how truly important that doily was to Pete. Once Reynold realized that, he had gladly apologized for his behavior.

In the end, Pete and Reynold parted friends, each having forgiven the other; but she wasn't sure the same could be said for Brad and Reynold. Brad had not said another word to Reynold after that. Nor to her. He had brought Pete back into the kitchen from outside and let her handle it from there. He had watched the three work through their problems, then checked the telephone pager he often carried in his pocket as if it had gone off, and left the house without a word to anyone.

That was a good part of the reason Jillian was unable to fall asleep afterward. Brad had been so nice to go after Pete and return him for an exchange of apologies, but then disappeared before anyone could thank him for his help. Obviously, he had not done it for thanks. He had done it for Pete. In the few short days he had been there, he and their son had become close friends.

This made it even harder for her to get up out of bed the following morning. Eventually, she had to face the inevitable. She had to tell Brad about Pete, which in turn meant she would have no choice but to tell Pete about Brad—and Reynold about both of them.

With all that ahead, she did not look forward to leaving the bedroom. She most especially did not look forward to breakfast with Brad seated directly across from her, studying her with those intense blue eyes.

Just his presence made her stomach knot, her guilt pulling at it like a heavy lead weight.

Moving at a snail's pace, by the time Jillian showered and dressed in a comfortable pair of white cotton shorts and a light pink sleeveless blouse, with matching tennis shoes, the morning had slipped well past nine o'clock. Breakfast was long since over when she finally entered the dining room to find only a plate with several blueberry muffins and a box of cold cereal still on the table.

Eating cereal meant making a trip into the kitchen for milk, and in her depressed state she was in no mood for added exertion, so she chose a muffin instead, which she had with what was left of the coffee still warming on the buffet.

From where she sat breaking her muffin into tiny pieces and nibbling each one, she had a nice view of the front yard that included part of the gardens to the south, a small section of the main road beyond, and the tree-dotted cliffs that stood sentry over the glittering ocean.

How peaceful the morning felt after such a long, tormented night. She closed her eyes to listen to the different birds calling from the large trees that gave the dining room windows their cool afternoon shade. Her father was so right about this place. Just being there had a certain healing quality.

If only it could heal the wrong she had done Brad. Heal it enough he would understand her reason for that wrong, and forgive her.

If she ever found the courage to tell him.

But how did one bring up such a subject after so many years? *Oh, by the way, Brad, did you know that you and Pete share a little more than a genuine love for baseball and the ability to belly-laugh at really bad jokes? Did you also know that Pete isn't really six years old, like you seem to think? Oh, I guess I should have corrected you—Pete is actually seven. He'll turn eight this coming Saturday. Why, yes, I guess that does mean he was conceived during our last summer together. Imagine that. I suppose that makes you the father. Hmm. I wonder why I never bothered to mention any of that to you? I guess I've been so terribly busy since he was born and since you arrived here, I haven't had time to think much about it.*

She blew out a shaky breath at just the thought of what Brad's response would be to that.

Telling Brad the truth now, after withholding it all this

time, especially after father and son had actually met and become close, was unforgivable. And she knew it. Were the situation reversed, would she find it in her heart to forgive him? Would she be able to excuse him if she learned he had lied to her about something so important? Probably not. It just wasn't easy to forgive something of that magnitude.

Oh, and Pete. He would have a fit if he found out she had been keeping him from someone like Brad all these years. But who knew Brad had changed his mind about the prospect of having kids in his life? That is *if* he truly had changed his mind. She still was not quite sure he had told the truth upstairs about wanting children of his own. He had been too convincing the day he had told her differently.

And what about Reynold?

She groaned and pressed her hands over her hot cheeks at yet another complication. Reynold was not going to be any too pleased to find out Brad was Pete's father. It was the sort of thing he would think she should have shared with him that first day he had arrived to find them both there. And she really should have. Reynold was her fiancé, for heaven's sake. He was the man who, after only months of knowing them, had so dutifully vowed to take over her and Pete's care for the rest of his life.

Damn. Though she had truly had the best of intentions, she had betrayed them all. Still, she could not bring herself to amend those betrayals. Not yet. Maybe not ever.

She was not ready for her whole world to be turned upside down. Nor Pete's.

If only the Seascape Inn would give her the courage to figure out what was right, then act on it. This was Monday. She had only three days before Brad's free week was over, and he left for home. Three days to find the nerve she would need to tell him the truth. Three days?

She grimaced. Would she even have an opportunity to be alone again with Brad in those three days? Reynold had these next few days scheduled tight.

"Hi, Mom. How long have you been up?"

Not having heard Pete's approach, Jillian jumped at the unexpected sound of her son's voice. She turned toward the hall door to find him standing in the doorway, his red shirt tucked into a pair of cuff-legged blue jeans, his scuffed sneakers tied, and his baseball cap on perfectly straight. Obviously, he had already run into Reynold that morning. "I guess I've been up about half an hour. Why?"

"No reason," Pete shrugged then walked over to stand at the end of the table. "I just didn't know you were up yet. You sure slept late."

"I was tired." She studied her son. He looked like a different child after Reynold tucked, tugged, and straightened everything for him—Reynold, who so wanted him to be Peter, instead of just Pete. What a task he had ahead of him.

"From having worried about me being so sick yesterday?" He pulled at the corner of the lace-edged table cloth, twisting it with his fingers. Clearly, Pete did not like the thought of being the one who may have caused her that much concern.

"Partly," she admitted, thinking it extremely important to be honest right now. Especially with so much dishonesty hanging over her like an ax ready to fall. "But mostly because I just couldn't seem to fall asleep last night when I was supposed to. I kept being distracted by the distant sounds of foghorns, crickets, and night owls." *And by things that had nothing to do with their surroundings.*

"Yeah, they kept me awake the first night here. But I sort of got used to them." He glanced at her plate, now scattered with crumbs. "You've already eaten?"

She nodded, set her napkin aside, then stood. Her arms and legs felt achy from having tossed and turned so much. She needed to limber them with exercise. "I've eaten all I want and I'm ready to take a nice morning walk out by the ocean. Want to join me?"

"Can't." He shook his head and wrinkled his freckled nose to emphasize the fact.

"Why not?"

"I gotta go into the village with Mr. Johnstone and Mr.

Nelson to rent us the right fishing gear for our fishing trips these next two days. Mr. Johnstone says I gotta be there so they can get the right equipment for my height. He said we'd be leaving here in just a few minutes.''

''Already?'' How long had she sat there? She glanced at her watch rather than at the old clock on the buffet. Ten o'clock?

''Yeah, they want to go in time to rent everything we'll need and still get back here by lunch. Afterward, we're all to practice using the equipment out by the pond so we know exactly what we're doing once we get out on the water. He said everyone but Mrs. Nelson plans to fish. Even you.''

''Shelly isn't going to fish?'' That didn't surprise her. Shelly was not all that fond of the ocean anyway. The only reason she had come was to be with her husband, who, like Reynold, spent long hours in board meetings or in his office getting his work done. As Jillian understood it, the opportunities for Shelly to be with David were few and far between, which was all the more reason Shelly wanted a child. She was lonely. Jillian certainly understood that—if it weren't for Pete, she would be incredibly lonely at times.

''No, but she's going with us on the boat so she can watch Mr. Nelson fish and maybe work on her suntan, plus she's got some book she bought at the airport on her way here she wants to read. In fact, that's where she is right now—sitting outside in the garden, reading her book. She said she isn't going with us into the village, but would take pictures later on after we were all outfitted. You going to stay here with her?''

''I wasn't planning on it,'' Jillian admitted. ''I have to rent my fishing gear, too.''

''But that would leave poor Mrs. Nelson here all alone and she's still pretty sad from what was said yesterday about her not having babies.''

''She is?''

''Yeah, so it might be a good thing for you to take that walk you wanted to take, then come back here and keep her company some. Besides,'' he hiked his boyish shoulders with much aplomb, ''picking out fishing gear really should be a guy thing, don't you think?''

A guy thing? Jillian chuckled. Where had he heard that expression? From Troy and his father perhaps? Likely, it would be good for Pete's self-esteem to go with just the men to pick out the equipment they would need. ''Well, then, can I trust you and Reynold to make sure I get everything I'll need? Including one of those life preservers that zips up the front instead of ties?'' She hated the type that made her feel like Dolly Parton. ''And some sunblock for my face? We'll be out all day for two days. I'll need more than my usual suntan lotion.''

''Of course, we will.'' Pete glanced at the ceiling a moment, then twitched a dimple. ''You just stay here, take your walk, and let us guys handle all that other stuff.'' He took two struts toward the door, then stopped. ''And you might like taking your walk down by the beach. The sun has turned the sand nice and warm. Just right for taking your shoes off and curling your toes in it.''

''Sounds like you've been out there already.''

He nodded, then blinked. ''I just came back from there.''

Seeing a special sparkle in his pale blue eyes she would dearly love to share, she agreed. ''Then I'll make it a point to go walking down by the beach while you're gone.'' She probably would have ended up there anyway. ''I'll see if Shelly wants to go along with me.''

''No.'' Pete shook his head so hard, his cap slipped sideways, popping unruly brown curls in all directions. The thickness of his dark hair had definitely come from his father and not her.

Jillian's heart did a tiny flip at that last thought. How she had loved running her hands through Brad's thick, wavy hair. Almost as much as she had loved teasing the crisp, curling hair in the center of his chest.

''No sense even asking her,'' Pete continued, his words coming in a youthful rush. ''She's already said she doesn't want to move from where she is. She just wants to sit out there in the sun and enjoy her book.''

''Still, I should ask.''

''I tell you what,'' he responded brightly while repositioning his cap so it was straight again, though now with hair sprigged out in all directions. ''I'll go ask her for you.''

Before Jillian could offer to go ask the question herself, Pete was out the French doors, sneakers flying, headed toward the largest sitting area nestled in one of the many flower gardens south of the house. Jillian followed as far as the open windows and watched while Pete asked his question, and Shelly smiled but shook her head.

Within minutes, he was back, breathing hard from having run so hard. ''No, she says she's fine right where she is. But she thanks you for thinking of her and hopes you'll enjoy your walk. Meanwhile, Mr. Johnstone and Mr. Nelson are ready to leave. I'm supposed to meet them at the car, so I gotta go.''

He headed back out the doors, pausing to close them this time, then shouted so she could hear him through the tall windows that defined the adjoining wall. ''If you see any nice, unbroken seashells while you're out there on the beach, be sure to pick them up and save them for me.''

Pleased and surprised by Pete's eagerness to spend some ''guy time'' with Reynold, Jillian watched happily while her son again ran as hard as he could toward the back of the greenhouse where the cars were parked.

Perhaps there was hope for those two yet.

Desperately needing some peace of mind, Jillian tried not to focus on the serious problems that still threatened. She had dwelled enough about the inevitable for now and, for her sanity's sake, needed to free her heart from worry.

Hoping to do just that, she breathed deeply the merged fragrances of evergreen, honeysuckle, and salt while she headed along the flagstone path, across the freshly mowed lawn, toward the cliffs, eager for an invigorating walk along the water's multileveled edge.

With the steep, craggy cliffs that made up so much of Maine's midcoast, divided by long, rocky fingers of land pointing randomly out to sea, there were few flat beaches to stroll in the area. Fortunately, the Seascape Inn had one of the nicer stretches along the water's jagged way, but it was accessible only from the steep-angled stairs built ages ago— or directly from the water.

As a girl, that curving strip of gray sand and stone had been a favorite spot, especially at low tide, when the sea fell away to reveal some of the most remarkable treasures her young heart had ever seen.

What wonderful vacations her family had shared there. That was why she was a little surprised Sea Haven hadn't developed into just another tourist trap, like the larger resort towns farther along the coast. Even with Mayor Horace Johnson fighting tourism at every turn, she would have thought word about this small bit of paradise would have spread far and wide, bringing a lot more solitude-seeking vacationers than it had.

That was the wonderful thing about Sea Haven. It was far enough away from the tourist traffic of Route 1 that outsiders ventured there more by chance than by design. As tucked away as Sea Haven was, any visitors to the village had either followed a map because they meant to be there, or they were lost. Why, even after locating the village itself, often guests had to stop and ask for directions to the Seascape Inn.

Even with part of the roof in sight, the narrow main road to the north of town looked like little more than a wide, patched private driveway when in fact it bumped along the jagged Maine coast all the way to New Harbor. But because Horace had such strict rules about road signs, only the locals knew that. With the only sign that marked the road on the other side of town, most folks turned back rather than risk getting lost along a wooded, black-paved road that might lead to nowhere.

That was a big part of Sea Haven's charm. It was quiet, secluded, and simple. For miles, there were no major hotels, no fancy restaurants, and no nightlife of any kind. Just quiet strolls through the wilderness, picnics at the beach or on an empty island, boat rides along the majestic coast, dining in a quaint cafelike atmosphere, cold-water fishing, Grange dances, and the occasional potluck supper—sheer paradise to the vacationer wanting to escape the rush, glitter, noise, and pollution of the city.

Again, she closed her eyes and breathed deeply the fresh, clean air. Even in the more fashionable suburbs outside Dallas, where there were thick trees, rerouted creeks, and houses with large, sloping lawns, the air was never this clean, never this invigorating. Even at low tide, when the pungent salt smell outweighed the tangy scent of the wilderness, the air along the Maine coast exhilarated her.

If only there was a way to pluck off this part of Maine and move it to Texas.

Squinting against the morning glare off the water, Jillian adjusted her sunglasses and glanced off toward the Fisherman's Co-op. Although she continued along the flagstone path toward the stairs that would take her down to the beach, she was reminded that Sea Haven Village had what locals called a working harbor.

Proof lay in the different-sized lobster traps stacked high along one side of the floating wharf and the brightly painted buoys than hung in clusters from the posts and down the side of a small, wood-shingled shed like grapes in the sun. Beyond them, what few fishing boats and skiffs had not gone out for the day shifted with the water from their moors in the marina, where very few pleasure craft ever docked.

Since so many of the locals took their living from the sea as fishermen, lobstermen, shrimpers, urchin divers, or clammers, few business existed that were not marine-oriented. Oh, there was Miss Millie's Antique Shoppe and, down the way, a craft shop she occasionally visited, but most local businesses thrived from the money earned directly from the sea.

To these people, that was as it should be.

Jillian smiled as she neared the narrow coastal road. Although there were "summer people" who lived in the sun-bleached houses several miles down the southern shore, and most certainly there were the Seascape Inn guests, who came in a steady stream from the end of May until early September and sometimes beyond, Sea Haven Village was not a community to beckon visitors. Still, it never turned away a friendly face.

"Ahoy!" she shouted, spotting Hatch on the wharf, standing alone, smoking his pipe.

Having heard her over the ocean's gentle clamor, he bent low, squinted, then stood erect again and waved a hearty hello. She considered foregoing her walk on the beach and heading over to the wharves instead to have a friendly chat with the weathered old man who maintained the local lighthouse, but she remembered her promise to Pete to look for unbroken seashells and save them. How she would love to have a nice assortment collected when he returned from the village, enough shells to share a few with Troy, who in all his travels and his many moves around the country had never been to the coast.

Stepping across the sand-strewn, two-lane street, she headed down the stone marked path that crooked through a sloping field flaming with yellow, white, and red wildflowers, still headed toward the granite cliffs rather than the wharves.

A few yards from the angled steps that commenced at one edge of the cliffs and descended the steep bank with sharp turns to the beach below, she caught her first glimpse of rocky shore jutting out into the frothy water. Glistening blue waves cast brilliant fountains over the wave-smoothed boulders that blocked the far end of the sandy beach below.

Having always loved the ocean, Jillian savored the same giddy leap of her pulses she always felt whenever she stood at the helm of such breathtaking beauty. Her heart soared high above the many problems that weighted it earlier. For the moment, all that existed in Jillian's world was contentment.

A pair of playful white gulls dipped overhead, jesting in the unusually warm morning breeze while she stepped from between two sprouting pockets of fragrant fir and young poplar. Pausing, she watched the squabbling birds a moment before starting down the steep steps that ended on Seascape's secluded beach, not far from where lapping water gently stirred the gray sand and rounded pebbles.

Once on the beach itself, the sound of splashing surf surrounded her, bouncing off the granite walls with quiet applause. Eager to feel the coarse, sun-warmed sand beneath her feet, she hurried to a small, isolated boulder, about the size of a small steamer trunk, where she always placed her towels and lotion whenever she came to swim.

Quickly, she set aside the plastic bread wrapper she had brought to gather the seashells, tugged off her canvas shoes, and put them all inside a hollow near the top of the large rock to keep as much salt spray off them as possible. With that done, she headed toward the water, eager to shock her warm toes with the cold, moving water, but stopped short when she noticed she was not alone.

Her soaring heart sank like a rock in water when she noticed, not all that far away, on a mammoth pile of rocks that spilled right out into the water, the seated figure of Brad, clad in a pair of pale-blue cut-off jeans, his dark blue shirt whipping gently behind him.

Perched, Indian style, on the largest boulder, Brad stared idly out across the glittering horizon. Even from a distance, she could make out his grim profile, one that indicated he was lost to some very serious thought. Whatever held his attention, held it so completely he hadn't noticed her yet.

With pulses pounding at twice the normal rate, Jillian glanced at the stairs, not that far away. Her first inclination was to run away before he spotted her, but her conscience reminded her of the very real need to tell Brad about Pete. This could easily be her last and only opportunity to do that.

It was also the perfect opportunity. Although the splashing sounds over near the boulders did little to encourage a quiet chat, at least they would be alone when she told him.

Still, it would be better to talk in a quieter location.

If she could coax him off the rocks, to the more secluded area of the beach where the water rolled gently across the sand rather than slapped briskly against rocks, she would gather her courage and tell him. She wouldn't worry anymore about the consequences. She wouldn't worry how this would affect Reynold, who her son just now started to accept. Nor would she worry how this would affect Pete, who would want to know why she could not have revealed this secret earlier. She also would not worry about herself, though she would rather face the wrath of a hurricane than have everyone know the harmful decision she'd made.

No.

She would simply gather her courage and do what had to be done.

With that purpose now firmly in her heart, Jillian curled her hands into determined fists and marched toward the rocks much like a soldier headed off to war. *Too much like a soldier headed off to war.* Aware that she looked more like someone prepared to meet her death, she relaxed her hands and took several short, deep breaths before starting her climb up the uneven rocks. Because of the water's noise, and with Brad's attention so keenly focused elsewhere, he did not notice her until she sat down beside him.

He blinked twice, as if she were the last person he expected there. "Jillian?"

"Hi. How long have you been sitting here?" she asked, shouting to be heard above the ocean's din. She thought it best to start out with general conversation.

"Since before Pete left a little while ago." He watched her cautiously, as if uncertain what to expect from her.

"Pete knew you were here?" Was *that* why her son was so adamant she take her walk along the beach? He knew Brad was there? But why would Pete be trying to bring them together?

"Yes, I walked down with him earlier. He wanted to look for seashells, but the tide had just barely started to go out so there was little point in looking yet." His gaze returned to the sea, now fully retreated.

After a moment of silence, Jillian glanced in the same general direction, the wind tossing her dark hair back from her face like it did Brad's. "What are you looking at out there?" Off to the right were a half-dozen or more islands of different sizes, shapes, and distances, but they obviously were not what held his attention.

"Nothing, really. I was just looking. Into the past, I guess."

Jillian's heart gave a tiny little leap. *Into the past? Their past?* "And what do you see?"

She turned sideways to study his solemn expression, wishing desperately she had the ability to read thoughts.

"Us. The way it used to be."

The perfect lead-in for what she had to tell him. "Brad, we need to talk. Let's go over there near the lagoon." She gestured to the tiny part of the beach that curved inward.

He nodded his agreement and, with the push of one hand, stood.

Jillian, still trying to decide just how to word her life-altering news, didn't get up right away, giving Brad time to offer his hand. Feeling more like the giddy college girl she had been those nine years ago than a twenty-eight-year-old mother responsible for an eight-year-old son, she accepted that hand and let him pull her slowly to her feet.

Brad stood close, the wind tossing his hair to one side as he stared deep into her eyes and held her hand a moment longer than necessary. Clearly he searched for something. But what? Maybe she would find out after they reached the beach. There, they could talk and be heard without shouting.

Walking a few steps ahead of him, Jillian rubbed her hands together to remove some of the warm tingle Brad's touch had caused, balancing carefully on top of the rocks until she reached the area easiest to descend. There, Brad hopped down ahead of her with the agility and surefootedness of a cat, then turned to offer his hand again.

Filled with that same giddiness as before, she took the proffered hand and was inordinately pleased when this time he kept it. Even after they both stood on flat, even sand, he continued to hold her hand in his, swinging their arms lightly between them as, together, they headed for the quieter, more secluded part of the beach.

As if the past nine years had never happened.

❧ *Chapter 11* ❧

Jillian felt weak with wonder yet sad with regret when she and Brad finally reached the more secluded section of beach and Brad immediately let go of her hand.

"So what is it you want to talk to me about?" he asked as he sank cross-legged onto the warm, dry sand, using a smooth, rounded section of the rock wall behind him to prop his back. With less breeze near the small inlet to ruffle his thick, dark hair, he took the opportunity to comb the loose strands away from his face with his long, skilled fingers.

Joining Brad on the sand, Jillian sat with one leg bent and the other stretched out in front of her, oddly pleased at the way Brad gave that extended leg a second glance. For some reason—probably because he had just been thinking back on a time when there were no barriers between them—Brad smiled at her. He smiled that same adorable, dimple-encased smile that had stolen her heart all those years ago. *If only she didn't have to tell him what she had to tell him.*

Her heart ached with the desire to reach out and touch that sexy, flirtatious smile just once before it faded from his face forever, which it would—at least around her.

Instead, she lifted her knee and draped an arm over it.

"Us," she answered simply. The same answer he had given her earlier when she had asked what he saw when he gazed into the past. She took off her sunglasses and fiddled with the nose brace. Where they sat—a narrow curve of land blocked the morning glare off the water—made the sunglasses unnecessary.

"*Us?*" Clearly he had not expected that answer from her anymore than she had expected it from him earlier. He uncrossed one leg, allowing him to sit straighter and turn toward her, his navy short-sleeved shirt twisting across his broad shoulders. "What about us?"

"I-I—" Why did this have to be so hard? Her blood raced icy trails down her arms and up her neck while she folded the sunglasses and slipped them into the breast pocket of her sleeveless pink blouse. "I think we need to talk about some things and come to a sort of understanding."

"I agree. We do. For your son's sake."

My son? She groaned. This was not going to be easy. She dropped her forehead to her arm, wondering if she would really be able to tell him. Would she really be able to ruin this odd moment of friendliness between them?

"Jillian? What is it?" He touched her hair lightly, enticing her to lift her head and look at him. It was almost her undoing. He stared at her, truly concerned. "Is there something wrong with Pete?" He glanced in the direction of the stairs as if worried he should go check.

"No, Pete's fine. Right now, he has gone into the village with Reynold and David. I was supposed to go with them, but I thought it would be a good idea for Pete and Reynold to spend some time together without having me there to get in the way."

"Oh." Brad's hand dropped back to his side as if suddenly repulsed by the thought of touching her. "So you're not even considering what I said to you yesterday about Reynold. I'd hoped you would give it a lot of thought and start to see him for what he is. Especially after last night."

Jillian blinked. Why were they back to that? Why did every serious conversation with Brad lead back to Reynold? "A lot of thought? About what? About Reynold not being good father material? I already explained that to you. You're wrong about Reynold. He cares about Pete. And he cares about me. That's all that really matters."

"Cares?" He narrowed his pale blue eyes just enough that she noticed. "Yesterday, you told me how much he *loves* Pete and how much he *loves* you. Today, you use the word 'care.' Big difference." He studied her, speculatively. "Could it be that you have already started rethinking this situation? Could it be that after the incident last night in the kitchen, you've started to think about what could happen if you actually married him? Did at least some of what I said about him sink in and suddenly ring true?"

"No. But that's because you haven't had a chance to see the real Reynold Johnstone. You have no idea all the good he'll do for Pete."

Brad's expression turned as rigid as the granite wall behind him. "I guess you're going to have to explain that one to me because I don't quite understand the reasoning there. How will Reynold making Pete's life miserable be good for anyone?"

Exasperated, she waved her hands in rhythm with the accented syllables in her words. "How will Reynold make Pete's life miserable? By being there for Pete whenever he needs a man to talk to instead of his mother? By being there to teach Pete those things only a man can teach a boy? Or by taking him to museums and to cultural events where Pete will learn something other than how to swing a metal bat or when to slide into home plate—yet at the same time still be entertained? Tell me, which of those generous acts could possibly make Pete's life miserable?"

"Multiple choice?" He crossed his arms stubbornly, exactly like Pete always did whenever he became as angry as he was frustrated. "Then I pick number three as the most correct answer. What six-year-old boy wants to spend hours inside a museum or at a concert or whatever? And how often do you really think Reynold will follow through and do anything at all with the boy. Think about the three days since he's been here. How much time has Reynold spent alone with Pete?''

"That's not fair," she answered, ignoring the fact that Brad had just stated Pete's age wrong again. Another missed opportunity to correct a misunderstanding, and tell the truth. "This is not the sort of trip in which Reynold can take time out to be alone with Pete, though he really wishes he could. With David here, Reynold has to put business first. He has no choice.''

Brad shook his head. "Jillian, how can you be so blind to something that's so obvious? That man is all surface and no depth. His values are so botched up they almost don't exist. You can tell that by the sort of topics that carry his conversations. Reynold will *always* choose business over Pete. Think about it. Have he and Pete *ever* done anything alone? Just the two of them?''

"No, but that is not Reynold's fault. Pete has proved very slow to accept him. Truth is, until this trip, Pete avoided Reynold like he had the plague. The only time Pete hung around long enough to have a conversation with him was when I made him.''

"Sounds to me like Pete is a pretty darn good judge of character. He knows a pretentious phony when confronted with one—which is more than I can say for his mother, who obviously cannot see past that polished, pretty-boy smile Reynold plasters across his face, or that suave sort of sophistication he effects.''

Frustrated by such an unreasonable appraisal, her fingers curled into hard, angry fists. This was not the conversation she had planned when she had lured him over to the quiet part of the beach. "Why don't you like Reynold? What has he ever done to you?''

Brad studied her a long moment, the muscles in his lean jaws pumping a slow, steady rhythm, then abruptly he stood up. Suddenly, Jillian faced a pair of lightly tanned, well-muscled legs, braced equally.

"Nothing," he finally answered, teeth clenched while he

glowered at her. "The man has done nothing to me. But, then, I wouldn't care if he did. It's Pete I'm worried about; Pete, who wants a father he can feel close to, a father he can play baseball with on Sunday afternoons, one who will buy him greasy corn dogs with mustard and who will take him fishing if he wants, or who will help him build things he doesn't know how to build."

"But Reynold *is* taking him fishing," she pointed out, latching onto that one fact as if it were her only lifeline. "That is exactly why they are gone. They went to Landry's Landing to buy some of the fishing gear we'll need for our next two days of fishing and rent the rest."

He shook his head, as if unable to believe she had not yet grasped his point. "I meant alone. Just the two of them. Not in a small group of adults where Reynold is likely to spend more time kissing up to David than he is to showing Pete how to bait his hook or tie on the correct fishing lure."

Feeling at a disadvantage to have Brad looming over her like that, Jillian stood, too. She dusted the sand off her shorts. "I don't understand why you are so angry." It wasn't as if Brad knew the truth yet. "Why do you care what sort of relationship Reynold and Pete have?"

"I don't know. I guess because I like Pete as much as I do. He's a great kid, one who deserves a great father—not someone like Reynold Johnstone."

Stunned by how bitter Brad sounded, Jillian watched with silent outrage while Brad turned and stalked away, the muscles in the backs of his legs contracting then releasing with each angry step.

What was it between him and Reynold? True, no two men could be more opposite, but that gave Brad no reason, nor the right to declare Reynold an unfit father for Pete. So, what was the deal here?

"Well, that certainly went well," she muttered aloud as she headed back for her shoes and plastic bag. No longer was she in the mood to look for seashells. Not only had she failed to accomplish what she had hoped, she had made matters worse by letting the dastardly secret ride even longer.

God, but that woman could infuriate a saint.

Brad marched toward the lighthouse, his cross-trainers digging sharp trenches in the sand and shell-strewn path. How could Jillian want to marry someone like Reynold Johnstone? How could she possibly do something like that to Pete? Pete was her own flesh and blood. Could she really be so blind to Reynold's multitude of shortcomings? Or was it just plain selfishness?

Why, if Pete were *his* son, he would do everything in his power to make sure the boy had a good, stable father, one who could contribute to a happy home environment. Not some self-serving, egomaniac like Reynold Johnstone. Could she really be so uncaring?

And to think, he had actually hoped to make up and be friends with Jillian again. He had wanted to explain some of the hurtful things he had said to her nine years ago.

As if she'd care. Couldn't she see she was putting her own needs above her child's?

The truly sad thing was that he'd thought she had changed. And because of that mistaken change, he had honestly believed there was a chance, however slight, they could overcome the differences between them, and be together at last. Then *he* could have been Pete's father and would have made damn sure the boy had someone he could rely on during the tough childhood years ahead.

As it was, about all Brad could do for Pete now was try to help prepare him for an existence with a stepfather who cared about no one but himself. He could try to reassure Pete ahead of time that he was not to blame for the neglect he would eventually suffer. Pete needed to understand, so he could adjust to the sorely emotionally lacking life that lay ahead for him. Pete was smart. He could be made to see the truth.

Still, it made Brad's stomach turn sour. Pete deserved better.

* * *

Squealing with laughter, Pete ran into the house well ahead of Reynold and David, wearing a dark green fishing vest with lots of neatly buttoned pockets over his bright red baseball shirt. He also wore a matching starched hat that was pulled down level with his pale blue eyes and shaded most of his face, ears, and neck, making it hard to see anything that stood above him—which, unfortunately for Pete, was most of the visual world.

"Mom? Are you here?"

"Yes, I'm in here," she called to him, having just left Shelly out in the garden to come inside to see if Cora and Miss Hattie needed any help in the kitchen. That one muffin she had nibbled for breakfast followed by that brisk, angry walk she had taken barely an hour ago had left her a lot more hungry than usual. "In the dining room."

Having caught sight of Pete's outfit when he shot across the veranda just seconds earlier, Jillian was not surprised by his odd appearance when he marched in, wagging his half-hidden head proudly. "Now do I look like a Maine fisherman?"

"Very much," she told him, although she wanted to laugh at just how little like a Maine fisherman he did look with his starched vest, matching hat, and a wide leather belt with different-sized fishing hooks imbedded in grooves so narrow, they looked impossible to pry out. Maybe this was the way some of the big-time sports fishermen from far away dressed, but not the local guys. Why would Jacky Landry bother to stock such unorthodox gear?

"Where's Brad?" Entering further, he glanced around, clearly expecting to find him there.

"He was headed toward the lighthouse last I saw of him," she answered, then resumed the task of setting the table. Brad was the last person she wanted to talk about. "Probably wants to do some thinking." Too bad it wasn't to take a flying leap into the ocean. "He used to go there a lot to do that when he was younger."

Pete's happy expression melted with disappointment. "You mean he wasn't at the beach when you went for your walk?"

"He was there," she admitted, gaze narrowed but eyebrows arched. What had Pete hoped to accomplish by luring them both there? "But he stalked off shortly after we had another argument."

"Argument?" He tugged off his hat and slapped it across the back of a chair. "What did you two argue about this time?"

"That's really none of your business." She refused to tell Pete the ugly things Brad had said about Reynold, even though it would show Brad for the petty person he had turned out to be. Or maybe she didn't tell *because* it would prove him to be so petty. Even though he infuriated her, Brad was still Pete's father. She needed to remember that.

"Shoot fire." Pete kicked dejectedly at the floor, then turned and skulked toward the hall, shoulders slumped.

"Where are you going? Lunch is nearly ready."

"Upstairs. I left something important in the attic."

Before Jillian could ask why he had been up in the attic of all places, Reynold entered all decked out—an enlarged replica of Pete—followed by David, who easily made the third clone. Shaking her head, she was reminded of the Three Stooges and wondered if these guys would be the type to buy woolly chaps and silver spurs just to ride a horse.

"Lunch ready?" he asked, coming across the room to kiss her lightly on the cheek in an uncommon gesture of affection. As usual, his blond hair was immaculate, even after having worn that silly hat. "We have had a busy morning. We're hungry."

Still studying their odd attire, Jillian held a straight face. "Yes. Go wash your hands. Miss Hattie saw you pull in and went to the kitchen to tell Cora it was time to serve." She waited until Reynold and David were nearly to the door before quietly adding, "And you might want to take off that fishing gear while you eat. I'd hate for you to get food on the new duds."

Reynold nodded he agreed, unbuttoning his vest just before he and David disappeared from sight.

Shortly after enjoying a light shrimp and rice salad without Brad's troublesome presence, the men retired to the pond to practice casting the large fishing rods they had rented, while Shelly stayed behind to help Jillian and Miss Hattie clear the table. As soon as the dining room was tidied, Shelly headed out to the carriage house to get her camera and then take pictures from the gazebo.

Since Jillian did not need to be taught the proper way to cast and place a line, she remained in the house even after finishing the cleanup, watching occasionally from the windows, waiting for Pete to appear so Reynold could also show him the proper handling of the large-style fishing rod. Having opted for shoreline fishing over deeper water, casting a considerable distance while placing the line properly was important.

But Pete never showed.

With the dining room cleared and Shelly gone to take her photos, Jillian went upstairs to find out what had become of her son. He had scampered away right after lunch and she hadn't seen him since.

"It's right down here," Pete told Brad as he flipped on the overhead light then headed down the steep, planked stairs that led into the daylit basement. "Miss Hattie said it was in a bright red box with big green letters stored up near the ceiling. Said we couldn't miss it."

"But I thought you were supposed to be out there learning how to cast for the fishing trip tomorrow," Brad said, following right behind.

"They're going to show me how to do that later. After Mr. Nelson is sure he knows how. It's easier to teach one person at a time than to try to teach two together." Having taken off his new fishing gear for now, Pete wore a baseball cap again, backward.

As did Brad. "So, in the meantime, you've suddenly decided to take up croquet?"

"Mom told me it's a game my grandma and grandpa used to play all the time, and Miss Hattie said tonight was supposed to be a lot warmer that the past few nights, which means it would be a good evening for me to learn how to play." He paused on the bottom step and glanced around. To the left, just ahead, was a large washer with a matching dryer, and to the right stood lots and lots of metal shelves filled with mason jars and canned food items.

Behind him was a big heating unit and a set of stronger shelves made from thick lumber built right onto the walls. There were also boxes on the floor, a barrel in the corner, and two long windows up next to the ceiling that gave in more light than the bare bulb hanging overhead. "Don't worry, you can go find something to eat just as soon as we're done here. Besides, you should have been here earlier when it was still time to eat." He cut a quick look at Brad, then pointed to a Ranger-red box near one of the windows. "Is that it?"

Brad passed him, circling around behind the stairs with long, athletic strides. "Looks like it."

"Can you get it down by yourself, or will you need help?"

"I should be able to get it down without any help."

"But it looks like you're gonna have to climb the shelves to get to it, huh?" He stepped down from that last step and headed toward him.

"No, it isn't that high up," Brad told him, looking around. "I should be able to use that chair over there and reach it easily enough."

Pete frowned. They hadn't figured on that. "Why bother dragging that chair over? Why not just climb up there and pull it off the shelf?"

"Because it would be a lot safer for me to use the chair." He backtracked to the laundry area, snatched up the narrow wooden chair Miss Hattie sometimes sat in while waiting for her clothes to dry, and returned with it. "I'll have that croquet set down in just a second."

Pete cut his gaze around, but didn't see evidence of Tony anywhere. How was this going to work without Tony there to run interference somehow? "There's no hurry."

Brad tested the chair's sturdiness by pressing down on it with his palm then shaking it. Assured it wasn't ready to collapse, he climbed up onto the slatted seat and leaned forward to slip his hands underneath the large box. *He wasn't even going to touch the shelf below it.*

"You want me to help?" Pete hurried forward but before he could reach for the faulty shelf and give it a tug, suddenly the wide board creaked twice in warning, then gave way on one end.

"Watch out!" Brad made a quick grab and caught the slow dropping plank by the edge before much more than a couple of half-empty paint cans could topple off it. Fortunately, neither popped open from the fall.

"That was close," Brad exclaimed over the clattering cans, breathless from his save. "How'd that happen?" Already he looked around for a way to correct the problem. "I didn't even touch that shelf."

"I don't know," Pete said, shaking his head with what he hoped was just the right amount of bewilderment. "The thing just broke loose for some reason. See?" He pointed to where Tony had tampered with the nails. "There, near the wall, it broke loose from the bracing." Exactly like Tony said it would.

Brad bent low to look at the underside of the shelf. Continuing to hold the board level with one hand, his muscles bulging from the strain, he reached underneath and felt the break with his fingers. "You're right. It feels like the nails holding it pulled straight out for some reason."

Sliding his hands to a better position, he bent again and peered at the underside of the shelf, then glanced around at other areas of the cellar, searching for something. "Go ask Miss Hattie where she keeps her repair tools and then bring me a hammer and at least four large nails so I can fix this."

"You going to hold that shelf in place until I get back?"

"I just about have to," Brad said with a flat expression. "It's either that, or let all this stuff clatter to the floor. So hurry." He glanced at the many paint cans and other such supplies still on the shelf. "I don't want to have to be here all day."

"One hammer and four big nails," Pete repeated the request aloud, then saluted Brad in the same manner Tony had saluted him earlier. "I'll be right back."

Turning to face the opposite wall so Brad couldn't see his grin, Pete hurried back up the stairs, through the room-size pantry, and into the kitchen.

"Hi, Mom," he called to his mother just entering from the main hall. He slowed his pace to a casual walk the moment he spotted her. Happily, he winked at Miss Hattie, who had entered right behind her, while he strolled quietly toward the mudroom.

"Where have you been?" Jillian called after him, stopping him just as he reached the doorway. "I've been looking for you."

"Down in the cellar."

"In the cellar? Why?"

"No reason." He started walking again.

"Where are you headed now?"

"Outside. I figure Mr. Johnstone should be about ready by now to teach me how to cast that big-sea fishing rod he rented for me." He slid his hands into his back pockets just before he ducked innocently out of sight.

For a long moment, Jillian studied the empty spot where Pete had stood. Something was not quite right about Pete's behavior just then, but she wasn't exactly sure what was off about it. Was it something in the all-too-innocent way he looked at her?

"I think maybe I'd better go peek downstairs and see what trouble Pete might have caused while he was down there."

"Do you mean in the cellar?" Miss Hattie queried, headed toward the old, cabinet-style radio near the fireplace to adjust the station. She did not wait for Jillian's answer. "Would you do a favor while you're down there? Would you bring up a couple of jars of sliced peaches? I'm considering a nice, piping-hot cobbler for dessert tonight.''

Jillian darted her tongue across her lip. Miss Hattie's peach cobbler for dessert sounded wonderful. "You bet. Do you need anything else while I'm down there?"

"No, the peaches are the only thing I need." She bent low to see the numbers on the round, lighted dial while turning one of the wooden knobs barely a fraction until her favorite station was again tuned in. Soft music from the big-band era drifted from the gleaming wood cabinet. "You do remember where they are, hmm? Across the cellar, near that far wall?"

"Of course, I remember. How many times have I had to go down there to use that washer in my lifetime? You can go ahead and pull out everything else you will need for that cobbler; I'll be right back with the peaches.''

"No need to hurry yourself." She straightened and smiled brightly, her green eyes twinkling as she smoothed an imaginary wrinkle from her apron. "Since Cora took the afternoon off to go see her granddaughter in that school play, I have several other things to do, too. Even so, there's all afternoon to get done what I want done.''

Glad Pete was headed out to be with Reynold so when Brad returned from the lighthouse he would see the two together practicing for tomorrow's fishing trip and have to eat some of the cruel words he'd spouted earlier, Jillian started downstairs to get the peaches. Also to figure out what Pete might have been up to earlier.

First the attic, now the cellar, was there no part of this house Pete hadn't explored? Why, even she had never been in the attic and she had pretty much had the run of the house when she was young.

Frowning to see the cellar door left open, thinking to reprimand Pete for that when next she saw him, she reached for the light switch out of habit. Her frown deepened when she realized Pete had left the light on, too. It wasn't like Pete to do that.

Padding quickly down the stairs in her light pink tennis shoes, Jillian was nearly to the bottom before she noticed Brad, standing on a chair, facing the wall, holding a plank shelf in place. He had shifted his weight to one leg, his other knee bent, as if he had been there awhile.

With both arms held chin high, his dark blue shirt stretched taut across his broad shoulders, part of the hem pulled out from his snug-fitted cutoffs.

The norm of late, Jillian's first inclination was to flee the room. She was not ready to face yet another confrontation with the insipid man. She was still far too angry over that last one.

"Did you get the hammer?" he asked, not bothering to look over his shoulder at her. He shifted his weight to the other leg, rippling the hard muscles in his calves. "I think I could probably reuse these same nails if I could just come up with a hammer. For some reason, they aren't even bent. It's like the shelf was pulled out instead of pushed down."

"I have no hammer."

Brad tensed, quickly giving equal weight to both legs, but he did not bother turning around. Clearly, he wasn't any more eager to deal with her than she was with him. "I didn't know it was you."

"Don't worry. I'm just down here to get a couple of jars of peaches for Miss Hattie. I'll be gone in a minute."

Taking a deep breath to steady a suddenly racing heart, she continued down the stairs as intended and crossed to the shelves that held the jarred fruit. She had made it halfway back to the stairs with two jars in hand before Brad said anything else.

"You haven't seen Pete, have you?"

Although she had vowed not to glance in his direction again, for fear he might be looking her way and mistake her interest for something it was not, his question nevertheless pulled her attention to him.

He continued to stare at the shelf he held, not caring enough to as much as glance her way. "Yes, just a few minutes ago. I saw him as he was on his way outside to join Reynold and David down by the pond.''

"Outside?'' Brad turned to look at her so abruptly, the bill of his turned-around cap struck his shoulder and knocked off his head. It fell to the chair at his feet at the same time his eyebrows dipped low over darkening blue eyes, a clear indication he did not want to believe her.

"Yes, he went outside.'' Halting, she gave a defiant lift of her chin. "To be with Reynold and David awhile so Reynold can teach him how to use some of the fishing equipment they rented this morning.'' Feeling triumphant, she smiled. "I guess that works against your little theory about Reynold, doesn't it? They managed to find time for each other after all.''

"You must have ordered Pete to go out there,'' Brad insisted, clearly not ready to believe that Pete could have done so of his own accord. He obviously didn't want to accept that Reynold had finally started to win her son's favor. "Pete wouldn't have gone otherwise.''

"He would, and he did,'' she informed him happily, then started toward the stairs again, eager to get far away from his stifling presence. Something about being in the same room with him made it hard for her to function.

She was halfway to the top, her gaze locked on the painted wall beyond the open doorway, when a sudden, phantom wind came out of nowhere and blew the door shut.

Cripes. The whack made her jump nearly out of her skin. Her heart raced faster still.

"What was that?'' Brad cried, clearly just as startled by the unexpected sound.

"Just the door.'' she answered between great draws of breath. "I'll open it again.''

Needing to escape him more than ever, she reached for the knob, dumbfounded when it refused to turn. She tried again. Twice. Nothing. Then she tried turning it the other direction. Still nothing. "Brad, I'm not sure, but I think we're locked in.''

❧ *Chapter 12* ❧

Panic did not set in until Jillian tried knocking as hard as she could to try to get Miss Hattie's attention, and no one came. The only sounds she heard were those from the radio.

"Brad, we are *really* trapped down here."

She gripped the banister hard as she looked at him still standing on the chair awkwardly holding the huge wooden shelf in place.

"How can we be?" He scowled over one shoulder, looking more annoyed with her assessment than worried. "The only lock on that door is the little metal twist lock Hattie had Jimmy put on several years ago to keep curious youngsters from opening it. Somebody had to be out there to turn it to make it work."

"I don't know how, but I've tried several times and I cannot get that door open. I can't even get the knob to turn." She stepped back up and tried it again. It gave just a little, but not nearly enough. "It's like somebody strong is out there holding it."

"That doesn't make sense." He glanced around as if trying to figure out what to do with the shelf, his eyes stretching when his gaze fell on a small hammer atop a stack of corrugated boxes in the far corner. "Where'd that come from? I didn't notice it a few minutes ago."

Seeing what had his attention, she hurried down the stairs. "Here, I'll get that for you."

The sooner he freed his hands, the sooner he could help her open that door. She didn't like being locked in the cellar, didn't like it one bit.

Brad shifted the weight of the shelf to his left hand and took the hammer she offered in his right. "Can you help me hold the board in place while I align those nails again?"

Not thinking about the odd fact they now worked together at something, Jillian set the peaches aside then used both hands to steady the shelf. "Is that about right?"

"No, just a little higher." He tugged it up another half an inch.

She tiptoed to accommodate.

"Right there." With the nails hammered through the back of the shelf at an angle, he aligned the ends to go directly into the bracing still anchored to the wall. He then hammered on the board itself, driving all the nails in at the same time. As soon as wood butted against wood, he pulled his hand away to test it. When that appeared to give Jillian no added strain, he bent to snatch his cap off the chair then knelt low to double-check his handiwork. "I think you can let go now."

"Good." Her arms had started to ache near the shoulders. "Now go open that door."

Flexing his left hand while he walked, Brad slid the hammer through a belt loop on his cutoffs, plopped his black ball cap on his head, and headed up the stairs. Seconds later, he too stood back, staring at the door, baffled. "There's no reason for that knob not to turn. Even if the jolt did cause that little lock to snap in place, the doorknob should still turn. The two aren't in any way connected."

That had been her thought. The lock wasn't in the knob. Also, even if the inner doorknob workings had broken, the handle would still turn. This was just so weird. "So what do we do now?"

Like her, Brad tried knocking on the door to attract someone's attention. Again, nothing stirred inside the house. He took his cap back off, folded it, and tucked it into his waistband then tried tucking his arm against his body and slamming a braced shoulder against the door. But the doorframe proved too stout and he did not have enough room on the narrow, steep stairs to get a running start at it.

"Let's try it together," she suggested, and moved up to the top stair to stand beside him. Facing each other, only inches separating them, they waited until the count of three then slammed the door in unison. Still it did not budge.

"Too bad she didn't get whoever put that door together to build her storage shelves, too," Brad commented, running his hand over the surface. "That's as solid as those cliffs out there."

Jillian watched his hand, mesmerized by its smooth movement, while she tried to figure out what to try next. She could not stay down there in the cellar for the rest of her life, especially not with Brad there, too. Her stomach rose and tumbled at the mere thought. "What next?"

Brad studied her for a long moment, his blue eyes reflective in thought, then just when she thought it might be in his head to kiss her, he spun about and clamored down the planked stairs. "We need to find something long enough to knock on the ceiling. We'll get Miss Hattie's attention that way."

"Good idea." It didn't need to be much, the ceiling was not very high. Sucking tiny little breaths past the constriction in her throat, Jillian followed. "There's an old broom over by the washer."

Brad had already spotted it. Seconds later, he stood in the area closest to the kitchen and pounded the ceiling with the broom handle several times, then paused to listen for movement.

Nothing.

He tried again.

Still nothing.

"She can't hear us. What about the windows?" Jillian asked, ready to move on to the next idea. She glanced at the two long, narrow panes of glass built into the opposite wall, near the ceiling, and then down at her own slender frame. "I'm probably thin enough to wiggle through."

He eyed her speculatively a moment then nodded as he dragged the chair he had used to the closest window to reach the release lever. "Just don't forget about me being down here because I don't think I'll be able to fit through such a narrow space."

Climbing up, then tiptoeing, he worked with the window several seconds before muttering. "It's locked." He moved to the other window. "It's locked, too."

"Here, let me try. Maybe there's a trick to it." She wasn't about to give up as easily as that. She climbed up onto the chair with him, very aware when their bare legs bumped, and tried the window herself. He was right. It was locked. But then, why wouldn't it be? The days had not grown quite warm enough to warrant opening them, though the room could certainly use the fresh air.

"And there's why Miss Hattie hasn't come to our rescue," Brad said, tapping the dusty inside pane with his fingertip. "She's on her way out to the pond to serve lemonade."

When Jillian leaned close to have a better look, her shoulder brushed against Brad's arm, sending a shock wave of tingling warmth through her she fought hard to ignore. This was not a good time for acute sensual awareness. She turned her attention toward the yard instead.

Sure enough, there was Miss Hattie crossing in front of the gardens, carrying a white-handled tray with a clear pitcher of what looked like iced lemonade and a stack of plastic glasses. "Oh, great! And with Cora having the afternoon off, there's no one else in the house to hear us."

Brad let out an annoyed breath. "Door jammed. Windows locked. Unless you happen to know of some secret way out of here, it looks like we have no choice but to wait until Miss Hattie returns."

They stood a minute longer, both on the same chair, both looking forlornly out the window like two puppies in a pet store, then suddenly Brad jumped down and headed toward the stairs. There, he sank down on the left side of the third step, his feet braced on the second. With his knees so conveniently placed, he crossed his arms over them and propped his chin. "I just hope she doesn't plan to stay and have lemonade with them. I haven't eaten since breakfast. I'm hungry."

Remembering he had missed lunch, likely due to their argument, she suggested he open a jar of Miss Hattie's peaches or maybe her pears and help himself. He eyed them a moment, but in the end did not move from the stairs. "No, I'd rather wait for something more substantial. She can't be too long down there."

Hoping that proved true, Jillian stepped off the chair and considered sitting in it, but her insides were in far too much turmoil to allow her to be still. She paced the floor instead, restlessly aware of the silence that filled the space between them.

"Sorry about the argument we had earlier," she said in an effort to avoid a continuation of the same. She glanced at him, hoping to see the same regret she felt, but could not read his emotions from there. "It was not the sort of talk I had planned."

"I know." Still slumped, he shifted to look at her briefly, then turned his attention to a hairline crack in the wall in front of him. "It wasn't what I had in mind either. It's almost like we're doomed to argue." He lifted his chin off his arms but didn't bother to look at her again.

Back to strained silence. Whatever happened to those long, easy conversations they used to have about anything and nothing? She let out a soft, wistful sigh, longing for those days again. Then unable to think of anything else to occupy her motions, she returned to the chair and sat down, glad it was in an area more behind Brad than beside him where he couldn't easily look at her. She felt uneasy enough just being trapped there with him.

In desperate need of distraction, she glanced around at the miscellaneous items on the shelves beside her, but found nothing to interest her. Her attention returned to Brad instead. *There was plenty to interest her there.* Plenty to interest *any* woman. But, unfortunately, he did not feel the same interest in her. What little magic they had once shared was gone. It had died that cold September day he told her good-bye.

Suddenly sad again, and not wanting to be, Jillian stood. She had to find something to think about besides the past.

Wandering about, she fiddled with the knobs on an old eight-track tape player then poked her finger in the hinged door, breaking a mass of spiderwebs. It had been awhile since that thing had been in use. Didn't Miss Hattie ever throw anything away?

Next, an old phonograph lured her attention to the shelf below. It was the type that had a plastic carrying handle and looked something like an old, boxlike suitcase. Fat, metal buckles held the lid down and part of an electrical cord poked out from underneath the lid. When she bent to have a closer look, she noticed a stack of dust-covered photograph albums beside it. The top one slid off the shelf just as she tilted her head to read the faded writing across the front.

"What's that?" Brad asked, having turned to see what had hit the floor.

"An old scrapbook of some sort," she told him. She brushed away the dust with the side of her hand to read the date written in bold black marker as she picked it up. "1987 & 1988."

The same two years she had dated Brad.

Fighting mixed emotions, she flipped it open. Despite the turmoil inside her, she couldn't help but smile fondly at the first photo to catch her eye. "Hey, here's a picture of my parents. Out at the marina holding hands with Bill Butler in the background."

"Yeah?" Brad stood and came toward her, clearly curious about the album.

"Oh, and there's Hatch the day he caught that raccoon that had such bad breath. Or should I say the day that raccoon caught him." She balanced the book in one hand, allowing her to point at the photograph in question. "My parents have that same picture."

"As I recall, your dad was the only one around here with a camera during most of that summer. He must have taken these and sent copies to Miss Hattie." He moved to stand behind Jillian, bending over her shoulder for a closer look. Although he did not actually touch her, he stood close enough to send a shiver over her. "Oh, no, there's Jimmy Goodson out on the beach. He looks about fourteen years old there. Look at those gangly legs."

"Poor kid—all skin, bones, and ears." Jillian laughed at the strongman stance Jimmy had struck for the camera. He had arched his shoulders and sucked his stomach in to display a fine set of scrawny ribs. "Oh, look, and there you are helping Preacher Brown, Bill, and Fred Baker move that new piano into the church. Look at that expression."

"Hey, it was heavy," Brad retorted in ready defense, laughing at his grimace along with her. "Come on, bring that thing over here so we can both look at it."

Thinking that fair, and eager to see what other treasures were inside the album, Jillian followed Brad to the stairs and sat down beside him. Balancing the bottom of the oblong album in her lap, she opened it again, resting the top cover on Brad's knees. Together they explored what photos were still glued to the pages, a few spots now empty, probably from the glue having given way over the years. Soon, they were able to distinguish the ones her father took from those other guests had taken by the fact that her father's had the year imprinted along the right edge. Leaning forward, they waded through a dozen or more pages of photographs taken in the year 1987 before coming to those taken in the summer of 1988.

That was when looking at the photos turned a little uncomfortable. It was clear by the way Brad and Jillian were then touching each other, or looking at each other in practically every photograph that they had fallen in love by then.

Or at least, they *thought* they had. For a moment, Jillian longed to go back to those happier times. If only for awhile.

Glancing at Brad, she wondered what it would be like to stroll again along the beach, arm in arm, without a care in the world.

Her heart gave a tiny twist at the mere thought.

"Oh, goodness, look at that one," Brad said, unaware she had turned her attention to him. His blue eyes glittered when he pointed to a particularly embarrassing shot of them both sitting in the same swing, her in his lap and leaning back against his shoulder, dewy-eyed. "I wonder whatever happened to that old swing."

"I don't know. I think that whole tree is gone." She could not remember seeing it behind the church the few times she had been in that part of the village since returning.

"Too bad. We had a lot of fun in that old swing."

She nodded. It would be darn hard to argue the point with that photo right in front of them. She looked at it again and smiled sadly at the two young lovers still weeks away from reality. Odd, how little Brad had changed in the passing years. He still had his thick, and at times unruly, dark hair, and he was every bit as slender and fit. Amazingly so.

"We had some good times that summer," he admitted, lifting his gaze to hers. Absently, he rubbed his hand down the front of his lightly tanned leg while studying her. "Seems like a lifetime ago."

Jillian's stomach twisted, pulling at her heart. It *had* been a lifetime ago. Pete's lifetime. She swallowed hard. Should she tell him now?

They stared questioningly at each other a long moment before Brad dropped his attention back to the album. Although the handsome lines of his face revealed no identifiable emotion, his voice sounded strained when he continued to browse, "Look, there's your mother and father having a picnic together. Out on our island."

Our island? Although quite content to continue looking at Brad, Jillian could not resist taking a peek. The island was where she and Brad had first made love. "I guess I must have taken that picture."

"I think you must have taken that one, too." Brad's finger slid to the next photo, which was a close-up of his swimsuit-clad posterior. And what a fine posterior it was.

Jillian wet her upper lip while heat slowly climbed the back of her neck. What was *that* doing there? It was as hard to imagine Miss Hattie allowing a butt-shot of Brad in her photo album as it was to imagine her father having sent it to her. How embarrassing. "Yes, I suppose I did."

"Interesting angle." He lifted an eyebrow, looking at her again, humor evident in the sparkling blue of his eyes. "I think you managed to capture my personality perfectly. By any chance do you have a copy of that at home? Perhaps an enlargement on the wall above the family fireplace where you can look at it often?"

She knew he was kidding, but for some reason she wanted to stay serious, probably because it was too easy to forget the past nine years of heartache while they were laughing. "No, I put away all my pictures of you right after you told me you didn't love me anymore." Which, was true. She didn't throw them away, because Pete would want to see them one day, but she had put them in storage years ago. "It hurt too much to have them around after that."

Brad's expression fell instantly solemn. "I never said that. I never said I didn't love you anymore."

"Same as." She shrugged, trying not to let on how very near tears she was. She had sworn years ago never to let him see her cry again. "You told me you didn't want to marry me."

"I never said that either."

"Yes, you did." *Why was he saying that? Why was he lying?*

"No, I didn't. What I said was that I didn't think marriage would work for us. I never once said I didn't love you or that I didn't *want* to marry you. Never once."

Jillian frowned, trying to remember back, but for the life

of her could not recall his exact words. Just the results. She had run away in tears, and he did not come after her. "But after I hinted to you that I did not want to be apart from you again, and that it might be a good time to consider marriage, you became very upset and told me you didn't want me bringing you down. You didn't want a wife hanging around your neck. You told me that your education was much too important, that becoming a doctor was much too important. Wasn't that the same as having said you don't really love me?"

"No." Brad looked down a moment. "And that's not exactly what I said." He chewed at the corner of his mouth a moment then lifted his gaze to hers again. "I think what I said was that I didn't need the burden of a wife at that point in my education—any wife, not just you—and that I certainly wasn't ready to have children taking up what little time I could call my own. But I had a reason for saying that."

"Yes, and that reason was to break it off with me. Forever." Trying hard to get this all straight in her mind, she set the album aside. Besides, she had relived enough of their happy times together to make her ache for yet another nine years. "Why don't you just admit it? What feelings you had for me, if any, had grown cold and, as a result, you wanted to break up with me."

Brad lifted his hand as if about to touch her cheek, but then thought better of it and dropped the hand back in his lap.

Jillian had to learn what he was thinking. "It's true, isn't it, Brad? Wasn't that what you wanted that day? For us to break up forever? We'd had our fun. But the summer was over, and you had made other plans to fill the rest of your life, plans that in no way included me." She curled her hands into fists, frustrated by the fact he wouldn't admit such a simple truth. "Why won't you just say it? I never meant as much to you as you did to me."

"I can't say that. You meant the world to me," Brad stated in a voice so deep and so sincere, Jillian had a hard time not believing him.

She was dumbfounded. "How can you say that?"

"Because it's true."

Confused by the emotions raging inside her, and by the candor displayed in his blue eyes, Jillian tried to look away, but couldn't.

With memories of what it had been like between them still so freshly rekindled, Brad lifted his hand again and this time caressed her cheek with trembling fingers. His eyes darkened with something not quite identifiable as he slowly leaned toward her. "Jillian, I've never loved anyone as much as I love you, but I know as well as you do that marriage has always been out of the question for us. We would have just made each other miserable."

Love? Although little of what Brad said made sense to her, Jillian couldn't help but notice the present tense when referring to what he felt. Could seeing her again have somehow reignited what he had once felt for her? But was it really love he had felt even then?

"Brad, I—" Jillian started to say something, but the moment she realized he meant to kiss her, all words deserted her. Dazed and with her heart beating nearly out of her chest, she swallowed back whatever it was she had been about to say and turned her attention to his parted lips.

Her next several breaths came in short erratic bursts. *Oh, God, yes, please do let him kiss me. I'll suffer whatever the consequences, but please do let him kiss me. Just once more.*

With a longing she had not felt in nine unbearable years, Jillian's eyelids lowered as she parted her mouth and prepared her senses for the wonder only Brad could offer.

When his lips touched hers timidly, the magic turned out to be even stronger than Jillian remembered, jarring her right to her toes. It was like that first kiss all over again—the one he had stolen out in the gazebo, the one that in the end had left them both breathless and wanting more.

When Jillian did not pull away like she should, the kiss deepened. Brad's lips felt warm, tender, and persuasive, making her wish the moment would never end. Suddenly, Jillian was nineteen again. Nineteen, and madly in love with Brad

Pierce, the most handsome man in all of Maine, the most handsome man in all the *world*.

With passion climbing to a maddening intensity, Brad pulled her to a standing position then down two steps to the floor, away from the stairs, where he immediately wrapped her body in his. Jillian responded eagerly. She slid her hands up his shoulders, holding him as close as was physically possible. In a natural response to all that happened, she dipped the tip of her tongue into his mouth, eager to taste as well as feel him.

Oh, how she had missed him.

Driven by nine long years of need, Jillian moaned softly and dug her fingers into the strong muscles covering his back, pressing him closer still. He moaned, too, as he ran his palms over the tops of her shoulders, down her sides, then up again toward her breasts, making her weak with awareness.

So like the past.

So *very* like the past.

Desperate to relive more than just his heated kiss, and still not caring what the consequences might bring, she did not brush his hand away when it gently cupped her breast. She continued to let him overwhelm her with kisses. For the next few minutes, she would pretend Brad still loved her every bit as much as she still loved him, every bit as much as she would always love him.

"God, how I've missed you," he whispered, his eyes dark with passion when he pulled away far enough to move that same hand to the top button of her blouse. Warm, skillful fingers dipped inside, grazing the sensitive skin between her breasts while he worked to release the stubborn button.

She was too caught up in the physical response to his touch to voice her thoughts, but willed the button to do his bidding. Finally, the tiny disk slipped through, as did the next one, allowing the material to gap enough for a hand to slip inside. When his fingers moved between the silk bra and her heated skin, and brushed a sensitive crest, she shivered in response.

In the nine years since Brad, no other man had touched her

there. No other man had roused her passion enough for her to *want* him to touch her there. Not even Reynold, who had never really tried, but would never have succeeded, despite their commitment to marriage.

Determined not to think about Reynold or her engagement and chance spoiling her desire by weighting it with guilt, Jillian reached for the next buttons herself, ready to be free of that blouse.

Suddenly, it was a blessing that they were locked in that cellar where no one could get to them. Although she was not sure where in that small room they would manage it, she wanted to make love to Brad one last time. Wanted it more than she remembered ever wanting anything in her life. Her whole body throbbed with need.

Finished with the blouse, Brad worked with the clasp of her bra, finally releasing it, allowing her breasts to burst from the silken restraint. She closed her eyes and arched her shoulders back, her breasts aching for his touch while he pushed the bra down until straps slid over her shoulders enough to drop the contraption out of his way. In the next motion, he cupped both breasts, lifting them full and high as he caressed the nipples with his thumbs. Shock waves of white-hot pleasure shot through to Jillian's very soul, filling every fiber of her being with a need so powerful, it hurt—a mere sampling of what was to come.

"We shouldn't be doing this," Brad muttered, dipping his head to trail tiny kisses down her neck then across her collarbone, his chin brushing the tops of the breasts he still taunted with his thumbs. The nubs were so taut now, they quivered at the same time the ends of his hair tickled her shoulders.

"I know." The words were barely audible above her heavy draws of air, but she was no more able to stop than he was.

Releasing one breast, he slid his right hand up between the blouse and the front of her shoulder, and had just started to push the material back, further clearing his way, when the rattling of a doorknob brought them screaming back to reality with a jolt.

Unable to fully grasp the situation, they broke apart, both heaving deep, shuddering breaths and eyes dark with need.

"Someone's coming." He forced the husky warning through an emotionally clogged throat.

He glanced down for one last look just before she gasped and pulled her blouse together, clearly as alert as she was to what they were both about to lose. This very well may have been their last opportunity to know one another in that way.

The doorknob rattled again.

Jillian's heart jumped when she glanced at it and noticed it turn. Before, it wouldn't do that. For some reason, they were no longer locked inside.

"It could be Pete," she cried, her voice a harsh whisper as she ducked under the stairs, hoping to get her bra fastened and her blouse buttoned and tucked again before anyone spotted her. What would she do if it was her son? How could she explain being down there half-undressed with a man she was supposed to hardly know?

Brad moved to the other side of the room, likely to draw attention from her. He turned as if studying the many jars and cans stacked on the far shelves.

"Oh, hi, Brad. I didn't know you were down here."

Jillian did not have to look up to know it was Jimmy Goodson. Frantically, she worked with her clothes, praying he would not glance down before she finished. Her fingers trembled when he started down the steps.

"Oh, hi," Brad returned over his shoulder. "Yes, I came down here hoping to find a jar of Miss Hattie's pear preserves." He snatched up a jar then headed immediately toward the stairs. "I thought I might like to have some on my rolls at supper." Obviously, he hoped to head Jimmy off before he made it much further.

"They're good eating all right," Jimmy agreed as he stepped to one side to give Brad room to pass, but continued on his way.

"What do you need down here?"

Jimmy paused and turned but fortunately looked up instead of down. "I came to borrow Miss Hattie's hedge clippers. I saw her out by the pond a few minutes ago and she told me I'd find them in the garage, but it seems to me I remember them being down here."

"No, I think she's right. They are in the garage." He continued up the stairs, never faltering a step. "Come on. I'll show you where."

Jimmy tapped his foot once, then shrugged and followed him back up the stairs.

Jillian's heart refused to beat, knowing all Jimmy had to do was look down and he would see her through the open steps. But his attention was on Brad, who continued to rave inanely about Miss Hattie's pear preserves.

Just before Jimmy stepped through the doorway, he reached back and turned out the light, then gently closed the door behind him. She prayed the knob didn't jam again, but knew if it did, Brad would eventually return for her.

Flooded with relief, she stepped out from under the stairs for more room and quickly buttoned the last two buttons of her pink blouse, then tucked the hem back into her white shorts nice and neat. By the time she had climbed back up the stairs to test the door, her heart hammered at a more normal rate, but her body still ached with unfulfilled need.

Guilt washed over her as she curled her fingers around the cold, metal knob and turned it.

She ached for the wrong man.

❧ *Chapter 13* ❧

Pete listened distractedly while Mr. Johnstone again explained how to work the large fishing rod they had rented for him at Landry's Landing. Although Pete didn't much like the idea of Jimmy Goodson going up to the house alone while his mother and Brad were still locked in the cellar, at least he wasn't headed any farther than the garage where Miss Hattie stored a lot of her summer stuff. With any luck, Jimmy would never know the two needed help getting out of the cellar.

"Bring the rod back over your shoulder to two o'clock, push down on the little lever with your thumb like I showed you, or with your other hand just seconds after you start to quickly whip the rod forward to ten o'clock," he repeated, demonstrating with his own rod, clearly twice the length of Pete's.

Pete watched from several feet to his side while the practice weight tied to Mr. Johnstone's line flew high across the dark blue pond then dropped into the water with a plop.

"It's as easy as that. Two o'clock, then ten o'clock."

Easy, sure, if you happen to know how to tell time that way. Pete scowled as he gripped his own rod again. Hadn't the man ever noticed that most of the clocks in their house were digital?

"Now you try it again. But this time, concentrate."

Pete did his best to mimic the moves, but instead of his practice weight sailing out and hitting the water on the far side of the pond, it fell near his feet with a dull thud. He screwed up his face in disappointment. That attempt was worse than the last.

"You aren't trying," Reynold scolded, bringing his weight back in for another demonstration with short, brisk turns of his reel handle.

Pete watched that tiny muscle at the back of Mr. Johnstone's cheek jump in and out sort of like it did last night when Brad made them apologize to each other for not seeing eye to eye about his grandmother's doily. "Show me again."

"Maybe it would help if he stood closer to the water," Miss Hattie offered from the gazebo where she and the Nelsons sat sipping lemonade. Being in on the scheme to trap Brad and his mother in the cellar, although thinking it all Pete's idea and that he had somehow rigged the door to stay shut, she was in no hurry to return to the house. "Then he wouldn't have to throw the weight so far."

When Pete turned to smile at her, he noticed Tony seated beside her, his tall frame slumped down, an arm draped casually around her shoulders. Surprised to see him there, Pete tilted his head questioningly, then glanced in the direction of the house.

Tony responded with a wink and a smile. *They needed their privacy.* He wiggled his eyebrows to give further meaning to that silent response.

Although not totally understanding, Pete laughed, then aware no one else knew what suddenly had him laughing, he thought quickly and said, "Imagine what will happen if I get *too* close to the water and fall in during the next time I try to cast the weight to the other side."

"Well, as you can see, *my* shoes are still drying," Mr. Nelson muttered, pointing to where two leather shoes and a pair of light blue socks sat sunning on the gazebo banister. Though his expression stretched flat with annoyance, Mr. Nelson's eyes glittered with humor as he wiggled his toes to emphasize his problem.

Mrs. Nelson chuckled. "Quit complaining. You are the one who suggested we all try to get in a little fishing this week. Can we help it that you've gotten a little rusty from not having taken the time to do any fishing during the past eight or nine years?"

Obviously, Mr. Johnstone did not want to discuss the reasons for Mr. Nelson's clumsiness as much as Mrs. Nelson did. "Let's try it again, young man. Two o'clock, then ten o'clock, and be sure to flick your wrist just so."

But before Pete had a chance to turn around and watch yet another demonstration, the man had already casted.

"Peter, you aren't paying attention. How can you possibly learn anything if you don't pay attention?"

Pete sucked in his earlier grin, knowing it went against Mr. Johnstone's present scowl and would make him scowl even worse, then turned to face the pond squarely. "I'm sorry. Show me again."

After several more tries, and failing each time, Pete again rolled in his weight, and was about ready to give up when he felt someone's hands curl around his wrist. At first he couldn't see the hands, but slowly they formed a faded image.

Here, let me help you.

Although there was no warmth to it, Pete felt Tony's presence behind him while Tony carefully adjusted his grip on the rod, moving his fingers farther down the handle. He then lifted Pete's other hand to the metal reel, singling out the index finger and placing it over the release.

When I say now, you press down on that lever as quick as you can.

Pete nodded and relaxed his arm so Tony could move it around easier. Watching intently, he allowed the rod to pull back over his shoulder until it was a lot farther back than he had taken it before, then felt it flip forward with a different kind of motion than he had used. It felt sort of like throwing a baseball overhanded, only balking at the last minute so the ball really didn't go anywhere but the runner on base would think it did. A nifty trick his coach had taught him.

Now.

Pete pushed the lever as quick as he could and watched, amazed, as the gray weight sailed high into the air then fell to the water with a plunk.

"I did it!" He glanced back at the others to make sure they had all watched. "I did it!"

The Nelsons and Miss Hattie applauded.

"About time," Reynold muttered softly, still reeling his weight in from his last cast. "It's not the most difficult thing in the world to accomplish."

But sometimes you have to have hands-on help, Tony suggested, but only for Pete's benefit. No one else knew he was there.

"Thanks."

Glad to oblige. He felt Tony move away.

"I'm just glad I was here to help," Reynold said, thinking that thanks had to have been for him. Having reeled in his weight, he gave it a slight shake to rid the line of a piece of dripping moss then prepared to cast again.

Ready to give it a second go, this time on his own, Pete quickly wound the weight back. Without looking around to see where Tony had gone or who watched, he flicked the rod back then forward again, amazed when the weight did exactly like before. Wait till his grandpa saw that. No more pole fishing off the spillway for them. Way cool.

"Looks like you're ready to learn about putting live bait on your hook," Reynold said, staring at where the weight hit the water. "I bought just enough today for us to practice that."

"Live bait?" Pete flattened his eyebrows. He didn't like the sound of that.

"Yes, that's where you put your hook through a smaller fish so it'll wiggle on the end of your line and attract a larger fish. It's great for fishing off the side. If you pierce the fish just right, it'll wiggle around for quite some time."

Pete curled his nose. What a disgusting thought. "I'm not watching anything like that."

"Watching? You'll have to learn to bait your own hook."

Not if I can help it. "We'll see," is all Pete dared say on the matter as he prepared to cast for a third time. He'd rather stick to using plain lures. "Right now, I think I need a lot more practice casting. I can learn that other stuff tomorrow." That is if his mother still wanted to go after having finally worked out her problems with Brad.

Uh-oh.

Pete froze. He did not like the sound of that "uh-oh" and spun around to see what Tony had found to "uh-oh" about. Something heavy filled his chest when he spotted Jimmy and Brad headed in their direction. Jimmy carried the hedge clippers he had gone after and Brad carried a half-eaten sandwich and an empty glass.

How did Brad get out of the cellar?

I guess I should've stayed in the house rather than come down here to give them more privacy. Evidently, they figured out the door wasn't being held shut anymore.

Maybe Jimmy had something to do with that.

Or maybe they just weren't quite as— Tony paused, as if searching for the right word—*occupied as I thought they were.*

"Where's Mom?" Pete called out to them, hoping to get some idea about whether she and Brad had at least cleared the air like they were supposed to while stuck downstairs. If Brad still acted annoyed just talking about her, Pete would know they were still upset with each other.

"She was in the kitchen last I saw of her."

He looked somewhat uncomfortable at the mention of her, but not all that angry. That much was good.

"A-yuh, she's in the kitchen, all right," Jimmy put in, glancing at Miss Hattie. "She was pouring herself a glass of milk and looking real thoughtful about something just before we left." He lifted his eyebrows as if sending secret messages her way. "Oh, and I found the shears right near where you said they'd be, although I thought I remembered seeing them in the cellar.''

"In the cellar?" Miss Hattie's green eyes widened as she pressed a hand to base of her throat. "You didn't go down there, did you?" She glanced at Brad, now pouring lemonade into his glass, then at Pete, standing stone still listening, but the question was clearly for Jimmy.

"Not really. I made it only about halfway down the steps before Brad here convinced me these things were indeed in the garage and I followed him back out. I didn't even get a chance to ask Miss Westworth what she was doing down there. It looked almost like she was down there trying to hide from someone, though I can't imagine who."

Brad had more than a little trouble swallowing that first gulp of lemonade and ended up sputtering part of it before he could talk again. "Hey, Pete, I saw that cast you just made," he stated, quickly changing the subject while he blotted a couple drops of lemonade off his chin with part of the bread that made his sandwich. "Impressive."

Pete glanced at Tony, who had his hand splayed over his eyes, then at Miss Hattie, who blinked rapidly a half dozen times before he turned to see what Mr. Johnstone's expression might be. Like Jimmy, did Reynold also wonder why his mom was down in the cellar looking like she might be trying to hide? "Thanks," he answered politely. "But I have to admit, I'm not exactly what Coach Stover would call a natural at this. I had a lot of problems before I finally got it right."

Mr. Johnstone looked as if his mind was on other matters while he worked to untangle his line from something in the water, which was fine with Pete. The less the man knew about what was going on, the less trouble he could cause.

"A-yuh," Jimmy put in, nodding in agreement. "It was a fine cast. I sure wish I didn't have to work on Fred's truck tomorrow or I'd go with you to see how big a fish you catch. I could also show you some of the better places to anchor."

Pete cut his gaze to Reynold, afraid he was going to insult Miss Hattie's good friend by pointing out that he wasn't invited, but Reynold was still too preoccupied with whatever held his line.

"Speaking of work," Jimmy went on, "I need to go put these to good use." Holding the shears by the handles, he rested the blades on his shoulder, like a soldier carrying his rifle. "But, first I think I need to go by the Blue Moon and take care of one small matter." He cut his gaze back to the house almost like he was pointing to it, then winked at Miss Hattie before waving good-bye to Pete. "If I don't see you before, I'll see you Saturday afternoon, and have I ever got a great memory saved up to give you."

"Saturday?" Mr. Johnstone called out to Jimmy, who had already started off around the pond to the village. Evidently, Mr. Johnstone had caught at least part of the conversation. "What makes you think you'll see Peter on Saturday?" With his line finally freed, he quickly reeled in his weight.

"Because I'm coming to the party," Jimmy called back, slowing his steps but not completely stopping. "I wouldn't miss it for the world."

"What party?" he asked, but in a voice loud enough only those close by heard. Having brought in his practice weight, he prepared to put his gear away. "What's he talking about?"

"My birthday party," Pete answered, beaming a natural response. "Remember? It's my birthday Saturday."

Not having heard the question from a distance, Jimmy continued on his way, so Miss Hattie sat forward to explain. When she did, the sunlight hit her hair and made it look like a shiny cloud encircling her head. Sorta like an angel. "And we certainly couldn't let such a momentous occasion go without just celebration. That's why we've invited everyone around here to a little party we're having in Pete's honor."

"We?" Reynold's scowl deepened. "Who's this 'we'?"

"Why his mother and me, of course." Her forehead notched with concern. "I thought you knew. We're going to have cake, and ice cream, and party hats. But instead of asking everyone to bring a lot of toys Pete says he won't have room to take home anyway, he has asked that everyone come with some memory of his grandmother. It is really a lovely idea. He wants everyone who knew her from all her summers here to come prepared to tell the memory at the party, but I've asked them to also have their memories written down so he will have them to keep." Her green eyes sparkled. "I'll admit, I'm looking forward to it."

"But I've already made plans for that day," Reynold stated. Having closed his tackle box, he propped his rod against a nearby bench, then moved closer to the gazebo where Miss Hattie, Brad, and the Nelsons sat. "I've already made reservations for five at Tavern on the Green in New York, which will be followed by a Broadway play that's opening that weekend."

"But I don't want to go to New York," Pete protested, instantly angry. What gave this man the right to mess up his birthday? Wasn't it bad enough he wanted to mess up his life? "I want to stay here and have the party Mom and Miss Hattie have planned for me. I want to show all the people who come that doily Grandma made."

Miss Hattie pressed a finger at the corner of her puzzled frown, studying Mr. Johnstone a moment. "Does Jilly know about these plans?"

"No, it *was* to be a surprise." Mr. Johnstone threw up his hands as if they had all conspired to ruin those plans for him. "The tickets were almost impossible to obtain."

"But if Pete doesn't want to go—" Brad started to put in, clearly as annoyed as Pete was, but Mr. Johnstone wouldn't let him finish.

"The boy will have a great time in New York. Perhaps the party can be put off until Sunday. We can be back by noon."

"But Sunday won't be my birthday." Pete curled his hands into tight fists at his sides, wishing he had the nerve to punch the skinny man in the stomach.

"Reynold, if he doesn't want to go—" This time it was Mr. Nelson coming to Pete's aid. "You can always try to exchange the tickets for another date. It doesn't have to be part of this trip, does it? Besides, I've always found the cast performs better once it's over opening-night jitters. To tell you the truth, I think I'd enjoy the little party they plan to have here far more. I like talking with the locals." He turned to Miss Hattie. "Is Hatch Tyler coming? Such an interesting character, that Hatch. Imagine, spending all your life married to the sea."

"Of course, he's coming. Hatch wouldn't miss the chance for a piece of my chocolate cake for anything." She smiled, looking grateful to Mr. Nelson for what he had said. "Besides, he has several stories about Pete's grandparents he's eager to tell."

"I'll just bet," Shelly put in, laughing as she rested her head on her husband's shoulder, something she liked to do when her own shoulder was under the crook of his arm. "I met him yesterday and he was just full of wonderful stories."

Miss Hattie chuckled. "That's Hatch, all right. Never at a loss for something to say."

"So what about it, Reynold?" Mr. Nelson asked, obviously wanting to get the matter settled. "Can't you change the overnight trip to New York City to another weekend? Besides, you have to remember, Shelly and I are *from* New York, and although attending an opening night is fun, it's not something worth missing a birthday party for." He smiled at Pete, who still stood at the water's edge. "How old will you be?"

Pete's already flopping stomach flopped even harder. Not only was it pretty clear his mother didn't want how old he was known, it was something his ghost friend, Tony, also had said he shouldn't tell aloud for fear it might cause Brad to realize the truth before hearing it from his mother. Knowing Brad might never forgive his mother if he found out any other way than from her telling him, Pete tried to decide some way not to answer.

For the first time Pete could remember, he was glad when Mr. Johnstone interrupted, "I don't know about this. I still think the trip to New York is a better idea. As I understand it, Peter has never been to a Broadway play. It would be good for him."

Mr. Johnstone studied Mr. Nelson's half-frowning expression a few seconds before deciding. "I know how to solve this. We'll let Jillian choose which would be better for Peter. How's that?"

"Works for me," Mr. Nelson said with a shrug, as if that meant the matter was solved. His half-frown disappeared behind the smile that had been there earlier.

"Me, too," Mrs. Nelson agreed, snuggling closer to her husband. Except for when the two were kissing each other on the mouth, which they did a lot when they thought people weren't looking, Pete liked the way those two acted around each other. Sort of like Troy's parents did. Like his mom and Mr. Johnstone never did, which was fine with Pete.

About all his mother and Mr. Johnstone ever did was hold hands, and, thank heavens, they didn't even do that very often. Why, in the three days Mr. Johnstone had been there, he had seen them touch only that once out on the porch. But he noticed her and Brad bump elbows or brush hands at least a half-dozen times. Pete knew some of the times they brushed up against each other may not have been on purpose, but they couldn't *all* be accidents. Some had to have been on purpose. Just like with Troy's parents.

"Good. Then it's settled." Reynold hurried to gather up his fishing gear. "I'll go ask her right now."

"We'll go, too," Miss Hattie said, already reaching for the serving tray she'd brought with her. After Brad had poured the last of the lemonade into his glass, there wasn't much point leaving it behind. "That way we'll all know what to expect."

After everyone had left but him and Brad, Pete set his rod aside and sat down only a few feet from Brad in the sunny part of the gazebo. He drew up his legs until his knees pressed against his chest then wrapped his arms around them. "I don't like him."

He didn't have to say who.

"I know. And I can't much blame you." Brad glanced over his shoulder, in the direction of the house where the others were just disappearing inside the house—even Tony, who'd obviously gone along to watch the outcome. Pete figured Tony would report everything said when they slipped off to the attic later.

"I wish he'd go away."

"You aren't the only one."

Not having expected that comment, Pete cut his gaze to Brad, then laughed. "Yeah, he's a real pain in the butt, isn't he?"

Brad's eyebrows arched as he, too, laughed and turned to face the pond again. "Not exactly how your mother would want it phrased, but, yes, he is—a royal pain in the butt."

The sunlight fell across their backs, warming them, while Pete considered how very much alike they thought. "I wish I didn't have to go fishing with them tomorrow."

"Oh, but you'll have fun. Especially now that you know how to cast like that. Why, I wouldn't be surprised if you were the one to catch the biggest fish. I'll bet you catch one even larger than your mother, who is quite a fisherman, as I recall."

"But I'd rather stay here and play some catch with you. Or maybe get in some more batting practice. Ever since you showed me where someone as short as I am should hold the bat, I've been getting a lot better."

"Do you want to do that now?"

Pete thought about it, but decided he was in too foul a mood from having just learned his birthday plans might be ruined to do anything he enjoyed. "No, I don't really feel like it now. Maybe later."

After several minutes of companionable silence, Pete commented further, "I wish you didn't have to go home Thursday. I wish you could stay long enough to be at my birthday party."

"I take it you think your mom is going to say no to the trip to New York."

Pete shrugged. The weird way his mother had been acting lately, he couldn't be entirely sure what she would decide.

"She already knows I want to have a party here, and it is *my* birthday. I'm figuring she'll let me do what I want. Especially once she finds out that nobody else really wants to go to New York—except Mr. Johnstone, of course." Having stuck his folded cap in his waistband to get it out of the way while he learned to cast, he pulled it out and snapped it open. "I should have known he would try something like this. He doesn't know what fun is. I can't imagine why my mother wants to marry the man. He's such a dweeb."

Brad nodded in agreement, then fell deeply silent again.

Pete wondered what had his thoughts, and hoped it was his mom, but decided not to ask him. Instead, he waited a few minutes, then tried repeating what he had hinted at earlier.

"Yeah, I sure do wish you didn't have to go home Thursday. Having you at my birthday party would even make up for Mr. Johnstone being there." He sighed. "Yeah, I sure do wish there was some way you could talk that doctor friend of yours into taking care of those patients of yours for a few more days. Didn't you say he owed you for the *two* weeks you took care of his work back in March?"

From the corner of his eye, he watched Brad's expression turn even more thoughtful. So much so, Pete filled with hope and proceeded along that line, "I wonder what would happen if you called your doctor friend and asked him to continue taking care of your patients a few more days?"

A smile slowly formed on Brad's face, shaping two dimples right about the same places Pete had dimples. Remembering how they looked a lot alike, even if they weren't shaped exactly the same, Pete hoped he would turn out just as handsome as Brad when he got older.

"I guess I won't know until I ask him, will I?"

Pete's hope grew again. "Then you'll stay?"

"I'll try. I won't know if I can swing it until I've actually talked with Kelly, but if he's willing to continue seeing my patients through the weekend, then I don't see why I should have to miss your birthday." His eyes sparkled. "And since Kelly told me just last night when I talked to him on the telephone that he's had no real emergencies yet, I suppose I had better be thinking about what I want to tell about your grandmother, shouldn't I?''

Great! If Brad stayed for his birthday, that meant they had at least two more days to try to bring him and his mother together. But, they really needed to get it done before then, since how old he was bound to be announced at the party, if not right before. Heck, it might even be written out right on the cake. Once Brad knew that about him, it wouldn't take two seconds for someone as smart as him to figure out the year Pete was born.

They still had to act quickly.

Since Reynold had hauled the tackle box with him, all Pete had to carry back to the house was the fishing rod while all Brad had to carry was his empty glass. With their hands pretty much free, they stopped twice to pet Walter the lop-eared community dog who had shown up minutes earlier and followed them from the pond to the sun-dappled screened porch just outside the mudroom.

Knowing the dog was always welcome and had been for years, they propped open the screen door so it could come and go when it wanted, and went on inside.

At Brad's suggestion, Pete leaned the fishing rod in the far corner of the mudroom then followed him to the small sink to wash his hands. When he noticed Pete lather his wrists, he had to ask, ''Did your grandfather teach you that?''

''What?'' Pete asked, taking the fingernail brush and scrubbing hard.

''How to wash your hands like that.''

''Like what?''

Brad chuckled, washing his hands in exactly the same way. It was funny how many things they had in common. ''Never mind.''

Once finished, they each took one of the small, tasseled hand towels stacked nearby.

''Wait'll Mom hears that you're gonna stay at least until

Saturday,'' Brad said, finished drying his hands. "Is she ever going to be surprised.''

To say the least. "Wait a minute, Pete. It's not for sure I'll be able to stay. It all depends on what Dr. Mack has to say.''

"He'll say yes. He just has to,'' Pete proclaimed and dropped the hand towel into the tiny hamper. Without glancing back, he hurried into the kitchen.

Brad moved to follow, worried Pete would tell Jillian while Reynold was there. For some reason, he did not want Reynold to know just yet. Perhaps that was because of the guilt he felt over what happened down in the cellar, and over what else would have happened had Jimmy not interrupted. Had there been no intrusion, they would have made love right there on top of all those boxes. He was certain of that. And even though that was exactly what he wanted, it was not right. Not with Jillian engaged to someone else.

Brad might not like Reynold, and he might truly believe a marriage between those two would be one of the worst things that could happen to Pete, but the fact remained, the two were engaged. Had Brad finished what was started downstairs, he would have selfishly taken that which now technically belonged to another man. It would have gone against the most basic of human principles. How could he have lived with himself after that?

Even so, it was difficult not to consider how willingly Jillian had come into his arms and how eagerly she had returned his passion. If Reynold was really all that important to Jillian—if he had truly claimed her heart—she never would have given in to the kiss so easily.

Or would she?

Judging by how quickly she had to have gone from his arms into Pete's father's arms, Jillian did not have the same regard for love that he did. It could be she didn't consider being engaged to someone quite as limiting as he would. Maybe she thought faithfulness came only after the vows were spoken and until then she was free to play.

Or, could it be that Jillian still felt something toward him?

Could there still be a passion so strong, so overwhelming, it had left her unable to turn away from it earlier? True, she may never have truly loved him, but she had indeed desired him, or they never would have made love those nine years ago. Not Jillian. No, the truth was she had desired him every bit as much as he had desired her. Then, as well as now.

Following close behind Pete, Brad stopped a few feet from the kitchen, then turned back. He had been so lost in thought, he had forgotten to put his towel in the hamper. He was still too bewildered over the fact that, despite the years, despite the major differences in their lifestyles, and even despite the painful fact she was now engaged to another man, there remained that chemistry between them—a chemistry so strong, so overpowering, that even now he wanted her as much as he ever had.

But did she feel the same way? Now that they'd had time to steady themselves after that unexpected burst of passion, was she disappointed or relieved that Jimmy had interrupted them? If disappointed over the interruption, could she now be having second thoughts about her engagement to Reynold? Could she also be having second thoughts about *him*? In some small way, did she now regret never having contacted him again as much as he now regretted never having contacted her?

His heart sank to the bottom of his stomach as he dropped the wadded towel into the hamper. Was it possible he had made a serious mistake breaking up all those years ago? Could they have worked around their differences, after all? More importantly, was it in any way possible he still had a chance with her even now?

He did not want to leave there until he had found that out. He could not live the rest of his life not knowing, always wondering.

If there was even the remotest chance he and Jillian could be happy together, despite all that had gone wrong between them, he needed to know.

He had to find some way to be alone with her again—then

screw up his courage enough to confess to her exactly how he felt, and hope she would do the same.

Drifting aimlessly about, Tony waited for Pete in the attic, frustrated that yet another likely plan had been foiled. This time by Hattie's good friend, Jimmy, who was not supposed to have gone any farther than the garage.

They had come so close this time. When he left the cellar earlier, Jillian and Brad were so deep into the throes of passion that, had they not met such an untimely intrusion, they would have consummated their love again. Tony knew that as well as he knew the third step on the main staircase creaked at the slightest weight.

Surely, that lovemaking would have led to the intimate conversation the two so desperately needed to have, the one in which Jillian would finally confess the truth to Brad, the one where she finally admitted that Pete was Brad's son, and that the only reason she agreed to marry Reynold was because Pete had reached the age where he needed a man's influence in his life.

The moment Brad learned he was the boy's father, he would insist *he* be that man, which would leave Jillian with no further reason to marry Reynold. Having come to realize she still loved Brad with all her heart, she would instead let Brad back into her life.

Tony was so certain of it, he could hear the jingle of Brad and Jillian's wedding bells in the shadows above him.

But until the two had that conversation, until Jillian finally broke down and told Brad the truth, Pete was stuck with Reynold's unwanted interference. Poor kid.

"Tony, you up here?"

"Yes, over here."

With it still midafternoon, there was enough sunlight in the attic for Tony to see Pete's excited expression as he scampered into the room in the disheveled way only Pete could.

How odd. He had expected Pete to be just as disappointed as he was that their 'foolproof' plan had indeed proved them fools—although clearly some progress had been made. To Tony's surprise, Jillian had decided against Reynold's New York plans for Saturday. Days earlier, she probably would have knuckled under and agreed to whatever the persistent man wanted. But today she'd held her ground.

"What has you smiling so big?" he asked. Pete had viewed his face several times now, so Tony didn't bother rising into the shadows. Instead, he drifted forward where they could see each other better.

"I'm smiling because I'm dying to tell someone my good news, but everyone's too busy to listen. Mom's washing her hair. The Nelsons are locked away again in the carriage house. Kissing again, I'll bet." His face screwed up at that last thought. "And Miss Hattie's off to get vegetables or something."

"Well, as you obviously have guessed, I'm not too busy. So what has you smiling like that?"

"I'm smiling because it doesn't matter so much about the two fishing trips now. Even with those taking up nearly two whole days, we should still have a couple more days to work with."

"How's that?"

Pete beamed as he took his cap off, shook it once, then put it back on. Probably because of all the dust, since Hattie had such a hard time coming up there to clean. Just too many memories.

"Brad's planning to call and ask that doctor friend of his to cover for him a couple more days so he can stick around and go to my birthday party." He thought a minute before the excited expression suddenly fell. "I am getting the party, aren't I? Mom didn't go and agree for us all to fly to New York on Saturday, did she?"

"No, the party is still on. You won't have to go to New York until that following weekend, after you leave here."

"Might not have to go at all if we could just get Mom to go ahead and tell Brad about me. I got a feeling that's all it'll take now to get them back together. Whatever happened down in that cellar made a real difference in how they feel toward each other. When I talked about mom just a little while ago, Brad seemed more sad than angry, like he was before. I think he wishes he and mom could get back together. I think that's why he was so willing to go make that call.''

''Ah, now we also have Thursday and Friday, too.'' Tony nodded. This was definitely good news. "That will give us time to try to get them alone together at least once more before Saturday, and if that doesn't work out as hoped, we should still have enough time left to try at least one more different strategy.''

''Any ideas what that might be?'' Pete looked as if he was already trying to come up with something himself. That was one thing about Pete. He liked to be prepared.

Tony shrugged and thought with him. They could try the direct approach maybe? No, he would really rather the problem be handled indirectly. It would be better all the way around if it was Jillian's own decision to tell Brad, not one he'd helped plant in her mind. If it came to that, so be it. But for now, they would try to get Jillian to find the courage to follow her own heart.

''About all we can do is take it one step at a time, Pete. Before worrying about the next plan, let's wait and see what happens after we get them alone together again.''

❧ *Chapter 14* ❧

Miserable with guilt and yet brooding for the past, Jillian sat staring out at the front lawn from the second-floor turret windows, watching while Brad showed Pete and David Nelson how to play croquet and while Shelly snapped photos galore and laughed at some of the poses they struck.

Sadly, Jillian thought back on all those sultry, late afternoons she and Brad had played teamed against her parents. What fun times they'd had together.

What fun times Brad and Pete were having even now.

How she longed to go outside and join them in that fun.

But that would be wrong.

Especially after what had happened earlier that day.

It wouldn't be fair to Reynold and she had to consider his feelings. Especially now, after having nixed his New York plans. He really thought he had done something wonderful.

Sighing, she turned away just as Pete doubled over with laughter from David having tried to ''knock'' his ball away from the nearest hoop, but having hit the side of his foot with the mallet instead. Even her son's high-pitched laughter did nothing to lift her spirits.

What a mess life could be. If only she hadn't run into Brad again after all these many years. The timing could not have been worse. If it had to happen, why now? Why, after everything had finally started to come together for her—*and Pete*?

She had fought so hard to get over Brad for almost a decade. Fought so hard to get over all the insecurity and heartache he had caused. Why couldn't her life have continued along without ever seeing him again? Without being so painfully reminded what his mere presence was capable of doing to her?

Damn. Everything had seemed so steady and safe before coming back to Seascape and running into Brad again. After all those years of floundering aimlessly, she had finally found a direction in her life that made sense. True, she might never be quite as genuinely happy being married to Reynold as her mother had been to her father, but at least she would finally have stability in her life. Better yet, *Pete* would finally have stability in *his* life. Giving Pete that made it worth the compromise. With Reynold, she might not get all that a woman needed from the marriage, but Pete would certainly get everything a little boy needed.

Her frustration deepened when she flopped onto the bed then rolled over onto her back to stare at the all-too-familiar ceiling. *No one* was more stable than Reynold. He had set a life plan and worked toward it, allowing few distractions. He was as constant, kind, and courteous as he was confident and secure—and he offered her the sort of lasting companionship she needed. He was also very shrewd and nicely handsome. Always immaculately groomed. Never a hair out of place.

So why couldn't she stop thinking about Brad, who was the exact opposite of all that? Except maybe for being handsome. Brad actually topped Reynold in the looks department. But then Brad topped every man in the looks department. Still, he was not constant, nor did he make a woman feel at all secure like Reynold did. So why couldn't she put what had almost happened between them while trapped in the cellar out of her mind?

Her heart skipped at the mere memory of Brad's lips on hers again—soft, warm, and persuasive, tempting her beyond all normal reason.

Her eyelids drifting shut of their own accord as she replayed the moment in her mind. How magnificent it had felt to be in Brad's strong arms again, to feel his body pressed against hers, and his trembling hand trail lightly over her skin. Although she had no right to give even a small part herself to him—having now promised her life to another—for a moment, she had truly wanted Brad to return her to that ultimate height of passion. That realm of ecstasy so wondrous, only a few ever found it. *One last time.*

How she had longed to have that one final memory of him to cling to, one last wondrous moment to keep tucked inside her heart during all those long, lonely years to come.

What? Eyes suddenly wide, Jillian sat bolt upright, baffled by that last thought. How could she possibly stamp the years ahead as being long and lonely when she would soon have both Reynold *and* Pete to keep her company?

"This is ridiculous," she muttered. She swung around and slid off the bed. "I'm moping around this room like some lovestruck teenager while Reynold is bound to be out there somewhere waiting for me to surface."

Glancing at the clock, she noticed it was already nearly time for supper. Where had the last two hours gone?

Feeling guiltier still, she combed through her hair and changed her rumpled blouse, then headed downstairs to find Reynold. She wanted to be extra nice to him that night to make up for his earlier disappointment. He had so wanted to make Pete's birthday special by taking them to New York. It wasn't his fault Pete would rather stay here and meet all the people his grandmother knew. Nor was it Pete's. Still, Reynold's feelings had been hurt.

Calling on extra willpower, Jillian decided to put what had happened with Brad out of her mind and not think about the incident again. Nor would she allow herself to be alone with him again—for any reason.

She had already proved herself far too weak for that.

"Seasickness," Brad announced after examining Pete thoroughly. Turning away from the bed, he dropped the stethoscope back into the side pocket of the medical bag he normally kept locked inside his Blazer. He had already put away everything else he had just used. "Looks like the son doesn't take to the water quite as adeptly as his mother."

"Seasickness?" Jillian wrung her hands like she always did when worried about things she thought she should worry about. "Are you sure that's all it is? This is the second time Pete has had stomach trouble in less than three days. Are you sure he hasn't picked up some sort of virus?"

While listening to his mother, Pete rolled over onto his side and moaned while wondering if death would prove quick and merciful, or be slow and long-suffering.

"Brad, you know as well as I do that there are always viruses going around."

"I thought about that," Brad assured her, "but I've checked him from head to toe and the only symptoms are the violent stomach and his unwillingness to focus long when I ask him to look at something."

Pete closed his eyes against another sharp stomach cramp, but immediately opened them again. For some reason, it was worse with his eyes shut. With them shut, he felt almost like he was still out on that stupid fishing boat, anchored in one spot while constantly rocking up and down. Up and down.

His stomach retched at the mere memory and he leaned way over so this time he would hit the basin Miss Hattie had brought him. Geez, how did anyone survive being out on the ocean for days at a time? How had Brad survived it back when he used to work on the fishing boats in the summer?

As soon as Pete eased back down onto his pillow, he looked at his mother pleadingly. He wanted her to wipe his face again with that nice, cold, wet rag in her hand. At least once more before he passed on. Although normally he ran like the dickens whenever he saw his mother armed with a face cloth of any kind, this afternoon, it felt so good to have his cheeks, neck, and forehead bathed.

"A-am I going to die?" he managed, but in a voice so

weak he barely heard it himself. And if he did die, would they let Troy come to the funeral?

Both Brad and his mother chuckled at his question. Odd, how they both considered death such a funny subject.

"No, Pete, you aren't going to die," his mom assured him. The bed squeaked under her weight as she sat back down beside him where she had been until Brad returned from getting his medical bag. "And as soon as that medicine Brad gave you does what it's supposed to do, the cramping should stop and you'll feel a lot better."

"That is if you'll keep it down long enough to have any effect," Brad cautioned, kneeling. He glanced briefly at the contents of the bowl and didn't even grimace at what he saw. How'd he do that?

"But if you keep tossing out your medicine like that, I'll have to give you a suppository instead."

"What's that?"

Brad's eyes glimmered from the light coming in from the windows across the room as he looked at him from just a couple of feet away. Still kneeling, Brad's chin was level with the top of the bed. "Believe me, you don't want to find out. So for now, we'll try it by mouth again, okay?"

Pete sat up long enough to swallow another tiny gray pill. The water Brad handed him felt good swishing in his mouth, but lousy once it slid down into his stomach.

"Keep in mind, these pills are to stop the severe cramping you have and relax your stomach. I only have a few with me," Brad warned as he put away the packet again. "I don't generally keep a large supply of medicine in here. Just what I consider basic."

Pete nodded his understanding. "I'll try to keep it down."

His mother leaned over to wet his face again with that cloth. "You would probably have a better chance of doing just that if we all left the room and let you try to get some rest. Brad said the medicine will also make you sleepy, which is good."

Hearing the word *all* reminded him that Mr. Johnstone was

in the room, too, standing near the door, scowling. Clearly, he wasn't pleased to have had his fishing trip cut short, especially in this manner.

Geez, it wasn't as if he'd gotten sick on purpose, or that he was deliberately faking it.

Well, at least not *this* time.

"Will you come back and check on me?" Pete asked, turning his attention back to his mom. He would sure want them to know if for some reason they were wrong and he did die.

"Of course." She trailed her finger down the curve of his cheek, making him want to close his eyes. "I'll check in on you every fifteen minutes or so to make sure everything is okay."

"Thanks. I'll try to go on to sleep now."

With that promise, everyone walked out of the room, leaving the door blocked open with a chair, like they had last Sunday. He waited until he heard them walking quietly down the stairs as a group before rolling over on his back and closing his eyes briefly.

It didn't take long to figure out that forcing himself to fall asleep was *not* going to work. Not when he could not keep his eyes closed for more than a few seconds at a time before the bed started to pitch and roll beneath him just like the deck of that boat.

"Good job."

Pete cut his gaze to the turret where Tony stood, leaning against the wall. How'd he do that when, if he wanted, he could walk right through that wall? "It's not what you're thinking. I really am sick this time." Man, was he.

"Oh, I know that. I can tell just by looking at you. You look about as green as grass around the gills. But you have to admit the timing couldn't be better. You losing your lunch all over Reynold's shoes the way you did made everyone eager to come back early, even him, and it proved the perfect way to get your mom and Brad in the same room again. Ever since that cellar prank, your mother has avoided Brad like he's suddenly carrying some tropical disease."

He moved closer to the bed. "Not only that, but tomorrow no one is going to demand you go on that boat again. And with any luck, you should be able to convince the others to go on but talk your mother into staying here with you. I already know Brad has no important plans for tomorrow, so sticking around here to keep an eye on you will be logical for him. And after what you did to Reynold's shoes, I'd think it's a safe bet you'll not be invited to go fishing again this entire trip."

Pete laughed, but then groaned at how unsettled that made his stomach feel. "He didn't look too pleased to have his shoes plastered, did he?"

"No more pleased than he was last night when that cup of coffee poured over into his lap *accidentally*."

Pete continued to grin, but avoided laughing again. "Yeah, too bad Mom followed him up to be sure he put those pants in water. Then get the stain rubbed out as soon as he got them off. The way the Nelsons were making goo-eyes at each other, it was pretty sure they weren't sticking around much longer. That would have left just her, me, and Brad watching the ballgame."

"Until you suddenly felt the need to go to the bathroom and never come back."

Pete sighed. "Oh, well, it was worth a try. I just wish the coffee hadn't been so cold." He grimaced when he felt another sharp twinge in his stomach. "Oh, man, I sure hope this bellyache is worth the good thing that might come of it."

"Still hurts that much? I guess I'd better leave you alone for now. Besides, with everyone having returned early, and on the day Hattie makes her weekly trip into the village for several hours, she and Cora suddenly have their hands full trying to have supper ready a few hours sooner than originally planned. I like to help out at times like that."

"But I thought they didn't know about you." Especially Cora. Pete had talked to Cora and knew she'd jump right out of her skin if she suddenly discovered that Beaulah Favish and some boy named Aaron Butler had been right all these years. There really were ghosts at the Seascape Inn.

"They don't have to know about me for me to slip around and help get things done. Each just assumes the other did the work. Truth is, it's kinda fun seeing how much I can get away with before anyone starts asking questions." He winked, then slowly sank through the floor.

Tony now gone, Pete tried closing his eyes again. This time, to his amazement, the bed stayed still and sleep came quickly.

With Reynold still downstairs swapping business war stories with David, Jillian stood just outside the open door while she listened to Brad read to Pete from the book about the history of baseball he had found on the tidy bookshelves out in the alcove. Since the small rollaway wasn't sturdy enough for both of them, having been broken once before, and it was nearly time for her to appear for bed, too, they had moved to the alcove and sat side by side on one of the blue-cushioned window seats.

"Look at those baggy uniforms." Pete laughed, pointing to a photograph on the lower half of the page. Although Pete had already put on his pajamas, he still wore his favorite baseball cap. Backward, of course—like Brad's. "You could fit at least three of those guys inside one pair of those britches."

Brad nodded his agreement as he read the caption below.

Pete listened attentively.

What a heart-tugging picture they made. Father and son. Reading at bedtime. Not a care in the world.

Jillian combatted a sudden rush of tears. She did not want her vision impaired while she watched and listened to the natural camaraderie between the two.

"You mean they really had baseball back in the 1800s? Wasn't that even back before you or Mom were born?"

Brad chuckled, glancing at Pete with such humor glittering in his blue eyes and such true adoration that Jillian had a very real urge to rush inside and blurt out the truth. A truth that so rightfully needed to be told, yet she didn't dare be the one to tell it. Not after all the time she had allowed to pass.

Even though in her heart she now believed Brad would not reject the idea, and in fact might now welcome being told that he was Pete's father, he would still be impossibly angry with her for having kept such a pivotal secret. Angrier now than had she told him when he first arrived.

Her heart sank like a lead weight. If only she'd had the courage to tell Brad the truth that first day. If she had, everything might already be resolved and she would not be standing there, wishing he had somehow figured it out on his own. Had he asked the right questions about Pete, she would have had to tell him everything. The decision would have been taken out of her hands, as would the consequences.

But for reasons she could not fathom, Brad still hadn't a clue that he was Pete's father. And he so deserved to know.

Clasping her hands, she wished now she had pooled the courage to do what was right from the beginning. But how could she have known?

While the temptation to walk inside and announce everything to both of them continued to burn inside her with blistering heat, the courage needed to do so remained lacking. She had waited too long. They would both hate her for keeping secret something they had both had every right to know from the start. They would hate her even though at the time she thought she was doing the right thing for everyone involved. By keeping her secret, she had hoped to save Brad the guilt of rejecting his own son, and Pete the anguish of suffering that rejection.

It had all seemed so simple then. And so complicated now.

The hard, throbbing ache that nagged at her increased to unbearable proportions when she watched Brad shove Pete's cap forward over his blue eyes in playful admonition over some outrageous comment. How could she have been so wrong about a situation? Brad and Pete were great together.

"Mom?" Pete's voice broke Jillian's anguished thoughts shortly after he had pushed the cap back and noticed her outside the door. "What are you doing standing out there in the hall all alone?"

Brad looked up, questioningly, while she then entered the room but he didn't say anything. Even his expression revealed nothing.

"I was waiting." She did her best to keep the strangled emotion out of her voice. "I wanted to give you two a chance to find a stopping place in your reading." She pointed to the clock. "It's about time for bed."

Pete studied her a moment, then glanced again at the book he and Brad held balanced precariously on his right pajama leg. "But I'm not all that sleepy after that big nap I took this afternoon. And this is a great book." He pointed to one of the pictures. "Come look at it."

Feeling a little overwhelmed by Brad's presence in their bedroom but knowing Pete was the one who had invited him there, Jillian sauntered over and sank gratefully on the window seat, left of her son. She tried not to look across at Brad, who sat on the right of him, while Pete pointed to an unsmiling man in a sagging uniform, holding an odd-looking sports cap over his chest.

After several minutes of glancing through the glossy pages of the book, she reminded Pete again of the time. She expected yet another argument but he surprised her by popping up off the seat and heading immediately for the still-open door, the book tucked carefully under his arm. "I'll be right back. I have to brush my teeth and all that."

He paused just long enough to kick aside the chair they had used to keep the doorway open most of the day to allow a breeze through the room, then judiciously pulled the door closed behind him.

With Pete suddenly gone, Brad now sat only about a foot away from Jillian with nothing between them but the alluring scent of his men's cologne. Her already rapid heart rate did double time when she remembered the last time she had breathed his cologne that close. It had been down in the cellar. Just before—

"Looks like he's fully recovered from this afternoon," Brad said, first to break the awkward silence that followed Pete's departure. "But, even so, I don't think it's a good idea for him to go out on the boat again tomorrow. He can stay here with me if you would like. I have absolutely no problem with that."

Jillian sucked a quick, unsteady breath. It hadn't dawned on her that by having agreed to stay behind with Pete the following day, she had the same as agreed to stay behind with Brad, too.

The tiny hairs across the back of her neck prickled at the mere thought, but she couldn't decide whether the odd sensation was from guilt, fear, or excitement. Or perhaps a combination of all three. "Thank you, but with Pete well again, there's no reason for you to have to stick around here tomorrow, too. It's bad enough you had to give up your plans for today. I know you and Vic Sampson had planned to sneak off and do a little pier fishing as soon as he finished with his mail route. Besides, I've already explained to the others that I plan to stay behind with Pete. They're going out tomorrow without us."

"Oh?" Brad arched an eyebrow, looking far more interested in that fact than he should. "Then we're going to be here alone tomorrow?"

Jillian tried to swallow, but her throat refused to cooperate. Fortunately, that didn't affect her ability to talk. "No, not exactly alone. Pete will be here. So will Miss Hattie."

"No, Miss Hattie will be gone most of the day. It was while she was still at the cemetery putting the flowers on those graves she always puts flowers on that she noticed your boat returning to the wharf early. Worried something serious was wrong, she came straight back here to find out what the trouble might be. That meant she never finished her usual Tuesday errands, nor did she have her weekly visit with Miss Millie. She plans to finish everything tomorrow."

"That still leaves Pete," Jillian pointed out, wondering why suddenly the room felt as if it had no air when all the windows but two were open wide. Enough night breeze drifted through to ruffle the dark hair curling out from under Brad's backward cap. So why couldn't she breathe?

Brad studied her a moment longer, his blue eyes glittering with untold thoughts, until eventually he nodded. "You're right. That still leaves Pete. He'll keep you safe."

"Safe?" She blinked at the unexpected comment then lifted her hand to play idly with the gold pendant at her throat. "What do you mean 'safe'?"

"From me. Isn't that what you are thinking? That Pete being here tomorrow might be all that keeps you safe from me?" He slowly dampened the inner rim of his lips with a maddeningly sensual swipe of his tongue, as if purposely luring her attention to his mouth. "There's no reason to be that afraid of me, you know."

"Afraid? Me? Of you?" She dropped her hand to her lap and forced a sickly smile. "I don't know what you're talking about."

"Yes, you do." He slid closer, taking in much of the small gap Pete had left.

Her pulses rushed madly. Only inches separated them now and already she wished his arms were around her. How could she be so weak?

Brad's pale blue eyes bore deeply into hers while he scooted closer still. "What happened in the cellar yesterday afternoon has left you afraid to be alone with me. You're afraid of what might occur if something like that happened again. You're afraid that the feelings we still have for each other will get the best of us, only next time there might be no interruption."

"Don't be absurd." Unable to look at him while discussing something so intimate, she dropped her gaze to the small, round braided rug in the middle of the turret floor. "What happened between us in the cellar was some sort of weird fluke. Nothing more. It just so happens that I got over whatever I felt for you a long time ago."

"I think you're wrong." Moving closer *still*, his thigh

touched hers and sent out an electric shock wave so strong it caused her to gasp aloud.

Unable to cope with such a sharp, volatile reaction, Jillian willed her body to move away from his, but no part of her responded. She budged not an inch.

What was happening to her? Why did she sit there like a lame duck when she should be halfway across the room by now?

"Brad, you're wrong," she told him, though it was hard to be all that convincing when she could not drag her gaze off that blasted blue and gray rug on the floor. She should look him in the eye and be firm. "I'm over you and have been for quite some time."

"I thought the same thing about you." He settled his hand beneath her chin, gently lifting it with his fingers, forcing her to face him while she breathlessly awaited the rest of what he had to say. "That is, I thought so until last Thursday when I saw you again. After that, my doubts surfaced immediately. Then yesterday, when we kissed and I nearly melted into the floor, I knew right then I had never really gotten over you— and never would."

His eyes darkened with such familiar passion when his gaze dipped to her mouth, it sent Jillian's heart rate racing well beyond the comfort zone. She had to stop this. And stop it now. Before Pete returned and caught them sitting only inches apart, gazing longingly at each other. *Or worse.* What if Brad kissed her and, again, she could not find enough resolve to pull away? What would Pete think then? What would *Brad* think?

"Brad, you seem to have forgotten something extremely important." By then, Brad's mouth hovered so electrically close to hers, his minty breath caressed her lips with warmth. "I'm engaged to Reynold."

It was like someone threw ice water in Brad's face; his head snapped back that quick.

"Thanks for reminding me," he replied, already on his feet. The muscles in his arms flexed rhythmically. "I'd never forgive myself if I were in some way responsible for breaking up the social couple of the century.''

He aimed straight for the door, but paused and turned to blast a few last words at her before opening it. ''I hope for your sake you really are in love with that jerk. But after what happened between us yesterday, I have serious doubts that you are.'' His eyes turned black with emotion. ''Tell me, do you respond with that same degree of abandon when Reynold touches you in the places I touched you?''

What a hurtful question. ''Reynold has never touched me in those places. Our relationship is not like that. He's too much of a gentleman, and I respect him for that. It's one reason I'm so willing to marry him.''

Brad looked surprised to hear that, but still very angry. ''Respect is not the same as love. I think you need to do some deep soul searching during the next few days because before I leave here, I have the horrible feeling I'm going to tell you exactly how I feel about you.''

Before Jillian could comprehend what he might have meant by that, much less offer an intelligent response, he had jerked the door open, slammed it shut, and was gone.

Chapter 15 ❧

After suffering through yet another restless night in a place that was supposed to be known for peaceful sleep, Jillian awoke early Wednesday with a pulsating headache. But a hot breakfast without Brad's stifling presence and two Tylenol broke the pain in time to get ready for a day with her son.

Since Pete had not yet seen the inside of the little non-working lighthouse nearby, and was extremely eager to do so, she stuffed just enough money in her shorts pocket to buy soft drinks should they end up in the village afterward, then headed back downstairs to find out if her son was ready to leave.

To her dismay, Pete was outside sitting on the front steps with Brad, who had reappeared since missing breakfast, watching while Candy the cock-eyed cat tried futilely to capture a lively yellow butterfly.

The task would have been hard enough for a normal cat, but for an animal that had to see two of everything, batting down the flittering insect proved next to impossible. Both Brad and Pete chuckled as the black cat did her level best but never came within inches of the fluttering butterfly.

Listening to the mingled laughter through the screen door and knowing how quickly it would come to an end the moment she stepped outside, Jillian's heart sank. She couldn't help but recall Brad's last words to her. He was very close to telling her exactly what he thought of her. She just hoped he would not decide to tell her off in Pete's presence. She did not want Pete in a position where he might think it his duty to take sides against the very man he would one day be told was his father.

"Come on, Pete. Let's get a move on." She drew in a deep breath and held it several seconds while waiting to see what Brad's expression would be when he turned to face her. After last night, she expected to see nothing short of pure hatred. Even though she still wasn't entirely sure what had enflamed him so quickly, he had been nothing short of furious with her.

Responding to her voice, they both twisted around at the same time. Pete still smiled over the cat's antics, but Brad's expression leveled to reveal no emotion at all. Good or bad.

"Mom, would it be all right if I ask Brad to go along with us?"

Jillian's heart clenched, mid-beat, then resumed at twice the already accelerated rate. That was exactly the question she had hoped would not come out of her son's mouth. She sought frantically to come up with an answer that would not enrage Brad further and still let him know she needed to be away from him; but nothing came out of her mouth.

Pete seemed oblivious to her panic. "What about it, Brad? You want to go with me and Mom to the lighthouse? You could point out some of those islands you've been telling me about. The ones with all the lazy animals who do nothing all day but lie in the sun."

Brad returned his attention to the cat, which had given up on the butterfly and now batted at her own tail. Although Jillian could no longer see his face, his strong shoulder muscles remained taut.

"I'm sorry, Pete, but I can't. I promised Dr. Mack I'd call the hospital where we both practice so I can check in on some of my patients this morning. A couple of them have said they'd like a chance to talk to me about a few details concerning their medical care. It's the least I can do, considering he was so nice about agreeing to cover for me an extra week.''

Extra week? Jillian's legs felt suddenly hollow as she took a few steps sideways and gripped the gray banister with one hand. Nobody had told her Brad planned to stay an extra week. She thought he planned to leave tomorrow, which meant if she hadn't found a chance to tell him about Pete before then, she would not have to until she was a lot more prepared. ''What's this about staying an extra week?''

Pete shoved to his feet, excitement brimming in his big blue eyes as he tugged the legs of his red shorts back down. Brad glanced at him questioningly, as if he also wondered why Pete had kept that one little fact a secret.

''Didn't I tell you, Mom? Brad called that doctor friend of his to see if he would work in his place another few days so Brad can come to my birthday party Saturday. And his doctor friend was so nice he offered to let him stay a whole 'nother week. He said he more than owed it to him. Didn't I tell you that?''

''No, you didn't tell me.'' How oddly calm she sounded for someone whose world had just taken another wild, unexpected turn. ''When was this decided?'' She gripped the banister harder. Brad was supposed to leave. Even if she told him, he was supposed to leave tomorrow.

''Monday afternoon, right after Jimmy accidentally reminded everyone about the party. I went upstairs to tell you all about it, but you were in the bathroom washing your hair and, I guess after telling everyone else, I forgot I hadn't told you.''

Brad had also stood, facing her and dwarfing Pete even though he was one step lower than the boy. He tucked his hands into the back pockets of his jeans as if lacking anything else to do with him. The gap in his half-buttoned shirt widened. ''You don't have a problem with that, do you?''

Only in that you're bound to find out Pete's real age at Saturday's party and will realize the truth immediately. Her stomach coiled into a hard, painful knot.

"No, of course I have no problem with that." And maybe she didn't. Truth was, his being there could turn out to be for the best. When Brad saw Pete's age emblazoned across the huge chocolate cake Miss Hattie planned to bake, it would finally force the issue into the open. But would that be best for Pete?

"Good, because I've been looking forward to being there. A lot of our old friends will be there."

Still too stunned to think through the best way to handle this situation, Jillian held her hand out to her son, pleased it did not tremble. "Tell Brad good-bye, and let's go see that lighthouse."

Several hours passed before Jillian concluded the inevitable. If Brad stayed, she would have to tell him about Pete before the party. Though dreading that more than she had dreaded anything in years, it was the fairest thing to do. No more chickening out. Brad would have a hard enough time accepting the truth, but to have the knowledge forced on him while in a room filled with old friends would be unforgivable.

She needed to find an opportunity to tell him about Pete well before the party Saturday afternoon. Then together they could inform Pete about Brad. But first, she had better find a way to tell Reynold. Brad wasn't the only one who was going to have a hard time accepting the graveness of her mistakes.

Not ready to confront the issue just yet, with Reynold still having to be told first, Jillian did her best to avoid running into Brad that day until it was time for supper. Except for one incident in which they had both entered the mudroom at the same time and muttered a brief hello before passing through, she was remarkably successful all day. But supper was the one occasion she could not avoid his company. Not entirely. Not when he sat directly across the table from her.

Even so, there was was no law that said she actually had to look at him or talk to him. Nor did she want to—not knowing the conflict that lay ahead for them. If Brad thought he was disgusted with her *now*, wait until he discovered the horrible lie she had kept all these years. She cringed to know she was indeed guilty of lying to Brad. Lies by omission were still lies, no matter how she tried to justify them. The very fact that she'd misled him by not correcting Pete's age when the opportunity first arose was the same as having purposely lied to him.

"So what do you want to do with all those fish you caught?" Miss Hattie asked David, who had caught almost all the fish brought back that day.

With Jillian's woeful thoughts effectively shattered by Miss Hattie's fresh attempt at conversation, she glanced at David, who was still very excited over his catch.

"I don't know." He sat forward, eyes rounded. Clearly, he had not thought about doing anything with the fish.

"Well, we can't leave them in the sink forever." Miss Hattie pulled her napkin off her lap to dab lightly at the corner of her mouth where just a trace of butter sauce had landed, then returned the napkin to her lap. "For one thing, I'll run out of ice."

Pete looked up from what was left of his lobster, fork still in hand. "I have an idea. What about we have a fish fry tomorrow night? We could have hush puppies and coleslaw and everything."

Miss Hattie blinked, then looked again at David. "What about that? Would you like to have a good, old-fashioned Southern-style fish fry with those fish? Cora and I will clean them and fry them, if you six will eat them."

It didn't take long for everyone at the table to vote in favor of fried fish, after which David regaled the group with yet a third round of stories about how he caught them. Clearly, he had never experienced such success at fishing before.

"I want to go back out tomorrow."

Shelly wrinkled her pretty, sun-pinkened nose and looked at him pitifully. "But we've already spent two days fishing."

"That doesn't matter. I enjoyed today. I want to go back out tomorrow and catch even more—before that cold front Bill was telling us about comes through late tomorrow night and makes the weather too cool for going out on the water to pleasure-fish.''

"Sounds good to me," Reynold put in, eager to back David in any decision he made. "We can go back to that same little cove tomorrow morning and use up the rest of that bait we bought." He nudged Jillian. "You'll come too, of course. That way Shelly won't have to be so bored."

Jillian looked at him, surprised he would suggest that. "But I can't go. You know being out on the boat makes Pete sick. We have little choice but to stay aground."

A muscle near the back of Reynold's jaw pumped spasmodically, alerting her to his anger. Evidently, something else was bothering him. Something more than the expected fact she would want to stay with Pete.

Was it possible Reynold had found out the truth about Brad? Had Reynold discovered that she and Brad had been more than just good friends all those years ago? Her shoulders tensed when she realized Bill Butler could have told him how close they had become, though she didn't think Bill would be the type to deliberately cause trouble. Still, he had been their skipper for the day.

"Jillian," Reynold spoke through a forced smile, his voice barely loud enough for her to hear how he grated out each syllable. "It's bad enough you didn't come with us today, and that you weren't with us Sunday, surely you aren't planning to stay behind tomorrow, too."

Thinking this neither the time nor the place to discuss such matters, she returned her attention to the lobster on her plate and pretended she hadn't heard him. "We certainly can't have Pete getting sick again, can we?"

As if the situation wasn't disturbing enough, Brad set his fork down and studied first Jillian then Reynold. No clue to his thoughts lay in the strong lines of his handsome face. "If Pete's a problem, he can stay with me tomorrow. I have no real plans, at least nothing that I can't change or that can't involve a boy, too. And I love having him around." He glanced at Pete and winked.

Reynold's rigid smile turned instantly genuine. "That is certainly very good of you, Doc. That would leave Jillian free to come with us on the boat tomorrow. Yes, that solves everything."

"But what if I don't care to go out on the boat tomorrow? What if I *prefer* to stay mainland with Pete?" Jillian asked, angry that Reynold thought he had the right to decide something like that for her.

"Yeah," Pete piped in, sitting forward so Reynold would see his freckled scowl—had he looked. "What if we've already planned to go seashell hunting for a little while tomorrow, then into the village to have two more of those strawberry sodas?"

David blinked, clearly uncomfortable with the quarrel he had so unwittingly started. "Hey, if it's going to cause problems, we don't have to go again. I just thought it would be fun to get out there one more time before the weather turns cooler. Shelly isn't going to want to come along if she can't at least get a little sun while we're out."

"And it will be fun," Reynold put in firmly, then smiled. "Jillian and I will discuss this later and come to a rational compromise. You can consider the fishing trip an absolute. We'll work this out to be what's best for everyone."

He certainly sounded confident in that.

"Yes, David," Jillian conceded, an equally insincere smile in place while her annoyance continued to shift around inside her. "One way or another, I'm sure you'll go fishing again tomorrow." Reynold would see to it. *But I won't be there because I'll be mainland with my son.*

Pete continued glaring at Reynold a moment longer, then sat back and yanked his napkin off his lap and flopped it into his plate. "May I be excused now? I've got some stuff I'd like to think about up in the attic."

Jillian figured it might lessen the tension a little if Pete did leave the table, although why he kept running off to the attic was beyond her. She had peeked in the other day and found little to interest a young boy. "Only if you are sure you don't want dessert. Miss Hattie has some of that peach cobbler left.''

''I'm sure I don't. I'm full.''

''Want some company?'' Brad asked, having tossed his napkin aside, too. He already reached for his plate, his silverware, and his half-empty glass.

''No, thanks. I like doing my thinking up there alone.''

''Well, I'll walk you as far as the kitchen sink. I believe I've had about as much as I can swallow for now, too.'' Having tossed out that double-edged comment, he pushed his chair back and stood. ''Miss Hattie, dinner was delicious as usual.'' The natural smile he offered their hostess fell into a grim line when his gaze shifted first to Jillian, then to Reynold. ''I'll be off outside getting some *fresh* air.''

Both angry and miserable, Jillian watched Brad and Pete walk out side by side—broad shoulders teamed with skinny ones, and both with folded baseball caps tucked in their belts. If it were not for the chance she might end up outside alone with Brad at a time she had not quite screwed up her courage to tell him what she needed to tell him, she might have pushed her chair back and gone with them.

Not about to put up with the silent treatment Reynold deigned to bestow upon her, and too worried about the all-too-serious predicament she still faced, Jillian opted to leave the others in the front room watching Miss Hattie's favorite comedy and take a short walk alone before bedtime. She hoped the fresh night air would help clear her thoughts enough to decide just how to handle the situation with Brad, who had never returned after supper and still didn't know she had held her ground and would spend the next day with Pete.

If Reynold wanted David to enjoy another day of fishing, they would have to go without her. Pete's health and happiness were far too important to her. If Reynold didn't understand that yet, then it was time he did. It was time everyone understood that. Pete wasn't just someone she felt accountable for, he was the love and joy of her life. He was the only person she could count on to be there for her no matter the circumstances, and she very well intended to be there for him.

Headed toward the cliffs, she didn't bother stopping for a flashlight or a lantern. The moon glowed brightly enough that night she wouldn't need either to make her way across the lawn.

All she needed was a sweater, which she had thought to grab, and a little thinking quiet. With Pete's birthday party less than three days away, she had to secure enough time alone to come up with what Pete would term a workable game plan, one that resulted in father finally knowing about son, but without a lot of hurt, rage, and retribution.

The first step remained obvious. Even though she was angry with him, it still made sense that Reynold, as her fiancé, be the first one she told about the true circumstances behind Pete's birth. But then, as childishly as he was still behaving over her decision to stay behind with Pete tomorrow, the opportunity to tell him anything so important would not be presenting itself anytime soon. Perhaps she could tell him tomorrow night, after he had had time to think through the unreasonable demands he had made of her since coming here, and after he had realized how unrealistic he had been to ask her to desert Pete for an entire day of what was supposed to be Pete's vacation, too.

After all, it was at Reynold's suggestion that Pete was there. Reynold had hoped for a chance to get to know the boy. Could she help it if Pete had turned out to be so unsuited to the rocking motion from being anchored out in the ocean?

Slipping her hands into the pleated pockets of her dark blue slacks where they would be snuggly warm, having had the foresight to change out of her maroon shorts just before dinner, Jillian headed for the cliffs. There was a bench just down the trail where she could sit far away from the house and look out over the ocean. And think.

Breathing deeply the invigorating blend of evergreens and the sea and feeling better already, she watched the ground to keep from stumbling in the dark on her way to her favorite oceanside bench. She did not realize Brad was anywhere around until she felt some force bring her to an abrupt stop.

"What the . . . ," she muttered, looking around for whatever had blocked her path. Her first thought was that it had to have been a protruding tree branch, but the nearest copse was several yards away.

While trying to figure out what had held her in place, she spotted Brad a short distance away. He stood, legs braced and arms crossed, at the very edge of the granite cliffs, his back to her. A light wind circling from the south that night molded his loose-fitting, soft cotton shirt against one side of his strong, lean body while the excess fluttered gently on the other side. His long, dark hair danced from under his backward baseball cap and caught the glimmering highlights from the not quite full moon.

Though it was not yet time to have that long talk with him, and although he had not yet noticed her, which meant she could easily walk away, she felt drawn to him—in more ways than one. Not only did her heart long to be at his side if for no other reason than to see that incredibly handsome face in the silvery moonlight, her arm felt as if someone had hold of it, tugging her by the elbow in Brad's direction. Odd, the tricks the psyche could play once the heart became involved.

Not questioning fate in this instance, Jillian stepped lightly across the large rocks until she was on the one just a little behind and to the side of him. She did not quite have the courage to step right to the edge of the cliff where Brad stood with the toes of his shoes jutting into thin air. The movement of the water so far below tended to make her a little more cautious of what could happen if a rock slipped than it obviously did Brad.

"Thanks for offering to stay with Pete tomorrow," she said loud enough to be heard over the rhythmic rush of the water against the shore below—her way of letting Brad know he was no longer alone.

Startled, Brad turned to face her, blinked twice, then stepped down onto the flat, oblong rock where she stood. "I didn't do it for you," he responded, but barely loud enough to be heard above the ocean. "I did it for Pete. I wanted him to know that someone cares about him."

Jillian tilted her head. Brad had meant to hurt her with that comment. "Pete knows how much I love him. He knew that even before I stood my ground and told Reynold again that I'd be staying behind tomorrow, keeping Pete company."

If her determination to stay with her son surprised Brad, he didn't let on. "Yes, well, I find it hard to believe that Reynold had the gall to expect you to go out with them instead." Brad moved farther from the ocean, onto a grassier area away from the rocks. There he had the needed room to pace around and wave his hands in frustration. He was always such an animated person when angry.

"I don't think he fully understands that my primary resposibilities must go to Pete," she admitted. "Having no children of his own, he hasn't yet grasped just how strong a commitment I have had to make to my son."

"The man doesn't understand that sort of thing because he can't see past his own needs," Brad replied. His mouth flattened with disgust. "And why you have yet to recognize that simple fact is beyond me."

Jillian followed him to the wide grassy knoll between the cliffs and the wooded walking trail, trying to decide how best to respond to that. Part of her felt it her duty to defend Reynold further, while another part of her agreed with Brad wholeheartedly. Reynold had acted very childishly about tomorrow. And he continued to act childishly. When she left the house for a walk, he had refused to as much as look at her.

"Brad, I did not come out here to rehash the same old argument with you."

His angry expression turned immediately questioning. He stopped pacing about to study her a moment. "Why did you come out here?"

"To think." Feeling uncomfortable to have his gaze probing hers, as if trying to analyze her deepest thought, she glanced south, facing the wind. She could just make out the lights on the gated cove further down the shoreline. "Believe it or not, I have been known to do that from time to time."

"Do what? Think?" He moved to stand beside her, though she didn't brave a glance in his direction to see if he, too, studied the distant cove, or whether he now studied her.

"Yes. It's a somewhat complicated process, but I manage it now and again."

He chuckled, relieving much of the tension between them. "And what is it you came all the way out here to think about? Or is that none of my business."

Oh, it's your business all right, she thought, but refused to acknowledge that aloud. She wasn't ready to get into any of that. Not yet. "Would it gratify you too terribly much if I admitted I came out here to think about how angry I am with Reynold?"

"I would think it certainly a step in the right direction. You should be angry with Reynold. That's why I'm out here. I'm furious with him. I hate it when his thoughtlessness hurts Pete like that."

Jillian breathed a little easier. At least Brad hadn't insinuated Reynold had hurt her boy on purpose. "Reynold still has a lot to learn about Pete. I really think the problem lies in the fact the man has never had children of his own, although through no fault of his own. It'll take him awhile to adjust to a child's special needs."

"He was married before?"

"Yes, four years ago he was married to a woman named Karen who refused to give him children. She was a very selfish woman who was so adamant that they not have a family, she eventually gave him an ultimatum. She told him either quit bothering her with the annoying prospect of having children or she would divorce him." Jillian braved a look at Brad and could tell he wasn't quite sure what he thought of her disclosure. "Reynold opted for the divorce. He said if she didn't love him enough to have his child, their marriage was doomed anyway."

Brad looked perplexed a moment, then sad. "Does he plan to have children with you?"

"Not right away." Jillian wondered why that prospect didn't cheer her like it usually did. "For now, Pete is enough. We'll probably have a child later, after Reynold has met his career goals and has the time he would need to give a second child."

She shifted her weight from one leg to the other at how uncomfortable she suddenly felt. The truth was, she and Reynold had discussed the matter only once, and she really couldn't remember what had been the outcome of that conversation. She supposed they had left it hanging. "The really sad thing about Karen and Reynold's divorce is that barely a year later, Karen married someone else, and due to some miscalculation on her part, she soon ended up pregnant with twins. Once she actually had children to care for, she changed her entire outlook on motherhood. The day I met her, she seemed very happy and very proud of her two toddlers."

"You don't suppose it's possible Reynold lied and it was really him who didn't want kids," Brad suggested, clearly still looking for the bad in Reynold.

Jillian frowned at such a ludicrous thought. "Of course not. Reynold loves kids. He has told me that many times. You should hear how bitter he sounds whenever he talks about his ex-wife and her children. I think it truly enrages him that she refused to give him children, yet now she has two adorable daughters. And rumor has it she is pregnant again."

"I think there was a lot more wrong in that marriage than he wants known."

"I'm sure that's true. No one is comfortable revealing to others *all* the painful details behind a failed relationship." Jillian braced the back of her lower lip against her teeth to keep it from trembling while her own pain raced to the forefront. "It can hurt immeasurably to discover that the one person you thought loved you more than life itself never really cared, and was in fact using you."

"You sound like you've had personal experience in that area." He sounded sympathetic.

She turned away again, afraid he would see the tears forming and know they were because of him. "I've had my share of heartache."

Brad reached out and touched her cheek from behind, making her long to lean back and seek further comfort in his arms. But pride prevented her from making such a fool of herself. She would not let him know how deeply his touch affected her. Besides, she was still committed to Reynold, and she was not one to turn her back on her commitments, no matter how much she wanted to.

"Is Pete's father the one who hurt you?"

Her shoulders tensed, then shook, in a combination of anguish and mirth. How could any man be so on target and at the same time be so completely without a clue? "Yes."

His arms came around her and held her close, forcing her at last to give into the desire to seek comfort from him. "I'm sorry someone had to hurt you like that."

It was just as ludicrous that he should apologize for himself and not know it, as it was for her to close her eyes and lean back against him, accepting his strength. Still, that is exactly what she did.

"Maybe you should have given the relationship more time before becoming so intimate."

"But then I wouldn't have Pete," she commented, stating the one obvious wonder of the whole situation.

"That's true. It would be hard to consider anything that resulted in Pete being a mistake."

She could almost hear his pained smile.

"Even though it hurts me to realize how quickly you fell in love with someone else after we'd parted, I can't say that the relationship was mistake. Not when it gave you Pete." His voice caught, then twisted. "I wish I had a boy like that. Sometimes I wish it so hard, I almost see myself in him. Which is ridiculous, I know, when he looks so amazingly like his mother."

A sharp pain tore through Jillian's heart so severely it caused her to clamp her eyes shut tight. She could not have been handed a more perfect opportunity to tell Brad, but she hadn't told Reynold yet. She also did not want to risk breaking this tender moment between them. She so loved having Brad's arms around her, his strong body warm and supportive against her back. So much like old times. So very much like old times.

But there was no getting around it, Brad needed to be told.

❧ *Chapter 16* ❧

Pete caught a slight movement at the outer edge of his vision and turned in time to see Tony coming toward him from the corner closest to the bookshelves. He had to have come right through the grandfather clock ticking on the other side.

"So did you manage to get them together?" Pete asked, thinking the words rather than speaking them aloud so the others in the front room would not hear him talking and decide he had gone nuts.

Tony nodded, his gaze on Miss Hattie rather than him. "They are out on the cliffs talking about you right now. Even though the truth hasn't been mentioned yet, I think this just could be the night. I may be wrong, but I think she's trying really hard to work the conversation around so she can tell him in a way he won't get too angry with her."

Not wanting anyone to think him loony for staring off at an empty corner of the room, Pete looked again at the television, but seeing there was now a commercial, he felt it okay to glance away again. Nobody was expected to watch commercials. "If that's so, what are you doing in the house? Get back out there and watch over them until they've finally had it out. We don't want anything interrupting them until everything has been said and he's decided to forgive her." His heart raced at the thought that before this night was over, Brad would know he was his father.

"I plan to. I just wanted to come give you a progress report and make sure Reynold wasn't on his way out to check on her. Just in case that crosses his mind, I've hidden his jacket again to slow him down." He swapped his gaze from Miss Hattie to Mr. Johnstone, who shifted uncomfortably on the sofa as Tony moved farther into the room, at just about the same time Mrs. Nelson stood and headed for the hall door.

Pete's eyes rounded when she passed right through Tony on her way to that little bathroom near the registration desk without missing a step. How come people could walk right through him and not feel a thing? He was tempted to get up and try it himself but decided to stay put.

This time, it was Tony who hesitated a moment, just long enough to glance back at Mrs. Nelson, then continued on out of the room, drifting right through the turret windows and back out into the night.

When Pete turned his attention back to the television program, he was so full of hope and excitement that he could hardly concentrate.

Jillian stood silently facing the cove, Brad's arms still around her. While enjoying his glorious warmth, she tried for what had to be the hundredth time to figure out the best way to word her confession. She did not want him hating her forever.

"Brad?" Her blood pounded with such painful force, she could hardly hear her own voice. The hour of reckoning had arrived.

"Hmm?" Clearly in the time she had been silent, his thoughts had wandered.

"There's something I must tell you about Pete's father that you are not going to like hearing." Drawing in a deep, steadying breath, she pulled away and turned to face him. He looked at her so puzzled, and at the same time so clearly afraid of what she had to say, she nearly backed out again.

"I'm not sure that it's any of my business." Moonlight

splashed through the trees, across his handsome face. His eyes glittered from some distant thought.

Jillian curled her hands into fists in an effort to keep her determination alive. In a very few minutes he would know all about her deceit, and would despise her for it. Still, the time had come. She just hoped he would stay and talk it out enough to understand why she had kept such a secret before confronting Pete with the news. "But it is your business. It's something I wish I had revealed to you a long time ago."

"Why? Because you feel guilty after having lied to me about what you felt for me back then?"

"Lied? I've never lied to you about how I felt." She tried to recall even one time she might have misled him and couldn't. "Why would you say something like that to me?" Evidently he was trying to push his own guilt off on her. But what purpose could that possibly serve? "I'm not the one who pretended to feel something that was never there. I told you I loved you, and *I* meant it."

Brad's eyes narrowed. "Are you saying you never once lied to me?"

The walls of Jillian's chest caved in around her, making it suddenly very difficult to breathe. *Well, no, not if you put it that way.* "Brad, what is this all about? What is it you think you have figured out?" Had it finally occurred to him how very much alike he and Pete were? Was she about three seconds too late in telling him the truth?

"Nothing," he snapped. "I just wanted you to know that you aren't the only one who knows what it feels like to have been used in the past."

What did his later love life have to do with her telling him something about Pete's father? "I never said I was."

"I just wanted you to know, I've got scars, too."

"Brad this is not a competition to decide who's been hurt the most. I have something I want to tell you. Something you should have been told ages ago."

"If it has anything to do with Pete's father, I'm not sure I am ready to hear it."

Jillian stared at him a long moment, trying to reason past this latest outburst of anger. "Are you saying you already know?"

"No, I'm saying I don't want to know. It just so happens I have enough on my plate right now without you piling on more. A man can only take so much."

Jillian arched an eyebrow while trying to figure this out. Brad has just said he didn't want to know whatever it was she had to tell him, but did he have any idea the importance of what it was he didn't want to know?

Becoming more confused, she shook her head in an attempt to clear her thoughts so she could start over.

Brad evidently sensed she intended to try again and backed away. "Jillian, I'm just not ready to hear it, okay? Let's end this conversation right now. I don't want to hurt anymore than I already do."

"Well, I guess you can't get much clearer than that," she said, feeling vastly relieved but at the same time annoyed to have had her attempt to tell him the truth so readily refused. "I'll keep my secrets to myself then."

She felt as if a great weight had been lifted. If he did suspect the truth, he was not going to force her to tell him, yet if he didn't suspect but later found out, she now had a perfect excuse for having continued to keep him in the dark. He had ordered her not to tell.

For the first time since Brad's arrival, Jillian knew she would have no problem falling asleep that night. Oddly, it was Pete who would prove the restless one before finally dropping off.

She had thought her vow to stay there with him the following day would have eased any aggravation Reynold's demand had caused, but obviously it hadn't. The moment she returned from her walk, Pete had come running out of the parlor all excited to see her, but after only seconds his mood had fallen again and for the rest of the night, he had moped around like he had lost his best friend, which in a way he had, having earlier found out that Troy would be moving again soon.

Knowing how that must be affecting her son, she waited until Pete had finally fallen to sleep before snuggling under her own covers and closing her eyes. How unusually relaxed she felt now that the responsibility of telling Brad had inadvertently been taken off her shoulders. It was now his own fault he didn't know.

Drifting peacefully toward a much needed night of blissful slumber, she was on the very edge of oblivion when a clatter followed by a deep guttural oath startled her alert again. Thinking the noises had to have come from Pete tossing and muttering in his sleep, something he occasionally did when he was as restless as he had been earlier, she sat up and glanced toward the rollaway, surprised to see Pete perfectly still. There was none of the twisting and turning that always accompanied Pete talking in his sleep.

She must have imagined the noises. They had sounded too close to have come from the outside.

Grumbling, she socked her pillow twice then laid back down but was not yet asleep again when awhile later she detected a voice a second time. This time it came as a deep, masculine whisper barely heard above the night breeze rustling through the heavy tree limbs outside her window.

It called her by name.

"Who said that?" she replied, also in a whisper but a little more strident than the one she had just heard. Sitting again, she swallowed back her reflexive fear and quickly searched the shadows for movement. "Who's in here?"

"This is your conscience speaking to you." The voice sounded a little louder this time, as if it now came from right beside her bed. But even so, it still was not much above an annoyed whisper. "You are supposed to be asleep by now."

"My conscience has a male voice?" She continued to search the shadows, trying to figure out where a grown man might have enough room to hide, while she leaned over the edge of the bed and picked up one of her shoes off the floor.

It wasn't much, but it could be used in defense should whoever it was plan to attack her or Pete. "I hardly think so."

There was a long pause. "Okay, then this is someone else's conscience speaking to you."

Whoever it was sounded irritated with her.

Heart pumping while she continued to scan the darkness, she tossed back the covers and swung her legs over the side of the bed closest to the door, ready to run for help if necessary. With toes now touching the cold floor and her shoulder toward the sound, she continued to grip her left shoe in a tight fist. "If you're someone else's conscience, then why is it *I* hear you?"

Again, there was a lapse. "Okay then, you're right, this is a bad dream. It has to be. What other explanation is there?" All attempt at a whisper was gone for the moment. "Just sit there and listen to your dream for a minute, will you?"

That confused her. She felt awake, but like the voice just said, what other explanation was there? She had to be asleep. This had to be one of those weird dreams where you think you are awake but really are not. "Rather testy for a bad dream, aren't you?"

"Isn't that what bad dreams are all about?" He was back to whispering calmly.

Okay, that part made sense. But nothing else did. "So what is it you want?" Using her empty hand, she pinched her other arm and felt decided pain. But she could have dreamed the pain. She had certainly dreamed panic before. Many times.

"What I want is to tell you that it's high time you get your act together." The voice had moved around to the end of the bed, near where her feet would have been were she not sitting off to one side. "You've put off telling Brad about Pete long enough."

Jillian scowled. Yes, only a *bad* dream would point that out to her. "But I did try to tell him. Just a few hours ago when we were outside alone. He told me he doesn't want to know."

"But still he's going to know," the voice pointed out with

loathsome accuracy. "Whether he wants to or not, he'll have no choice but to realize the connection the second he finds out how old Pete really is. Then what are you going to do?"

Jillian slumped back onto the bed, having given up trying to find the source of the voice. There was no one else in that room but Pete, who was still asleep. "You really are my conscience, aren't you?" She let the shoe fall back to the floor. It would do little good against her own psyche.

"If I'm not, I should be. Something has to convince you to do what you know is right. Time is running out. Check the clock. It is Thursday morning already. Pete's birthday party is in two days. Everyone will be aware of his actual age after that. The sooner you tell Brad, the better."

"But don't you think I should tell Reynold first?" She pulled the bed covers back over her, suddenly cold. "After all, he's my fiancé. He's the one who'll be taking care of Pete in the many years to come."

"Are you sure of that?"

Jillian blinked. Why would her own conscience doubt Reynold? Were Brad's suspicions starting to get to her again? Or was she doubting Reynold's love? Would he want to marry her once he'd learned her secret? Or maybe she was doubting herself. Did she really want to marry him? Would it even be fair to marry him, when Brad still stirred her heart so? Or did any of that even matter? Reynold rarely spoke of love. Did love really matter to him? Did she?

"Don't you launch in on Reynold, too. I've got enough to worry about with the situation involving Pete and Brad."

"Mom, who are you talking to?"

Pete's groggy voice startled Jillian into sitting up again. She had not meant to wake her son.

"Myself," she answered, thinking it the most honest answer, though in truth, she had never had a conversation quite like this with herself before. Wondering if Pete was really awake and talking to her, or if his voice was simply a part of the strange dream, she couldn't help but feel a little batty. "I'm just talking to myself, Pete."

"Why?"

Good question. "I've got a few problems I'm trying to resolve and I guess talking them out helps me. I'm sorry I woke you."

"That's okay." Being one to accept just about whatever he was told, Pete rolled over and went right back to sleep.

Jillian, too, laid back down but had not closed her eyes yet when she heard the voice again. This time the sound drifted from over near the door. Obviously, her restless conscience liked to wander about the shadows.

"Look to your heart and do what you know is right. You hold the futures of many people in your hands."

Oh, there's a comforting thought. She rolled over on her side and sighed. This was going to be another long night after all.

A loud knock on the door woke Jillian with a start. She rolled over to take a bleary look at the clock. "*Eight-thirty?*"

She'd overslept again.

Shoving to her feet, she glanced first at Pete's empty roll-away then at the mirror behind the vanity. Her hair was a mess, but she did not care enough about that to take the time to brush it. Having already spotted the door key still on the table, she figured it was probably just Pete having accidently locked himself out again.

Somebody needed to do something about that eccentric door lock.

"Coming."

Blinking several times to try to force herself more fully awake, she opened the door and was befuddled to see Reynold there. "You guys haven't gone yet?"

"No. David overslept and Shelly did not bother to wake him, so it'll be a few minutes yet before we leave. I just thought I'd come up here and give you one more chance to go with us. I really could use your help out there." Even though he could not actually see the carriage house from there, he glanced briefly in that general direction. "Shelly's bored stiff without you around."

Jillian did not really believe that true. Shelly liked being with her husband too much. "Then have her stay here. I've already explained why it is far more important for me to be here with Pete than be out on the boat with you guys. Being a mother does bring certain obligations with it."

"I tried convincing her to stay, but she doesn't want to spend an entire day without David." He sounded more annoyed with the situation than genuinely concerned. "She says she does too much of that back home."

"I can understand that." Still not fully awake, Jillian rested her shoulder against the side of the partially open door. "She loves him."

Reynold opened his mouth to respond to that comment but hesitated after looking again at her. One eyebrow arched while his gaze dipped to take in her full appearance. "Did you have a hard night?"

Remembering what she looked like, she grinned and ran a hand through her tousled hair. "Yes. I suppose I did."

"You look awful."

She chuckled her agreement. "Just think what I would have looked like if I'd had to get up even earlier to go off with you guys. Pete very well may have saved the world from a truly terrible fright."

He stroked his chin at that comment, obviously not seeing the humor intended. "This is not working out, is it?"

Jillian's smile dropped like sudden dead weight as her cheerful mood turned instantly cautious. "What's not working out?" Was he about to drop her, too?

Why did that thought not hurt as badly as it should?

"Having Peter here." He gestured he wanted to come in so she backed away and let him inside. Dressed in his usual pleated slacks and pullover, he glanced about the disheveled room, noticed an empty chair, and headed for it. "I thought it would be good to have him here with us, especially knowing how very much Shelly loves children, but Peter's being here is getting in the way.''

Confused, Jillian closed the door and followed him partway. Knowing how Reynold hated clutter, she absently started putting things in order. ''But it *is* good having Pete here with us.''

Reynold paused near the chair, but didn't actually sit. He turned to face Jillian instead, his expression grim. It occurred to her then that when he was not smiling and pouring on the charm, he really was not too appealing. Odd that she had never seen him quite this way before.

''It's not good when it keeps you from doing what's important.'' He narrowed his green eyes just enough to notice. ''I've been considering it a lot these past couple of nights, and I think we should ship Peter back home on Sunday. That would let him stay for his birthday but still leave us nearly a week up here without him getting in the way all the time. Since your father will probably be too busy, you can call Ruby with the time of his flight arrival and have her pick him up at the airport. She can take him back to your house and watch him there.''

Jillian couldn't believe what Reynold just suggested. Clearly, he had not thought the matter through. ''But Ruby has all next week off.''

''She *had* all next week off.'' He moved forward and rested his hands on Jillian's shoulders as if that might help her see matters his way. ''All you have to do is explain the importance of the situation to her. Explain that we need her to return to work early so she can take care of Peter for us. Offer her a nice bonus for being generous enough to give up part of her vacation.'' He started running the crook of his finger through some of the snarls in her hair, as if unable to look at them a moment longer. ''Ruby should like that. All employees like bonuses. Since she'll be getting a proper bonus for giving up part of her vacation, you could even suggest she use the bonus to spend part of her next vacation here. She used to live in Maine, didn't she?''

"Yes, and she envied us coming. But I still don't see why we need to send Pete back." She stepped away, not wanting the distraction from him working with her hair. "Except for when he's on a boat that is anchored in one spot, he's just fine. Truth is, he's enjoying it up here a lot more than either of us expected."

"But only because you are doting on him every minute." There was a bitterness in Reynold's tone that surprised her. "Besides, didn't Peter himself say he didn't want to come? Doesn't he have important baseball games to attend?"

"Yes, but—"

"I know." He interrupted any argument she planned with a fresh thought. "Maybe he could stay with that Troy friend of his. Then Ruby wouldn't have to return to work early, and you wouldn't have to offer that bonus." His green eyes glimmered, truly believing he had struck the perfect solution. "Don't you think Peter would like staying with his friend for several days? Didn't you say those people love to have Peter over?"

"Oh, Pete would enjoy it, I'm sure." Especially after having found out during that telephone call yesterday that Troy's family planned to move again before the end of summer. "But I wouldn't. I like having him here."

She especially wanted him there next week after Brad had finally realized the truth. It would give the two time to get to know each other as father and son instead of just a couple of good friends who had met by chance. Pete being there would also give *her* a logical reason to be around Brad during that week, so she could try to earn back his good favor, yet at the same time she could continue to help Reynold gain David's business. "I want him to stay."

Reynold met her gaze a long moment, then shrugged as if it hadn't been all that important anyway. Already he headed toward the door again. "At least think about it. Peter would probably be a lot happier back in Texas where he would have someone his age to play with."

Jillian crossed into Reynold's path to keep him from leaving just yet. The mood was not right to tell him her secret, knowing if he found out while that angry, he might march out and announce it to Brad himself, but the time had come to find out how Reynold really felt about Pete. "Tell me, are you really that concerned for Pete's happiness? Or are you more concerned for you own?"

When he stopped short in his tracks, looking truly hurt, she felt guilty for even asking. Still, all this about wanting to send Pete back home bothered her.

"I'm concerned for us both, Jillian. As long as Peter is up here getting in the way like he is, he can't be happy. Neither can I. It's turned out to be a no-win situation for both of us. And now that I realize I'm not going to be able to spend any time with him anyway, there is not really much point him being here at all. I never should have forced the issue. I should never have demanded he come."

"But you did, and now he is here enjoying himself. I don't want him to leave." Her protective instincts bubbled to the surface. "And I most especially don't want him traveling back home alone. If he's so badly in your way that you absolutely cannot put up with him, then I'll return with him. You can book two fares for Sunday."

"Don't get so upset. I was just making a suggestion. If you feel that strongly about it, the kid can stay. Maybe we can find something to do next week that won't involve boats. If the weather turns as cool as they say it will, it won't make a lot of sense to be out on the water after today anyway." He walked over and placed an arm that felt more possessive than comforting around her shoulders. "Don't talk about leaving. I need you here helping me."

With so many doubts already nagging at her, she decided to find out if Brad could be right about this guy. "Just as long as we've reached an understanding about Pete. He is very important to me. Just as important as our own children will be."

Reynold dropped his arm. "I do understand about Peter." With stiff movements, he headed toward the door. "More than you realize. Peter means the world to you."

Clearly, he had avoided the issue of having more children. Was that by design? "But what about our own children? Will you understand when they turn out to be just as important to me as Pete is." He did intend to have more children, didn't he? She had told him several times how important a large family was to her. She studied his stiff movements.

"Of course, I'll understand." He reached for the knob. "That is as it should be."

"Then you aren't opposed to having children?"

He opened the door then paused, holding it half open. "If I were opposed to having children, why would I have been so upset to find out Karen didn't want to have a family?" His grip tightened on the doorknob just before he looked away. "But if it turns out that one reason Karen and I never had children during the years we were married is because I am unable to produce them, I hope you'll understand and not hold such an inability against me."

Jillian stared at him, floored. Could that be the real reason he and Karen hadn't had any children? Was Reynold sterile and ashamed to tell her? Was he afraid she would think him any less a man? Slowly her anger gave way to concern. Was it possible the bitterness she had detected earlier in Reynold's voice had been aimed at himself rather than Pete? Could it be she was not the only one harboring a dark secret here? "If that turned out to be the case, we could adopt. There are lots of children out there in need of a home."

Reynold tensed, took a short breath, and continued out into the hall. "We'll talk about such matters later." He started to close the door behind him, but looked back at her one last time. "Are you absolutely sure you can't go with us? It would certainly mean a lot to me if you went."

Was that his way of asking if such a flaw made a difference in how she cared about him? "I'm sorry, but I can't. I have to stay here with Pete. I've already promised."

"But surely he would understand if you would rather be with adults."

Tired of arguing about something already decided, she crossed her arms and leveled her gaze at him. Sterile or not, she didn't like him nagging at her. "I'm staying right here with my son."

Angered by the acrid tone in her voice, he narrowed his eyes into a harsh glare, then clattered the door shut.

"We will discuss this more later," she heard him mutter just before he clamored down the stairs and out the front door.

You can bet on it, she thought, and headed for the vanity to gather her toothbrush and a washcloth. In fact, when Reynold returned later that day, they would have a good long discussion about *a lot* of things. By tomorrow, they would know exactly where they stood with each other.

✿ *Chapter 17* ✿

Jillian was not all that surprised when Reynold returned late Thursday in as much of a snit as he had been when he left. Even though she had had a quite enjoyable day, what with Brad at the lighthouse helping Jimmy and Hatch sand and paint the metal railings around the top walk most of the afternoon, Reynold had suffered nothing but setbacks from the onset.

After a late start from David having overslept, the three had hurried to the wharf only to discover that the boat set aside for their use had sprung a small leak during the night, which meant transferring all the food and gear they had already carried on to a larger, more cumbersome vessel.

Once out on the water, the engine of that second boat stalled, leaving them stranded for hours in an area too deep to use their shallow-type fishing equipment. They had ended up playing cards and frivolous party games most of the afternoon while Bill had someone jetty out with the parts he needed to repair the engine.

An hour later than expected, Shelly and David returned to Seascape Inn sun-pink and tired but in a very good mood, while Reynold trudged in ten minutes behind them, fit to be tied. To him, the day was a washout simply because it had not gone according to his plans. He was so irritated that he did not care to talk about it. All he wanted to do was go upstairs, bathe, and change for supper, which was being de-layed because Bill had radioed land how late they would be returning.

With no one around most of the day to cause Jillian prob-lems, she and Pete shared an opposite experience. They spent the morning collecting unusual seashells, then consumed most the afternoon having Jacky Landry at the Landing identify them. For lunch, Jillian and Pete had split one of Lucy's su-per-deluxe hamburgers with all the trimmings and an hefty order of french fries at the Blue Moon Cafe and drank it all down with a couple of creamy strawberry sodas.

Still feeling down to have learned his new best friend, Troy, would soon be moving to Vermont, where it looked like they would stay awhile, Jillian did what she could to make the day special for her son. As a result, she managed to avoid thinking about what loomed ahead for her during most of their time together. It was not until Brad returned from the lighthouse late that afternoon while she and Pete were sitting out in the main garden enjoying a moment of companionable quiet that the uneasy feeling of doom befell again.

With such an agonizing night ahead, Jillian's thoughts shifted to the most logical of the plans she had concocted, the one she had pieced together in those last long hours before dawn while still unable to sleep, the same plan she had avoided thinking about all day but now deemed deserved full consideration.

As soon after tonight's supper as possible, she would take Reynold off somewhere where they would be alone when she explained about Brad's relationship to Pete. Once he had fully grasped that Brad had been much more than a mere friend in years past, she would find out how that affected where they stood as a couple.

After Reynold's little outburst that morning, Jillian had no idea what his reaction would be, but did not think he could get too much angrier at her than he had been that morning.

A shiver washed over her at having witnessed a side of

Reynold she had never seen before. Not once in their several months of dating had he acted the least bit annoyed with her—or anyone else, for that matter. He had always been such a tolerant man. But even the most tolerant man had a breaking point.

That was why, however he took her news, whether calmly or irrationally, she wanted plenty of time afterward for a long, sensitive discussion about how much Brad being Pete's father would affect everyone. She and Reynold could then decide what they, as a couple, should do about it.

If Reynold thought it a reason to postpone their wedding, then so be it. She would postpone that however long he wanted or needed. After all, this problem was not of his making. He deserved the opportunity to decide just how he would let it affect him.

She just hoped Reynold would not take hearing about Brad's blood relationship to Pete as a hurtful reminder that he could not have kids of his own—*if* that was indeed the problem that came between him and Karen. He had not said for certain he was sterile, but after his comments that morning, she thought that might be the case. Maybe Reynold would prove more willing to discuss such matters tonight. So much needed to be brought out into the open and carefully examined. In the end, the exchange could prove very healthy for them. Airing their different concerns could carry their friendship to a new, higher level, one that would make the coming marriage stronger in the end.

Then, as soon as she had smoothed the waters with Reynold and reassured him she was not the type to let something like this affect her commitment to him, it would be time to tell Brad. Either that, or face another ugly round with her conscience that night.

Her heart thudded at the thought of how that second conversation might go. If only she had some idea how he would react and how long it might take to convince him she only thought to do what was best for everyone, then she could also plan how and when to tell Pete.

If the evening was not completely shot by the time she and Brad finally finished their discussion, she would give him the opportunity to be with her when she next told Pete. Or should she wait until the following morning to tell Pete—after he'd had a good night sleep?

That portion of the three-part plan could be decided after she saw what time it was by then. For now, it was enough to know she would be telling Reynold and Pete that night, before bedtime.

With Pete having already gone back inside to find out how much longer until supper, and with the wind having risen considerably in the past half hour, she, too, headed into the house to see if Miss Hattie and Cora needed any help.

Entering through the front, she passed the dining room doorway and nearly crumpled to her knees when she glanced inside. For a moment, she thought she saw her mother sitting at the dining table in her usual spot, smiling at her. Her hands rested around the plate in front of her and there was a silvery glow around her.

Jillian shook her head at the unexpected sight and it immediately disappeared, but not before having filled her heart with a painful longing. How she wished it had not been her mind playing tricks on her and her mother really could be there for her. Her mom would be able to tell her if she was indeed doing the right thing by divulging the secret after all these years. Her mother always knew about such things. In fact, she was the one who thought Brad should be told from the outset.

That certainly would have avoided a lot of problems.

Sighing heavily, and no longer feeling much like helping in the kitchen, Jillian strolled across the vacated room to the tall, guillotine-style windows along the south wall and gazed sadly out at the yard. It was the same yard where she and her mother had spent many a carefree summer afternoon, the same yard where her mother and father had enjoyed endless, stress-free hours in each other's company. It had been the perfect haven for the Westworth family, which was why they came nearly every year.

My, how the years could change things. After her mother's death, her father refused to return, afraid he could not cope with the memories, and Jillian had been gone even longer than that and for similar reasons, ones that concerned her feelings about Brad. But for what? She had stayed away nine long years only to find the results of her past mistakes still waiting for her upon her return.

Blinking back the tears, she glanced beyond the gardens with their colorful spring blossoms to the carriage house, splattered with what little afternoon sun still flickered through the distant trees. Such serenity, despite the brisk wind tugging at the tops of the tallest trees, a sign that the cold front Bill Butler had warned about was not far away.

It seemed appropriate somehow. Might as well have a wintry bleak storm beating down on her world as it slowly fell apart.

Jillian crossed her arms to cradle her aching heart. Seeing her mother's image had reminded her of how suddenly life could end, of how brief their time on this earth could be. There were only so many years a person had to be happy and loved, and she had already taken eight of those years away from Brad and Pete.

So why did she still have doubts about her plan to tell them what they had every right to know? Was it because of all the pain she knew it would inflict?

Perhaps what she needed was another woman to talk to about this. Since it obviously could not be her mother, maybe Shelly would listen to her and offer advice. All she really needed was for someone she trusted to assure her that she was indeed about to do the right thing, someone to offer her the courage she needed to follow through.

Yes, Jillian, you are. You are about to do what you should have done ages ago.

Jillian's eyes widened against the sharp pain her mother's voice had caused. An icy chill skipped across her shoulders as the tears she had been blinking back since imagining her mother at the table spilled down her cheeks. Although she knew her mother was not really there, for a brief moment it *felt* as if she stood right behind her, supporting her. And that was all that mattered to Jillian.

She now had the courage to do what was right. She would start as soon as they finished eating, as planned. By morning, everything would be out in the open, and their lives would be forever changed. But how long after that until Brad, Reynold, and Pete finally forgave her? She pressed her forehead against the cool glass. Probably never.

"Mom?"

Pete's voice startled her. She wiped at her tears with quick strokes of her fingers then turned around.

"Yes?"

As soon as she spoke, he took a tentative step into the room. Obviously, he sensed her misery. "Miss Hattie told me to go find everyone and tell them supper is finally ready. Brad already knows and said he would go tell the Nelsons. I'm supposed to tell you and Mr. Johnstone." Standing only a few feet away, he studied her with a deep notch just above those big, beautiful, dark-lashed eyes. "Were you crying?"

Jillian blinked several more times, then smiled, feeling suddenly very foolish. It was not at all like her to cry simply because she faced a lot of trouble, but then rarely did she face the sort of trouble that could change lives and hurt others.

"Yes, I was," she answered honestly. "For some reason, I thought about Grandma again, and realized how much I miss her. It made me sad."

"Me, too," Pete said then slid his little arms around her waist and hugged tight. "I've heard so much about her summers here and how happy she was that sometimes I think I see her, too. Once, out in the garden where all the chairs are, it felt like she saw me back. She smiled at me."

Again, tears filled Jillian's eyes. That exactly described what she had just experienced. How odd that it made them feel sad to be in a place that had made her so happy. "We have a right to miss her, you know. She was a wonderful, caring person.''

Sniffing loudly, and fearing she was about to start crying all over again, she gently pulled away from her son. ''Better go do as you were told so we can eat. I think Reynold is still upstairs in his room.''

Even though tramping upstairs to knock on Reynold's door was clearly not something Pete wanted to do, he headed dutifully toward the hall. He was such a good kid. How she dreaded turning his whole world into one big confused mess.

''Pete?''

Stopping just short of the doorway, he turned and looked at her quizzically and for a moment she saw a bit of her mother in his curious expression. ''Yeah?''

She swallowed, not really certain why she had called out to him. Perhaps she wanted apologize for what was about to happen, but that would be putting the cart before the horse. The apologies would come later. ''I love you.''

He blinked, then flattened an eyebrow, more puzzled now than ever. ''I love you too, Mom.''

''I just wanted you to know that. I love you and would never do anything intentional to hurt you.''

''I know that.'' He tilted his head, both eyebrows now flat. ''Mom, are you all right?''

''I will be.'' She chuckled at how bewildered he looked. Such a cutie. ''Now, go.''

Pete studied her a second longer, then shrugged and scampered out of the room. By the time he returned with Reynold, Miss Hattie and Cora had brought the food in and set most of it on the buffet against the west wall and the rest on the table.

A minute later, Brad, David, and Shelly entered through the French doors from the veranda. All three were laughing about an answer David had given in a game David, Shelly, and Reynold had played while stranded on the boat that afternoon.

The three paused with the door still open until Shelly finished telling her part of the story, then continued on inside. Although it was not quite dark enough yet to necessitate artificial lights, Jillian noticed Miss Hattie had already turned on the outdoor lighting. Probably because the storm was coming a lot sooner than planned. Little yellow lights twinkled in the wind-tossed gardens beyond.

"Sure smells good," Pete said, stopping to have a look at the golden mountains of food before heading for his chair. "I love fried fish."

"So do I," Brad chimed in as he, too, took his chair. He looked to be in a lot better mood than he had been the night before and he reached eagerly for his napkin.

But Reynold wasn't in a better mood. Reynold said nothing to anyone as he pulled out Jillian's chair and waited impatiently for her to sit.

Soon everyone was seated, the blessing had been asked, and the hot food brought to the table a platter at a time and passed around family-style. The condiments, already on the table, were picked up and passed around as needed, as were the rolls.

"Tartar sauce?" Miss Hattie asked, handing a small glass bowl to Brad, who in turn would pass it on to the Nelsons.

"No, thank you. I don't care much for tartar sauce. I would rather have plain old ketchup with my fried fish." He passed the white-filled bowl on to Shelly.

"See, Mom?" Pete piped in, having caught Brad's comment while shoving the fish he had just piled on his plate to one side, making room for everything else. "I'm not the only one."

Jillian glanced at Pete's bright smile. Clearly, he was pleased to learn that someone else would rather have ketchup than tartar sauce.

She wondered if tastebuds were hereditary.

"You hate tartar sauce, too?" Brad asked, already pouring a generous strip of bottled ketchup in the small space between his fish and french fries.

"Can't stand the stuff."

Pete wrinkled his freckled nose while Brad nodded complete understanding. "Well, it looks like we have yet something else in common."

Shelly smiled at Brad's comment. "You two are just like two peas in a pod. It's uncanny how much alike you are."

Brad looked at Pete curiously, then shook his head as if dismissing a thought.

"Yes, exactly like two peas in a pod." Miss Hattie put in, then looked at Jillian knowingly.

Although Miss Hattie would never be the one to reveal such an important secret, Jillian shifted uncomfortably as she accepted a large bowl of coleslaw from Reynold. She put a tiny serving on her plate. *By tomorrow, everyone at this table would know exactly how much Brad and Pete did have in common.*

Her insides buckled at the thought. Within an hour, she would already be explaining it to Reynold.

"Is that all the coleslaw you're gonna have?" Pete asked, clearly surprised. He pointed to the tiny mound on her plate with the skinny end of the half-empty ketchup bottle Brad had just handed him. "You usually pile half your plate with that stuff."

"I'm not very hungry tonight." *With good reason.* She glanced at the clock, again reminded of how soon the world would fall apart and tumble to her feet.

Pete cut her a puzzled expression. "Man, those strawberry sodas at the Blue Moon sure do stick with you forever. I was hungry again hours ago." If Pete suspected there was another reason she suffered such an overt loss of appetite, he didn't show it. Instead, he turned his attention back to Brad as he twisted the cap off the ketchup and set it aside. "So how come Hatch and Jimmy asked you to help them paint that lighthouse today? You're just a guest here. You're not supposed to be asked to work."

"We didn't paint the entire lighthouse, just the metal railings and window trim," he answered. He stopped spooning green tomato relish onto the last empty spot on his plate to watch Pete pour a long strip of ketchup beside his fish. He glanced briefly at the identical strip of ketchup on his own plate. "I suppose they asked if I wanted to help because I tend to spend so much time there. I do a lot of good thinking while standing up there, looking out over the ocean."

"Yes," Miss Hattie put in. "That's where he always goes whenever he needs to think. Same with Jimmy Goodson and Vic Sampson. Some folks say standing out there on that walk-around is soothing to the mind. Now, to me, it is a bit more spooky than soothing. I like to go up from time to time and look around, but from inside the main compartment where I have all that glass to protect me. I especially enjoy going up there in the fall after the trees all take on their brilliant colors, even though I readily admit I'm not all that fond of heights. Why sometimes I get a fluttery feeling just standing out on that widow's walk off the second floor." She glanced toward the ceiling.

"I don't know why," Pete said, stabbing a small piece of fish and drawing it through his ketchup as he, too, looked ceilingward. "You are as safe as a person can be here. Believe me, nothing bad is ever going to happen to you, not in this house anyway."

"I know the feeling," Shelly put in as she glanced about the room. "Even with those dark clouds rolling in outside and the wind stirring them around like that, I also feel so very safe and secure being in this house." She gestured toward the windows behind Miss Hattie just as a gust of wind ruffled the curtains. "It's so nice here, I can't remember ever having enjoyed a vacation spot as much as I have enjoyed this one. Believe me, David and I will be back. I also plan to tell all my friends about this little piece of heaven."

"Just don't send so many people here that I can never get a reservation," Brad commented, winking at Miss Hattie as he stood to go close two of the windows. "I don't know what I'd do if I couldn't spend at least a couple of weeks here every summer. I'd probably go nuts."

Jillian watched the muscles in his arm flex while he pulled

the lower window in place. It wasn't until he turned to go back to his chair that she noticed how dark it had gotten outside. Apprehension gnawed at her when she glanced again at the clock. Time passed that evening with amazing speed.

"According to that answer you think I should have given while we were playing Encore today, you *are* nuts," David put in, then laughed.

Jillian pushed her food around her plate with the tines of her fork while watching the camaraderie that flowed around her. Everyone laughed and talked and enjoyed each other's company, having become amazingly good friends in the few days they had been there. Everyone, that is, but her—and Reynold, who still had not said two words since he sat down.

She hoped that did not bode ill for the conversation to follow. He would have enough to be upset about without having started out in a foul mood.

Her stomach coiled tighter still. She could well imagine what Reynold's mood would be after being told about Brad. Black as the night sky that had fallen outside.

Maybe it would be better to wait until tomorrow, *after* he'd had a chance to get over the assortment of aggravations he had suffered that day.   But, no, she didn't have time for that. Tomorrow was Friday. Miss Hattie would start getting everything ready for the party, which meant Pete's birthday would be the main topic of discussion. His age could be mentioned to Brad at any point while making the cake or deciding on the flavor of punch. Jillian couldn't allow that.

She no longer wanted Brad to have to figure it out on his own, not after having already gone a week without doing so. No, he deserved to be told in an open, honest manner.

Rocking her fork handle between her fingers, she dared a quick glance at the subject of her tormented thoughts. He looked so happy and so unsuspecting while laughing at something Pete said that everything inside her body that could ache, did ache. How she hated knowing what lay ahead. Soon that deep, dimpled smile would find no room on that attractive face.

Already hurting more than a person should ever have to, she tried to stop imagining the talk that lay ahead but couldn't. So much hinged on whatever happened during those next few hours. What if Brad ended up hating her forever? She did not think she could stand it if he did. Even though there was no chance she could ever have a future with him, she did not want him to hate her. That would be more than she could live with.

As if feeling her gaze on him, Brad glanced up and notched his forehead. His deep blue eyes studied her questioningly, making the ache inside grow all the worse. Her heart rate accelerated to twice the normal speed in a futile effort to banish at least some of the anguish tugging at her.

He was such an incredibly handsome man. How she wished he had loved her as much as she loved him. Things would be so different now. The three of them would be so happy.

"Jilly, I know you said you weren't very hungry, but you have hardly eaten a thing," Miss Hattie commented, breaking Jillian's dismal thoughts. "Is there something wrong with your fish?"

Jillian pulled her gaze from Brad's. "No, the fish is fine." To prove it, she placed a small bite into her mouth and smiled as she chewed it. It may as well have been cardboard.

"At least you'll have plenty of room for dessert. After dessert, though, I'll be retiring early." She turned sparkling green eyes to Pete. "I have a birthday present to finish putting together."

Jillian's apprehension took another leap at Hattie's mention of a birthday present. She did not want Pete's birthday discussed in any way for fear Pete's age might yet be mentioned. But how did she keep them from talking about something so important to Pete without them questioning her motive?

"You're giving me another present? But, Miss Hattie, you already gave me the bestest present I could ever hope to have," Pete replied in earnest. "You gave me Grandma's doily. And you're making me a three-layer chocolate cake. You don't have to give me anything else."

"Oh, but I am putting together something special for you, something else that will remind you of her."

Pete's eyes lit up. Gone was any intention he may have had to convince her to keep her present. "Yeah? What?"

"I can't tell you." She wagged a lily-white finger in playful warning. "That would spoil the surprise."

"That's true, Pete," Jillian put in quickly. "I don't think we should discuss your birthday at all right now. Hearing too much about it will only spoil it for you later."

"No it won't. Besides, I want to know what she's going to give me that will remind me of Grandma."

Brad shrugged, then chuckled. "Of course you do, but that would take the fun out of it. You'll just have to wait."

Clearly outnumbered, Pete scowled and ran his hand through the most disheveled part of his hair when he cut his eyes to Brad. "Okay, I'll wait. But I won't like it."

Shelly studied Pete's sulky frown a minute, then studied Brad beside her. After a second she pursed her mouth into a thoughtful expression. "You know, I can't decide which of you two has the longest eyelashes. Or which has the bluest eyes. It really is amazing how very much alike you two look. Almost as if you were brothers. No, given the age difference, I suppose it would be more like you were father and son. Interesting."

Brad cut her a perplexed frown, then looked again at Pete.

In that next second, Jillian's heart screeched to a near-halt.

❧ *Chapter 18* ❧

Shelly's earlier comment had planted the first seeds of any real suspicion in Brad's mind, but that last comment had caused him serious thought. "Father and son?"

Pete stared at Shelly with eyes round as half-dollars, as if unable to believe anyone had said such a thing.

"You're right, Shel, those two do look a lot alike," David chimed in, reaching for his water glass. "I've thought that myself."

Everyone joined Brad in staring at Pete, who had yet to blink. Everyone except Jillian, who kept a fearful gaze locked on Brad.

For the longest time, the only sound came from the gusting wind outside, until Reynold finally broke the silence with his flat voice. "I don't see that the two look anything alike." He leaned forward far enough to get a better look at Pete seated on the far side of Jillian. "But, then, Peter doesn't really look like anyone I know, not even Jillian."

That comment stirred a whirlwind of controversy.

No longer able to concentrate on the animated discussion around him, Brad's gaze narrowed while he continued his own perusal of Pete's wide-eyed expression.

Reynold couldn't be more wrong. Pete definitely had his mother's eyes—not in color, but in shape and in their ability to display mischief. Pete also had her adorable, turned-up nose; and whenever he wrinkled it in disgust, he wrinkled it up high, exactly like Jillian wrinkled hers.

But, then, too, Pete did have long, thick eyelashes like his, and he had the same strong chin and the same-shaped forehead. Also, like Shelly pointed out, their eyes were the same shade of blue, and now that he paid closer attention, their hair held nearly the same blending of dark brown with a blond tint, whereas Jillian's hair had reddish tints.

His stomach tightened when he noticed Pete's hair also kicked up in the exact same places as his. It also parted just off-center like his. Why hadn't he noted any of that before? Obviously the others had. Shelly and David had both just commented on the odd coincidence. But was it coincidence? It had to be. How could Pete possibly be his son? Pete was almost two years too young. *Or was he?*

"Pete, how old will you be Saturday?"

Pete cut his still-rounded gaze first to the ceiling, then to his mother. "I-I'll be eight."

Eight? "You're seven years old?"

Pete nodded then looked again at his mother. "Why? How old did you think I was?"

Not seven years old, he thought, already doing the math. If Pete was born eight years ago this Saturday, that meant he was likely conceived in late July or early August of the second summer he and Jillian spent together. *Not long after they had become intimate.*

Stunned, he cut his gaze to Jillian for verification or denial and his heart sank like lead. Her guilty expression told him it was true. Pete was his son.

His son.

Brad had never felt such numbness, nor such confusion. He had fathered this child and Jillian had shown neither the decency nor the common courtesy to tell him about it.

Why all the secrecy? Why all the years of deceit? What had been the reasoning? Was she afraid, if he knew they shared a son, he might be able to force her to marry him?

Had she loathed the thought of marrying him so much she was willing to keep his own flesh from him?

That would explain her nervous behavior when she mentioned the word "marriage" during their last day together. Could it be he had miscalculated her reason for having asked him for his opinion about such things? Was it possible she hadn't hinted for them to get married after all? Could it be that what she had been about to tell him was how opposed she was to the idea rather than suggest they consider it?

He blew out a shaky breath when the next question struck him. Did he go through that entire song-and-dance about not wanting to be tied down for no reason? Had he gone out of his way to save her from something she was in no danger of wanting?

Obviously. Hadn't she later proved how little she cared about him by never contacting him again?

Not even to tell him about his son.

Angry, hurt, and unable to put together coherent answers to all the questions spinning inside his head, Brad shoved back from the table and rushed out of the house, out into the coming storm, leaving the French doors open behind him.

He glanced back only after he heard a crash behind him but did not break his stride.

Pete, clearly terrified by Brad's sudden burst of anger, had been in such a hurry to get to his feet and follow, he had knocked his chair sideways then stumbled over it. Poor kid had no idea what was happening. "Brad, wait for me."

Pete called out again from inside the house just seconds after Brad jumped off the veranda, but he was no longer emotionally equipped to answer the child.

Instead, with tears blinding him, he headed in a dead run toward the forest. He had to be alone.

"Brad, come back. Wait for me."

Frustrated, Pete stumbled a second time over the chair in his attempt to follow Brad outside.

Horrified by the rage she had witnessed in Brad's eyes, Jillian made a grab for Pete's shirt, but missed by mere inches as he scrambled to his feet a third time and headed immediately for the door.

"Pete, don't go out there."

Pete never looked back. Within seconds he, too, had disappeared through the open doors.

She stood to run after him, but Reynold snared her arm. With one hard jerk, he spun her around to face him as he stood to shout at her, "What the hell is going on here?"

"Reynold, let go of me. I have to go after Pete."

"Not until you've told me what exactly is going on here."

Jillian cut her gaze first to Shelly, who looked at her apologetically, then to Reynold, whose eyes were black with rage, and blurted the truth. "I'm not sure, but I think Brad just figured out he's Pete's father."

"*What?*" The word was spoken in unison from both Reynold and David, but neither Shelly or Miss Hattie looked surprised.

"I think Brad just figured out he's Pete's father," she repeated, tugging to free herself. "I have to go after them. I don't want Pete facing Brad's anger alone."

"He's Pete's father?" Reynold's hold on her arm tightened until it cause her to yelp with pain. "You and Brad were *lovers?*"

"Yes, it's a long, pathetic story." She twisted with all her might, freeing her arm at last. "And I'm sure Miss Hattie can fill you in on a lot of it. If not, we can talk about it when I get back."

Not giving Reynold a second chance to stop her, she flung herself immediately toward the French doors. A blustery wind coming through the one window that remained open had pushed them almost closed again, but when she neared them, they parted wide as if some invisible doorman had thrust one aside for her.

With the oddest sensation she was not alone, she paused at the edge of the light pouring from the veranda. Gut twisting, she searched the night-shadowed yard, eager for a glimpse of Brad and her son. But they were nowhere to be seen—not in the garden, or the drive, or the sloping field near the pond, or anywhere else where they would have still had light.

"Pete! Brad! Where are you?"

With no answer, she folded her arms against the sharp wind, and headed in the only direction that made sense.

"Jillian, you need your sweater," Shelly called out after her, but she didn't have time to go back after it. She had to find Pete and Brad before Brad had a chance to say something he would later regret. She hurried toward the point.

"Jillian, come back here!" That time Reynold called after her. "I demand to know how Brad can possibly be Pete's father. Why wasn't I told? Don't you think I had a right to know? Jillian! I said to come back here." He sounded more angry with her disobedience than her deceit. "Do so. *Now!*"

Even though Jillian could hardly view the ground in front of her, she broke into a run. She was too concerned over what Pete might face, and over what Brad surely felt, to care that Reynold was angry with her, too.

With her heart pumping hard and both lungs burning more with each blistering breath she took, Jillian paid no attention to the cold chattering of her teeth as she approached the lighthouse in a half-trot, having had to slow down after tripping over a piece of wood she hadn't seen along the shell-strewn path. Her right palm throbbed from having landed on it.

Coming up to the side, she swelled with hope. The lighthouse door was open. She must have guessed right. Brad had come there in his quest for solitude.

She slowed more, glancing up while she listened for voices above the wintry wind, but heard nothing but the sound of the ocean crashing harder than usual against the rocky shore below. A flare of orange in the shadows beyond drew her attention to Hatch standing outside near the picnic table, smoking his pipe while awaiting the storm. There was just enough light coming from the main part of the attached house for her to make out his shape as he waved her toward the tower.

Certain now she would indeed find both Brad and Pete

inside, she hurried through the open door. Except for a tiny light halfway up the circular stairs, it was creepy-dark inside the tower. Neither Brad nor Pete had bothered to turn on the overhead lights in the crown, and they certainly hadn't bothered to light the main lamp, which might not even be working now that Hatch was under orders no longer to use the lighthouse as a warning to boaters.

"Hello?" she called out as soon as she had made it halfway, her feet level with the night-light marking the spot. The hollow darkness above and the dampness from the night air forced her to take the metal steps a lot more slowly than she wanted. "Hello? Are you guys up there?"

With the wind howling forlornly through the open door and echoing up the curved walls in such a way it drowned her voice, she didn't call out again until she reached the top. "Hello?"

Brad stood at the windows facing the ocean, an unmoving silhouette against a churning black sky, but spun around at the sound of her voice.

"Why didn't you tell me?" He moved from the other side of the compartment, his words sharp with betrayal. Though she could not see his face, the wavering undertone indicated he had been crying.

A gentle nudge moved her in Brad's direction, as if someone else was there encouraging her closer, but she refused to take more than two steps. She did not want to be too close to Brad while he was in such an emotional state.

"I don't understand it, Jillian. Why didn't you tell me?" he repeated, angrier now because she had failed to answer.

"I had planned to." She trembled from more than the cold while trying to make out his expression. She hadn't meant to hurt him, hadn't meant for him to find out the way he did.

She blinked against a fresh onslaught of tears. He had gone a full week without figuring out the truth. Why couldn't that unenlightenment have lasted a couple more hours? "I know you aren't going to believe me, but I had planned to tell you later tonight."

"You are right about that. I don't believe you." Clearly disgusted, he turned away again, his body rigid.

Jillian wanted to go to him, touch him in some way, and beg his forgiveness, but his hatred stood like an iron wall between them. Still, she needed to hold someone. She hoped her son would prove not nearly as angry with her as Brad. She glanced around the shadows, but couldn't make out his shape. Not even when lightening skipped across the distance, offering a few flickering seconds of light inside. "Where's Pete?"

Brad spun to face her again. "What do you mean, where's Pete? Why are you asking me that?"

Her legs ached as a new danger wove into her heart. "Because he followed you out of the house. Isn't he here?"

Concern replaced the hurt in Brad's voice when he moved a step closer. "Didn't he go back inside?"

"No." Thunder rolled past with an ominous quake.

"Not even after it became apparent he couldn't keep up with me?"

"No." The room felt as if the last presence of hope had left.

"*Damn*, Jillian. I'd lost him long before I ever reached the woods. Why didn't you stop him?"

"Me? I couldn't stop him anymore than I could have stopped you."

"You could have tried." With no time for further accusations, Brad headed toward the stairs. "We have to find him before this weather gets any worse. Did he at least grab his jacket on the way out?"

"No, he went out the same door you did. His jacket is still on the coatrack near the front door. He never went near it."

The next sound Jillian heard was the echo of Brad's feet hammering the metal steps as he hurried down them. Not nearly as familiar with the steps as he was, she followed at a slower rate, but as fast as her uncertain footing allowed.

"Brad, where are you headed?" she called out as she saw his silhouette dart through the open door below. She did not like being left behind. Not when her son's very life could be at stake.

"To the woods," he shouted back, his voice barely heard above the wind outside. "I took the south trail here."

Expecting to find Brad halfway to the trees by the time she finally emerged from inside, she was surprised and grateful to see he had waited near the gate.

"We have to hurry," he shouted "The wind is gathering force about as fast as the temperatures are dropping."

And Jillian smelled rain. The storm Bill had predicted for the early hours of morning had come early.

Following while Brad retraced his route, Jillian called out at the top of her voice as they entered the forest. "Pete? Where are you?"

There was no answer, only the rush of icy wind through the trees. "Pete, answer me. Where are you?"

Slowing the pace after entering the trees, where the darkness was enough to make hurrying more dangerous, Brad reached back and took her hand. Clearly, he did not want her to fall. Despite all she had done to him, all she kept from him, he obviously did not want her hurt. "I took that path."

Fighting the shame over what she had done, she focused instead on her fear as she glanced at the treetops whipping back and forth overhead and noted an eerie glow in the churning clouds. "What if we don't find him before the rain starts? What if the wind gets even worse and snaps off a huge limb and it falls on him, crushing him?" She was becoming hysterical, but there was nothing she could to do stop herself. She shouted to be heard above the clamor of the wind-whipped branches overhead. "What if he's already hurt? What if he's been killed by a falling tree? It would be all my fault. I never should have kept the secret." She brushed her hair out of her face with hard, angry swipes. "I never should have kept you two apart. If he's out there hurt, I am the one to blame. Me. His own mother."

Letting go of her hand, Brad grabbed her by the shoulders

and shook her twice. "Jillian, don't. This isn't doing Pete any good."

"But I'm to blame for everything." Able to make out Brad's concerned expression even in the darkness, she broke into harsh, racking sobs. "Don't you see? I'm to blame for everything. I've hurt you and I've hurt Pete. My own son. My own flesh and blood. I'm an awful person."

To her surprise, rather than agree with her and chastise her for all the hurt she had foolishly caused, Brad pulled her into his arms and held her tight. Suddenly, she was surrounded by warmth and security. "No, you aren't. There is no way you would purposely do anything to hurt Pete. I don't understand the reasoning yet, but I know you well enough to believe that however wrong your logic, you think you did what's best for the boy."

She squeezed her eyes shut. How could he be so understanding after what she had done to him? "That's true. I had good reason for doing what I did. Or at least I thought I did. But that doesn't change the fact that Pete is lost out here somewhere, possibly hurt. Nor does it change the fact that it is my fault. I may not have meant to hurt him—or you—but I did." She trembled in his arms, wishing instead of holding her close, he would slap her hard like she deserved. "Oh, Brad, I should have told you about Pete the day you first arrived here. I should have swallowed my pride and my fear, and admitted right then the secret I'd kept."

"That's true, you should have. But how is knowing that going to help us find Pete?" He stroked her hair with a comforting hand while glancing in the direction they had been headed. "We can talk about this later. There just isn't time right now for you to wallow in guilt. We need to find Pete. He has to be freezing by now."

"You're right." Jillian pushed away, not sure what had come over her. She was usually so strong, especially in times of crisis. "I'm sorry."

"No need to be sorry. Not for that anyway," he said, already taking her hand again and leading her along the shadowed path.

While Brad said nothing more about what had just happened, Jillian resumed calling out to her son. "Pete? Can you hear me? Where are you?"

A splintering crack overhead caused her to gasp. She looked up expecting to find a tree limb crashing down toward them, but nothing fell. Still, there was the knowledge one could have fallen. "Pete! *Where are you?*"

Brad joined in calling for the boy, although his voice did not carry as well over the frigid wind and distant thunder. "Pete? Can you hear us?"

There was barely enough light beneath the trees to make out where the narrow path split just yards ahead until another flash of lightening ballooned to the west. With the woods around them suddenly bathed in a wavering blue light that lasted several seconds, Brad pointed to the left fork with his free hand. "I came down that trail."

After following Brad's route several more yards, Jillian thought she heard a child crying but could not be certain with all the other commotion around them. She pulled Brad to a halt and listened carefully.

"Pete? Is that you? Where are you?"

"Mom. I'm over here."

"*Pete!*" Relief washed away only part of her fear while she and Brad hurried toward the sound. Pete was alive, but had to be hurt or he would have come running.

The sky flickered again, followed only seconds later by a much louder rumbling of thunder. The storm was almost upon them.

Even with the added light, Jillian did not see her son.

"Pete? Where exactly?" This time it was Brad shouting.

"Over here."

A tree branch bent back, evidently caught by a sudden, strong gust of wind just as another spike of lightening shot across the clouds, allowing them to see Pete's tiny form, sitting on a fallen tree, holding his ankle.

Jillian's first fear was that the huge tree had struck him on the way down, but as they got closer, she noticed it had no limbs or leaves. It had been there awhile.

"Pete, what's wrong? Why didn't you answer our calls?"

"I didn't hear you until just a few seconds ago. The storm was too loud."

Jillian suspected part of the reason he hadn't heard them and responded was because he had been crying too loud, but she kept that thought to herself. She put her arms around his small form as she sat down beside him. His whole body rocked back and forth while he continued to grip his ankle. His arms were like ice. "What's wrong with your foot?"

"I tripped over something. It hurts bad."

Brad knelt in front of him and first felt of Pete's leg through his jeans, then rolled up the hem and felt of the ankle itself. When that caused Pete to whimper, he bent low to get a better look, but ended up shaking his head and standing again. "He's hurt it bad enough that it's swollen, but it's too dark for me to tell much more than that. We need to get him back to the house."

A nearby clap of thunder caused Pete to jump then start crying again. "I can't walk on it. I tried."

"That's okay. I'll carry you," Brad told him, already bending to do just that. He held him in such a way, the injured ankle remained higher than his heart. "You just hang tough until we can get you to the house."

Pete wrapped his arms around Brad's neck and squeezed his eyes shut while Jillian hurried ahead, making sure that whatever had tripped Pete earlier wouldn't also trip Brad. She kicked asked any fallen limbs or loose rocks while Brad followed closely behind.

Nothing else was said until they had cleared the woods and Brad picked up his pace. "Pete, it was foolish of you to try to follow me. Especially with a storm coming. You could have hurt a lot more than just your ankle."

Jillian's heart lurched forward while she hurried alongside

them. Pete would not have been out there if it weren't for her.

"I know, but I saw how angry you were, and it scared me. I came after you because I thought you might need someone to talk to."

"Still, when you saw that you could never catch up with me, you should have turned back."

"I know that. *Now*." He grimaced when Brad's heel slipped into in a small hole, causing him to jar his leg. "And I'm sorry."

"There'll be time for apologies later," Jillian put in, knowing hers should be first. "For now you just concentrate on keeping that foot still."

In a miraculously short time, they arrived at the house. The front door popped open just seconds before Brad's foot connected with the steps.

Having spotted them from inside, everyone but Reynold rushed outside to find out why Pete was having to be carried again. If still stunned by Jillian's announcement earlier, they did not show it.

"He's hurt his ankle," is all Brad took time to tell them, smiling his gratitude when David stepped back to hold the front door for him.

Reynold waited just beyond the entrance, a scowl deeply entrenched in his face. He waited till Brad had passed them then moved to block Jillian's path. "We need to talk."

"Not now," she answered, though clearly aware he was right. They did need to talk, and they would talk, just as soon as she knew Pete would be okay. After entering the light, she saw just how blue and swollen the skin looked above his rumpled sock. She prayed the ankle wasn't broken.

"Jillian." Reynold grasped her arm when she tried to side-step him so she could follow Brad and Pete upstairs. He ground his next words beneath a low, menacing voice, not allowing anyone to hear them but her. "Don't you think you have embarrassed me enough in front of the Nelsons? We need to talk *now*."

"Not now," she repeated and gave her arm a hard enough jerk, she freed herself on the very first try. With Brad and Pete already partway up the stairs, she ran to catch up. At the top, she skirted around them to open the door.

For the first time since their arrival over a week ago, the lock hadn't malfunctioned. It opened without having to dig the key out of her pocket and stayed open after giving it just one push.

"Put him on my bed," she said, already flipping on all the lights.

Brad did just that. Immediately he eased Pete's shoe off then peeled back his sock so he could have a look at the foot, too. It had swollen all the way down to his toes.

"What can I do to help?"

"Go get some ice," Brad answered without bothering to look up.

Jillian hurried back down the stairs to do just that. When she arrived at the kitchen door, she was met by Miss Hattie, who carried a large yellow mixing bowl already filled to the plastic rim with half-moon shaped slivers of ice. "Here."

"Thanks." Pleased Miss Hattie had been one step ahead of her, Jillian took the bowl and spun back toward the stairs. Halfway there, Reynold confronted her again. Rather than give him the chance to grab her a third time and possibly make her spill the ice, she darted around Shelly, who stood nearby, then shot up the stairs.

"Jillian, you're behaving like a child."

She heard his footsteps behind her, but she didn't have time to worry about it. She had to get that ice to Brad.

"Jillian, come back here."

Ignoring his shouts, she hurried on into the room and found Brad down on one knee, examining Pete's foot. "Here's the ice."

Brad did a double-take when he glanced at the bowl, obviously impressed with her speed. "Bring it over here. I don't think the ankle is broken, but I need to reduce the swelling before I can be sure."

He glanced around, as if looking for something in particular, then stood and peeled out of his shirt without unbuttoning it. Muscles rippling taut and lean as he spread the shirt across a portion of the bed they were not using and dumped the ice onto it. Quickly, he tied the corners together, hobo style, and draped the bundle around Pete's ankle.

Pete grimaced but didn't complain when Brad then applied gentle pressure around the makeshift ice pack.

Feeling helpless, Jillian hurried forward to brush Pete's windswept tangles from his face with gentle fingers, the only comforting thing she knew to do.

"Jillian, come out here and talk to me."

Reynold again.

Jillian glanced up, annoyed to find Reynold standing out in the hall, arms crossed like some imperious king. Why couldn't he just go away and leave her alone for now? She did not have time for such childish behavior. "I can't, Reynold. Pete may be seriously injured. I have to be with him."

"You can come back and see about your son *after* we've talked." He stepped back and pointed to the floor beside him, an obvious gesture to where he expected her to stand.

Jillian curled her hands into tight fists, unable to believe he could demand that she leave Pete right now, and was just about to march out there and tell him exactly that when a stray wind gusted through the turret windows and blew the door shut.

Right in Reynold's face.

Reynold uttered an oath she had never heard him utter before then, a second later, the doorknob rattled so hard the entire door shook. "Jillian, open this door."

The lock must have malfunctioned again.

"Later. I'm busy right now." Smiling at how helpful fate had been, she remained at Pete's bedside where she gently sat and held him in her arms while he gritted his teeth against the pain caused by the ice.

Reynold shouted twice more for her to open the door or suffer the consequences. But when it finally soaked in she would rather suffer the consequences, he muttered something about Pete being a worthless brat and the engagement being off before he stomped angrily toward the stairs.

Aware by that outburst how right Brad had been about him all along, she didn't care one bit that he had just broken their engagement. Nor did it bother her to know how badly she had misjudged him and how foolish she had been to want to marry him in the first place. All that mattered at the moment was Pete's ankle.

Eventually, Brad removed the ice, and with the swelling down, was able to resume his examination by gently pressing the main trigger points with the tips of his fingers and then manipulating the foot in several different directions. He watched Pete's face closely for reactions.

"Is it broken?" Jillian asked, studying Brad's expression closely.

"No. If it was broken, he would be doing more than just grimacing when I bent it too far. He'd be yelping with pain." He looked at the foot again. "Wiggle your toes again."

Pete frowned but obliged, then blinked with surprise as the toes wiggled freely. "It doesn't hurt as much as it did earlier, back when Mom was gone to get the ice."

Brad smiled at Jillian. "No, nothing's broken. All that ankle needs is a good, sturdy elastic bandage and about four days of inactivity. But if it isn't better by then, we'll want to take him to a hospital and have it X-rayed."

He bent forward and ruffled Pete's hair then headed for the door. "My medical bag is still in my room. I'll go get it, and another shirt." Gripping the knob, he looked back at Pete a long moment, then took a slow, deep breath and stared pointedly at Jillian. "As soon as I'm through here, you and I are going to go somewhere alone and have a nice, *long* talk."

Chapter 19

Jillian's heart gave a hard thump after Brad finished wrapping Pete's ankle and told Miss Hattie he could have the ice cream he wanted, but was not to leave that bed.

"I'll see that he doesn't," Miss Hattie said, then hurried forward with the small bowl she had held for the past several minutes.

Having already given Pete three children's aspirin for the pain, and his stethoscope to play with until their return, Brad gestured for Jillian to precede him out the door. "We'll be back in a little while."

"Take all the time you need," Miss Hattie told him. "I'll be here with Pete."

Jillian waited until they were in the hall before daring a quick look at him. "Where should we go?"

Brad glanced at the alcove where rain now pelted the windows in steady sheets and at the stairs where voices drifted up from below. Finally, he gestured to the door across the hall. "My room."

Jillian hesitated, not because she feared what he might do to her once they were alone, but because she had absolutely no idea what to say to him. Nothing could make up for the loss he had suffered at her hand.

Brad opened the door, then stepped back. When she did not follow right away, he returned to where she stood, her feet frozen to the white runner that cut a soft path down the center of the wooden floor. "Afraid of me?"

"No, just of what you might say to me. Brad, I never meant to hurt you."

He paused for a breath. "Then why didn't you tell me about Pete?"

His blue eyes registered so many different emotions while they searched hers, she could not be sure which was the most prominent.

"Because I thought you would be better off not knowing," she finally answered then dropped her gaze to the gleaming hardwood floor. Even to her that sounded lame. "You'd told me you didn't want a family and I believed you. It was a mistake. I know that now." She swiped at the tear escaping down her cheek. "And there's nothing I can do to make it up to you."

Brad stood stone still in front of her a long moment before finally lifting her chin, again forcing her to look deep into his probing gaze. "You could tell me you're sorry. Please, Jillian, just tell me you are sorry for having kept such an important secret from me."

Sorry didn't begin to describe what she felt. But before Jillian could quite gather the presence of mind needed to explain that to him, Miss Hattie leaned out into the hall and called to them.

"Could you two postpone your talk for a few minutes more?"

Brad's hand abandoned her chin immediately, but he didn't step back. Nor did he respond to Miss Hattie's question. Instead, he just stood there, staring at Jillian.

With her heart pulled in all directions, Jillian turned just her head and watched Miss Hattie hasten toward them. "What's wrong?"

Glancing back at the door left open, Miss Hattie frowned then answered in a soft voice filled with concern. "It's Pete. He has decided Brad is mad at him, and nothing I say seems to make him believe otherwise. Could you two go back in there and explain to the boy that although you were upset with him for having run off into the night like that, you are *not* angry with him? There is a difference.''

Not waiting to hear how Miss Hattie had arrived at such a preposterous conclusion, Brad returned immediately to Pete's bedside. Jillian followed only a few steps behind. Miss Hattie remained out in the hall.

''What's this I hear about you thinking I'm mad at you?'' Brad asked, pulling the desk chair closer to the bed then turning it around so he could straddle the back. He looked at Pete, perplexed.

''Aren't you?'' Pete asked in a tiny voice, pushing around his ice cream with his spoon.

Jillian's heart went out to her son in a tender rush. Pete was so worried about Brad being angry, he couldn't even bring himself to look at him.

Brad's forehead notched as he came off the chair and moved to the bed. ''No, of course not. Why would you think that?''

''Because of what you said outside about how foolish I was to try and follow you. And because ever since we got back here, you've had a frown on your face.'' His lower lip trembled. ''I'm sorry I turned my foot and fell down. I didn't do it on purpose.''

Brad lifted his gaze to Jillian as she quietly closed the door then came forward. ''Pete, Brad is not angry at you. He's angry at me.''

''I know, but he's angry with me, too, for running after him like I did.''

''No, I'm not,'' Brad asserted. ''Sure, I was upset with you for having scared me half to death like that, but I'm not angry with you.''

''But you're angry with my mother?'' He lifted cautious blue eyes to Brad's face.

Jillian drew a deep breath, aching for both her son and Brad. ''That's because he has every right to be. Just like you have every right to be angry with me.''

"I do?"

"Yes, you do." With her heart hammering a hard, brutal rhythm, she folded her hands together and sat down on the side of the bed, one leg bent, facing Brad. "I've kept something a secret that I shouldn't have and it involves you." Her voice caught on the emotions twisting inside her, keeping her from going on. She looked to Brad for help.

"What's she's trying to tell you is that I'm your father."

Pete blinked then grinned, his blue eyes lighting at the news. "You are? She told you that?"

"I was going to," Jillian said, having again found her voice, "but he figured it out before I could quite get the courage."

"I figured it out when you told me how old you are." He looked at Jillian with an arched eyebrow. "Someone had let me believe you were younger than you actually are."

"And you're okay with that? With being my father, I mean."

Brad quirked a smile. "Yeah, I'm okay with it. Like I told you days ago, I've always wished I had a son like you."

Jillian smiled, too, though she knew the dilemma between her and Brad was far from over, at least there was no discord between these two. Tears of gratitude filled her eyes. "I was wrong to keep such a secret from Brad. Not only have I cheated him out of the son he's wanted all these years, I've cheated you out of a father. All because I was too afraid if I told him, I faced another rejection from the only man I ever truly loved, the only man I ever longed to marry. I let my own insecurities get in the way of your happiness."

Brad's head shot up at those last two comments. He stood and walked first to the window, then back to the bed. "God, what we've missed." Tears shimmered in his eyes. "And I'm just as much to blame as your mother."

"You?" Pete tilted his head, as if finding that statement odd.

Brad blinked hard then looked toward the wall. "I took it upon myself to decide what was in your mother's best interest.'' He blinked again, then glanced at Jillian, his face so filled with regret she, too, started to cry when he then spoke his next words to her. "I wonder if my own insecurities weren't in play when I decided that I could never keep a woman like you happy, all because I was not wealthy, nor was I quite as sophisticated as your other friends. We were certainly happy enough until then. But by the time the word 'marriage' came up, I had convinced myself that I was all wrong for you, and that parting was the noble thing to do.''

He paused to swallow the catch in his throat. "Then, when you didn't bother to as much as telephone me or write a letter, I decided I'd been right. You had been stringing me along just to have someone to keep you entertained during your long summers here. I had no idea the reason that you hadn't contacted me was because you had a secret to hide.'' He gestured to Pete, who soaked this all in with wide eyes and a gaping mouth. "Had I known the truth, I would have been at your doorstep years ago. Instead, I learned to live with my sorrow.''

Jillian whimpered while a hard, throbbing ache filled her chest. So that was why he had said that about not wanting a family when it was so obviously not true. He had done it for her. "And I thought you pushed me away because you didn't love me enough to want to marry me. I thought *you* were the one stringing *me* along.''

"Hardly.'' He moved closer so he could better gauge her reaction. "I have never loved anyone as much as I love you. I just didn't think I had one chance in a hundred of competing with your lifestyle. Your family has way too much money.''

Filled with so much emotion that she hurt, Jillian reached out and took one of the hands hanging helplessly at his side, then stood to face him squarely. "Money is nice, I'll grant you that, but it is not essential to happiness. Or rather it is not essential to *my* happiness.'' His fingers curled around hers, sending hope through her every fiber. "I'm like Pete. I envy your simpler rural lifestyle.''

She held her breath while awaiting his response. That had

been a hint, pure and simple, but whether he understood it as such remained to be known.

Brad's gaze trailed from their hands, locked so tight they were like one fist, to her upturned face. "Then share that lifestyle with me. Move to Maine where you can still help run your grandfather's charities by using a computer with a modem, and by making frequent visits to Texas, but where you will live with me. I have a large enough house for all three of us." He pulled his gaze free long enough to glance at Pete. "Would that be all right with you?"

Pete blinked, not having expected to be included in this. "That depends."

"On what?"

"On if you plan to marry my mother." He crossed his arms, then added in his sternest voice, "I won't have my mother moving up here to live with you unless you plan to do right by her and marry her."

"The boy watches a little too much television," Brad chuckled to Jillian, then straightened his shoulders for emphasis. "Sir, with your permission, I'd be proud to ask for your mother's hand in marriage."

Pete's eyes glittered with devilment. "Don't you want more than just her hand?" A grin quirked at one corner of his mouth.

Jillian nodded then laughed. "Yes, I suppose he does watch a little too much television."

Giggling, Pete tilted his head again. "Is all forgiven?"

Brad returned his gaze to Jillian and for a long moment they simply stared at each other. "Yes, it looks like all is indeed forgiven."

"Then I think somebody ought to go downstairs and make absolutely sure Reynold knows that he is not going to be my father after all. Let him find some other kid to torture with his boring trips to the museum and his lessons on how to tuck in a shirt. As for manners, I'd rather learn about them from Coach. Oh, and Miss Hattie will also need to know."

"We'll inform everyone else later," Brad said, pulling Jillian into his arms. "But right now, with your permission, I'd sure would like to kiss your mother."

"On the mouth?" Pete wrinkled his nose.

"On the mouth."

He jerked the covers up over his head at the mere thought of it. "Okay, you can kiss her. But *I'm* sure not watching."

Epilogue

Tony followed Hattie and Cora into the dining room where the birthday party awaited. Reynold was gone, having been called away late Friday on what he had claimed to be urgent business; but the Nelsons stayed to finish out their vacation.

With guests scattered about the room in clusters, the birthday boy himself stood near the head of the table where the birthday cake would eventually sit, glancing curiously at Shelly's stomach. Ever since Tony had told him she had a baby growing in there, having felt the second presence when she passed through him nights before, Pete had not been able to keep his eyes off her. It was as if he expected to see the stomach swell up right before his eyes.

"Here it is—the extra-special present I promised you," Hattie said as she placed her brightly wrapped present on the table beside his grandmother's doily.

Tony knew from having watched her put it together, the gift contained a small album that held photographs of Pete's grandparents and his parents when they were younger. There was even one photograph of him, which she had put in after having guessed the special bond that had developed between them.

"Do I get to open it now?" Pete asked, already running

his hands over the colorful surface in an attempt to figure out what might be inside.

"No, not until after we've had cake and everyone is ready to start telling you their stories," Cora put in, setting the towering cake directly in front of the chair where Pete would eventually sit.

Pete frowned, but didn't argue while Preacher Brown came over for a closer look at the cake. "My, how delicious that looks."

"And it looks big enough to feed a whole army," Jimmy Goodson agreed, sticking a crooked finger out to capture a bit of icing, only to have his knuckled popped by the ever-vigilant Miss Hattie.

"A-yuh, it's plenty big," she agreed, laughing at how quickly Jimmy retrieved his hand, then looked at Preacher Brown again. "Why don't you take some to Miss Beaulah on your way home?" She glanced toward the windows filled with brilliant sunshine. "You'll find her out by the gazebo."

"Binoculars in hand, no doubt." A knowing smile broke his neatly trimmed beard.

Everyone who had heard him, laughed.

Tony drifted back to a better vantage point, content to be surrounded by such gaiety. How nice to feel such love and hear such warm laughter inside his grandfather's home.

While watching from that distance, his attention fell on Brad, Jillian, and Pete, who whispered to each other a moment before Brad stepped away, clanging a spoon against his water glass.

"Friends, if you don't mind, I have an announcement I would like to make, one I think will make several people here very happy."

Everyone in the room fell silent, including Lucy Baker, which Tony thought was an accomplishment in itself.

"Although I'm not sure if it comes as too much of a surprise to some of you, I'd like to announce that Jillian Westworth has at long last consented to be my bride. We are to be married next month in Dallas."

Before he could say anything else, Vic, Fred, Bill, and Hatch all scowled and dug deep into their pockets, coming out with money that was handed over to Jimmy Goodson.

Brad waited until Jimmy had time to pocket his newly found fortune, then continued with the announcement, everyone eager to hear more. "But because of my medical practice, my new wife, my son, and I will make our home here in Maine, where my son will be allowed frequent visits to Vermont to see his friend Troy."

Pete beamed at hearing Brad call him his son, but Vic studied Brad speculatively.

"Well, we all know now what day you announced the wedding, but what day are you two getting married?" he asked, glancing at the others in the room. Clearly there had been bets made on both dates.

"June 30th."

Vic's shoulders sagged again as he, Fred, Bill, and Lucy all dug into their pockets then handed Jimmy yet more money while Hattie, Shelly, and Pastor Brown ignored their grumbling and rushed forward to give Jillian a hug.

Wanting to offer his own congratulations, Tony drifted closer to where Pete could see him clearly.

Well, Pete, it looks like you got exactly the father you wanted. He smiled, then winked, delighted everything had turned out so well for the boy. *The one you should have had all along.*

Don't miss *Beside a Dreamswept Sea* by Victoria Barrett—the next magical SEASCAPE ROMANCE. Turn the page for your sneak preview . . .

T he child was going to drown.

The truth slammed into Tony Freeport with the force of a sledgehammer. A stunning one, considering she lay tucked safely in bed in the Shell Room of Seascape Inn and, in his fifty years of working with his beloved Hattie in assisting others here to heal, he'd never before seen anyone come to harm under the inn's roof. But in Suzie Richards' dream, all the signs of real-life drowning were evident: panic, an inability to breathe, and fear. So much fear . . .

Dream or reality, if Tony didn't do something quickly, the nine-year-old daughter of Bryce Richards and the deceased photo-journalist Meriam *was* going to drown.

What could Tony do? What *should* he do? Suzie, taking on the burdens of family no child should ever have to carry, had been the catalyst insisting he intercede this far. But to intercede in her dreams? Did he dare?

This had to be a near-miss warning. Had to be.

He looked through the closed bedroom door, out into the upstairs hallway. The paneled walls deepened the night's shadows and the only light was that seeping through the bank of mullion windows centered inside a small vaulted alcove at the far end of the hall. Tall mahogany, hand-carved book-shelves flanked those windows. Tony couldn't clearly see the books in them, but he didn't have to see them to know each book's title, to know each spine stood straight. Nor did he need to see the pillows on the thick cushions of the window seat nestled between those shelves to know they'd been fluffed. Hattie Stillman nurtured everything in her care, which included all of Seascape Inn, most of Sea Haven Village, and, at one time, him.

He scanned the polished planked-wood floor from the far end of the hallway back toward the end where he stood. On the left, facing the Atlantic Ocean, was the master bedroom, dubbed The Great White Room years ago, and the bath; on the right, the L-shaped staircase leading down to the first floor, and the Cove Room where Bryce Richards should have been sleeping but wasn't. Instead, the man dozed slumped on the hallway floor, his head lolled back against the paneled wall, his slippered foot rumpling the edge of the white Berber rug that stretched from the stairway's landing nearly all the way down to the Shell Room, about a yard from Tony's feet.

Bryce was a man on a mission. Two sets of his friends from New Orleans, T.J. and Maggie MacGregor and John and Bess Mystic, had found ''magic'' at Seascape Inn, and Bryce had come here with doubts but hopes that enough magic remained to grant his daughter peace from the emotional demons haunting her sleep since her mother's death two years ago. But even in sleep, Bryce was despairing; Tony sensed it. Despairing that, though armed with its angelic innkeeper, Miss Hattie, the charming old inn couldn't hold *that* much magic and, without it—God knew Bryce had tried everything else—Suzie's nightmares would be an endless source of her suffering.

And Bryce despaired that she'd dream and, asleep in the Cove Room across the hallway, he'd not hear her cries, not know to come and comfort her. So he had forsaken the luxury of a soft, king-size bed and had stood guard on the hallway's oak floor outside her door, listening, waiting, and praying he wouldn't be needed.

The agony of the situation had broken Tony's heart, and he'd aided the quiet of the house in lulling the reluctant Bryce to sleep, agreeing with his darling Hattie's assessment that Bryce was worn to a frazzle. But who wouldn't be? Worried sick about his three children overall, Suzie and her nightmare in particular, fighting a constant battle of wills with that dour-faced Mrs. Wiggins, who Bryce's wife had hired to care for the children when Jeremy had been born four years ago, and then—right on the heels of the narrow-miss divorce between John and Bess Mystic—that blasted Tate divorce case. It was a wonder Bryce Richards was still upright!

In the days since their arrival at Seascape Inn, Hattie had mumbled repeatedly that no more a devoted father than Bryce ever had graced the earth, and Tony wholeheartedly agreed with his beloved on that appraisal too. Bryce was a fine father, a fine man, and a fine attorney.

Yet that hadn't spared him from challenges.

As if he hadn't had enough on his plate already, he'd been tossed a moral dilemma on the Tate divorce case that would have brought even the most avid believer, the most confident man in the world, to his knees. It was a shame he had represented Gregory Tate. Not only disagreeable, the man had proven himself unscrupulous and coldly calculating. Though the divorce had been granted and the case was behind Bryce now, it had left him weary, his opinion even more jaded about the odds for successful, happy marriages—and it left him admittedly curious about the mysterious Mrs. Tate.

So was Tony. He leaned against the doorjamb, propped the toe of his shoe against the floor, then rubbed his neck. Why had the woman never once appeared in court? Never once attended the attorney/client meetings with Bryce, Gregory, and her own attorney? Her behavior was curious.

Now, Tony grimaced, because since he had given Bryce this brief but much needed respite of sleep, Suzie fought the fiendish nightmare alone. Tony shouldn't intercede further— dream intervention was expressly forbidden—but she was suffering uncomforted, and that was his fault. He couldn't deny responsibility and condemn her to this. Hattie would never forgive him. Worse, he'd never forgive himself.

Protocol be damned. Tony shoved away from the wall.
Rules and regulations, too. What more could be done to him?
Already he lived in the house with his beloved Hattie and yet
he couldn't talk directly with her, couldn't hold her, couldn't
love her as a man should love a woman—as he *would* have
loved her had he been given the chance. What could be more
challenging? And a child's life hung in the ballast. Likely her
father's, too—if anything should happen to her.

Theoretically, people didn't actually die just because they
died in their dreams. But what if Suzie did? In Tony's experience, dreamers *always* had awakened prior to actual
dream-state death. So why wasn't Suzie awakening? Soaring
heart rate. Gasping something fierce. She might not drown,
but she could have a heart attack. Drowning or a massive
coronary, dead was dead.

He tried several tactics to nudge her into awakening.

Nothing worked.

Now what?

Having no idea, Tony scowled, feeling inept and agitated.
The bottom line was Bryce Richards had little more left to
lose. Tony *had* to intercede.

He stepped into Suzie's nightmare, into a raging storm.

The wind stung, bitingly cold, whistling through crisp,
brown leaves that had fallen from the cypress and oaks near
the shore. Familiar cypress and oaks. Familiar low stone wall
running along the rocky ground to the pond. And familiar
white, wrought-iron bench, north of a familiar, freshly painted
gazebo.

Crimiy, Suzie was in the pond behind Seascape Inn!

Did she realize this yet? That her recurring dream actually
took place here?

Odd. Before three days ago, Suzie never had seen Seascape
Inn nor its pond, and yet she'd suffered this same nightmare
for the past two years.

Agitated by the blustery wind, Tony squinted against the
darkness and glimpsed the shadow of a little rowboat—the
very boat he himself with his lifelong friends, Hatch and Vic,

had fished from as boys. Rocking on turbulent waves, the boat dipped low, took on water. And—sweet heaven, it was empty.

"Suzie?" *Where was she?* "Suzie?" The wind tossed Tony's words back to him. Nearing the water's edge, he called out again and stumbled over a giant oak's gnarled roots.

His foot stung.

Startled, he winced. Physical pain? How peculiar. It'd been half a century since he'd felt physical pain . . .

He frantically scanned the dark water. Later, he'd think about the pain. He had to find Suzie now—before it was too late.

Midway across the pond, something flashed white. Her nightgown? No. No, it wasn't. Just froth from a wave. Fear seeped deeper, into his soul. *Where was she?*

Straining harder, skimming, probing, he spotted her. Near the bow of the boat, foundering in the water, arms flailing, head bobbing between the waves.

Oh, God, she really *was* going to drown. Unlike her other dreams, this one wasn't a near-miss warning!

He cupped his hands at his mouth. "Suzie! Hold on to the boat. I'm coming. Just hold on to the boat!"

"I can't!" she shouted back. Swallowing in a great gulp of water, she choked.

The sound grated at his ears, tore at his heart. Why in the name of everything holy did she feel it vital to hold onto the oars? Though wooden, they wouldn't offer enough stability in the turbulent water to keep her afloat. Still, she held them in a death grip.

He had to find out why. Though dangerous—fear of him, in addition to the fear and panic she was suffering already, could worsen her situation dramatically—to help her, he needed to understand her rationale.

She screamed. A shattering scream that pierced his ears and reverberated in his mind. A chiseled hollow in his chest ached. Whatever the risks, damn it, he *had* to take them.

Focusing, he tapped into the child's thoughts.

*You have to get both oars in the water and keep them there,
Suzie.*

Not her voice. A memory. Something she'd been told by
a woman. Someone older—twenties or thirties maybe. And
that accent—definitely not anyone from Sea Haven Village,
or from Maine. Southern. Distinctly southern.

The child took a wave full in the face, sputtered, then
coughed.

He hurried toward her, resenting that in her dreams he obviously lacked his special gifts, his abilities and talents with
the physical, that would allow him to fish her out without
getting so much as a toe wet. In dreams, it appeared he was
as weak or as strong as a normal man. And while at times
he'd love to again be a normal man, when Suzie was clinging
to life by an oar wasn't one of them.

What did it all mean?

He returned his cupped hands to his mouth. "Suzie, let go
of that oar right now and grab hold of the boat. Do it! Do
you hear me? Do it!"

Her wet hair swept over her face and clung to her tiny
cheek in a clump, her eyes wild with fear. "I've got to keep
both oars in the water! I've got to, or I'm not gonna get
better."

This was new ground, and Tony waffled on what to do.
His heart told him to go get her. His logic warned if he
touched her, with her body temperature as low as it surely
was already from the frigid water, the cold could result in
pneumonia and she'd die. But if he didn't physically get her
out of the pond quickly, she'd die, too. Simply put, he was
in a lose/lose situation here. Damned if he did, damned if he
didn't.

He had years of experience. He just had to not panic. Had
to think about this. He cleared his mind, then weighed the
pros and cons, mentally searching for alternatives less risky
to Suzie.

There were none.

He hated any but win/win situations, yet the core in this

one rested right where it had before he'd begun his search: She had a fighting chance with pneumonia; she didn't with drowning.

Tony dove in. Hit the frigid water that sucked out his breath, then stroked furiously toward her.

The lack of true physical exercise for too many years had him winded and tiring quickly. Soon, his arms and legs felt like lead and he couldn't seem to get enough air to feed his starving lungs. They throbbed and ached, and the physical sensations of weight and gravity and oxygen deprivation had him sluggish, tired, moving about as quickly as a hypothyroid snail. Without his special gifts, could he get to her in time?

"Please, don't let her die. Please, help me help her." She was so close. So close. . . . *"Please!"*

He dug deep, scraped the remnants of his reserves and pulled a mighty stroke.

His fingers snagged the collar of her nightgown.

He tugged, grabbed her more securely with his left hand, the boat with his right, then curled her tiny body to his and hugged her to him. She latched her arms around his neck, squeezed so hard he sensed she was trying to crawl into him. And then she began to cry. Deep, heart-wrenching sobs that jerked viciously at his heartstrings. "Shhh, it's okay, little one. I've got you now. I've got you now."

She breathed against his neck, her voice a rattled whimper of sound. "Promise?"

This crisis, she'd weathered. This time, she'd survived. Awash in gratitude and relief, he swallowed hard. "I promise."

Water swirled, tugging at his clothes. Awareness stole into him and he recalled stubbing his toe on the gnarled oak's root. His foot actually had stung. And now, more awareness of the physical dragged at him. Her moist, warm breath at his shoulder. Cold as she was from the frigid water, the warmth of her tiny body. The feel of her fingers digging into his neck. His own need for oxygen, for rest. The weight of his uniform. Sensations.

Lifelike . . . sensations.

His hands began to shake. Awed, humbled, he shook all over. He'd not felt any physical sensations since he'd returned home from the battlefield for burial back in World War II and, because he hadn't, now he couldn't be sure which of them, him or Suzie, groped with greater emotional turmoil.

She was alive.

And, for the first time in half a century, he was feeling the actual touch of another human being.

His eyes stung and a tear—a tear—slid onto his cheek.

An uneasy niggle nagged at him. He'd been in many situations in the past fifty years and had felt nothing physical. So why now? True, he'd never before entered anyone's dreams—and he fully expected to pay a steep penalty for trespassing into Suzie's now—but there had to be some deeper reason for this. His sixth sense screamed it. And it screamed that something about these particular "special guests" made this intercession, and their situation, different from the hundreds of other special guests he and Hattie had assisted at Seascape Inn.

Suzie wheezed. Feeling the rattle against his chest, he prayed Seascape would protect her from almost certain pneumonia. Over the years, many had called the inn *The Healing House*, and how fervently he hoped its reputation proved prophetic for Suzie.

These special guests are different. A woman's voice echoed through his mind. *This situation is different.*

She sounded urgent, yet calm and dispassionate. Who was she?

Who I am doesn't matter. My message is what is important, Tony.

Why?

You'll have to find the answer to that yourself, I'm afraid.

I see.

No, you don't. That's part of the problem. But you will, Tony, I'm rather, er, persistent.

Just what he needed. Another stubborn woman to contend

with. *Well, I'll have to figure it out later. Right now, I need to get Suzie out of this water and wind before she freezes to death.*

Ah, I'm encouraged. The woman sighed.

Excuse me? Kicking his feet, he steered toward the shore, holding onto Suzie and the boat for fear his strength would fizzle.

You're mired in a quandary yet still putting Suzie's needs first. I'm encouraged by that. And, yes, I expect you will figure it out—eventually.

Terrific. Stubborn and snooty. A barrel of sunshine. *I'm encouraged that you're encouraged.*

Save your sarcasm, Tony. The woman laughed, soft and melodious. *You're going to need your energy.*

He wanted to kick something. Actually, he wanted to kick "Sunshine." Wicked of him, but did she have to be right about the energy bit, too? His muscles were in distress; he didn't have the energy for this verbal sparring—or the time for it. Not right now. Suzie had stopped crying, but she still clung to him as if she feared he'd forget and let go of her. He'd promised, but promises didn't hold much value to Suzie Richards; that much was evident. At least not those aside from her father's. In the chaos of what had been their family life, Bryce somehow had retained his children's trust. That in itself, considering the circumstances, was a miracle.

To reassure her, Tony smoothed her frail back until her shudders eased. When they subsided, though vain, a sense of satisfaction joined those of relief and gratitude inside him. He'd catch hell for breaking protocol, but feeling Suzie inhaling and exhaling breath made whatever price he had to pay worth it. The last thing she needed was more tragedy in her life. It wouldn't do Bryce any good, either. The man had suffered his share of challenges and then some.

Unfortunately, from all appearances, he was fated to suffer a few more, but at least those challenges wouldn't include the death of his oldest daughter.

They might. Sunshine commented.

Tony's skin crawled. *Not if there's any way in the world for me to stop it.*

You might want to recant that statement, Anthony Freeport.

No way.

We'll see.

A shiver rippled up his backbone. Images raced through his mind. Images of Suzie again in the little boat, trying to do something with the paddles and falling into the pond. Images of her in the water during a storm, gasping. Drowning. And images of Tony standing alone on the shore, his hands hanging loosely at his sides, his shoulders slumped, watching and yet powerless to help her.

Powerless? Shock streaked through him. But he'd never before been powerless here. Never . . .

Until now.

Sunshine's softly spoken warning thundered through his mind. His knees collapsed. He locked them, stumbling and shuddering hard. God help them all.

This wasn't an ordinary dream.

***Beside a Dreamswept Sea*—A June 1997
Seascape Romance from St. Martin's Paperbacks.**